The Rocking Chair

The Rocking Chair

Dell O'Neill

The Pentland Press Limited
Edinburgh • Cambridge • Durham

© Dell O'Neill 1995

First published in 1995 by
The Pentland Press Ltd.
1 Hutton Close
South Church
Bishop Auckland
Durham

British Library Cataloguing in Publication Data.
A catalogue record for this book is available
from the British Library.

ISBN 1 85821 305 3

Typeset by CBS, Felixstowe, Suffolk
Printed and bound by Antony Rowe Ltd., Chippenham

To my dear late husband, Paul. I sat by your bedside gently holding your hands as you slipped quietly away to the Heavenly Land.

CHAPTER 1

The woman walked wearily up the hill to her big house which stood at the top of the cliff overlooking Loch Etive. The messages she was carrying were really far too heavy for her; every now and then she would rest at the side of the path. Years ago there was no hill, then as she sat staring across the calm water she wondered why life had treated her so cruelly. The afternoon was bitterly cold and she shivered in her shabby coat. Well, she thought, this will never get me home. She grabbed the two bags of messages and walked slowly on. When she let herself into the house she made straight for the kitchen, laid the bags on the clean scrubbed table then sat back in the rocking chair beside the blazing fire and remembered.

Her mind returned to the happy days of her childhood. The youngest of four girls, with two younger brothers; Nan the oldest girl, then Sarah, Vera next then herself. Billy and Ewan were the two young brothers. Such is the picture that I, Mary Scott, now present to the outside world: a picture of a tired old woman without a future and with a past that few would envy.

Before the heart-ache began the house was filled with laughter. My mother and father were always there when we needed them. Of course there were angry words from Mum when Dad came home drunk or if any of the children got into trouble but Mum was sure to blame the other children in the village. In her eyes her children could do no wrong. We all had our own special chores to do, making the beds, cleaning the windows, helping mother on wash day, carrying water from the well. I liked school days best; it took us an hour to walk to school and an hour back. Those days we didn't do any work then. On the way to school and back we usually got up to some mischief. I liked summer time best; we always managed to gather wild blackberries and Mum would make lots of lovely jam. Saturday morning was baking time; we were all kept out of the big kitchen while Mum baked the week's supply of scones, cakes and dumplings.

Dad took all of us down to the loch out of Mum's way in the summer. The

1

loch was home to all kinds of sailing boats; while we played, Dad would just sit and smoke his pipe and fish. He always went home empty handed. I still remember as I sit in my rocking chair the appetising smell of the home baking as we all approached the house. My sisters and brothers rushed in first then Dad and of course our lovely dog Rusty and last but not least myself. Dad always took our beautiful black and white collie with him to his work as the head forester. His work was to look after the stately trees of firs, pines and yews on the estate. The landowner lived in a beautiful house on the other side of the loch; his mansion surrounded by large fir trees. The landowner was a powerful man with a vicious temper. People said his wife Jean lived in fear of him; he was a law unto himself. Dad very seldom saw him, his weekly pay and his working sheet were brought to him by his boss's butler who rowed over from the other side of the loch every Friday. After our tea of home baking Dad would always disappear while we children were left to our usual chores. My sister Nan was always the bossy one telling us younger ones what to do. She was a lovely looking girl, fair hair, large blue eyes and lovely fair skin and tall for her age. At school she made sure nobody bullied her younger sisters and brothers but at home sometimes she was hard to live with.

Sarah was completely different, as dark as my sister Nan was fair. Sarah had jet black hair, large brown eyes like her father yet there was always a sadness about her which I could never understand. Vera and I were closer as there was only one year between us, in fact we were more like twins, both of us good looking, according to what I heard people say about us. My younger brothers whom I always looked upon as nuisances were really lovable rogues, always up to some mischief. Dad tried to tell them off but behind his threat there was always a sly smile. On Sundays we all got ready to go to church; staunch Roman Catholics, we were all dressed in our Sunday best, Mum and Dad with my two older sisters leading the way, while the rest of we younger ones trailed behind. We walked the mile to church every Sunday, hail, rain or snow. It was considered a 'mortal sin' to miss Mass on a Sunday and the fear of going to Hell prayed on your mind all week if you missed Mass. Of course it was different if you were very ill, then you were excused.

Mother made all our clothes on her large sewing machine and the younger children always got the hand downs. Vera and I didn't mind when we were young but as we grew older I for one resented it. Always second hand clothes, never anything new. Our childhood though was a happy one, mother nursing us through all our different kinds of illness, from scarlet fever to a septic toe or finger. Father never had a day's illness, he was always laughing and joking and enjoyed the best of health. Mother had her usual ups and downs and Nan usually looked after mother when she had one of her off days.

Our house had three bedrooms, a large parlour, large kitchen, and outside toilet. From our parlour window we had a lovely view of the loch. I enjoyed the changing moods of the loch; some days she would be dead calm like a sheet of glass with the sun glinting on her waters. Other times the waves would rise high over the craigs with the white spray on top. Then there were times when she was shrouded in secrecy by the heavy mist which blocked everything from our view. Our nearest neighbours were half a mile down the road from us. Their name was MacLean. Very well off, Mr and Mrs MacLean had a small son Hector and a daughter Flora, both at boarding school. I used to think we were better taught at our school than they were. Of course, some people are gifted with brains but are too lazy to use them. I often thought to myself, money doesn't buy everything.

On Mondays after coming home from school we all helped Mum with the chores. Each one of us had our own special task to do; the boys being the youngest got off scot-free. They would come home from school, throw their school bags on the floor then grab a few scones and quickly disappear down to the loch. Every Friday night was bath night. Mum and Dad would fill up the big zinc bath with lovely hot water which was heated in a big black pot on the range. Nan and Sarah were always the first to have their bath, Vera and myself next; lastly it was the boys time. By the time they were finished the whole of the kitchen floor would be flooded. I don't know when Mum and Dad took their bath; when we were young we never gave that a thought. After we all had our baths we went straight to bed. Mum and Dad had the biggest room. All us girls were in the one room with two double beds. Nan and Sarah shared one while Vera and I shared the other. The two top drawers in the big chest of drawers belonged to Nan and Sarah while the two bottom ones were Vera's and mine and woe betide anybody who touched the two top drawers. Their hair would have been pulled out.

I was always frightened of thunder and lightning storms; usually the wind would be howling down the chimney and the rain lashing against the window panes. Whenever that happened Vera and I would jump into our big sister's bed till the storm passed over. Nan was the storyteller; it was always during the storms that she told stories to keep us younger ones quiet. The one I liked best was the one about the Laird's wife; she would start her story like this:

'Once upon a time many years ago, a proud powerful Laird and his wife lived in a big mansion, his wife was very lovely. As they had never been

3

blessed with children, one Christmas the laird's wife went to the orphanage and arranged for a little girl called Rose to be allowed to stay for the Christmas period at her home. The butler would call for her the next day and give the child a special Christmas. Rose was a bonnie child; the laird's wife took to her right away, what with her long red hair and big blue eyes so after the Christmas festivities were over she decided to let her stay on in her house for good. She decided Rose would help cook in the kitchen and in the afternoons she was allowed into her ladyship's bedroom to read to her while she was resting. Rose loved the large spacious room with its lovely dressing table; often she would stand beside it and wondered what all the little glass topped bottles were for and all the different jars of cream. Then there was the silver topped hair brush, comb and hand mirror and last of all her large jewel box. Often after a late evening out her ladyship would take her jewels off and leave them just lying on the dressing table till the next morning then put them away when she got up. Her large oak bed where she lay looked out onto the front lawn and at the edge of the lawn stood a large oak tree. In the mornings when she awoke she loved to watch this large tree and watch its leaves change with all the different seasons.

'In late spring the tree was a busy place, birds from the proud magpie to the little thrushes building their nests. In the warm weather she would ask Rose to open her bedroom window wide and leave it like that so that she had a good view of all the different birds busy making their nests. One late spring morning little Rose was busy in the kitchen helping cook; the butler came in and told Rose that her ladyship wished to see her right away. Rose ran straight upstairs to the bedroom where the laird was standing by the window.

'"Sit down, child," her ladyship said. "I want the truth from you. Have you taken the diamond rings from my dressing table?"

'Rose was frightened. She had never seen her mistress so angry. Bursting into tears, she said, "no, I have never touched any of your rings."

'"Well, Rose, you and cook are the only two who come in here and I fully trust cook who has been with me for eight years so I am sending you back to the orphanage. Go and pack your things at once. The butler will take you back."

'Rose left the room; the tears streaming down her cheeks. She knew she had not taken the rings but no one would believe her. She left the lovely house in disgrace.

'Years later a terrible storm raged all over the country; thunder and lightning and gale force winds. The large oak tree standing at the edge of the Laird's lawn was split in two by lightning. The laird ordered it to be cut down immediately as it was a great danger, ready to topple at any minute. The workmen arrived and felled the huge oak tree and to the workmen's amazement there lay on the ground a large bird's nest full of all kinds of gold trinkets; among them were her ladyship's diamond rings. They carried the nest up to the laird; he was amazed at the contents of the magpie's nest. He hurried up to her ladyship's room and showed her the rings. Her ladyship could hardly believe what she saw then she burst into tears. She thought of the sad little girl she had so wrongly accused of stealing her rings. Right away she sent word to the orphanage for Rose to be brought back but no trace of the little Rose was found. It seemed after that her ladyship lost the will to live; she never got over how she had wronged that lovely orphan girl and was never the same again.'

My sister and I were so engrossed in the story we forgot all about the storm and went back to our own bed to sleep thinking of little Rose.

In the long hot summers during school holidays all the blankets and bedspreads got their annual washing. One bed was done at a time; mum would gather large stones and place them in a circle. Inside the stones a big fire was lit, then a large black pot was placed on top of the stones. The girls were kept busy keeping the big pot filled up with water from the well. The fire was always lit near the well. Dad carried the big wooden washing tub down beside the fire for mum. When the tub was filled with warm soapy water, we all took turns tramping the blankets with our bare feet until the blankets were clean. We all enjoyed doing that, even the boys; Dad would help Mum to rinse the blankets and wring all the water out of them with their bare hands then the blankets were hung up on the clothes line to dry.

There was a post office in the village and one or two other shops. You could buy almost anything. They all had a good trade except the baker as many of the wives did their own baking. There was also a smithy. The blacksmith, Bill Ross, had a dour looking son called Grant who would barely spare you a glance.

Nan, six years my elder always seemed to get everything her own way even with Mum and Dad, who in their own way were very strict with the children. Every morning everyone sat around the big kitchen table for breakfast except Dad. He left for work with Rusty at 6 a.m.. That of course was in the summer. It was different in the cold winter. Days were short, indeed it was dark from 4 p.m. till 8.30 in the morning. Sometimes in the most severe weather he did not work at all; then he spent most of his days sawing logs for the fires, most of our fires just burnt wood. In the evenings he would disappear. Later I found out he spent most of his time and money in the only hotel the village had. It was during the winter that Dad and Mum were always quarrelling. I learnt later it was Dad spent what little money we had on drink. Late every night we could hear Dad singing happily on his way home from the hotel.

When Nan was sixteen she had grown into a beautiful girl. Every Sunday when the whole of the family sat in their own special pew in the church I noticed Nan was always turning her head looking sideways at someone. One Sunday I also looked and found the youngest of the MacPherson's sons, Donald, smiling back at her. The MacPhersons owned a large farm on the other side of the loch; they also owned a small boat which they used to bring them all over to church on Sundays. Donald was a fine looking boy, well built. He spent most of his time helping his father and brothers on the farm. They owned about twenty milking cows; as we all left the church, Nan, instead of walking beside Mum and Dad, would linger behind to talk to Donald. At first Dad did not pay attention but as the weeks went by he began to smell a rat. One Sunday after lunch he called Nan into the parlour and told her she was to stop seeing the MacPherson boy as she was still too young. We younger children wondered what wrong Nan had done; Nan came back into the kitchen and just started helping Mum clear the lunch dishes away. Not a word was spoken, all that we could hear was the clatter of dishes.

Every Christmas time a big dance was held in the church hall. We were all too young to go the night before Christmas Eve. Dad and Mum were wakened at two o'clock in the morning; it was Rusty barking and howling. Dad put on his slippers, he never took time to put a dressing gown on and hurried down the stairs. He went straight into the kitchen and caught Nan climbing in through the kitchen window. He waited till Nan was standing at the table, took one look at her, his face like thunder and turned and walked back up the stairs to bed. Mother wanted to know what the trouble was, but wasn't told.

In the morning we sat down at the table for breakfast; Dad always sat at the head when he was not working. Nan did not come down and Sarah was sent to fetch her at once. Five minutes later the two of them took their place at the table. After breakfast Dad called to Nan to follow him into the parlour.

Nan rose from the table even though she had not touched any food; Mum followed them into the parlour. Their voices were raised angrily at first then all we heard were whispers. After what seemed an eternity the parlour door opened and Nan and mother came out, Nan went straight upstairs to her room and stayed there for the rest of the day. Mum came back into the kitchen and shouted to Sarah to help her with the breakfast dishes, the rest of us disappeared down to the loch to play.

When we all arrived home before tea time Mum called us into the kitchen and handed Vera a letter. 'Take this letter to the post office straight away, Vera, and take Mary and the boys with you.'

It had been snowing earlier in the day, now it was very heavy, still we had to do what we were told so the four of us set out to the post office. After we posted the letter who did we see but Grant Ross the blacksmith's son with a beautiful new sledge, real steel runners and steel handles right round the sledge. He asked us if we wanted a ride and we all accepted at once. It was such a big one, the five of us managed to squeeze on to it, Grant taking the rope. I believe the whole village must have heard our screams of laughter. Grant left us at the door, then he made his own way home. From the day on Grant and the boys were the best of pals. We all went into the house covered from head to toe in snow; Sarah came into the hall and helped the boys to get their soaking clothes off then we went into the kitchen for tea. Dad and Nan were there also; we all ate in silence. The atmosphere was terrible and Vera and I were glad to get to our room.

About a fortnight later the postman brought a letter addressed to Mum and Dad. Dad opened the letter, read it and then handed it to Mum. After Mum read it she said to Dad, 'Well that's settled.' We found out later that Mum had written to her sister Kate who lived on the Isle of Mull and had asked if it would be all right if Nan could stay with her for a short holiday. Auntie Kate, who was a schoolmistress at the local school said she would be delighted to have Nan to stay with her. Next day Mum started packing Nan's few belongings; Mum was going to travel with Nan. It would be a long journey; first of all Mum and Nan would have to walk to the railway station to get the train to Oban then the boat from Oban to the port of Craignure where Auntie Kate would meet them. I felt so sorry for Nan who went about the house as if her thoughts were miles away and she looked so sad. Dad still went about with his face like thunder. Next morning Mum and Nan set out on their long journey to the Isle of Mull. The ground was still covered in snow and Dad was hoping that they would not have a rough crossing over to Mull.

It was a fortnight later before Mum came back, she said Nan had settled in nicely and Auntie Kate was asking how we all were. Life went on as usual in our house, the only difference being Sarah was in charge of us in Nan's place. Every Sunday we went to Mass as usual. The MacPhersons went also; I often would give a sly look over to Donald but he always kept his eyes down. His father and mother were at Mass also; Dad never spoke to any of them. After Mass we all hurried home. About two months later Mum got a letter from Auntie Kate, saying Nan was ill and that she had better come and take her home. After a long talk with Dad, Mum left on the long journey to bring Nan home; it was a fortnight later that both of them arrived back. Nan was sent straight off to bed and Dad sent for the doctor.

After the doctor had seen Nan, Dad flew into a raging temper and said that Donald MacPherson was to be sent for immediately. On Sunday after Mass we all waited outside for the MacPherson's family to come out. Dad went straight up to Donald and told him to come straight up to the house with them as he had to talk to him. Donald said he would have to see his Dad first and was told to make it quick before dad lost his temper! Donald just shook his head and followed Dad and Mum and the family home. When we arrived home Dad told Mum to set another place for lunch as Donald would be staying awhile. After our meal Dad, Mum, Nan and Donald went into the parlour. What seemed like ages they all came out again. Dad went with Donald to the door, shook hands with him and said he would make all the arrangements. Then he came into the kitchen and announced, Nan and Donald were getting married in three weeks time.

The Banns would be announced in the church for the first time on Sunday. Mum and Nan came into the kitchen and for the first time in months Nan was smiling. Years later we found out that Nan was expecting a baby and had to get married. Nan and Donald's wedding was a very quiet affair, just our family, Auntie Kate and the MacPhersons. Nan and Donald lived on the farm with his family; the house was never the same after Nan got married, we all missed her, most of all her storytelling. Sarah took over Nan's place. The following year Nan's baby was born, a boy. We saw him only once when he was being christened in the church; his name was Michael. I often went into the parlour to find Mum would be standing staring out of the window looking across the loch thinking of Nan and her little grandson. Dad had told Nan to never darken his door again. I didn't understand why as Nan was always his favourite daughter.

Sarah was three years older than Vera and the clever one at school. When she was 16 she won a bursary for college. She spent three years at college learning typing and commerce. When she was 19 years old she got work at a RAF station in Inverness in the office. Sarah had a room of her own; once a month she came home for the weekend, so that was two of the girls away from home. When Sarah left Vera took over her work helping Mum, in fact both of us helped her for as the years went by she had more and more of her 'off days'. Dad was never the same after Nan left; he was getting old, so was our dog Rusty. Nan by this time had five of a family; she had had a baby every year since she got married. By this time Vera was 16 years old, I was 15, Billy the oldest boy 13, and the baby of the family 11 years old. Dad still worked at the forestry, also he drank most of the money he earned. I often wondered how mother managed so well on so little.

On September 3 1939 World War II broke out; Britain was at war with Germany. Mum got a letter from Auntie Kate in Mull telling her she must stock up as much food as possible. She must have sent money, also. After lunch Mum, Dad, Vera and the boys set off to the village. Dad got a loan of a barrow from the blacksmith; we all trooped into the shop, Mum with a long list in her hand. She handed it to Fred Walsh the grocer who took one look at the list, just nodded to Dad and started getting everything ready. Dad was kept busy loading the large barrow; eventually everything on the list was ready and paid for. Before Mum left the shop she asked Mr Walsh to order blackout cloth for the windows.

We all arrived home laden, even the boys were carrying parcels. After Dad unloaded the big barrow he went straight down to the shop for another load. Off our big kitchen was a big larder; stone floor and stone shelves right round the walls. Most of the food was stored there, self-raising flour, plain flour in ten stone sacks, oatmeal, raisins, currants, sultanas, lentils, barley, dried peas, all in 10 lb. bags. By the time Dad came back with the second load the larder was full. Upstairs in Mum and Dad's bedroom was a big cupboard. It was also packed with all kinds of rolls of material, bags of different coloured wool. Vera and I wondered what on earth was going on. It was only when Sarah came home at the weekend that we were told the full story. Where she worked she was told everyone in the country was to be issued with an identity card with a special number and name and address. Also, we would all get ration books and clothes coupons. The babies and expecting mothers would get a free pint of milk a day, pint of orange juice and a bottle of cod liver oil. All the school children would also be allowed one pint of milk a day at school.

Sarah could not stop talking, 'and who do you think I met today at the station. No other than our proud neighbour's son, Hector MacLean and to crown it all he is an officer. I was busy typing away when he came into the office; as he passed my desk he said hello. I could hardly believe my eyes and oh, he looked so handsome. In fact we travelled on the same train home; don't let on to Mum and Dad. I really do like him.'

9

Vera and I were quite excited at Sarah taking us into her confidence for when she was young she was so secretive.

Farmers and miners were exempt from call-up because the country needed all the food and coal it could get. Father was too old and so he joined the Home Guard.

The following week the blackout cloth for the windows arrived. Mr Walsh delivered it himself. Mum started right away to sew the curtains. When she was finished Dad helped her to put them up. The following morning Dad called me into the parlour; he said I would have to start work right away. Auntie Kate had a friend in Glasgow, very well to do, who needed a girl to help her cook. As everything had all been arranged I was to leave home on Monday and start work right away. Mum of course would travel to Glasgow with me. I was 15 years old and sent out to work without a thought of how I felt. That night I cried myself to sleep and many a night after that I cried silently in bed in the tiny attic bedroom I shared with the parlour maid.

We were wakened at six every morning by Ina the cook, a big woman with a rotten temper, who made our life hell if we didn't rise immediately. It was bitterly cold, even in early October, and I shivered as I washed then dressed in the plain grey dress I had been given.

On my first day I was drinking a cup of tea before starting work and was amazed at the number of all the kinds of pots, pans, frying pans, fish kettles in different sizes and big black kettles. Most of the cooking pots and pans were in copper and hung up in rows on the wall. The big black range was twice the size of the one we had at home. Cook shouted at me, 'You won't get much work done sitting there all day dreaming.' She flung a coarse grey apron at me and told me to start peeling the days vegetables. I didn't realise that any household could consume so much food in a day. The rest of the day was spent cleaning all the big pots and pans cook used. After that I had the big stone floor of the kitchen and the pantry to scrub out. The servants all got their meals in the kitchen, even the toffee nosed butler.

Theresa was the kitchen maid before me so she showed me the ropes, what to do and what not to do. 'On no account get on the wrong side of cook or she will make your life hell.'

I still cried myself to sleep. The first week I was at the Ramsays I was so dead beat I would crawl up the stairs to the attic and fling myself on the bed without even washing myself and fall fast asleep as soon as my head touched the pillow. When I was wakened in the morning by Theresa I felt so sore and tired and did not want to get up. Theresa was so full of life as she went about her work cleaning all the big rooms upstairs. She had lovely rosy cheeks, dark flashing eyes and jet black curly hair. Cook, besides doing all the cooking, had to wash the front hall and door steps every morning; also, she had to clean the front door brasses. She was so stout that when she walked it was more of a waggle. I often used to laugh when Theresa would imitate her.

I very seldom went out as I did not know my way about and by October the days were short and with the black-out, you were apt to get lost. Anyway I had no money; that's what made me so angry with Mum and Dad. They had sent me down to this big strange house without a penny in my hand. My monthly wage then was one pound, five shillings; of course we got our food and board, though everyone was rationed. I often wondered where the Ramsays got all the food. Cook, Theresa and I had to give our ration books to her ladyship. His lordship spent most of his time in the grounds; he had two gardeners who were past the age for being called up to war, so in a way he was lucky to have them. They, of course, had their own small cottages.

About the second week I had been working I got a letter from Mum. Dad still kept up his spite against Nan and Donald and his grandchildren. Nan now had five of a family, Sarah was going steady with Hector; she was missing him as he had been moved to Coldishaw in England where the Spitfire planes were. Vera was called up for the Land Army; she had written to Mum and said she enjoyed the work. Billy and Ewan were still at school, too young to be called up, thank God. I loved my little brothers. The two of them were great pals with Grant Ross. The three of them were inseparable. The blacksmith now had a small boat which Grant, Billy and Ewan were allowed to go out in, so long as they kept near the shore of the loch.

I missed home and the carefree days spent beside the loch with Nan, Sarah, Vera, Dad and the boys. Those days were gone. Three weeks before Christmas, Master James and Master John came home for the Christmas holidays. I very seldom saw them as I was always busy in the kitchen skivvying away there. What a life, every day the same; up at six in the morning dead tired, the never ending vegetable peeling and pot scouring and scrubbing stone floors. My hands by this time were covered with sore hacks; cook gave me some horrible grease to rub on them but it was a long time before they got hardened. Cook lorded over everyone; I think her ladyship was very careful what she said to her as she was a good cook and Lady Ramsay did not want to lose her.

When Master James was home, Theresa used to spend a lot more time upstairs, and sometimes at first I had imagined that someone sneaked into our room at night. Theresa's bed and mine creaked terribly when we got into them at night. One night the noise of Theresa's bed woke me up; it was pitch black, all I heard was the bed creaking and someone whispering; 'Come on don't be afraid.' At first I thought I was dreaming but as my eyes got used to the dark I made out a tall figure in a night-shirt, tip toeing out of our bedroom. This went on regularly while Master James was at home. Theresa carried on as usual, her cheery self.

On Christmas Day we all had to line up in the hall to get our Christmas presents from her ladyship. The two gardeners, butler, cook, Theresa and myself. My present was a pair of black stockings which I badly needed; I had saved up and sent Mum a lace edged handkerchief, also a lovely card. I watched for the post every day to see what Mum would send me but nothing came. I think it was then I realised that both Mum and Dad did not give a thought for me. I often wondered why; I had done no wrong yet both of them treated me as if I had.

Master James and his brother John went back to university. I think Theresa was quite pleased. I spent my days off in my room reading. What with the blackout and the cold wet weather, I still did not know my way about Glasgow. Cook said when the days lengthened she would take me round the shops. When the postman came he would linger at the back door hoping to catch a glance of Theresa. If Theresa caught sight of him she would give him a big smile and a wave.

The months went by and I settled into my daily routine of scrubbing, and true to her word cook one day took me out shopping. I was amazed at all the big shops in every street. With cooks help I got a few personal things which I needed; also a nice dress for five shillings. After shopping we went into a tea-room and had a lovely tea with cream cakes which I had never seen before. We arrived back in time to get the supper ready. For the first time since I left home I felt happy. What I had bought I had earned with my sore hands. A week before Easter, Master James and his brother John came home for the Easter holidays. I often wondered why the two grown up sons were not called up for the Forces while boys much younger than they were. That I was never to find out. On the first night the boys were home I was wakened again by the terrible noise of Theresa's bed creaking. After quite a while I watched Master James creeping on tip toe out of the bedroom. This went on all through the holidays. I was getting a bit tired of all the sneaking out and in of my bedroom. I asked Theresa what it was all about; 'You will hear soon enough about everything, Mary,' she said.

It was a week later after James and John went away that Theresa was called into the drawing room. Theresa by this time was getting a lot stouter, but in my innocence, I never bothered about it or gave a thought that anything was wrong. Cook went about tight lipped; she obviously knew. About an hour later Theresa came into the kitchen and told cook and me that she had been given a month's notice to leave then she sat at the big table and burst into tears. The whole story came out. Master James had got her pregnant but when Theresa told her ladyship all about the goings on at night, her ladyship would not believe her and called her a lying slut.

'I have seen you,' she said, 'carrying on with the postman when he calls. The child will be his so don't try and blame Master James, he is just a boy. So from today you will be given a months notice to leave.'

I felt sorry for Theresa. She helped me a lot in my first year then again my mind went back to my sister Nan when she came home in disgrace. Why was it always the girls who were disgraced but never the boys; I thought that was most unfair.

I had never kept in touch with Nan since she got married so I thought on my Sunday off I would write her a long letter. I told her about the work I was doing, more like slavery if you asked me then mentioned the story about Theresa. Nan, of course, would understand how miserable Theresa felt. After I finished writing it I thought since it was a nice spring day that I would go out and post it. The letter box was just at the corner of the road. When I came back in, cook, Theresa and Jack the postman were all sitting at the big kitchen table drinking tea. Cook invited me to have a cup also. Then Theresa blurted out that Jack and she would be getting married in three weeks time. She also said Jack had got his call-up papers and would be leaving in a few days after they were married. I got up from my chair and gave Theresa a big hug and wished Jack all the happiness.

I had asked Nan in my letter to try to find out Vera's address for me as I would like to write to her also. Mum and Dad never wrote to me; I often wondered how my little brothers Billy and Ewan looked right now. Oh, how I missed my brothers and sisters. At times in this beautiful big house I felt so lonely. When Theresa left I was made parlour maid; cook took me shopping for morning and afternoon uniforms. Her ladyship paid but at the end of the month half a crown was deducted from my pay towards paying for them. In fact you got nothing for nothing. My work as parlour maid was pretty hectic. I rose as usual at 6.00 a.m. and gulped down a cup of tea before I cleaned and lit all the fires, carried scuttles of coal up to each room, took tea to her ladyship and his Lordship in bed, set the breakfast table, cleaned out the dining room, drawing room, bathroom and the library. Cook in the meantime was busy cooking the breakfast.

To replace me in the kitchen a new girl called Katie Brown was started. I felt sorry for her, she was so small and frightened looking and I could see the tears in her eyes. I gave her a big smile and told her not to worry as cook's bark was worse than her bite, then down to breakfast. Katie hardly ever spoke; the big pots and pans were a bit of a struggle for her to clean at first. Cook lost her temper with Katie as the heavy pots would more or less go crashing on to the floor as they were much too heavy for her. Then cook would lift them into the sink for Katie to clean; also the poor girl hadn't the strength to scrub the stone floors. Cook would just look and shake her head.

The long summer days arrived and I was able to make my way about Glasgow. I liked most the beautiful big shops; all the clothes on show in the windows were out of this world, to me anyway. Also, besides the price of a dress, would be the amount of clothes coupons that were needed. It was coupons for everything, food as well as clothes.

Cook and I went to Theresa's wedding which was very quiet and took place in a Register Office. There were about four other couples getting married that same afternoon; some of the young husbands would be going to the war in a few days time. Ina, Jack and Theresa and I wished the newly married couple all the happiness in their future years. When we were leaving Theresa pulled me aside and whispered that Jack knew the baby wasn't his but he said that he always loved her.

Cook and I got back to our usual footing, she was the boss in the kitchen and I was just a parlour maid. In the long summer days, Master James and his younger brother John were a pain in the neck. They thought because we were maids they could do anything they liked with us. One day when I was cleaning out her ladyship's bedroom James sneaked up behind me while I was making the bed. He said I had turned out to be a pretty little thing and gripped me round my breasts. At first I was taken by surprise then I realised what his intentions were. Well I flew into action, took the duster out of my pocket and struck him across the face. He jumped back calling me a spitfire and saying that he would fix me later. I was angry, also frightened he would go to his mother and tell her a pack of lies; I had my position to think of. I did not want to be sent home in disgrace.

After the supper dishes were done Katie and I made our way up to our dreary attic bedroom. The pair of us must have fallen fast asleep straight away; as usual we were dead beat. I was wakened by someone on top of me.

I opened my mouth to scream but a big hand covered my mouth.

'Shut up you slut, I am going to put you in your place.' I opened my mouth wide and with all my force, clamped my teeth into a little finger. The intruder let out the most awful scream and jumped off the bed and out of our room. The noise woke little Katie and she started crying; I had to go to her bed till she fell asleep.

Next morning I carried on as usual, handling all my different chores. While I was serving breakfast I noticed Master James was missing; when I went back to the kitchen I mentioned to cook that Master James was not down for breakfast.

'Oh,' she said, 'didn't you hear, his lordship had to drive him to the Western General hospital, he nearly lost his finger in an accident last night.'

I thought to myself, he was lucky it was just his finger.

The following morning the postman delivered a letter for me. It was from my sister Nan; I was so excited but had to put it away in my apron pocket till lunch time when I would have peace to read it. The news was mostly about how hard she had to work with all the young children to look after and she herself never keeping well. Donald's mother just sat in the chair beside the fire all day and expected Nan to dance attendance to her. Donald and his brothers and dad were kept busy with the cows and sheep and the work on the land. She went on, the only time she saw mum and dad was when they all attended church, but dad still ignored her. Also, Sarah our sister was going steady with Hector MacLean, who was now high up in the RAF. She hadn't heard any word about Vera so could not send me her address. She saw Billy and Ewan at church every Sunday and both were looking well, 'lovely boys'. The letter finished, 'all my love Nan.' I sat down on my bed and cried, I missed them all so much.

During the summer it was a pleasure to work in this lovely big house, the windows usually were kept open and the lovely lace curtains would blow gently with the warm soft breezes. The only snag was I dreaded when Master James was at home. I used to think he hated me, he would be always up to some dirty trick. The first day he saw me brushing the stair carpet with the banister brush and dust pan he ran up the stairs two at a time. I leant against the wall to let him pass. As he passed me he gave me a sly punch and kicked the dust pan all the way down the stairs and ran up the rest of the stairs laughing, leaving me to start the stairs all over again. This happened quite a few times, and always when there was no one else to see him, until I came to the end of my tether. I said to myself, I will be ready for you next time.

15

The staircase consisted of seventeen steps to the first landing, then another ten steps to the next landing. Making sure that my employers were out, for I did not want them to get hurt, I decided to put a piece of string along the third step from the first landing, tying it tight so that Master James would fall flat on his face. I thought to myself, maybe after that I will get peace to do my work. The next day true to form while I was brushing down the stair Master James came in the front door. He looked up and saw me kneeling brushing the stairs. With a sneer on his face he flew up the stairs but never reached the top. He tripped on the string and let out a loud cry as he went toppling down the stairs. I flew down to the stair and hid the string in my apron pocket then went up to the next landing. I was there when cook came out of the kitchen and found Master James lying his full length in the hall.

I shouted over the banister to cook, 'What is wrong?'

She shouted up to me, 'come down right away, Master James is ill.'

I ran down the stairs showing such concern and said to cook that we better phone for the doctor. Just then her ladyship came home followed by the butler; she took one look at her son and ordered the butler to carry Master James up to bed. I looked down at my tormentor and, seeing him lying on the floor looking so helpless, for the first time since I became parlour maid felt really sorry for him. I found out later in the day from cook that Master James was to stay in bed for a week as he had got a nasty knock on the head. I was relieved to hear that he would not die. Of course he lived to cause more trouble. Not to me but to little Katie whom I tried to look after as she was such a delicate girl.

A nurse came the next day to take care of Master James while he lay ill in bed. She looked a right old battle-axe, but she was a good nurse, very strict. I was never allowed into James's room, thank God, otherwise I think I would have finished him off. I usually carried all his meals up for him, laid the tray on a small table at the door. After I had knocked at the door, nurse would appear and take the tray into the room. It was a great feeling to be able to go about my work with the knowledge that I would not be pestered with Master James. John, his younger brother, was completely different, I think he knew what was going on for when he passed me at any time he would just smile and give me a sly wink.

The war was into its second year now and the food rations were poor. Two ounces of everything, even the sweeties, but still the Ramsays seemed always to have plenty of food. Of course when war broke out his lordship ordered the large lawn at the back of the house to be dug up and the gardeners planted all kinds of vegetables. That in itself helped us a lot and there was the hot house with the tomato and cucumber plants. At the other end of the large plot were rows of fruit bushes. In the autumn cook was extra busy making all the different kinds of jam.

Cook and I were getting along a lot better; she could rely on me if any crisis came up. Katie, also, was growing taller and stronger. I think she must have been starved before she came to us. Theresa would visit us often, while we were all sitting round the big kitchen table drinking our tea, and would give us all the news about herself and Jack her husband. She said Jack was such a thoughtful person. She lived with him only a week before he went off to war.

The next week a new postman came with our letters, much older than Jack, and I got a surprise as there was a letter for me. I pushed it in my apron pocket till I got time to read it after lunch. After I had attended to serving lunch in the dining room, I gulped down mine in the kitchen then flew upstairs to my bedroom to read my letter. At first sight I thought it was a letter from Nan, instead it was from my sister Vera who worked in the Land Army.

Her work was even worse than mine, in all kinds of weather she and another three girls had to start work at 5 a.m. First of all the cows had to be milked, forty in all, then the pigs fed, and the pig stye cleaned out; that was before they had any breakfast. She said the food was good, 8 a.m. was breakfast time. They always had a big plate of porridge, boiled egg and toast and as much tea as they liked. Lunch and supper, too, were good. After breakfast they went into the fields to plant potatoes and every kind of vegetable you could think of. In the summer the long days were too much for them; at the end of the day the girls were dead tired. After a wash they all would just flop down on their beds. The four girls lived in the one hut which was specially built for them. Vera was now 17 years old and very fed up. The big farm where she worked was in Angus and quite a distance from the nearest town. She complained that the issue of clothing coupons was terribly inadequate. I still had quite a few of mine left but thought to myself I would hang on to them in case I had a daft spending spree. I noticed that Vera never once mentioned mum and dad or the boys so I did not know what was going on at home. Oh how I longed for the peace and stillness of the loch.

Life went on as usual at the big house of the Ramsays. Master James was up and about again but he kept out of my way; my worry was how was I to keep a watchful eye on Katie. I was sure Master James would look upon her as easy prey. I could look after her at night because before I went to bed every night I would jam the handle of the door with the one and only chair we had in the room. I warned Katie against him and that was the best I could do.

17

Cook and the new postman became very friendly and often I would find them sitting at the table drinking tea and laughing their heads off. It was a change to see cook happy.

In the third year of the war things were becoming a lot more frightening. The sirens would sound more often and we all had to leave whatever we were doing and run downstairs to the cellars till the all clear went off. Sometimes we would be downstairs for hours; those were the times when Clydebank was bombed. We would sit huddled together, frightened to death. Cook would give us all the news at breakfast the next morning. It seemed a lot of damage was done to the shipyard and the houses at Clydebank. The people had to be evacuated to different parts of the country; what a mess the whole place was left in.

The summer came to an end and the dreary dark days returned. It was really dark, not a light could be seen anywhere. Most people stayed indoors, it was safer. It was Nan my sister who wrote to tell me Sarah and Hector were getting married in the village church on 7 December 1943. Nan said it was to be a big wedding. Mum, it seemed, was making all Sarah's trousseau, from the beautiful white satin dress to her lace panties. It was then I remembered the big cupboard in mothers and dad's bedroom filled with all different kinds of bales of material, yet never once did she make any kind of dress for Nan, Vera or me. Why was Sarah so special? Mum never even wrote to me inviting me to come home for the wedding. That night when I went to bed I cried myself to sleep. After the wedding Sarah and Hector were to go back to Inverness for a fortnight's honeymoon then Hector would return to his flying base.

On my seventeenth birthday cook made me a lovely cake and her ladyship gave me a little purse with sixpence in it. I went into the drawing room specially to thank her. While I was there she told me to sit down as she wanted a few words with me. She asked me right away if cook or I had ever seen Theresa since she had her baby boy. I told her that Theresa had stopped visiting us when she became very stout, in fact none of us had seen her since. Her ladyship said if anytime she calls, tell her I wish to see her. I got up from my seat and said that cook or I would give Theresa the message; she thanked me as I left the room. My mind went back to the day of Theresa and Jack's wedding when she told me that her baby was not Jack's. I was beginning to think that her Ladyship knew all along that Theresa's child was Master James's, her grandson. But, sadly, Theresa never came back for years, in fact cook and I were beginning to forget all about her.

It was drawing near Christmas and cook was extra busy making the plum puddings, mince pies and shortbread. The lovely smell of the baking took me back to my childhood days when every Saturday dad and the children ran into our big kitchen and saw all the lovely fresh baking mum had made, covering the table. Billy and Ewan were always the first to snack a hot scone off the table and run outside again, never taking time to wait for tea. It was cook's voice which brought me back to the present. She said Master James was bringing a guest home with him and I had to prepare the guest room right away for her. I thought, at last Master James must have a steady girlfriend. I spent the whole morning thinking what sort of girl she was; in a way I felt sorry for her as I alone knew how cruel he could be. Anyhow I aired the room, changed the bed, put flowers on a table at the window and hoped the girl would have a pleasant stay. I certainly would go out of my way to make her stay a happy one. While I was serving at dinner that evening, I got a good look at Margaret, James's girlfriend; she was simply stunning, jet black hair, large dark eyes and very pale skin. I would put her age about 19 years. Master James was 22. When I went back to the kitchen I told cook what I thought.

'Yes,' she said, 'I know, I have seen her and she is as cold as ice.'

I wondered at the time what she meant but before Margaret left I was to find out for myself.

The next morning her ladyship came into the kitchen and said that Margaret would be having her breakfast in bed while she was her guest. I looked at cook who just nodded. Katie of course was always in the background working, cleaning the never ending dirty pots and pans. I set Miss Margaret's tray and carried it upstairs to her bedroom. After I had pulled the black-out curtains back I woke Miss Margaret and helped her to sit up. Also, I put extra pillows behind her back then laid her breakfast tray on the bed. I was on the verge of starting to pick up her clothes from the floor when I heard an enormous crash. Miss Margaret had flung the tray and its contents on the floor. I was taken aback at the suddenness of it all. I just left the room and went downstairs to the dining room and asked her ladyship if I could have a word with her. She excused herself and rose from the table leaving his lordship and his two sons sitting there. We went out into the hall and I told her what had happened when I had taken Miss Margaret's breakfast up to her.

Her Ladyship never said a word but went straight up the stairs to the guest room. I went back into the kitchen and told cook what had happened.

'I was expecting something like that to happen; we will just have to wait and see what her ladyship says.'

19

Katie and I had just sat down at the table for breakfast when her ladyship came in.

'Mary,' she said, 'before you start your breakfast I would like you clean up Miss Margaret's bedroom as I will be phoning for the doctor to call in to see her, also take Katie with you, that's quite a mess to clean up,' and as she turned to the door, 'I am sorry, Mary, about all this.'

Katie and I made our way up the stairs to the guest room.

I knocked at the door and a voice answered, 'come in'.

I got quite a shock, Miss Margaret was sitting up in bed with the loveliest smile you ever seen on her face. She looked beautiful; her first words were, 'Mary I am so sorry about all the mess on the floor, the tray of course just slid off the bed.'

I thought to myself who does she think she is fooling. I answered, 'Don't worry, Miss Margaret, Katie and I will have it cleaned up in no time.'

What a mess the carpet was in, marmalade, porridge, bacon and egg and sugar. It took the two of us a good half hour to get the room back to normal. Of course the lovely carpet would take some time to dry as Katie had to scrub it. As we were leaving I wished Miss Margaret a pleasant day.

'Thank you, Mary,' she said, 'and the little one.'

Both of us were glad to get out of that room and downstairs to our breakfast. By this time Katie and I were starving and cook had made us a bit of bacon and egg. I enjoyed it and had two cups of tea.

After breakfast I had my usual chores to do. The family had all gone up to the drawing room so I started cleaning the dining room first. The windows looked out on the long driveway to the front door. I noticed the doctor's car there and I wondered how long he had been in the house – everything seemed so quiet. After I had finished in the dining room I started brushing down the long staircase; that way I was sure to see who was going out or coming in. I often heard it said that the servants knew more about the house than the lady of the house knew herself, which to a certain extent was true. The doctor came and went but we never found out what was the matter with Miss Margaret.

She must have moved in the upper classes for she wore very expensive clothes in the latest fashion. Master James and Miss Margaret went everywhere together, both of them in a world of their own. For the rest of Miss Margaret's stay she behaved the perfect lady; as for Master James I thought he had grown up and forgotten his hatred for me, until the night that her ladyship was giving a big dinner party in honour of James and Margaret's engagement. Margaret's parents, Lord and Lady Liddle, were there. So, too, were our doctor and his wife and the minister and his wife. It was while I was serving the second course that the accident happened. The butler carved the meat at the side table then I took the plate and placed it in front of each guest. Katie was helping with serving the vegetables and I went round to each guest with the gravy boat. Master James was the second last one I had to serve. Just as I was about to pour the gravy he purposely nudged my arm and I spilled the gravy over the beautiful cloth. He put his napkin up to his mouth to hide the sneer but his eyes told me all. Her ladyship was upset, worried in case Master James had been burnt with the hot gravy. Her ladyship did not know that besides the nudge, Master James also gave me a vicious kick on my leg. It had taken me all my strength not to cry out with the pain in my leg. I think Miss Margaret was a bit suspicious but she just looked at Master James with those lovely dark eyes of hers. I, of course, was banned from the dining room for the rest of the evening. I resolved to bide my time to get my own back on Master James even if it took me years.

I told cook the truth. She was blazing.

'That Master James,' she said, 'he is a bad one; I don't like the thought of Miss Margaret being with him alone.'

At the end of the week Miss Margaret came into the kitchen to say goodbye to cook, myself and Katie. She handed something to Katie then with that special smile of hers she was gone. My first thoughts were, the three of us in the kitchen would have a lot less work to do. Katie went up to cook, opened her red sore hand and showed her what the lady had given her. It was a shining new shilling. I thought I saw cook wipe a tear from her eyes. Next minute she yelled that well we all better get on with the work but first would have a nice cup of tea and a big slice of that nice fruit cake. The three of us sat down to our fly cup of tea which we all enjoyed. After tea we were ready to do battle again to attend to the never ending chores.

It was getting near Christmas and cook, Katie and I went shopping for presents. Katie hardly ever went out and it was a delight to see the expression on her face when confronted by all the lovely things. I had plenty of coupons but wasn't sure I had enough money even though my pay was now thirty-five shillings a month. There were so many people to buy presents for – all my sisters, my brothers and, of course, cook and Katie. Before going home we had tea and cream cakes in the tea-room. When we got back the butler told me that her ladyship wanted to see me immediately.

I ran up the stairs to my bedroom, dropped all my parcels on the bed then ran down the stairs to the drawing room. I knocked on the door then went in. Her ladyship was sitting beside the fire. She said, 'Come over her Mary and sit down. While you were out shopping your mother phoned to say she wanted you to return home straight away as your dad had taken ill and she needed your help to nurse him.' I thought to myself, what a cheek mum had expecting me to drop tools and run whenever she asked. I just sat in silence then her ladyship said, 'I don't like the idea of you travelling that long journey by yourself especially in the black out.'

I said, 'My Lady I am not going home.'

At first I thought she had not heard me because of the long silence that followed then she said, 'If you don't want to go Mary I won't force you. I will write to your mother and explain everything.' When I was walking towards the door her ladyship said, 'Mary, you have a big hole in the heel of your stocking, see to it that you change them right away.'

I flew up the stairs, changed my stockings then flew down them again. I went straight into the dining room to set the supper table for my employers and Master John. It was a pleasure serving John, he was as different from Master James, as day is from night.

When I went back into the kitchen cook had the supper ready so I struck the gong, waited till everyone was seated, served their meal then went to the kitchen for my own supper. Cook and Katie had already started theirs; it was a mixed grill. Joe, the butler, was also there but none of us girls paid any attention, he could have been a block of stone for all the attention he got from us. I told cook and Katie about what had happened in the drawing room. I knew cook was gasping to hear what was going on. I waited until the butler left then gave cook the full story. At first cook just sat at the table slowly drinking her tea then all of a sudden she shouted, 'In my opinion your mother has got a good cheek expecting you just to drop everything and run.'

'Funny, cook,' I said. 'That was the very thought that crossed my mind.'

Then she asked when I would be leaving.

The room was in silence then I said I wasn't going home. Both cook and Katie shouted, good for you. That night before I fell asleep I thought of the last two and a half years that I had slaved away in this big house and not a single letter from mum or dad. Also, I wondered why they had not asked Vera to go home. Maybe they had and she also had refused.

On my next Sunday off I spent most of the day writing letters to Nan and Vera. I asked both of them if they knew anything about Dad's illness. I did not understand how such a powerfully built man always in the best of health suddenly turns ill. When I went down to the kitchen for my supper, Steve the new postman was laughing and joking with cook. When he saw my letters he offered to post them for me and I was pleased to hand them over. I did not realise how hungry I was till I sat down at the table and cook placed a big plate of trout in front of me, filled my cup up with tea and placed lovely new baked scones just out of the oven. One thing, nobody could beat Ina at cooking and baking. After supper I went straight back up to my room, thinking of dad and feeling so sad that he had kept up his spite to his lovely daughter Nan who lived just across the loch from them.

Next morning her ladyship told me to get the guest room aired again as Miss Margaret would be staying with us the week before Christmas. Also Master James would be home. I thought to myself, trouble. Then again it could be me who would get in first. I would take each day as it came. One thing Master James taught me was to stand up for myself. I was well educated in the wily ways of men. It's funny, on my days off I loved reading love stories but men in real life were completely different. I never really knew how to treat them. I was still young, only 17 years and most of my life spent in the Ramsay's big house. Katie was turning into a bonnie girl, but still on the shy side. I was different at 15 years, I always had my brothers and sisters to play with and at school we had plenty of friends. I don't know if Katie had any family, she never once mentioned anyone. Anyhow, with Master James home again, Miss Margaret or not, the chair was getting used to jamming our bedroom door. For Katie's sake, also mine, I wasn't going to take any chances.

Miss Margaret was as beautiful as ever when she came into the house leaning on the arm of Master James. I went up to the guest room with her to see her settled in. Her room looked so cosy with the big coal fire burning brightly. I laid out her night-dress and dressing gown and slippers, told her when supper would be ready and left. I ran down the back stairs so I would not need to pass Master James's room. I was always on edge when he was home, wondering what dirty trick he would get up to. The week passed without any incident happening, maybe he was so much in love with Margaret that he had eyes only for her.

On Christmas Day the butler, the cook, Katie and I all lined up in the hall as usual with the two gardeners, to get our Christmas present from her ladyship. As each one was handed their present she wished them a Merry Christmas. Then she and his lordship returned to the drawing room while we went back to the kitchen. Cook wasn't in a good mood, what with all the extra guests coming. I helped Katie and cook with the vegetables, mashing the potatoes, making the gravy. The big dining table was already set with all the extra decorations, lighted candles, crystal glasses shining, large crackers and a little present set at each place. As the last course was being served, His Lordship rose and raised his glass in a toast to Master James and Miss Margaret. Everyone raised their glasses and wished the young couple all the happiness. Margaret and James just sat smiling at one another.

During our Christmas dinner I had time to open her ladyship's present to me, a pair of woollen gloves. The following week I got two small parcels, one from my sister Nan, the other from my sister Vera. I opened Nan's present first; it was a woollen scarf which she had knitted herself; also a letter was enclosed. She said that the only time she saw mum and dad was at church on Sunday. No, she did not knew that dad had taken ill; also she had seven of a family now to look after. She could not very well leave Donald to take care of them. As for her mother-in-law, all she did was sit at the fire all day. Nan thanked me for the present I sent her, a bone hair comb.

After I read the letter, I thought to myself what a terrible life women have to lead after they were married, having babies every year. I wondered how Sarah and Hector were getting on; nobody seemed to know anything about them. Of course they lived in a different circle. I then opened Vera's present, a pair of silk stockings, they were beautiful. I wondered where on earth she could have got them from; in her letter most of her talk was about her new boyfriend, an American in the Air Force. She said she was madly in love with him and on her days off from the Land Army she met Andy Carter, her boyfriend, and he usually gave her a good time. At the latter part of the letter she said mum had not written to her about dad's illness, anyway she had no intention of going home as the Land Army needed her. I thought to myself, why me of all my sisters. Why did mum have to send for me when she needed help, when I was the only one who was sent out to work at 15 years. Again the bitterness I felt two and a half years ago came back to me and I vowed to myself, for now on I would put myself first. I told her ladyship that I would be looking for a better position and that I would be giving a month's notice.

'There is no need for you to do that, Mary, I am very pleased with your work so I would like you to become housekeeper. Your work will be to check every morning the time and place of all his lordship's and my social engagements, attend to any telephone calls, keep a list of all the linen and various other things I have to attend to. Also, your pay will be two pounds ten shillings a month starting from your eighteenth birthday which is months away. Will you be able to wait that long?'

'Oh yes, my Lady,' I said.

'But before you go, Mary, no mention of this meantime to the rest of the staff.'

The next four months I went about in a dream thinking of my promotion. By the time that came about, Theresa would have been away three years. Her little son would be 2½ now. I often wondered if her ladyship thought about him. If he looked anything like his mother, he must be a beautiful baby. Funny I should be thinking of Theresa because the next morning the postman brought cook a letter from her. Steve the postman stayed for a quick cup of tea. Katie and I sat and waited till cook read it. She told us Theresa lived in a room in Partick. Jack was home on leave last week but is away to the front line again, he would not say where. Both herself and Alan her son were keeping well. She had her weekly pension so she was not too badly off. She hated the blackout, that was why she never travelled much. When Katie went outside to the bucket, I asked cook if we should tell her ladyship. 'I'll think about it,' she said. I knew I gave my promise to her ladyship for cook and I to let her know if at any time we heard word about Theresa. It was not me who got the letter so it was up to cook to tell her.

The months seemed to drag on but at last my eighteenth birthday arrived; I had kept my secret from cook and Katie about my promotion. Cook again baked me a lovely birthday cake, also she gave me a box of handkerchiefs; Katie gave me a hair clasp. When I went to the dining room to serve breakfast, her ladyship wished me a happy birthday and said she wanted to see me in the drawing-room after breakfast. As I was leaving she handed me a small parcel. I thanked her and hurried into the kitchen to see what she had given me. When I opened the parcel I was very disappointed to find a pair of black stockings. Cook and Katie sensed how I felt. Both of them in one voice told me to cheer up. There was a card from my sister Nan; also one from my sister Vera but nothing from mum and dad. Why worry, they never gave a thought about me anyway. After breakfast I told cook that her ladyship wanted to see me so I left to go up to the drawing-room. I knocked on the door before I went in. Her ladyship told me to sit down. Then she rose from her seat and went and stood looking out of the big bay windows.

'Mary,' she said, 'I know I promised you the position of housekeeper but his Lordship says I will have to cut down as the food situation is becoming serious. Britain is surrounded by German U-boats. Their aim is to sink every British ship in sight and food on the black market is becoming too expensive. The result is we have to live within our ration allowance, so you see, Mary, I am afraid you will be remaining as parlour maid.'

What her ladyship did not tell me was that the government had called up all women to work in the munitions factories; also the wages the girls got were much better than working as a servant in the big houses and they had better conditions and more time off to enjoy themselves. If I had known I'd have left there and then. As it was, the thought was in my mind, anyway. But, I was offered a ten shilling rise and agreed to stay until after Master James's wedding.

Another, longer, letter from Vera told me how she missed her boyfriend, who had been posted overseas, and the chocolates and stockings he had been giving her. She thought she might be pregnant. Also, Nan had written to her saying that dad had had a stroke.

I was 18 years old by then and felt really grown up; the last three years all I had ever done was work and slave in that big house. Katie was also grown up, 17 years, but the poor girl hardly ever saw the sunshine in that big kitchen, doing nothing all day but wash dirty pots and pans and scrubbing stone floors. What a life I thought the two of us endured and to crown it all that night after Katie and I dropped dead beat on our bed and fell fast asleep I was wakened by someone in my bed. I was about to scream but a big hand was put over my mouth.

'Don't dare make a sound or I will see that you are sacked first thing in the morning.'

I didn't say a word. I opened my mouth wide and clamped my teeth full force down on the man's fingers. With one loud scream he jumped off the bed and hobbled out of the room in his night-shirt. At first I thought it was Master James but lo and behold it was the dirty old man himself, his lordship. I was glad he never went near Katie's bed and woke her up.

Next morning, Katie and I went about doing our own chores; I set the breakfast for my employers in the dining room and went back to the kitchen. Her ladyship was already there telling cook that his lordship had to go to the hospital as he had hurt his hand and that there would be just one for breakfast. Like father like son, I thought. I told cook what had happened and said I was giving a fortnight's notice; also I would be taking Katie with me.

'Oh don't do that to me, Mary,' she said, 'if you and Katie go, so will I. Sit down and eat your breakfast first then the three of us will discuss what we are going to do.'

I told cook I was giving a fortnight's notice to her ladyship when I took her breakfast up to her.

'All right,' cook said, 'but don't say anything else.'

I handed in my notice to her ladyship; I think she had a good idea what had happened. She accepted my notice and told me to get on with my work. His lordship came into the hall while I was brushing down the stairs. I was ready for him if he came near me but luckily I was saved by the doorbell ringing. It was the postman, not our usual Steve who always came to the back door, with a telegram for his lordship. Lord Ramsay took the telegram to his study and told me to ask his wife to join him. I had to drop everything and climb the long stairs again to give her ladyship the message. I really was beginning to get sick fetching and carrying all day long for those two people whose only thought was for themselves.

I was halfway down the stairs when I heard her ladyship calling my name. Up the stairs I went again, knocked and entered the drawing room.

'Mary,' she said, 'that was a telephone message from your mother saying she needs you at home. She wants you to leave immediately as your father has taken a turn for the worse.'

I said I would finish my notice and would write, telling my mother when I'd be home. I turned and went down to finish the stairs then, after serving lunch, went to the kitchen for mine. After I had finished my lunch, I told cook about my mother's telephone call and that I would be leaving as soon as my notice was finished.

Cook said, 'Well Mary, that alters everything now; Katie and I will be staying on. I am sorry you are leaving but your parents come first.'

I thought to myself, no one seems to think I should come first; one day I vowed, I would do that. In the meantime I had three letters to write, one to mother and one each to my sisters Nan and Vera telling them I was going home.

That night before Katie and I settled down to sleep I sat down beside her and told her all about Master James and his lordship. I told her straight to make sure that she jammed her bedroom door with the chair. I showed her how to do it. 'Remember, Katie, it will be either them or you, make sure it is not you.' I felt better after our talk then jumped into bed and fell asleep. The next morning I gave my letters to Steve to post who was sitting drinking tea when I went into the kitchen for my breakfast. Now that I was leaving soon I was going to make sure that I would take it easy.

CHAPTER 2

The day I left Rutherglen House was bright and sunny; I was happy. The night before I had packed my small case so I was ready to leave for home as soon as I had my breakfast and had my pay and ration cards from her Ladyship. During my three years here I had saved most of my pay so I was quite comfortably off. I made sure nobody else would know. I had worked hard for the money. I said goodbye to Ina and Katie saying I would keep in touch with them then set off on the long journey to Loch Etive and home.

I had forgotten how beautiful the countryside was. All the different shades of green, the little well kept cottages with their trim gardens, the tall stately trees with their lovely green leaves rustling in the winds, the lochs so peaceful as the packed train flew by the countryside. Cook had made up lunch for me, lovely ham sandwiches and a big slice of her special cake. I had to change trains at Crianlarich; when I boarded that train I found it jammed with people. I wondered where they were all going, all the young men were in uniform. When I eventually arrived at our village station I thought I was the only one getting off so I was taken aback when all the men jumped off also. I wondered where they were all staying. I was feeling very tired after my long journey and still had two miles to walk before I reached home. Thank goodness it was still light so if I hurried I would arrive home before blackout. As I walked along the quiet country road I wondered how mum and dad would look; also my young brothers Billy and Ewan. My mind wandered back to our carefree days when we were all young. Yes we had happy times then.

At last I was home. I thought I'd better knock on the door first instead of just walking in. In a way I felt a stranger; I had been away so long. Mum answered the door, she just stood looking at me then said, 'come in, Mary.' Not as much as a hug or kiss or welcome home. I followed her into the big kitchen and was horrified at the filthy state it was in. I told my mother I was tired after my long journey and that after I had a meal I was going to bed.

'Make yourself tea,' she said, 'but there's no food.'

I just could not believe what I was hearing. After my cup of tea I made my way up to my bedroom where another shock awaited me. There were no clothes on the bed so I just sat down on the chair and fell asleep. I didn't even bother to take my coat and shoes off. When I woke the next morning I felt cramped and sore. The toilet was still outside and we had no running water so I filled a basin with cold water and washed, changed my clothes, brushed my hair then went back to the kitchen. Mum was just sitting on the rocking chair looking out of the window, her face very pale and tired looking. I asked her where dad was.

'In there,' she said, pointing to the parlour.

I walked into the room. My dad, once a powerfully built man with lovely rosy cheeks and always a big smile for us all lay on a single bed near the window and what lay on the bed was just a shell of my dad I knew. I said, 'Hello, Dad. Feeling better?' There was no response. The stroke had left him speechless. I sat and cried. It seemed after he had had a stroke there wasn't the money to pay the doctor. Later Mum found out from the hotel where he spent most of the time drinking that he owed them a lot of money; it was the same at all the local shops. After a while I thought, I suppose I will have to take charge of the sorry mess Mum and Dad are in. When I went back into the kitchen I asked Mum for the ration books intending to go to the shops for food since there was none in the house.

'Books in the shop.'

I nearly exploded, 'In the shops. What on earth are they doing there? You are supposed to keep them.'

'Owe them money,' was all she said.

I thought to myself what on earth is going on. I will go straight down to the shops and find out for myself. Then I asked where were Billy and Ewan. At Nan's was all I got. I was glad to get out into the fresh air again; it was a lovely day, the loch was calm and small boats were going back and forth. I just walked slowly thinking all the time what would be the best thing to do to get my parent's ration books back for them.

I went first to the grocer, Fred Walsh, who did not recognise me. After explaining who I was, I had to listen to his insincere expressions of sorrow about the state my family was in. I was blazing and angrily demanded the return of my parents' ration books, threatening to report him to the Ministry of Food. He reluctantly produced them but refused to let me have any rations until he was paid the four pounds owing to him. I paid him and refused to move until I had all the items on my own list.

When I reached home I went straight to the kitchen; I was starving as I had not eaten since lunch the day before. Right away I filled the kettle; while waiting for it to boil I had to scrub the big kitchen table before I could put any food on it. I would have to find out later what really went wrong with mum and dad. After I made the tea I had two fresh rolls and butter and two big cups of tea. I felt a bit better after that and took dad's breakfast in for him. I had made porridge for both of them. Dad was just lying the same way as he was when I had seen him last night. I thought, dear God, has he lain like that all night. I tried to feed him a little porridge but it was hopeless as I could not open his mouth. I saw down on the chair and cried. After a while I thought this will not get you anywhere. I heated some water and with a face flannel and soap set about washing my father. I changed his bed linen which was filthy and worn, attended to his back sores and shaved his face, cut, washed and brushed his hair then I got a drinking cup up to dad's lips till the cup of tea was empty. I was exhausted by the time I finished. I didn't know why mum didn't get the doctor in to see dad; come to think of it there was no money. I decided to ask Grant Ross to take me over to the other side of the loch on his boat to visit my sister Nan to see what help she could give me. In the meantime mum would have to be attended to.

I found Mum sitting upstairs in her bedroom; she, also, looked as if she needed a bath and change of clothes. First of all I had to coax her to eat some porridge. I took her arm gently and helped her downstairs; she was skin and bone. I laid the plate in front of her, also a jug of fresh milk but she just sat and stared ahead.

'Come on, mum, eat.' I spoon fed her then gave her a cup of tea. Dear God I thought, the two of them would have died of starvation if I had not come home. Our dog Rusty was dead I supposed; it was starvation also, poor loveable dog. I helped mum to change her clothes, seated her in her rocking chair then made my way to the village. I had to get hold of Grant Ross to ask him to row me over to the other side of the loch to visit Nan right away. Luckily I met Grant outside his father's smithy.

'Grant,' I said, 'will you row me over to the other side of the loch?'

He stood and stared at me then said, 'Who are you?'

'I am Mary Scott, Billy and Ewan's sister.'

A big smile spread over his face, 'Of course, Mary,' he said, 'wait till I tell dad first.'

It was a much larger boat than the one they had three years ago; also it had an engine. While we were racing across the loch I took time to study Grant.

When he was young he was so dour looking, now he was 16½, very tall and slim with lots of confidence. When we reached the other side I asked Grant to come back for me in one hour. He said he would. My sister Nan's house was a large two storey building with lots of barns and out-houses. I wondered how Nan looked after nine years and eight children. She was such a beautiful girl before she got married to Donald MacPherson. I made my way up to the big house, knocked on the front door. Nobody answered it so I made my way to the back door. There, at the back of the house, there seemed to be all the children from the village but they were Nan's children. They saw me, they stopped playing and ran into the house. A young woman came out and stood at the door. I could hardly believe the woman standing in front of me was Nan. Gone was the beautiful young girl; instead was a weary, sick mother.

'Nan,' I said, 'it's Mary.'

'Mary, oh my God Mary, how glad I am to see you. Come in dear and give me all the news. First of all I will make a cup of tea.'

Nan moved very slowly, I thought dear God don't say she is dying, also. I followed her into the big kitchen and sat down on one of the chairs at the table while Nan made the tea. The children were all taking turns at having a quick look at me then ran outside again. While drinking my tea I told Nan the real situation at home, the state Mum and Dad were in, both of them, starved and ill and helpless. I also told her the state the house was in.

'Why did they have to send for me and not Sarah or Vera.'

Nan just sat in silence then she said that Donald had forbade her to ever mention their names in his house. She also told me that she was practically a prisoner. The only time she was allowed out was to attend church on Sunday, therefore there was nothing she could do to help. I felt sorry for Nan. What a life. Then I remembered to ask about my young brothers Billy and Ewan.

All she said was, 'Donald works them into the ground.'

My hour was up so I gave Nan a big hug, both of us were crying as we parted then I made my way down to Grant's boat then back to the village again.

I was just where I had started that morning, nobody to turn to for help. I thought to myself while I am in the village I will call on Dr McKinnon. I waited in the waiting room till the last patient was seen than I rapped on the door.

He called, 'Come in,' without looking up and said, 'name please.'

I said, 'Mary Scott.'

He stopped writing, looked up and stared at me. 'Helen and Pat Scott's daughter?'

'Yes,' I said, 'I just arrived home yesterday; I really would like to know how the two of them have never received any help.' I then went on to tell him how I had found my parents and the house in such a terrible state.

He just looked down at his desk and started drawing lines on a bit of paper then he said, 'Sorry, Mary, there is nothing I can do. Both of them are dying; it's just a matter of time.'

I burst into tears; I was too late in coming home. Then again why was no word sent to Sarah and Vera. Why me who had to give up my post and deal with my parents' illness and debts and sorrow.

When I arrived home I heated water to bath dad and I put mum to bed and made her as comfortable as possible then I spoon fed both of them. The whole house needed scrubbing from top to bottom, also clean curtains put up and the windows cleaned but first of all I had to make myself some lunch, some scrambled eggs. I was starving. I only had a cup of tea at Nan's so it was eight o'clock in the morning since I had last eaten. After I had finished lunch I put on an apron, pulled my sleeves up and set to work. I made a start with the bedrooms then worked my way down the stairs to the parlour and finally the big kitchen.

I stopped to heat some thin soup for my mum and dad. Feeding then took me three quarters of an hour. I changed dad again then made myself another cup of tea. While I was scrubbing the kitchen floor, Dr McKinnon walked in. He told me that he had arranged for the district nurse to come in every day to bath dad and also help mum. He apologised for not being able to do more. As he left he promised to look in the next week. I knelt down and finished my floor then the door and outside steps had to be scrubbed also. When I went back into the house I felt a lot better. It was hard work and I was glad that mum and dad were going to get a bit of attention; perhaps maybe too late.

There was plenty of wood for the big range so the kitchen was nice and cosy. I had to write to Auntie Kate in the Isle of Mull and tell her the bad news about Mum and Dad, not that she could do anything as she was old herself. Also, to Vera; maybe she would come home and help me. Sitting at the table writing I felt so helpless, the tears started rolling down my cheeks, I was only 18½ years old and I had such a heavy burden to carry. How as it that my parents got into such a state and nobody in the village cared for them. I would make it my point tomorrow to find out. I fed and changed dad again and took some pudding up to mum. I had a terrible time trying to feed her but finally managed to get her to eat some, washed and made her comfortable. I fried a bit of fish and made some chips for myself. After my meal I would have a good look in all the cupboards and wardrobe.

When I left home I remembered how the big cupboard in my parents' room was jammed with all different kinds of bales of material and bags of wool. I will go straight up and see how much was left. When I opened the door I got the shock of my life; it was empty. What on earth had happened; it was the same with the wardrobe. I could not ask mum in case I upset her. Tomorrow when I went to the village to post my letter and get some messages I would make it my point to see the local priest, Father Joseph Nairn, to see if he could throw any light on the matter.

With that thought in mind I climbed the stairs to my bedroom and then to bed. The next morning I was up early, made some tea and toast for myself, lit the fire and boiled water for nurse to wash Dad and Mum, made porridge, took some to dad but could not get him to eat anything. Nurse came in then and looked and just shook her head. She introduced herself as Nurse Duncan and said she would attend to my father. I went up to Mum but, like Dad, she refused to eat any food. I sat down beside mum and stroked her hair gently. Nurse came running into the room and told me to run down to the village and get Dr McKinnon to come straight away. As I ran for the doctor I sensed that poor Dad had passed away. At last I reached the doctor's surgery, the room was packed with patients. I stood at the door as I did not want to go before my turn when a voice beside me asked if I needed help. I explained the position and a message was sent in to the doctor who came out, apologised to the patients and said, 'Come, Mary, I will take you home.'

When we reached the house the doctor said, 'Just stay in the kitchen, Mary, Nurse and I will attend to your father.'

It must have been about five minutes when Nurse appeared in the doorway and offered to make some tea.

Just then the doctor came in to the kitchen, put his arm round my shoulder and said, 'I am sorry, Mary, but both your parents are dead.'

I just stared out of the window. I wondered if I had heard right; surely doctor was wrong. I was with the two of them about an hour ago. 'No,' I said, 'they are not dead, they can't be, I was going to nurse them better.'

Nurse came over to me, 'Drink your tea, Mary, I will help you to lie down on your bed for a rest.'

There must have been something in the tea because bright sunlight shining into my room woke me up next morning. At first I had forgotten all about the death of my parents then it all came back to me. I sat on the bed and started crying, sobbing my heart out. Why, why I said within myself had mum and dad left me. Dad had died without his forgiveness to my sister Nan. Also Mum never had the chance to tell me why, when I was just 15, I was sent out to service. I would never know now. Nurse came into my bedroom and told me Father Joseph was downstairs, was I well enough to come down. I said I would come down straight away.

Father Joseph was sitting in the kitchen and he got up and shook hands with me. 'Mary, I am here to help you; first of all we will have to send telegrams to all the family. Also there are the arrangements to be made for the funerals.'

I told Father that I did not know Sarah and Hector's address. He said he would phone the RAF base and tell them to trace Sarah and tell her of her parents' death. Also he would go over for Nan and would bring her back. I was on the verge of telling him about my visit but changed my mind. He would find out for himself what the situation was. I had quite a bit of money saved during my three years working. As I was paying for everything since I came home, now I supposed I would have to pay for the funerals.

I was beginning to wonder where it was all going to end when a strange woman came into the kitchen. 'Hello, Mary,' she said, 'I am Morag, I have come to lay out your parents.'

I wondered what she meant but then it dawned and I just put my head on the table and started crying again. I don't know how long I sat crying before I felt a soft hand on my shoulder. I looked up and saw through my tears, a beautiful little girl about 6 years old smiling up at me.

'My name is Helen, Auntie Mary. Mummy brought me over the loch to see you. She said you were not keeping well and I was to be a good girl and help you. See mummy is making some tea for us.'

I looked up to see Nan standing at the range. 'Oh Nan,' I shouted and I flung my arms about her. 'I am so glad you could manage to come,' then both of us burst into tears. Little Helen started crying also. Suddenly, both of us stopped and cuddled little Helen till she stopped crying. I asked Nan how she managed to get away.

It was no trouble, Father Joseph had a few words with Donald then told her to gather a few things together as he was taking her home. She took little Helen to keep her mind off things. It was only when they were halfway across the loch did he tell her about her parents' death. Father Joseph said he would come tomorrow to make arrangements for the funeral service.

The two of us spoke in whispers while we were drinking our tea; little Helen went outside to play, giving us a bit of privacy to talk. I asked Nan if she knew how Mum and Dad got into the state that I found them in when I arrived home. She said, the way she lived she hardly ever spoke to any outsiders; the children kept her busy all day. Also she had the cooking, baking and the never ending washing that had to be done. Many a night she said that she cried herself to sleep thinking of how dad treated her. She could only think that when Dad was drunk he gambled all the money away and mum would be too proud to ask for help.

We decided to go into the parlour and see what we could find in Dad's desk. The desk was locked but we found the key in a pocket of a jacket hanging on the door. The shelves were packed with unpaid bills; the hotel, gambling bills, grocer's; I had paid that one but no way was I paying any more of his debts. It would cost a pretty penny to bury both of them. Nan could not believe her eyes as she went through all the unpaid bills. I said we would just leave things as they were till after the funeral, then we would discuss everything with Auntie Kate, Sarah and Vera. That's to say if they came to the funeral.

My sister Sarah and her husband Hector, in a big Rover were the first to arrive. Both of them were blooming with health; as I looked at Sarah I thought to myself, no shortage of money or coupons here. Hector was in RAF uniform, while Sarah wore a lovely black costume, black silk stockings and black patent high heel shoes. As she walked into the house a slight shadow seemed to come over her face. I flung my arms round her and gave her a big hug and kiss, gave Hector a hug also. Nan also ran and hugged her sister and all at once we all started crying again. Hector went outside and started playing with little Helen; after a while we all settled down again.

Sarah said Hector and she would be staying with Hector's parents so we need not worry about them. Nan made tea for us all again, then Father Joseph came to say that he had made all the arrangements for me. The coffins would be taken right away to the church where they would lie all night and then the following day at 10 a.m. the Requiem Mass would be said for their souls. The telegram boy brought a telegram from Auntie Kate saying she would be arriving late that night. She wondered if anyone could meet her at the station. I told Sarah and she said Hector would meet her. Well that was one problem solved. I asked Nan about the boys, Billy and Ewan, if they would want to come to the funeral also. I really thought they should come over that night. Nan never said a word. I was beginning to think she was afraid of Donald. If it came to a showdown I would go over myself and bring the boys back with me, Donald or no Donald.

That night Auntie Kate arrived; she was completely exhausted, so after a meal I helped her to get into the makeshift bed. I think she was too tired and weary to care where she slept. After I saw she was comfortable I put the light out and prayed that sleep would ease her sorrow at losing her only sister. Nan and little Helen stayed the night also. We went into what used to be Vera's and my room. There was hardly any furniture in it. The bed was there so that was something but no bed linen or blankets. Nan and I were annoyed at the state of affairs. We went downstairs to the parlour, pulled all the large tablecloths from the sideboard, helped ourselves to all the coats that were hanging up in the hall, then made our way back to the bedroom. The tablecloths were used as sheets and the coats as blankets then the three of us settled down for the night.

When we woke up next morning the sun was streaming in the windows. Nan and I left Helen sleeping. When we reached the kitchen Auntie Kate was already up trying to get the fire in the big range going. I told her I'd attend to that while Nan made the breakfast. At that same time Helen appeared in the kitchen doorway crying. Nan lifted her up then Auntie Kate looked after her. After we had all been fed it was time to get dressed and walk down to the church for the service.

Vera had not arrived yet, or had my younger brothers. When I entered the church Sarah and Hector were already there speaking to Father Joseph. When he saw us he came right up to me and said Donald had not brought the boys over yet; would he send Grant Ross over for them in the boat? I said, 'Yes, Father,' and burst into tears.

Nan helped me into my seat followed by little Helen and then Auntie Kate. Sarah and Hector sat in front of us, and all I could think of was would the boys and Vera arrive in time for the Mass. Father Joseph and the two altar boys started the Requiem Mass and I prayed for my dear mum and dad. What wrong dad had done was over; now it was the family left behind who would have to pay the price.

The service was soon over. I followed the two coffins out of the church and was amazed at the crowd of people who were there. The church was packed. Dr McKinnon and Nurse Duncan were there. Then someone put their arms round me. I looked up to see my sister Vera. Standing beside her were my brothers Billy and Ewan. I put an arm round both of them. I was so glad that all the family were at our parents' funeral. After we all left the graveside, Sarah came over to me and said Hector and she had arranged a meal, for which they were paying, in the church hall for anyone who wanted to come. I walked with Nan, Vera, Auntie Kate, Helen and the boys to the hall thinking all the time why, when my parents were alive, nobody bothered about them. The church hall was packed. I wondered where all the people had come from. I thought of our big house on the hill with not a scrap of food in it for the two dearest people I loved most, yet here in this hall everybody, strangers to me, were sitting down eating their fill. Inside of me I was blazing and sick to think while my parents lay starving to death not one neighbour offered any help. I got up and left the table; Nan and little Helen followed me. I wondered how people could be so cruel and I noticed how thin and tired my brothers looked. When I mentioned this to Nan and suggested that they should stay with me, she looked frightened and said Donald would never agree.

Sarah and Hector said they would have to get back to base. Auntie Kate said she would have to leave straightaway also. Hector offered to drive Auntie Kate to the station, so Nan, Vera, little Helen and the boys hugged and kissed her goodbye. As she was leaving she slipped me an envelope which I hid in my coat pocket and said, 'Remember, Mary, whatever happens the house is yours.'

While we were all walking back home Nan said, 'What did Auntie Kate say to you before she left?'

'Oh,' I said, 'she told me I was to look after myself.'

We had just arrived home and settled down to discussing arrangements when who would walk in but Donald who immediately ordered Nan and the boys to come home. Little Helen was sitting on her mother's knee.

I stood up and said, 'How dare you come barging into my house without as much as a knock on the door? The least you could do was to give us a little peace so soon after our parents' funeral.'

At first he was taken aback; my sister Vera also got up and stood beside me, I suppose ready for battle if need be. Donald stood silent for a minute or two. Since the last time I had seen him he had grown into a mean, powerfully built man and if he thought he was going to bully me and Vera the same as he was doing with the rest of the family he was in for a shock. It was me who got the shock.

'Your house,' he said, 'that's a laugh; the money your dad owes me could pay for this house twice over.'

'How dare you talk about my dad like that and I want you out of my house this minute.'

Nan had risen from the chair and taken little Helen's hand; she went to the door and told Donald they were coming but before Donald reached the door I said that my brothers Billy and Ewan were staying with Vera and me.

He turned and said, 'You can't do that, those two boys have still another years' work to do for my father to pay for the loan of money your dad got.'

'My dad is dead now, so also are his debts. Billy and Ewan are staying with me.' With that I went to the door and shut and locked it. My brothers came running to me and threw their arms around me.

'Don't worry dears,' I said, 'I will look after you,' but within myself I thought I don't know how.

I suddenly remembered Auntie Kate's envelope which she had given me. I went into the hall and got it from my coat pocket. I went to the outside toilet where I could read it in peace. Inside the note was fifty pounds and in the note she repeated the same thing about the house saying it was mine. Also, she said, through time I would learn the truth about everything, but for now I was to buy with the money things for the house and plenty of food. I put the note and money in my pocket and went back into the kitchen. Vera had washed the dishes and told me she had got a week's leave from the Land Army.

'That's fine, Vera, I will need help for all the messages from the village shop right away, so if you and the boys can come with me to carry them home.'

Vera said, 'I am sorry, Mary, I don't have much money.'

'That's all right,' I said, 'we will manage.' So the four of us set off for the village shop.

It seemed like yesterday when the four of us were children, laughing and shouting and running down the same road. When we reached the shop it was quite busy. We waited our turn; I had plenty of coupons as I spent very little on myself. Eventually, it was our turn to be served. I gave Mr Walsh the list I wanted. He looked at it then he looked at me. I was ready to explode if he said anything but he just walked through to the back room and came back with a selection of blankets, sheets, pillow slips and the big bag of groceries. I picked two pairs of blankets, two pairs of sheets, pillows, pillow slips then he said that would be ten pounds please. I handed over the money, Vera and the boys stood and looked on. I told Mr Walsh to parcel the blankets and sheets for me. He said he would deliver them and that they were all sorry about the death of my parents. I just nodded and made for the door before I started crying.

We were just coming out of the shop door when Dr McKinnon drew up and he offered to run us home. When we got inside Vera and the doctor went into the parlour. I told the boys to stay in the kitchen. The doctor gave me the death certificates which showed that my parents had died of heart failure due to malnutrition. He told Vera and me to take it easy then he said he was glad the boys were back home and to look after them as they had been through a lot. I wondered what he meant. I thought it best if Billy and Ewan got a bit of freedom and suggested they went to see Grant Ross. They thought that a great idea. After warning them about Donald and telling them to go to Dr McKinnon if there was any trouble, I chased them out. It was after closing time before Mr Walsh brought the bed linen. When I answered his knock he said he was very sorry for being so late but he had been extra busy all day. I thanked him then closed the door. Vera helped me to make up the beds then both of us went back into the kitchen to talk. I asked Vera about her boyfriend in the American Air Force.

'Oh him,' Vera said, 'not a scrap of the pen since he went overseas. I was glad I was not pregnant; from now on I sure will take good care of myself.' She said she liked the Land Army; the days were long but they were well fed; also they had good billets.

I told her of my life of misery as a servant in the Ramsays' household. She roared with laughter when I told her what I did to Master James.

'Good for you, Mary, I am glad that you were able to stick up for yourself. Look out, Donald, here comes Mary,' then both of us burst out laughing.

There was a loud tapping on the window, I looked up to see the boys. I had forgotten I had locked the front door. I opened the door for them, both of them came into the kitchen, sat down and never said a word. After a while I asked Billy what was wrong.

'It's that Grant Ross, his dad has forbade him to speak to us.'

I asked why but he couldn't tell me.

We asked the boys what they wanted for supper.

'Bacon, egg, tomatoes and chips,' the said together.

'Right, bosses,' I said, bringing a smile to their pale, sad faces.

After we finished our supper, the boys went to their room. There used to be lots of books and games for them to play with when they were young but now the room was empty except for the newly made up bed. I told the boys that next day we were going to buy some furniture and that they could choose what they wanted. They were overjoyed and gave me a big hug before washing and going to bed. When I arrived back in the kitchen Vera had finished the supper dishes. I put more logs on the fire then sat in mum's rocking chair. Vera sat at the other side of the fire. 'Vera,' I said, 'I was wondering if you could take Billy with you and get your boss to give him work on his farm. You know in four months time he will be 17 and I would not like him to get his call up papers. If he was working on the land he would be exempt. Vera was enthusiastic and said she would write to the farmer, Mr Smith, and ask if he could give Billy a job.

I kept wondering what had gone wrong at home and why I was always left to carry the can, and it was a little odd the way Sarah and Hector left so suddenly. Perhaps Dad's papers held the answer. Vera agreed to help me look. Both of us set to work going through all the papers. I just could not understand how dad was allowed to run up such high bills. As Vera and I went through them I was beginning to feel a bit suspicious; no way could dad run up all those bills. In the first place, when we were children at home, when mum had no money, she would say tomorrow is pay day. The butler will bring your father's pay tomorrow so we will do without until he comes. Also the shops and the hotel where dad usually went for his drink never allowed any credit. I remembered when I went with mum shopping she always paid cash and I asked Vera, when I went into service, if she went with mum shopping.

'Oh yes,' she said, 'always, and the boys came too to carry the messages.'

'Did Mum always pay cash?'

'Yes,' Vera said, 'always.'

Then it suddenly dawned on her that something was very wrong.

Both of us looked through all the papers to see if dad owed any money to Mr MacPherson, Donald's father but we could not find anything. I thought to myself, I wonder what mischief Donald was up to. Maybe he never forgave dad for turning Nan, his wife, out of the house without a penny. I vowed to myself that I would find out then I said, 'Let's call it a day, Vera. After a cup of tea we will go to bed. You never know what tomorrow might bring.'

The following morning after we all had breakfast we set out to the shops. First of all we wanted to go to a second hand furniture shop for bits and pieces for all the rooms. While the four of us walked to the shops I asked Billy and Ewan if they ever came over with Donald in the boat to help with the shopping. Billy said he always made him go with him and after all the messages were packed he would hand the list to Mr Walsh who would write something on it, then give it back to Donald, then Donald would tell Billy to run home and drop it in the letter box.

'Was that before or after Dad took his stroke?'

'After,' Billy said.

Vera all this time was listening to our conversation and vowed to kill him; I knew who she meant but because of the boys I never said a word. We all went inside into the furniture shop. It was lovely to see the boys laughing again. I really needed bedside tables, chests of drawers, two wardrobes, a large chair for the parlour and a settee. That would have to do meantime. I let the boys pick them as I had promised the night before. The manager came and asked if he could help. I told him what I wanted and asked him to deliver them that day if it was possible. He stood beside me, looking at the list then I said I would pay cash. When he heard the word cash, his behaviour towards me completely changed and I had his undivided attention. He even opened the door for us as we left and promised delivery that night. I thanked him then we all went to the baker shop. I let the boys pick what they wanted for tea. Vera and I picked out cakes then I ordered bread and scones. The girl gave me a receipt without being asked. Before we went to the grocers Vera asked Billy to run and post her letter. We all stood and waited till he came back. I got a funny feeling that if I lost sight of him, something terrible would happen to him. At last after I had got all the messages from Mr Walsh's shop we all made our way home laden with everything that we needed.

When we all got inside I locked the front door, I hung up the key on a hook beside the door. The kitchen table was covered with all our messages. Vera and I were in the act of putting them away when Billy came in with a plain white envelope which had been pushed in the letter box. He handed it to me; I just pushed it in my pocket letting it wait till later after we had our lunch. Nobody said anything. Vera filled the kettle and put it on the fire to boil. The boys helped to get the table clear then it was set for lunch. I had managed to get a nice piece of fish for each of us. After lunch I sent the boys into the parlour to read some books I had bought for them then Vera and I settled down. I took the envelope from my pocket, inside it was a plain white sheet of paper. On it was written, *if you don't send the boys back, I'll see that you will pay for it.*

I handed it to Vera. When she had finished reading it she said, 'What on earth are we going to do, Mary?'

'Nothing,' I said, 'Billy and Ewan are staying with me meantime. I do hope your Mr Smith can offer Billy work. He would be quite safe with you.'

I thought I would have a talk with Father Joseph tomorrow about the note, also I needed Billy's and Ewan's ration books and coupons. He was the only one who could get them from Donald. I was beginning to see now why Nan, my sister, was so frightened of him.

A loud knock on the front door brought us back to earth. The furniture van was there and two men started carrying the tables and chairs and other things I had bought. Vera and I showed them where each piece was to go; when they were finished I gave them a tip, said goodbye and locked the door. I wasn't taking any chances by letting Donald MacPherson in.

Vera was full of questions to which I had no answers. Why was there no furniture in the house when I came home? Why were the cupboards empty? Why was there no food in the house? Why did our parents die of starvation? I pulled the note out of my pocket again and said to Vera, if we compared the handwriting on the note with the bills in Dad's desk we might find the writing would be the same. Let's go and see and we made our way to the parlour where Billy and Ewan were sitting at the window reading, they were so engrossed in their books they never even looked up as we entered. It was just as well as we did not want the boys involved. I compared the note with the bills and no doubt about it, the writing matched. What on earth was at the back of Donald's behaviour? It must have been he and his brothers who had stolen everything from our parents' home after father had the stroke. Come to think of it maybe it was through them that he had the stroke. The more I thought about it the more determined I was to fight him and to get back what belonged to me. It was tea time, we called it a day and eagerly devoured our cream cakes. It was decided I should write to Auntie Kate in Mull and ask for advice.

As I lay in bed that night I suddenly realised that the MacPhersons had been blackmailing my dad. It was funny that everything seemed to change after Nan had to get married. There was no sense asking Nan about anything; even if she knew she would be too frightened of Donald to do anything. Before I fell asleep I said to myself time will tell. After breakfast the four of us set out walking to the village. Auntie Kate's letter had to be posted then there was the visit to Father Joseph to see if he could help us. I would have to tell him everything. We all went into the church first and met Father Joseph on the verge of coming out. The Father sent Billy and Ewan out to play and I related all the problems.

'I think, Mary, after what you have told me about Donald it really is a matter for the police. We can't have him threatening you and Vera and the boys. If you don't mind I would like to have a look through your dad's papers. I could come tomorrow if this is suitable.'

'Of course, Father,' I said. 'In the meantime we better see if Grant Ross will row us over to the other side of the loch and get Billy and Ewan's ration books and coupons.' I told Father also about Grant Ross refusing to play with the boys.

'In that case,' he said, 'I'll ask Mr Ross himself but before we go I will get the housekeeper to make us some tea.'

I went to the window and told Billy and Ewan to come in. The housekeeper, a stout elderly lady with a lovely smile brought in the tea which the boys really enjoyed. Father Joseph just took a cup of tea. I felt quite hungry after our walk along the loch. Vera seemed the same.

Mr Ross rowed us over to the other side of the loch. When we were all leaving the boat Father Joseph said to Mr Ross, come also. Ross got out of his boat with a scowl on his face but followed us all up to Donald's house. I knocked on the front door, but just as the last time I was over there, there was no answer so we all went round to the back. The children were all playing and little Helen came running up to me. I gave her a hug and kiss and told her to tell her mum Auntie Mary wants to see her. The child ran into the house, the rest of the children ran inside also. After a while my sister Nan appeared holding both of her hands up to her face. Vera and I ran up to her and supported her as she gave out a loud cry. Her face was covered in blood, following her was her husband Donald with a large piece of wood in his hand. When he saw us he immediately dropped the piece of wood. Father Joseph said to Donald that he wished to speak to him right away. Father Joseph and Donald disappeared into the house. Vera and I took Nan into the kitchen; we asked Mr Ross to come in also but he declined. Vera put the kettle on for tea, I bathed Nan's face and stopped it bleeding. One of her eyes was nearly shut, the children just sat on the floor, silent. I wondered how long Nan had been suffering this ill treatment from that mad husband of hers. We all sat silent at the table; I tried to get Nan to sip some tea but her face was too badly swollen. Donald's mother just sat in her chair, motionless. I thought to myself maybe she has had all the stuffing knocked out of her also by her husband.

Father Joseph came back into the kitchen alone, 'Come on, Mary, I have got the boy's ration books, also their clothes coupons so we will make our way home. We will be taking Nan with us to get her face attended to. Donald can look after the children for once himself.'

Billy and Ewan were on edge all the time so we were all glad to get into the boat away from that house of fear. Vera and I looked after Nan, Mr Ross, I think , got his eyes opened where Donald MacPherson was concerned. When we reached the other side of the loch we all made our way to the doctor's waiting room. Father Joseph had a few words with Peggy the secretary, then left. Peggy came over to me and said Nan and I could go straight to the doctor's office where he would see us straight away. I told Vera to stay with Billy and Ewan.

Doctor McKinnon attended to Nan's face and head straight away; 'I think we better send you to hospital and get your head X-rayed right away. Will you be able to go with her, Mary?' he asked. 'Before I can do that I will phone the police station and tell constable Colin Campbell to come right away. This is a serious situation; Donald will be charged with assault.'

He rang for Peggy and told her to take us into the small room off the waiting room and to show constable Campbell in as soon as he arrived.

Nan by this time was crying; she was worrying about the children which was only natural. I thought to myself that it was about time that mother-in-law got off her backside and helped the children. The door opened and Constable Campbell came in; he was a powerfully built man in his forties, fresh complexion and large blue eyes. His presence seemed to fill the room. Just then Peggy came into the room and told the policeman that doctor would like to see him first. As he was leaving the room he told us not to go away. When he came back into the room he asked Nan a few questions. Just then Peggy popped her head round the door to say that the ambulance was here to take Nan for her X-rays. I went with Nan to the hospital after reminding Vera to lock the door when they got home.

It was quite a drive to the hospital, Nan cried all the time; she seemed to be suffering a lot of pain. As soon as we arrived Nan was taken in a wheelchair to the X-ray room. I waited outside with the other patients. Nan was a long time away and as one of the nurses passed I asked her if she could enquire about my sister, Mrs McPherson. The nurse came back and took me to see Nan who was in her bed near the door. The doctor must have sedated her because she was fast asleep.

The sister in charged asked me a few particulars about Nan, her husband's name, address, how many children did she have, etc., then told me to go home now as Mrs McPherson would be sedated all night. 'You can phone in the morning,' she said, 'your sister is a very sick lady.'

I got up and made my way out of the hospital. I had no money with me and there I was standing outside the hospital doors wondering how in earth I was going to get home when Constable Campbell drew up on his motorbike. 'Well, Mary,' he said, 'how is Nan?'

'Not very good, sir,' I said, 'there is no point in you going in to question her as she is sound asleep.'

'In that case,' he said, 'I'll call tomorrow. Hop on the back of the bike, Mary, and I'll give you a lift home.'

I did not know what to say as I had never been on a motorbike in my life.

He must have read my thoughts because he said, 'sit on the back there and grab me round the waist; hurry up I have got to get back to the station.'

The constable left me at my door. Vera opened the door as soon as I reached it. As Vera was making the tea of sausage and egg I gave her all the news about Nan, repeating what sister had said, that Nan was a very sick lady. That must have been a terrible blow that Donald gave her when the X-ray showed a cracked skull. My, I thought, she must have been in terrible pain all day before the doctors sedated her. I thanked God that sleep would ease the pain.

Vera's voice brought me back to earth, 'Sit here, Mary, tea is ready.' We all sat at the table; I asked Vera if anyone had called.

She said no but when they were in the shops everyone was asking how Nan was. 'To tell you the truth, Mary, I think Donald has been ill treating Nan since the first day she was married. Poor girl, I remember she was the one we all went to if we were in any trouble, and when she was in trouble she had nobody to turn to. What a state of affairs.'

After I had helped Vera wash the dishes and cleared the table I sat in the rocking chair, the boys had gone to their room so Vera and I could talk in peace. Suddenly I said, 'Oh God don't take Nan away from us.'

'Funny,' Vera said, 'that's just what I was thinking; also, what would happen to all those little children if their mother died.'

Then both of us started crying. It was barely a week since we buried both parents, now this terrible beating happening to our sister. I was beginning to wonder if there was a curse on us. Vera and I sat for a long while talking then decided to make a cup of tea and get ready for bed. We shouted to the boys for their tea before they went to bed.

The next morning the postman delivered two letters, one for me, the other for Vera. While we all sat eating our breakfast Vera said her boss Mr Smith would be glad of the help of another hand on his farm and if Vera could bring Billy back with her he would give him six months trial. If by that time he was suitable and hard working he would be kept on permanently which was good news.

I opened my letter; it was from Ina the cook at Rutherglen House in Glasgow. She said that they all missed me. Katie was parlour maid now and her ladyship had got another slip of a girl to help her in the kitchen. Goodness knows where her ladyship got her from for she looked half starved. Also, Master James and Miss Margaret were married now. The wedding was a big affair, Miss Margaret was beautiful. She went on to ask if my parents were keeping any better then she went on to say Theresa and her little son visited her quite often in the summer months. Ina never told her ladyship about the visits as Theresa did not want her to know. She said the postman Steve was just using her to get free cups of tea – he was married with three of a family. She finished by telling me to take care of myself and to write soon. I gave Vera the letter to read and said to myself, when I got time I would write to Ina and tell her about my parents' death.

Vera said, 'You stay at home tomorrow with the boys, I will visit Nan in hospital.'

At first I thought I wanted to go myself then out loud said, 'That will be fine, Vera, it will give me a rest.'

The next morning we were wakened by loud knocking on the door. I flew down the stairs and opened it. Father Joseph was standing there; 'Come in Father,' I said, 'what's wrong with Nan?'

'Sit down first, Mary.' By this time Vera had joined us when Father Joseph spoke. 'I have bad news for you, dear. Your sister passed away this morning; I was in time to give her the last rites, she died peacefully in her sleep.'

Vera and I started crying and Father Joseph went upstairs to have a word with the boys. When he came into the kitchen he lit the fire, filled the kettle with water and put it on the fire to boil. All the time he worked away he never said a word, just left us to cry our eyes out. By the time Billy and Ewan came downstairs the tea was ready. Father said he would have to go but would be back later to attend to all the arrangements for Nan's funeral. With that he left us all with our new sorrow.

I don't know how long it was we all sat at the table but we all jumped by the loud knocking on the door. Billy ran to open it. I heard Constable Campbell's voice asking to come in. He came straight into the kitchen and stood in the doorway cap in hand. 'I have just heard the news of your sister's death. I am afraid Donald could be charged with murder.' He never got any further because the boys and Vera and I started crying again. In the distance I heard him say he would come back later.

None of us had any idea how long it was we all sat at the table when eventually we all stopped crying and Vera made the breakfast. She sent the boys out for logs while I set the table. With us all busy it helped to keep our minds off Nan's death. After breakfast Vera cleared the table, washed the dishes then we all went to our different rooms to get ready. I had taken over my parents' bedroom which was above the parlour. I sat at the window looking out over the loch. Today it was calm with the sunbeams dancing on the tip of the waves. I loved the loch, just sitting at the window and looking at it gave a certain calmness. I was wondering what was going to happen to those innocent children who had been left orphans. Vera shouted to me to hurry up as we had a lot to attend to. I gave myself a shake, got ready and went downstairs to the kitchen. It suddenly dawned on me that Vera was taking charge of everything; after all she was one year my senior. When we were all ready we set out walking to the village. I called at the church first to see Father Joseph but when we arrived there was only the housekeeper arranging the flowers at the altar.

'Is the priest about?' I asked.

'No, he has gone to the hospital to make the arrangements for your sister's coffin to be brought to the church. He also told me if any of you called to tell you that he had sent telegrams to your sister Sarah and your Auntie Kate.'

I thanked her then said that we better leave some money for Father Joseph to pay for all the expenses we were involving him in. She was taken aback, 'Oh no,' she said, 'I can't take any money, wait till you see Father yourself.'

With that we all left and made our way to Dr McKinnon. The waiting room was full; when we walked in a deadly silence fell on the room. Peggy the receptionist popped her head round the door to see what was wrong. When she saw us she came straight over to me and said, 'Doctor will be calling at your house sometime this evening Mary so there is no need to wait.' She opened the door for us and as I passed her she whispered, 'I am very sorry about Nan, Mary. Bye for now.'

I made my way down to the loch edge; Vera and the boys followed. I sat at the water edge watching the little waves lapping against the stones. Vera sat down beside me, then she shouted to Billy and Ewan to go to the bakers for bread and scones and one cake each and gave them the money and coupons. When the boys were out of hearing she said we better put a face on things as our troubles were just beginning. As we sat waiting for the boys the two of us spoke about what would be the best way to deal with all the terrible things that were happening to us, then Vera suggested that once the funeral was over we should discuss the future of Nan's children with Father Joseph. The way things were it was probable that Donald would be arrested. When I thought of our lovely Nan, I could have murdered him. I then wondered if the old woman had moved from her chair to look after the babies. We could hear the boys laughing as they ran to join us. What a change had come over them since I took them home. Vera and I got up and we all made our way home.

The first thing Vera did when we went into the kitchen was to start making the lunch. I wasn't hungry but I supposed the boys were starving. We were eating our scrambled eggs, the usual dried egg powder, when in walked Father Joseph. I must have forgotten to lock the front door. He gave us all the news.

Donald had been arrested and was in gaol. He was to be allowed out, under escort, for the funeral. Father Joseph left, saying he would see us at Mass the next day.

We all sat in silence for a while; I was wondering how I was going to get through the next sad day. About 3.30 p.m. the telegram boy delivered two telegrams. I opened them in a hurry. One was from Auntie Kate saying she was sorry she could not manage to come to the funeral. The other was from Sarah, *will arrive home this evening*. We were disappointed about the news from Auntie Kate, also Hector it seemed wasn't coming either. I wondered if Sarah would be staying the night at home here or whether she would stay with Hector's parents.

About 6.30 p.m. Sarah arrived in a taxi; one thing about her she had poise and elegance. She paid the driver then with a nod of her head she walked smartly up to the door. Billy opened it for her and gave her a big hug then it was the turn of Vera and myself for hugs and kisses and tears. Sarah had on the same expensive black costume and beautiful silk stockings and black patent shoes which she wore at our parents' funeral. She was the clever one; our parents gave her the chance to be educated. If they had been alive to see her then they would have been very proud of her. Even with all her fine clothes Sarah was to us just our loving sister.

'Come on, everyone, into the kitchen and I'll make some tea.' We all followed Vera.

I asked Sarah if Billy should taken her case up the stairs for her only to be told that Sarah had promised Hector, who was serving overseas, that she would stay with his parents.

As we all sat drinking our tea I told Sarah the horrible story relating to dear Nan's death. After Vera and I finished talking Sarah just sat quietly at the table, her lovely face had gone ashen; I thought she was going to faint.

'Are you all right, Sarah, come on sit in Mum's rocking chair beside the fire.'

'I am all right, Mary; tell me, where is that Donald just now?'

'In gaol,' I said. Sarah got up from the table and started pacing up and down the kitchen floor. I was beginning to get a bit worried about her when at last she sat down again and asked what was the cause of mum and dad's death. Sarah was shocked when I told her it was heart failure due to malnutrition and demanded to know why she had never been kept aware of what was going on.

I didn't know and could only suppose that no one had her address.

Sarah was silent and thoughtful for a while then mused that perhaps she and Hector were too wrapped up in each other.

'You see, Mary and Vera, Hector and I are so very much in love, the only people we thought of were ourselves. When Hector and I were home for our wedding, mum and dad seemed so happy and the wedding was wonderful. The only sad bit was Nan could not manage to come over. Donald had said that she was not feeling well; I wonder if he was beating her then. As if she did not have enough to put up with having a baby every year. Oh my God, Mary, what on earth is going to happen to those poor children?'

'We will have to wait till after the funeral,' I said. 'I am sorry you are leaving so soon Sarah, Vera and Billy will have to go to Angus so I will be left on my own with Ewan. I will pray to God to protect and give me strength to do what ever has to be done to clear my parents' name.'

'What do you mean clear your parents' name?'

Vera and I then told Sarah all about the unpaid bills in dad's desk and Donald's threatening letters if we did not send the boys back to work on his farm. Sarah volunteered to get what information she could out of Hector's parents and his sister Flora. It was getting late so we all walked with Sarah till she reached her in-laws' house. As it was a lovely night we took our time getting back home. Billy and Ewan ran ahead of us; I felt more at ease since Donald was in gaol. Where he was he could not harm the boys.

Vera had been getting up first since she arrived home but the next morning I was up first, cleaning the big range out, lighting the fire, filling the kettle and standing it on the hob to boil. The table was set, the porridge was made, also the toast. When I went upstairs to waken Vera and the boys Billy and Ewan looked so peaceful asleep I wished I did not have to waken them to face another sad day, their sister Nan's funeral. I shook the boys awake and told them breakfast was ready. Vera was already up and dressed when I knocked on her door. By the time I got downstairs again Sarah was at the front door, sobbing her heart out. The five of us sat down to a silent breakfast. I persuaded Sarah to take one of the tablets Dr McKinnon had given me on the day of our parents' funeral.

Sarah stopped crying and drank her tea then she told us that Hector's parents made it plain to her that she was not welcome in their house, that's why she had arrived home so early. It was funny everyone in the village knew for years what was happening yet no one helped my parents or Nan. There must be some evil about when nobody was prepared to talk out loud. I said, come on everyone, get ready or we will be late for Mass. We all made our way to the church, Father Joseph had attended to everything. Nan's coffin lay in front of the altar with four big candles, two at the bottom and two at the top. On top of the coffin lay one wreath. The church was packed. Donald was there handcuffed to a young policeman. His father and two brothers and sisters were there also. The old woman must have stayed at home to look after the children. My sister Nan was only 25 years old and there she lay in her cold coffin, her short life ended by that brutal husband of hers. My thoughts were caught short by Father Joseph starting the Requiem Mass. Sarah had started crying again. At our parents funeral she had been so composed. At the graveside Billy and Ewan stayed close to me; the sight of Donald seemed to put fear into them. This time there was no meal for everyone in the church hall afterwards.

Sarah came back home with Vera and me and the boys. The MacPhersons all went their own way. I never so much as looked at any of them. We were all glad to get back home. Vera made the tea as soon as we all settled down; Sarah said she was sending a telegram to the RAF station saying she was taking another day off. 'I want to find out everything,' she said. Vera and Billy were leaving that afternoon to go back to work on the farm so I was pleased that Sarah was staying another day. After their tea the boys disappeared to their room. I told Billy to pack the few belongings he was taking with him.

When we girls were alone again Sarah said Hector's mother had said that dad had got what he had deserved. She asked what she had meant but the only answer she got was a shake of the head. It was then that Sarah had walked out and come back home. She had forgotten her bags and Billy and Ewan were sent to fetch them. Vera had finished her packing and was all ready to leave when the boys came back. The boys must have run both ways because they were back in no time. Sarah wanted to know if Hector's mother had said anything, but the boys hadn't seen her. It was Flora who had got Sarah's things and she had only smiled.

We all set out for the station which was a two mile walk. It was a lovely warm day, the loch was in one of her special moods. Just looking at the calm water gave one a sense of peacefulness. At last we reached the station, Vera was crying, Billy was putting a brave face on things. I was glad Vera would be working at the same farm keeping an eye on him. We all stood till the train was out of sight then Sarah said, 'I don't know about you two but I am getting a taxi.'

'The very thing, Sarah.'

We all made our way to the taxi; I didn't realise how tired I was till I sat down. I don't think Sarah was used to walking the same as were Ewan and I. That was why it was she who thought of it. It wasn't long till we arrived home, Sarah paid the man and with her special nod of the head walked proudly up to the door. There was not one card or letter of condolence from anyone. I took my coat and hat off and went out into the back garden, Sarah and Ewan followed me. The place was in a mess, the once proud garden of dad's was an overgrown mass of weeds. I wondered what had happened to all the lovely rose bushes we had. There was no sign of the garden seat which used to stand in front of the parlour window. The lilac tree had gone and I wondered what had happened to it. Ewan offered to try to clear the mess. Sarah just stood and looked round about her then went indoors. I thought to myself when Sarah leaves home Ewan and I will tackle this mess.

When I went back indoors Sarah was sitting on the settee in the parlour.

'Mary,' she said, 'what I want to know is what happened to all the furniture that was in the house?'

'I don't know, Sarah. The place was empty of everything, there wasn't a scrap of food in the house when I arrived home.'

'Have you looked in the attic?'

'The attic, I didn't know we had an attic.'

'Don't be silly, Mary, every house has one.'

'Well,' I said, 'I am afraid you better show it to me. Lead the way.'

Sarah and I went upstairs to my room which used to be our parents then she made straight to the large cupboard, telling me to lock the door. I locked the door then both of us went into the big cupboard. Across the top of the cupboard were two large shelves right round the walls. Below them was a wooded rail for hanging clothes. The place was empty. Sarah went up to the further wall, pressed something and a panel slid back showing a small flight of stairs. We reached the top of the stairs but the door at the top was locked. Sarah tried key after key till finally we got the door opened. The place was in darkness as the small skylight windows were covered with black-out cloth.

Sarah switched on the light; I was amazed at the size of the room. It must have covered the whole of the top of the house, then I got another shock. All of mum and dad's furniture was packed up here, even the children's cot and cradle. All our dolls and the boys' bikes. 'Oh look, Sarah, there's a doll in the cradle; I wonder if it is one of mine.'

51

'It could be mine,' she said, and went forward to have a closer look at it. The next minute she let out a piercing scream and fainted.

I wondered what was wrong and went over to the cradle. Instead of what I thought was a doll was the remains of a dead newly born baby. I felt the hair on the back of my neck stand up in fear, then I started vomiting; the cold sweat was lashing off me then I must have fainted also. We don't know how long we were out for the count; it was the hammering on the bedroom door that brought me round. I struggled to the door feeling really ill and opened it. It was Ewan, 'Mary,' he said, 'Father Joseph is downstairs in the parlour. Are you all right Mary, you look as if you have seen a ghost?'

'I am fine, Ewan, tell Father I will be down as soon as I get dressed. I must have fallen asleep. I shut and locked the door again then went to help Sarah. By this time she was sitting up, the colour of death. We covered the cradle and repaired the tear damage to our faces with make-up. Trying to hurry, we started to cry again. There was a knock on the door and Father Joseph walked in. He was appalled at our appearance and said he would ask for Dr McKinnon to call. Then, after he told me to rest, he left, saying he would see us next day.

When Father left, both of us just lay back on the bed, too weak to move. Ewan knocked on the door and shouted, 'Can I come in Mary?' When Ewan came in he just stood at the door and asked if Sarah and I would like a cup of tea. 'Don't worry Mary, I had to do everything on Donald's farm, I'll just go and bring the tea up here. I am starving.'

Ewan disappeared downstairs; the way I felt I did not care what happened, I think the both of us were suffering from shock. After what seemed ages Ewan brought a tray in to us, three cups, sugar, milk, the big teapot and biscuits. Ewan put the tray on the table beside the bed and helped me to prop Sarah up. I managed to get Sarah to drink the hot sweet tea then drank my own.

'Will you bring the quilt from Vera's bed, Ewan.' He ran right away and got it. 'Now cover the both of us with it and then leave us to rest. When Dr McKinnon arrives just show him up and Ewan, please take the tray away. The tea was lovely.'

At last we were left in peace. I must have dozed off and when I opened my eyes Dr McKinnon and Nurse Duncan were standing beside my bed.

'Hello, Mary,' Doctor said, 'so you are still with us then. I think Nurse had better get the two of you undressed and Sarah can go to her own bed. After that I will give you girls an injection to put you to sleep. Don't worry about Ewan, Nurse will be staying the night with you.'

Everything seemed to be happening in a daze. At last I was left in peace, after the injection I felt myself floating in space, sleep, sleep, where we forgot all our woes and troubles. The next morning when I woke up, I felt a lot better, got up but found my legs still felt weak. Oh dear God, I couldn't afford to be ill, not with the secret that attic held.

Nurse Duncan came into the bedroom with tea and toast. 'I think, Mary,' she said, 'you better take it easy for a few days more and I don't think Sarah is well enough to travel. We will see what Dr McKinnon says when he arrives.'

'Is Sarah up yet, Nurse?' I asked.

'No, she is sitting up in bed, I told her to eat the toast and drink plenty of tea. It's the shock you girls have had after all the funerals.'

Little did she know what was really worrying us. No way could we confide in anyone, not even Father Joseph. Nurse had other calls to make and left Ewan to look after us.

After Nurse left I made my way to Sarah's room and climbed into bed beside her. She was glad to see me.

'How do you feel now, Sarah?' I asked.

'I still feel so weak, I really don't understand why.'

'Believe it or not, Sarah, both of us suffered a severe shock, seeing the dead baby in the crib. When we feel better we will have to decide what's the best course of action to take. In the meantime I better fill that big cupboard up with all our clothes to hide that panel.'

Father Joseph, true to his word, came to see us at midday. Sarah and I by this time were up and Ewan was glad to see us in the kitchen again. The message Father gave us was that Donald's case would be coming up in court in three weeks time and that Vera, Billy and myself and Ewan, Mr Ross the blacksmith and the Father himself would all have to go as witnesses. Thank goodness, the three weeks would give us girls time to deal with our worries.

To Father Joseph I said, 'Do the boys really have to go?'

'Yes,' he said. 'When the time comes Constable Campbell will let you all know. I'll say goodbye to you, Sarah, look after yourself.'

Ewan wanted sausages for lunch. 'Well,' I said, 'you better run down to the shop for them.' I gave Ewan the money and coupons, 'While you are at the shops get two ounces of Spam for a sandwich for Sarah to take with her on the train. Also three scones and three cakes, off you go now.'

When we had the kitchen to ourselves Sarah said that she would arrange a long weekend pass to come home for Donald's case, that way we could bury the little baby in the garden. In the meantime I was to buy a new garden seat and get Ewan to dig over the garden. I thought to myself, please God, help me through the next three weeks. I was beginning to wonder if that was what Donald was blackmailing my parents with.

Ewan came back with the messages and I set about preparing the lunch. I loved working in our big kitchen; the big logs crackling in the range, the big black kettle always singing away to itself and mum's favourite rocking chair. All brought back happy memories. At last everything was ready; Ewan told us that he heard Mr Walsh's daughter tell another customer that Grant Ross had got his calling up papers. Grant was four months older than Billy. Who will ferry people across the loch when he goes? I was glad Billy was exempt working with Vera on the land.

Sarah finished her meal and said she would have to get ready as we all had a long walk to the station.

'Would you like a pair of my walking shoes, Sarah, till we reach the station?'

'Yes,' she said, 'that would be wise,' and went upstairs to pack the last few things she needed.

When we were all ready the three of us set out on the two mile walk to the station. It was good to get out in the fresh air after being laid up in the house for two days. Sarah still looked pale. Another day in bed was what was needed but with the country at war everybody who was able to work had to work, whether they wanted to or not. At last we reached the station just in time. Sarah ran on to the train. 'Change your shoes, Sarah,' I shouted, and handed over the expensive patent high heeled shoes. Ewan handed her case over then with a quick hug and kiss she was gone. Ewan and I just stood and waved till the train was out of sight then I turned to Ewan and said, 'How about a taxi home?'

'Oh that will be great.'

CHAPTER 3

When we arrived home Ewan said he was going up to his room for a while. I was quite pleased to be left alone. I sat down in Mum's rocking chair and hoped nothing would happen till Sarah came home again. That evening I rested. Ewan came into the kitchen and said he was starving. We had toasted scones with our tea. When I was working in the big house none of the servants had the worry of counting out our coupons, now at home I had to do that every day. I didn't realise how much one had to scrimp. Britain was into the fourth year of the war and the food situation seemed to be getting worse.

I wondered who was looking after Nan's children; maybe Father Joseph might arrange for them to put into care. I myself would have liked to look after little Helen, also maybe two of her sisters but with that terrible secret still in the attic I couldn't. I asked Ewan if he knew what had happened to our garden seat which was always under the parlour window. He said Donald had taken it over to his house without as much as a by your leave. He and his brother had helped themselves to a lot of things from the garden shed.

'Do you mean to tell me Dad just stood and let them.'

'I'm sorry, Mary, Dad was ill in bed; the two brothers were laughing and joking all the way down to the boat.'

I felt the tears in my eye's starting again but managed to brush them away before Ewan saw them. 'Well,' I said, 'where Donald is just now he won't feel like laughing. In the morning after breakfast both of us will start clearing the garden. It will take us a while to get it ready for planting vegetables. Also late autumn we will plant some fruit bushes. Remind me tomorrow to order a good garden seat. Also we will need cement and sand to slab under the parlour window. The garden really is in a terrible state.'

I felt I had to get out of the house so I said to Ewan, 'how about a walk down to the loch.' He followed me outside. I locked the door then we both made our way down to the water edge. 'I think Ewan we will get a dog once everything is cleared up. By the way, what happened to Rusty?'

'To tell you the truth, Mary, I really don't know.'

That was the answer to most of the questions I asked.

I was no further forward about mum and dad's affairs than I was the first day I arrived home. I thought to myself, will I ever be able to get to the bottom of all this trouble? I felt like crying again but managed to keep the tears back. They could wait till I got to bed then I could cry my heart out. 'Come on, Ewan,' I said, 'we better get home; its getting dark.' The two of us rose and made our way up to the house. I gave Ewan the key; he ran on in front of me. I loved my little brother and would protect him as long as need be. He, also, was an orphan and like his brothers and sisters had lost the three most important people in the world. Whatever sadness he suffered inside, he never showed outwardly. Maybe he also waited till he was in bed and his head was under the blankets, then the flood gates would open.

The following morning the postman delivered three letters, one from Auntie Kate, the others from Vera and Billy. I opened Auntie Kate's first; she said she was not keeping too great and wanted to know what had really happened to my sister Nan. Also she said she was sorry about not being able to come to her funeral. Her legs were giving her a lot of pain. She invited me to come for a holiday when things were back to normal. I wondered what and when 'normal' might ever be. I opened Vera's letter; it was a bit more cheerful. She had got another boyfriend. He was in the RAF, good looking and a lovely dancer but she missed Andy though, always bringing either chocolates or silk stocking. I opened Billy's letter. He liked the farmer even though he had to work hard. There was always plenty of food and he had good meal breaks, more than he ever got at Donald's.

I left the letters on the kitchen table for Ewan to read then went out into the back garden and made out a list of everything that was needed. Meantime Ewan was waiting patiently for his breakfast. The kettle was singing away merrily on the hob and the porridge ready just to dish up.

The two of us sat at the table in silence while we ate then I said, 'after we are ready we will make our way down to the shops; maybe, Ewan, you can get a loan of a wheel barrow from someone to carry the cement and sand and weed killer home. I'll carry the messages.' When we had finished breakfast and washed up we set off for the village. I told Ewan my plans for the garden so that he would understand what everything was for. Little did he know the deadly scheme Sarah and I were planning. Better for someone so young as he not to know.

When we arrived at Mr Walsh's shop, it was he who served me. I handed him the list; after he read it he said he would have to order the garden seat, cement and sand, also the weed killer. I told him I needed the weed killer right away so that Ewan and I could get the garden into shape. He went and spoke to his daughter. She just looked at me and left the shop. Mr Walsh attended to the rest of my groceries. Ewan had left his sweetie coupons in the house so we used mine to get him a big bar of chocolate. The girl came back with a package and handed it to her dad who went on attending to my order. When I had paid he said it would be a week before the rest of the order would be ready, then he gave me the weed killer, telling me to keep it in a safe place. I thanked him and left. I sent Ewan to the bakers for bread and a nice cake each while I went down to sit beside the loch. As I sat looking out over the loch, I thought of my poor sister Nan who lay now beside her dear mother and father in the cold cemetery and wondered what was happening to her lovely children.

A voice beside me said, 'hello, Mary.' I looked up to see Father Joseph; he sat down beside me, 'feeling a bit better?'

'A little,' I said. 'Father, could you possibly manage to find time to bless our house?'

'Of course, Mary, but not until next week as I am very busy just now. Oh here comes Ewan, his mouth covered in chocolate.' Father just ruffled Ewan's hair and left.

My aim in getting the house blessed was to have the baby in the crib blessed also before Sarah and I buried him or her in the garden. I got up and both of us made our way home. Ewan would be 15 years in two months time and at the middle of the month the school holidays would be over. I thought for his sake that I would try and get him exempt; the boy has been through so much already. Maybe when he was 15 years I could get him work beside Vera and Billy. I could write to Mr Smith the farmer later on, in the meantime the garden was first priority and I would need his help with all the hard work.

I thought I would have plenty of peace to attend to the garden but when Ewan and I arrived home who was sitting on the doorstep but Donald's father. Ewan ran away when he saw him; before Mr MacPherson could say anything I flew at him. 'What have you been doing to my young brothers? I suppose you treated them the same way as your son Donald treated Nan.'

He was the same well built man as Donald and, at first he was taken aback then he drew himself up to his full height and said, 'I came to help with the garden, also I want to speak about your father.'

'I don't want you near my house again; if you ever dare to come I'll report you to Constable Campbell.'

'Oh is that so, maybe it is I who will go to the Constable with quite a few tales about your mum and dad.'

'How dare you talk like that about my dead parents who are hardly cold in their graves. If it is the last thing I do I am going to leave no stone unturned till I find out why you MacPhersons were blackmailing my parents.'

His face turned purple with rage; I thought he was going to strike me but instead he turned and walked away down the road. After he left I felt exhausted and just sat down on the steps and started crying. The flood gates were opened again; it was only when I looked up and saw Ewan standing crying also that I stopped.

'Is that horrid man away, Mary?'

'Yes,' I said, 'come in the house and I'll make something nice for us and, Ewan, from now on, please always make sure the door is locked whether we are in or out.'

I felt so shaken with the appearance of Donald's father standing in our door after what he and his sons had done to my family that I just drank a cup of tea and went up to bed to rest. I told Ewan just to please himself. I fell asleep and woke to find Ewan standing beside my bed saying that Hector's mother was downstairs wanting to speak to me. Ewan had left her in the parlour. I hurried and washed and tidied myself then went downstairs wondering what news she had for me. When I entered the room she was standing looking out of the window admiring the beautiful view of the loch. Apparently Hector had phoned very angry about what she had been saying to Sarah and said that she owed an apology to all the Scott family.

'I am very sorry, Mary, I really should not pay any attention to gossip.'

'Would you like a cup of tea Mrs MacLean?'

'No thanks, Mary, I must get back home. When Sarah gets her leave tell her from me she will be always welcome. I love Hector, I don't want him upset.' With that and a wave of her hand she was off down the road. I shut and locked the door saying to myself, I will write to Sarah tomorrow and give her the latest news. I found Ewan in the back garden busy digging away.

It took Ewan and I a full ten days to get the garden looking respectable. Mr Walsh delivered my order the following week as he said he would. The garden seat was lovely; wrought iron in white. We kept it in the house till the ground under the parlour window was ready.

'Ewan, I want the whole of the back of the house dug up and properly evened then when Sarah comes home she can help us to cement right round the house to the front door.'

'I can do that, Mary.'

'Thanks Ewan,' I said, 'we will have a lot to do before that; also I want the garden seat cemented down so that those MacPhersons don't take it in to their heads to run off with it.'

'O.K., Mary. I'll need two patio containers to stand each side of the front door; later on we will plant some bulbs such as snowdrops and crocuses.'

'I forgot to order the fruit bushes; I will wait till later on in the year. I found an old watering can at the back of the shed also; this will do for spraying the weed killer.'

I was glad I had a lot to do; it kept my mind off the little dead infant in the attic. Ewan and I would go to Mass tomorrow. Both of us had missed the last two Sundays. People would be beginning to wonder what was wrong. I felt sore the following morning with all the gardening that had been done. After breakfast the two of us walked to the church. When we arrived we went straight into our own pew. Some of Nan's children were already occupying my parents' seats. Inside I felt like exploding, outwardly I just smiled at the children then Ewan and I knelt down and waited for Mass to begin. The MacPhersons were all there, except Donald of course. I wondered who was looking after the children. They all looked so pretty and innocent. Little Helen smiled over to me and I smiled back. Father Joseph started Mass. I prayed for the souls of my dead parents and my dear sister Nan. After the service was over I waited behind to speak to Father about the blessing of my house and getting Ewan exempt from military service. Father said to leave everything to him and he would be up to bless the house on Wednesday.

I felt a lot happier as Ewan and I made our way home. After lunch I went up to the attic to prepare the room. I covered all the furniture, also the coat and crib then made sure the slide door was secure then made my way down to the garden to write some letters that were long overdue. It was a lovely day and Ewan wanted to go down to the loch to fish but neither of us knew what had happened to Dad's fishing tackle. At first I just sat in the chair relaxing, feeling the warm sun on my face. I was only 19 years old, never had a boyfriend and I wondered if I would ever have one, what with all the cares of the world lying heavily on my young shoulders and wondering what next was going to happen.

I wrote first to Sarah, telling her of Mrs MacLean's apology. Then a note to Vera and Billy and one to Auntie Kate. I wondered if she knew a lot more than she let on; in a way she was a very quiet and proud lady. While I was writing my letters I felt the presence of another person near me. At first I thought it was Ewan but when I looked up it was a young woman. My first thoughts were of anger; what right had she to come bursting in on top of me like that. Before I could say anything she said, that as nobody answered the doorbell she had made her way round the back of the house to see if anybody was home. 'Don't you remember me Mary? I am Mary Kate Bell. I was in the same class as you at school.'

To tell the truth I didn't recognise her; the girl I remembered was a pale faced thin little girl for her age. She always seemed to have colds because her nose was always running but the young woman in front of me was beautiful. Her long fair hair was shiny and silky, her beautiful big blue eyes were her main attraction. Also the clothes she wore were expensive. I didn't like her intruding; all I wanted was to have my privacy until the little infant was buried. 'Well, Mary Kate, would you like a cup of tea?'

'Yes, Mary, I would love one.'

We made our way to the front door. We reached it at the same time as Ewan whom Mary Kate didn't remember as he would have been in a younger class at school. I thought it funny she should say that because when we were all young all the children in the village went to the Christmas party in the school hall. Every year it was always the highlight of the year. Also every Sunday all the families saw everyone else and usually had a chat before everyone made their way home from Mass. I was beginning to get suspicious but I just smiled and started to make the tea and asked Mary Kate what she did for a living. She told me she was a hairdresser and lived in Glasgow. She was home on a week's holiday to see her parents who owned the hotel now. Inside of me was raging; so it wasn't a school friend visit after all. She was here to find out what was going on. She must think I'm stupid if she thinks she will get any news out of me or Ewan.

'I am afraid, Mary Kate, I have just a biscuit for tea; what with the rations.'

'That's all right, I am just thirsty; it is quite a walk from the village to your house.'

Before she left she offered her condolences. She asked if she could call again before she returned to Glasgow. I said that she could if she wanted to.

After she left I shut and locked the door, went back to the kitchen and asked Ewan if he had seen Mary Kate walking up the road. 'She never walked up, Mary, a strange young man brought her up on the back of his bike.'

Why the two faced liar I thought to myself. I'll fix you the next time you turn up. Mary Kate was just away when Constable Campbell called to give us the summons to attend court as witnesses at Donald MacPherson's trial.

'What about Mr Ross, Billy, Vera and Sarah?'

'Oh the local police will see to that, Mary; and how is Ewan faring?'

'By the way Mr MacPherson called here the other day and Ewan was very upset at the sight of him; in fact Ewan ran away into the forest when he saw him.'

'If he bothers you in any way, Mary, let me know right away. I'll deal with him.' With a wave of his hand he was away.

I wondered if Sarah would be staying with us when she came down or down at the MacLeans house. I would be glad to see them all again especially Billy. I made tea for Ewan and myself and wondered how the government expected us to survive on two ounces of this and two ounces of that, counting every coupon spent. Luckily Ewan got free milk, orange juice and cod liver oil. Give them their due, they put the children first. After my tea and a rest I went upstairs to make the beds up for the family. While I sat resting in the rocking chair my mind went back to Constable Campbell; I really did not know what I felt for him but when I was in his company I felt safe and happy and every time after he was gone I felt lonely. What I wanted was for him to share the house with me but within myself I knew that was impossible. He would take heart failure if he knew what was in the attic. Also so much had happened in the last few weeks I hadn't given a thought to the papers in dad's desk. I decided to wait until Sarah and Vera were home. I supposed Sarah and I would have to take Vera into our confidence.

CHAPTER 4

The week passed and all the family arrived home. Hector came with Sarah; she was to stay two nights at Hector's parents' house, after that she would be coming home for the rest of the week. Vera and Billy got a week off work, also, so it was a full house. I was happy again. Hector drove all of us to the court house for Donald MacPherson's trial; when we entered the building quite a crowd were already there. Father Joseph and the MacPhersons and Mr Ross were at the front of the room. We were shown to a different seat. The jury sat stony faced and sad looking. Once the doors were locked the two police officers brought Donald in. He was handcuffed to one of them and I was shocked at the change in him. Gone was the bully, arrogant, heavy built man. Instead was a pale faced, hollow eyed young man. He had lost a lot of weight during his three weeks in prison for killing my sister Nan. The whole place was in silence while each person gave their story in the witness box. I had to go to the stand and tell what happened the morning my sister died.

After everyone had given their evidence the jury left the room. Constable Campbell said we could go outside for a breath of fresh air if we wanted to. We girls rose, followed by Hector, Billy and Ewan. Hector and Sarah went to the hotel for a cup of tea. The rest of us stayed behind and just sat in silence then Vera said 'who is looking after Nan's children?'

'I don't know, I suppose they would have to get help. I don't think Donald's mother is of any use. All I ever heard about her from Nan was she just sat in the chair beside the fire all day.'

'I wonder, Mary, if she was treated by her husband the same way as Nan was by Donald.'

Our conversation was broken off with the arrival of Sarah and Hector to go back to the court for the verdict. We all made our way back; each of us going to our own seats. The jury were already in their seats, then the judge came in to the room and we all stood up till he sat down. The judge asked the jury for their verdict then, having received it, pronounced sentence of five years for the manslaughter of his wife, my sister. You could have heard a pin drop after the judge finished then suddenly, the whole courtroom was filled with the noise of people leaving. Some were crying; I suppose they were Donald's family; Constable Campbell came over to me and said, 'I think Mary, you and the rest of the family better leave by the back way. I have already told Hector to bring the car round to the back door for you all. There's too many reporters out front.'

'Thanks, Colin,' I said; I thought to myself he always seemed to know what was the right thing to do.

Vera, Sarah and myself and the boys made our way to Hector's car. We all hurried into it then Hector raced down the road for home. I thought to myself, in five years time I would be 24 years old; I wondered if by that time I would be married. Within myself I thought it would be nice if I was married to Constable Campbell; the more I saw of him the more I wanted him but just now I would have to put him out of my mind as there were far more pressing duties to attend to first.

When Hector dropped us off at our house Sarah handed me a big parcel then both of them went back to Hector's house. Vera, Billy and Ewan were already in the kitchen when I got in. I hurriedly opened the parcel; what a lovely surprise I got when I unwrapped the brown paper. Inside was a lovely joint of lamb. We were well off for food. Vera's boss had sent potatoes, cabbages, beetroot, flour and eggs. We had to keep quiet about that. Mr Smith could have been in trouble. Vera made the tea and we all sat down to enjoy it. While we were drinking our tea I said, 'Vera, do you know, I don't even know how to bake a scone.'

'Don't worry, Mary, while I am home I'll teach you.'

Billy and Ewan laughed at the idea that their big sister Mary could not bake while she could face up to the bullying MacPhersons or anyone else who threatened them. Little did I know then how much the boys loved me. After tea the boys went down to the loch; Vera and I were left to ourselves. I told her that tomorrow everyone would be helping to get the ground ready for cementing right round the back of the house. I should have told the boys to bring some stones from the loch as a foundation before the cement was laid. But, I forgot. So I went in search of the boys and found them throwing stones in the water. Vera and I sat down beside them then I explained that I needed stones 'just like the pebbles that you are throwing just now' for a base before we cemented the garden. Also, we needed a loan of a barrow.

'No need for that, Mary, dad's barrow is across the road from the house lying among the trees. I saw it the day I ran into the forest from Mr MacPherson,' Ewan said. We followed Ewan to the exact place where the barrow lay. I noticed the branches of the tree nearest to the barrow were broken as if somebody had been fighting. Vera noticed it also; the two of us just looked at one another and went over to the barrow to have a proper look. Billy straightened it up and gave it a push. 'Good,' he said, 'we will be able to use it tomorrow, Mary. Ewan and I know the best place to get the type of stones you need.'

'Well, Vera, I think we better get home and get the range stacked up with logs so we can cook that lovely joint Sarah gave us. Also we will have Yorkshire pudding, roast potatoes, the lot. Billy and Ewan can bring in plenty of logs and put the barrow in the shed. In two and a half hours time we will have a feast.' I just hoped we did not have any unexpected visitors; the door would be locked just in case.

It was like old times when we were all children. The kitchen was filled again with all the delicious smells of cooking. I helped Vera by doing the vegetables while she attended to the roast and puddings. The boys wanted to go straight away for the stones but I said we would all be the better of a day's rest and also a good feast. That way the work would be done all the quicker. In the meantime till dinner was ready the boys were cleared out and Vera and I were left alone. I asked if she thought her boss Mr Smith would be able to take Ewan on to work on his farm.

'Oh I don't know, Mary, I'll speak to him when Billy and I go back. How about you, Mary, what with the house empty and only yourself here you will be bound to be lonely.'

'To tell you the truth, Vera, I am not a lonely person, in fact I quite like being on my own. When you have all left I will treat myself to a lovely dog; I would like one just like our old dog Rusty.'

'But,' said Vera, 'it is such a large house. Why not put it up for sale.'

'I'll think about it,' was all I said but within my heart I knew I never could.

Dinner was ready. I think it was the first decent meal that'd been cooked since I came home. The boys had set the table and were waiting patiently for it to be served up. I thought to myself, dear God don't let anyone knock on our door till we have all been fed and the table cleared. Vera carved the joint, I put the vegetable dishes on the table; also the gravy and the Yorkshire puddings. The next half hour silence reigned in the kitchen while everyone enjoyed their meal. If anyone had knocked on the door it would not have been answered – we even pulled down the window blind. At last we were all finished; the boys helped Vera and I to clear everything away. They also helped with the washing up. I heaved a sigh of relief and sat down in the rocking chair. Vera sat at the table, the boys disappeared. I hoped they hadn't eaten too much and were sick. I closed my eyes and thought of all the events that had happened since I came home and remembered, Father Joseph never came up on Wednesday to bless our house. I would have to get him to come the next morning as I wanted the infant blessed before we buried him or her.

Hector drove Sarah up to the house the next morning and we all said good-bye to him then with a hug and kiss to Sarah he was off to the base again. I told Vera and Sarah that I was going to bring Father Joseph up to the house to bless it. Sarah came with me while Vera stopped behind to tidy the house and the boys went to the loch for stones. When we reached the church I managed to catch Father as he was leaving in his car. 'Oh Father you never came to bless our house.'

'I am sorry, Mary, I have been so busy; just a minute I'll get some holy water and run the both of you home and do it right away.'

Thank goodness I caught him in time. When we reached home I told Sarah to cover the crib in the attic while I went with Father to each room. The panel was kept open so the attic and the infant were blessed also. Father was in such a hurry that he seemed to race from room to room; even in the attic he never hardly glanced at it, then he was gone. Everything happened at such speed that even Vera never knew that the attic was blessed. Sarah shut the panel as soon as Father left the room – a good morning's work done. I told Sarah I had planned to bury the infant under the parlour window around midnight and was still wondering if we should tell Vera. Sarah said we must tell her and the work would be done quicker if the three of us stuck together; no way must the boys get involved. We heard Vera shouting that lunch was ready; both of us made our way downstairs to the kitchen. The boys have already been fed; they are away down to the loch for more stones. Sarah and I sat down in silence.

'What's wrong?' Vera asked so I left it to Sarah to tell her the horror story. That was why the garden was getting prepared.

Vera suddenly rose from the table and flew out of the kitchen door and ran to our outside toilet. I was sure it was to be sick; we waited quite a while for her to come back. In the end I decided to see if she was all right. When I opened the door I found her sitting on the toilet seat, the place covered in vomit. She was the colour of death. I shouted for Sarah to come and help me to get Vera to bed. Thank goodness the boys were down at the loch. After

Sarah and I managed to get Vera to bed I washed her and made her drink a strong sweet cup of tea then we left her to get over the shock. I supposed Sarah and I would have to do the work ourselves. The full moon that night, would help us as no lights were allowed during blackout. Sarah just sat at the table staring straight in front of her. I thought how on earth am I going to manage to do everything myself, I could not postpone the burial any longer. I took my cup of tea and sat in the rocking chair, urging Sarah to drink her tea while hot and put plenty of sugar in it. Sarah came out of her daze and started drinking her tea then there was a loud knock on the front door. I went answered it; Constable Campbell was standing there. My heart missed a beat when I saw him.

'Just called, Mary, to see if everything is all right. I see the boys are busy.'

'Yes, Constable,' I said.

'Mary, call me Colin, that's to say when I am not on duty.'

'Right, Colin,' then I explained to him that the stones Ewan and Billy were collecting for the garden was to be a base before we laid the cement. Also I said I would be cementing the new garden seat down in front of the parlour window so that the MacPhersons wouldn't run away with it. 'Oh, while you are here, Colin, I want to show you something. I would have liked Vera to come with us but she had to lie down with a bad headache. It's across the road in the forest.'

I led the way and Colin followed me to the exact spot where the barrow lay.

'Yes, Mary, all the branches are badly broken, as if three or four people had been fighting.'

'That's just what Vera and I thought; it was Ewan who noticed the barrow that day he ran away from Donald's father.'

'I think, Mary, I better look into this further; of course I will have to make discreet enquiries on my own; in fact it looks to me like foul play. I have often wondered what really happened to your father. Come on, Mary, we better get back. I have got to report back to the station. When the family have all gone back to their work, would you mind if I called to pay you a visit.'

'I would love that, Colin,' then off he went on his bike; a bit of me went with him also.

When I got back to the kitchen Sarah was up in the bedroom to see how Vera was keeping. I was beginning to get worried. I hoped Vera would be able to keep our secret; maybe it would have been better if Sarah and I had kept silent about the whole business. Billy and Ewan came in; the two of them the picture of health. It was so nice to see both of them so happy again.

'We saw Constable Campbell, Mary, what did he want?'

'Oh, he just called to see if everything was all right. You two run and play at the loch for a while, you have worked well today.'

After they disappeared outside I went up to Vera's room. Vera was still sleeping, Sarah was standing looking out of the window. She turned and said, 'we better finish everything tonight Mary, I think the strain is telling on me also.'

'Yes,' I said, 'about midnight we will have everything done. I have got a bottle of holy water and a small crucifix which I will place on the child's remains. We have got to be firm Sarah, everything in the crib must be burned in the grate. I'll wrap the remains of the infant in a clean white cloth. For mum and dad's sake, both of us have to be strong. I know, Sarah, how you feel but think of me also, the state I found our parents was unforgettable. I have that to live with also.'

'I am sorry, Mary, I didn't realise how hard it must have been for you.' Both of us then went down to the kitchen and made a cup of tea. We all had been upset about Vera and that jolted us into the snap decision to get on with the macabre business there and then while Vera was asleep and the boys were away.

Outside I went, grabbed a spade and dug a deep hole in the ground in front of the parlour window then raced up the stairs, got the holy water and crucifix then grabbed a clean cloth and wrapped the remains of the infant, placed the cross also in the cloth then sprinkled it with holy water; raced downstairs and placed the bundle gently in the cold earth, sprinkled more holy water on the earth then filled it in. I had bundled all the material that was in the crib, carried it downstairs and pushed it all in the grate to burn. Sarah stood and looked on in amazement then I put more earth on the ground, levelled it out with a fork and placed some of the stones over the earth ready for cementing. I got Sarah to search for a piece of wood suitable for mixing cement on. The boys arrived back from the loch and I roped them in to bring me the sand and cement and pails of water. I mixed the cement, told Billy and Ewan to pour it over the stones I had scattered then I showed them how to level it over, keeping it moist. When the stretch under the window was finished I told Billy and Ewan to bring the garden seat out and place it in front of the window.

'We will be walking on the wet cement Mary.'

'Never mind that, do as you are told.'

The seat was placed where I wanted it. 'Now I said lift it away.' They must have thought I was bonkers but they just looked at one another and did what I wanted. I made deep holes in the ground where the marks of the legs of the bench were made and filled them with cement. We then put the seat back in place and the four of us sat on it, pressing it well into the cement.

'Don't worry, Billy about the mess we've made, just put another layer of cement over the lot and put extra round the legs of the seat so that it will be extra secure.'

Both boys started right away. Sarah and I laid all the stones right round the back of the house and Sarah said, 'you know Mary, I didn't realise you knew so much. Once all the cementing is finished it will look lovely and the two patio containers for each side of the front door will give the house a lived in appearance again.'

'Do you not see, Sarah, what was behind all the work that has been done? I placed the garden seat over the infant's grave as a tombstone. Every time I sit on the seat I hope I'll remember to say a prayer for the little soul lying underneath the ground. Well that's finished, now we don't need to creep about in the dark or even bother Vera. I don't think we should even tell her what we have done. Come, Sarah, we will leave the boys to the cementing, and we'll get the dinner ready. There's some of the joint left to have.'

Sarah looked at me and said, 'you sure are a cool customer. It's a good job somebody can keep a cool head, otherwise the whole family would be in the soup.'

Both of us got the dinner ready; I hated peeling vegetables. It took me back to my skivvy days in the Ramsay household, however it had to be done. When the meal was ready we shouted to the boys to come in and to leave their shoes at the door. Sarah took a tray up to Vera.

'How is she?' I asked when Sarah came in.

'Oh she is a lot better, I left her sitting up in bed and told her to eat everything up. I'll take her a cup of tea up later.'

When we were all finished and had our tea I told the boys to finish the cementing and I went up and saw Vera who was sitting up in bed looking a lot better. 'How do you feel now, Vera.'

'Oh a lot better; I am sorry about all the mess I made, Mary, but oh I felt so funny and faint.'

'It was only natural; Sarah and I acted in the very same way, only I think Sarah was worse than you, so just hurry up and get better. Everything has been attended to.'

'What do you mean?'

'The little baby has been buried. I blessed the child and the ground with holy water.'

Vera lay back on the pillows and gave me a funny look then she said; 'you know, Mary, I don't know where you get your strength from. It's funny but none of the rest of us has the guts that you have.'

I often wondered myself where I got the strength to deal with all the problems.

An overpowering tiredness came over me, I was glad to fling myself down on the bed, and soon I was fast asleep. It was pitch black when I opened my eyes. Father Joseph was standing in the lighted doorway and behind him stood Dr McKinnon. Father Joseph put the light on and came straight over to my bed followed by the doctor then Sarah. 'What's wrong?' I asked.

Doctor took my pulse, 'thank God, Mary, you are with us again. Do you know you have slept for two whole days?'

'Two days, you are joking.'

He shook his head. I made to get up but my arms and legs felt like lead.

'Just lie still, Mary, you are suffering from sheer exhaustion. I'll send a nurse up to look after you. Your sisters and Billy will have to go back to their work. Ewan will still be here; Father has come to give you Communion.'

I let everyone give me orders instead of me giving them. I really could not believe that I had slept all that time. The strain of all that had happened to me in the last month had taken its toll. I knew my task had been done; mum and dad's reputation was saved. I was at ease now and would follow doctor's orders with no worry on my mind. Sarah and Hector came in to say goodbye followed by Vera and Billy. I just nodded and smiled.

Ewan sat on the chair beside my bed. 'Nurse Duncan is downstairs in the kitchen, she's waiting till they all say their goodbyes to you. I'm glad you are better, Mary, we were all going about like lost sheep the last two days. Constable Campbell called every day also, asking if there was any change. I suppose he will call again tomorrow.'

Nurse Duncan came in, 'Well, young lady, what's this I hear you have been up to. I'll be sleeping here for the next two nights; your sister Sarah has made the bed up for me so don't worry about anything. I have brought up some hot milk for you. Hector handed it in just now and a few other things "which when I leave this house I have never seen". I suppose you know what I mean. Now drink this up, then after I have changed and washed you, you can just go back to sleep again; rest is your best medicine.' It was with a great sense of relief that I closed my eyes and drifted into peaceful sleep knowing that everyone was taken care of.

Constable Campbell did call the next morning with a small bunch of violets. Nurse kept him at the door but took the flowers from him telling him if he called tomorrow she would let him visit me for a short while. He left with a big smile on his face and went walking down the road beside his bike. Nurse Duncan told Ewan to find a little vase for her to put the violets in. Nurse arranged the flowers then put them on my bedside table so when I woke up I would see them right away.

The next two days I was still very tired then I asked Nurse if I could get up. 'Yes,' she said, 'after breakfast but only to sit at the window and rest. Oh by the way that girl Mary Kate Bell called yesterday; quite a forward madam. She was in the kitchen; Ewan and I didn't know how long she had been there, she never even knocked or I would have heard. To tell you the truth, Miss Mary I was quite rude to her. I asked her what she was doing here; "oh I am one of the family" she said. "I was in Mary's class at school; I just called to tell her I was leaving for Glasgow. Tell her I'll call the next time I am home. I am sorry to hear that Mary is ill." If I were you, Mary, I would watch her, keep her at arms length.'

I enjoyed sitting at the window looking across the loch; it was misty but there was still some boats sailing back and forth. I could see Nan's house in the distance and I started to cry thinking of my lovely sister who was so young when she died. Nurse Duncan came in as I was wiping my eyes. 'Now,' she said, 'we can't have that, Mary, here is something that will cheer you up.' It was a letter from Auntie Kate. She was worried about me being ill. Somebody must have sent her a telegram for her to write so quickly. She knew I had been having a terrible time and wished she could have come to me but hadn't felt up to the journey. She invited Ewan and me to come for a holiday when I was feeling stronger and enclosed two ten pound notes.

I often wondered why was it that Auntie Kate kept in touch with me rather than my three older sisters, even when we were all young. When she visited us when mum and dad were alive, it was always me she would take with her when she went to the shops. I used to think it was because I was the youngest of the girls but as I sit at the window my thoughts of Auntie Kate kept puzzling me, and I brought my thoughts back to the present. The violets that Colin had brought looked very pretty in the little vase. It wouldn't be long before Colin was calling again and I began to think I was falling in love with him. My mind wandered also to Mary Kate's visit, what a cheek she had just walking into our kitchen without even a knock on the front door. I'd fix her the first chance

I got. She would wonder what's hit her. I gave a little smile to myself thinking if she came in just then I would not have the strength to blow a feather out, never mind her.

Nurse Duncan came into the room carrying a tray, placed it on the round table beside me and said, 'I want to see all the plates cleared by the time I come again. Ewan and I are having ours in the kitchen then when you are finished it's back to bed again, young lady.' On the tray was a lovely piece of haddock, a slice of lemon, a chocolate biscuit, a large glass of milk. I knew where the biscuits came from, Hector of course.

After my lunch I felt very tired and was glad to let nurse help me back to bed. She was like a dragon, protecting me from everyone. Ewan also was on the watch in case any of the MacPhersons took into their head to pay me a visit. I thought to myself when I am better I will arrange for a joiner, if it was at all possible to get one, to make a strong gate at the back garden to keep any unwelcome visitors dropping in on us.

When I woke from a restful sleep Colin was sitting beside my bed; as soon as he seen I was awake he took both my hands and clasped them in his large ones. I was so happy to see him; 'oh Colin,' I said, 'thank you for the violets, they are lovely.'

'Well, Mary,' he said, 'you sure did give us all a fright. I am so glad to see you are a little better. Nurse Duncan says it was delayed shock; in fact everyone in the village wonders how you kept going.'

'Is Mary Kate Bell away,' I asked.

'Yes,' he said, 'her father ran her in his car to the station yesterday. I don't understand that girl. You never really know what she's up to behind that sweet smile of hers.'

I told Colin what nurse told me about her walking into the kitchen and nobody even knew she was there. 'That's why, Colin, when I am well again I'll arrange to get a gate made at the back garden.'

'No need, Mary, for you to wait till you are well. I'll attend to that myself, so don't worry your pretty head. Just you rest and get better.' Nurse Duncan came in and ordered Colin out of the bedroom. He gave me a fly wink then squeezed my hand and left.

I felt so alone after Colin left; I didn't know what had come over me lately, most of the day was spent thinking of him. I just hoped he felt the same way about me.

'I will be leaving tomorrow morning, Mary,' Nurse Duncan said. 'Other duties call, so take advantage of me while I am here and do what you are told and rest. Even after I have gone, Ewan is a good boy, he will get what you need. Dr McKinnon will be calling in tomorrow before I leave to see how you are and here are some magazines Sarah left for you to read,' then off she went and I was left alone with my thoughts, but not for long.

Ewan came in carrying a small parcel. 'I was down at the shops for a message for Nurse Duncan and as I was leaving Mr Walsh called me back and handed me this parcel. All he said was, "give this to Miss Mary and tell her I hope she is feeling a lot better."'

'What's in it, Ewan?'

'I don't know, Mary, you better open it yourself.' Inside the bag was an orange and a banana. Oh how lovely, I wondered where on earth he had got them from, for in the last four years I certainly had never seen any. Ewan could not believe his eyes.

'I'll tell you what, run down to the kitchen and get a knife and we will have a half of each of the orange and the banana.'

I never saw anyone disappear as quickly as Ewan did, in a couple of seconds he was back. The pair of us weren't long in finishing them off. My, they tasted good and we cleared the peelings away before Nurse Duncan could take the huff at not even getting a smell of them. Nurse Duncan smelt the orange in the kitchen and demanded to know where we'd got it. She wasn't at all pleased at not getting any and said she wouldn't share hers with us – if she could coax one out of Mr Walsh.

I told Ewan that Auntie Kate had invited us to Mull and thought we might go for a week in a fortnights time. He was delighted.

While Dr McKinnon was examining me he said, 'I think, Mary, you should take a holiday.'

'It's funny, doctor, that's what I was discussing with Ewan last night. I will be writing to Auntie Kate to tell her.'

'Do it right away, Nurse Duncan will post it for you. She will wait till you are finished; come and see me before you go. I'll have a word with Nurse now, bye for now Mary.'

I told Ewan to fetch me some writing paper. I wrote a few lines telling Auntie Kate that I would like a holiday in a fortnights time, addressed the envelope then pushed the note inside and sealed it. Nurse Duncan came into the bedroom to say goodbye and collect the letter.

'I'll post it for you when I am down in the village. The first shop I'll make for will be Mr Walsh and woe betide him if he hasn't kept an orange for me.' While she was at the door she said, 'Ewan, take good care of your sister,' then she was gone. I thought to myself, it's up to you now Mary to get on with life.

The house felt quiet after my brother and sister had gone. I supposed it would take time for me to get my strength back. Nature has a wonderful way of dealing with troubles of the body. It was lovely just to sit in mum's rocking chair again, watching the flames flickering away in the grate and dreaming of far away places. It's funny how some people sail through life with not a care in the world while the likes of me seem to be surrounded with trouble all the time. Ewan came in with a cup of tea and some of the biscuits Hector had left. I noticed how he had filled out since I rescued him from his brother-in-law's house.

I don't know if it was the heat of the fire or if I was still weak but I fell fast asleep. I don't know how long I slept but when I woke up a blanket had been wrapped round me. I felt so cosy I did not want to move then I said to myself, 'Mary Scott, it's time you gave yourself a shake and moved yourself. You can't have your little brother running after you when really he needs love and attention. I must not forget he, also, has lost his dear mother and father and his sister Nan. Nobody knows but him what he must be going through.'

I rose from the chair, feeling a lot better after my rest and started washing the few dishes that were lying about then I walked into the parlour. To my surprise I found Ewan lying on the settee sound asleep. The poor lad must be exhausted. I went to the kitchen, got the blanket and covered him with it then left the room and gently shut the door behind me. While I was passing the front door I noticed a letter lying on the floor. The post must have come while we were sleeping.

I picked it up and went into the kitchen to read it. It was from Ina, the cook at the Ramsays. She said her ladyship was trying to get custody of Theresa's son Alan; Master James was the father. Theresa said they can fight all they want but no way were they getting her son. I thought, what an awful cheek her ladyship had, thinking all she had to do was give the orders and everyone jumped. I thought back to the dreadful way they treated Theresa when she told them she was expecting his child. Lord and ladyship turning her out of the house. If I had been in Theresa's place, I certainly would not have given in to their demands. Kate, cook said, was still with them as parlour maid and she still follows your instructions every night. A few nights ago she had seen the door handle turning but that was all. Master James and Miss Margaret were still madly in love. The food situation was bad.

I made my way out to the back garden and was surprised at the amount of work the boys had put into it, the whole place had been weeded and the cementing round the back of the house was perfect. Perhaps when Ewan and I came back from our holiday we would be able to tackle the lawn; in the meantime it had been sprayed with weed killer. A voice behind me said, 'I hope you are not starting digging already.' I looked up and there was Colin standing there.

Oh how pleased I was to see him; he always brought a ray of sunshine into my life. We sat on the garden seat and Colin admired the new cement work, wondering how the boys had managed to do it so well. I said that I'd shown them and he laughed, saying he'd have to watch out for his own job.

Colin promised to make all arrangements for the garden gate while Ewan and I were at Auntie Kate's. That was another weight he'd taken off my mind.

Ewan, awake again, was demanding tea and we all went inside. Colin made the tea and we had it with some of Hector's chocolate biscuits.

I asked about Nan's children, thinking particularly of little Helen. How I longed to look after her, but feared being pestered by Donald's father. Colin said they were being taken care of by Donald's mother's younger sister.

Saying he had business that would keep him on the other side of the loch for two or three days and would see me as soon as he returned, Colin rushed away.

Ewan said, 'I wonder why Constable Campbell is always coming round to our house.'

'I really don't know, Ewan,' but within my heart I thought I did. Through time he would find out for himself. I sat still in the rocking chair planning the kind of gate I would order for the garden, in fact I drew it on a piece of paper then asked Ewan what he thought of it. 'Where do you get all your ideas from, Mary?'

'I don't know, they just come; well what do you think of the gate?'

'It's great, Mary, I like it. Oh I forgot Sarah left you a letter before she left. I'll run and get it for you; I am sorry, Mary, I forgot all about it.'

'It's all right, Ewan, all is forgiven.'

I read Sarah's letter; Hector was getting posted again and she was worried, the situation was serious. Also she had to be careful what she wrote in her letters but she said if at anytime I needed help or was in any danger to let her know right away. 'This is what you have to write and I'll make arrangements right away to come home. The passwords are "the sun was shining brightly this morning". You better burn this note right away but remember the passwords.' I was feeling cold and sent Ewan to fetch my cardigan. While he was away I burned the letter. On his return we talked about the prospects of his going to join Vera and his brother Billy whom he missed so much. Then we had hot milk and went to bed.

After breakfast Ewan and I made our way to the shops; the only thing I needed was bread as Sarah and Hector had stocked up all the cupboards with tins of food, flour, rice, sugar, tea and coffee. They certainly did not mean us to starve. I was glad to get out for a walk in the fresh air again. When I reached Mr Walsh's shop I thanked him for the gift. Mr Walsh told me that Nurse Duncan had been in and mentioned the orange Ewan and I had shared. He had been obliged to give her the two oranges he had been keeping for himself.

We discussed the garden gate I wanted. Iron was out of the question as every scrap of metal was being requisitioned.

I left my sketch with Mr Walsh then Ewan and I made our way to the baker. When we came out of the shop Ewan said, 'look, Mary, there is Constable Campbell leaving the hotel. My, I wonder who is the lovely looking girl he has hanging on to his arm.'

I looked over and sure enough in broad daylight there he was laughing and hugging the beautiful blonde girl. Inside of me I was furious, what a fool I had been to think for a second that Colin loved me. 'Come on, Ewan, we better get to the bakers then we will spend some time down at the loch before we go home.' As I sat down beside the loch I planned what I would do when Colin called again at my house. He must have thought little Mary would still be at home convalescing; what a cheek, telling me that he had business on the other side of the loch for the next two days while all the time he was enjoying himself with that blonde. I would play him at his own game and just lead him on then when it suited me I would just give him the heave. Then again, was he just coming up to our house to spy? Maybe Donald told him why he was blackmailing my parents before he went to prison. Well, from now, Colin, I mused, I will be on my guard and no more private family news will you get.

After I had settled what I intended to do I felt a bit happier. Ewan had wandered further along the shore so I got up and followed him. My mind went back to the happy Saturday mornings when dad took us down to the loch to give mum peace to do the weekly baking, he always seemed to be laughing and happy. To us he looked as if he had not a care in the world. By the time I reached home Ewan was sitting on the doorstep waiting for me.

I was still feeling weak so I sat in the rocking chair to rest a while. Ewan put some logs on the range, filled the kettle with water and set it on the hob. When I get my breath back I'll make some scrambled eggs for us. Inside of me I was feeling blazing mad at Colin. I just hoped I did not show my anger to

Ewan at the baker's shop. If I did he never let on. When we were sitting at the table eating our lunch there was a knock on the door. Ewan made to answer it but I stopped him in case it was old MacPherson, Donald's father.

I opened the door to a young man with his cap in hand; before I could speak he said he was Frank Lees the joiner. Mr Walsh asked him to come up and measure the width and height for my new gate. I showed the joiner where the gate was to go, and stressed that I wanted a strong lock on it and the job done as soon as possible. It was agreed I would pay for the work as soon as it was finished. He put his cap back on, covering a mass of black curls; his eyes were the darkest blue I had ever seen. I wondered why a young man like him was not called up for service as the war was still raging on. When I went back into the kitchen, Ewan had cleared the table and was on the verge of starting to wash the dishes.

It was nearly two days before I got a letter from Auntie Kate; she said to come as soon as possible. She would meet me at Craignure where the ferry docked and to remember to bring Ewan. She sent her love. I was so excited, I was 19 years old and the loch was part of my life, but to sail on a big boat from Oban to Mull was something to look forward to. First of all I had to write to Sarah, Vera and Billy to give them my good news. Also, I would have to tell them about Frank Lees the joiner who made my lovely gate and put it up for me. I was very pleased with the strong lock he put on it; I felt a lot happier. I found out Constable Campbell was double crossing me but even though he still called I never let on to him about his 'blonde'. Yes, I still invited him in and gave him my sweetest smile when he arrived. I just watched what news I gave him and waited my time for revenge.

The thought of going on holiday made me feel better. I had to see what suitable clothes I had to take with me. I was always thrifty and thought spending good money on myself selfish. Then again I thought of Sarah; she must spend a fortune; also that flirty blonde Colin was with wore expensive clothes. I wondered where they got the coupons from; 'black market' I supposed. It would do Ewan and me good to have some new clothes and I decided to spend all our coupons before we set off for Mull. I wouldn't mention to Colin when we are leaving; lately I have been confiding too much to him. Also, he has never bothered to investigate the broken branches on the trees. That was over three weeks ago; so far he had never mentioned anything. All he did was sit in my kitchen drinking tea. When I came to think of it his time was spent asking Ewan questions. I would have to put Ewan on his guard and tell him to be careful what he says.

After breakfast Ewan and I set off on our spending spree. I hoped I would be able to get the kind of clothes I wanted, a new coat, beret and scarf to match; a nice dark brown, pleated skirt and a woollen rust twin set. A nice pair of walking shoes and a few more things. For Ewan, trousers, two shirts, two pullovers, underwear, socks and a strong pair of shoes and a scarf. I hoped I'd have enough coupons. Before we went into the drapers shop I called at Mr Walsh's shop for salt. That was one of the things Hector forgot to leave.

'Can I speak to you a minute, Miss Mary, privately?'

'Of course,' I said.

He went to the far end of the counter and in a low voice said, 'did you know Donald's father Mr MacPherson senior has a key to your front door?'

'Oh dear God, no, how on earth did you find that out?'

'Well it was my daughter who saw him unlocking the door and going in.'

'In that case I'll need to change the locks. Maybe Nan gave the key to Donald; while I am here I'll buy the locks for the doors. I need one for the kitchen door, also two bolts. If you could be so kind as to ask Mr Lees if he could put them on for me as soon as possible. I don't think I'll be able to sleep tonight.'

'I'll attend to that straight away and send the joiner up tomorrow. I am sorry to upset you but I thought you better know. By the way did Constable Campbell ever tell you they had a spare key; he knew they had one.'

'No,' I said, 'I don't suppose he gave it a thought.' Within myself I was thinking you dirty underhanded skunk Campbell; outwardly I thanked Mr Walsh for telling me. Ewan and I made our way to the draper's the first time for three and a half years I had set foot inside it. The shop was quite empty and we were served right away. I managed to get everything I needed; Ewan was pleased with his new clothes. The girl parcelled them up for us. When we left the shop I asked Ewan if he would like to go to the hotel for tea. He had never been in the hotel and thought it a great idea. My mind went back to the days and nights when dad always left the hotel drunk; you could hear him a mile away singing merrily on his way home. I went back into the draper's shop and asked the girl if someone could deliver our parcels for us. It was arranged for a boy to deliver them after closing time. I was quite pleased to be rid of all the parcels as they were beginning to become too heavy for me. Ewan and I made our way up to the hotel; when we reached the entrance I felt like running away then I thought, I better put a brave face on in front of Ewan. He was so excited at the thought of getting inside the hotel. I suppose he would often wonder why dad spent so much of his time here.

Inside, the hotel was lovely and cool; I did not know what door to go through to but was saved by a young girl asking me if she could help me. The girl showed us to a small table for two; the table was already set. She disappeared through a swinging door. While she was away I glanced round the room. To me it was a bit on the dark side; I always like to see what I am eating, otherwise it was beautifully furnished. Right round the room were red plush covered settees; the chairs at the tables were also red covered, on each table were pure white linen table clothes and napkins to match. I thought to myself, this will cost me a penny then again I had to see for myself what the hotel was like inside. While we were waiting to be served a middle-aged gentleman came into the room; I could see the resemblance of Mary Kate's face in him so he must be the owner. 'Are you being attended to?' he asked.

'Yes,' I said, 'thank you.' Just then the young girl came in with a cake-stand, scones, cakes, jam and butter and tea. Ewan could not keep his eyes off the cakes. 'A scone first, young man, with butter and jam then you can have just one cake.'

'Oh Mary, can I not have two?'

'Oh all right, I just hope I have enough money with me. Remember I had to pay for those locks for the doors. Did you know, Ewan, that Donald had a key to our house.'

'Yes, I did; I am sorry, I forgot to tell you; when mum and dad were ill he seemed to go up to the house every day. He always told Mr Walsh that the messages he got on credit were dads but he always took the food over in the boat to his own house.'

Well I thought, I hope he rots in jail; he was feeding his big family at mum and dad's expense. That's why both of them died of starvation. I hoped some day I would find out the truth.

'Look, Mary, there's that girl with Constable Campbell.'

The room we were sitting in had a window that looked out on to the front path. My back was to it, when I looked the two of them were disappearing round the back of the hotel. When the girl came with the bill which was one and threepence I paid it and asked who was the girl with Constable Campbell?

'The fair haired girl you mean?'

'Yes,' I said.

'That's his wife, Alice, they were married about two months ago, she works in the bar here at nights. Her house is across the loch.'

'I was just wondering if we were at school together, Mary Kate and I were in the same class.' With that Ewan and I left the hotel; the mystery of the blonde was solved. As I walked slowly home I felt disappointed that Colin had never mentioned his marriage then I thought, he must be after something

78

since it was not me. I thought if he calls again I'll just keep him at the door. I warned Ewan that from now on he was to be careful what he said to Colin. Thinking of the devil, he caught up on us on his bike. 'Was that you and Ewan in the hotel, Mary?'

'Yes,' I said, 'any law against us going in for tea. The girl who served us told me about you getting married.'

His face turned scarlet; I think he wanted to keep his marriage a secret a bit longer. Before he could say anything I said that there would be no need for him calling again as I was feeling a lot better now.

'As you wish, Mary,' was all he said and went on his way.

Frank Lees the joiner and the boy with our parcels arrived at the house at the same time. I showed Mr Lees what I wanted done. Ewan collected all the parcels from the boy and gave him sixpence. I left the joiner to carry on putting the new locks on the doors. I went into the kitchen and sat in my favourite rocking chair to rest awhile until the joiner finished. Ewan and I will unpack all the parcels and do some of our packing. The young man came into the kitchen to say the front door lock and bolt were fixed and could he start on the back door. I told him to go ahead and to make sure the window snibs locked properly. Every time I sat in the rocking chair my mind would wander back to my childhood days. I always felt at ease sitting in it. The joiner brought me back to earth. 'That's the locks and bolts fixed, miss, and the windows are quite safe and here are the new keys. The old ones I have laid on the table in case you want to keep them.'

I paid him then he touched his cap and was off home. Peace at last I thought to myself. I had two keys for each door; the bolts would give me extra protection during the night when I will be in the house by myself when Ewan goes to work on the farm. Must see about getting a dog when we get back from our holidays. Ewan came into the kitchen starving. So was I. I looked in the cupboard to see what Hector had left. We chose Spam and beans and toast and tea. The kettle was already boiling so it wasn't long before tea was ready. After we had our meal we made a start packing our cases.

I decided to see Father Joseph and Dr McKinnon. I was still feeling very tired, maybe Doctor would give me a tonic. I did not need to call on Father Joseph as he himself called the next day. 'Well, Mary, how is everything working out and where is Ewan? Has Vera managed to get him fixed up yet?'

'I don't know yet, Father; to tell you the truth both of us were going down to see you as we will be leaving tomorrow for a weeks holiday at Auntie Kate's in the Isle of Mull.'

'My, that's the best news I have heard, Mary.'

'Also, Father, when I come back home I was wondering if you knew of any kind of work I could do.'

'Yes, there is the very thing that would suit you. Dr McKinnon's secretary Peggy is leaving to get married in a months time; I'll put in a word for you. Just leave everything to me; you and Ewan enjoy your holiday.'

Ewan and I made our way to the doctor's surgery. The waiting room was packed; mothers with young babies, older children running wild and old men sitting with heads bent, staring at the floor and looking as if they didn't care whether they lived or died. Much to the annoyance of other patients Peggy showed us into the surgery ahead of our turn.

Dr McKinnon said the forthcoming holiday would do more good than any tonic and wished us well.

I called at Hector's parents' house to see if they would keep a watch on my house while we are away. Their house looks right up to ours. I felt very nervous, both of us went up to the MacLean's door; this was the very first time I had ever called at their house. When we were young our family looked upon Hector's family as snobs. I don't know why because to me they were very nice people. Maybe it was because they always had plenty of money; what a lovely house it was. Everything outside so prim and proper. I knocked on the door and it was opened by Hector's mother. She was pleased to hear we were going to have a break and would be delighted to keep an eye on the house.

CHAPTER 5

The next morning Hector's father was waiting at the door to drive us to the station; what a relief it was to see him. I wasn't looking forward to the two mile walk with our cases. I looked around the house to make sure everything was in order; the fire put out, windows locked, back door bolted then Ewan and I made our way out to the van. Ronald, Hector's dad, put our cases in the back of the van; the three of us sat at the front then off we went. The day was misty and a slight rain was falling. I glanced over at the loch, it was covered in mist. It was in one of its secretive moods. You never knew what was going on underneath all that mist. Ronald hoped the weather would clear up before we crossed the water to Mull. Ewan was excited; it would be his first time on a train and like me the first time crossing the sea on the ferry. At last we reached the station; Ronald attended to our cases then he had a few words with the station-master, then he came back and said the train would be in any moment. True to his word it came puffing round the corner.

Ronald saw to our tickets and put our cases on the rack in our compartment then he wished us a happy holiday and waved us off. That was the first time I had the pleasure of meeting Hector's dad; he was such a gentleman, so different from my own dad but I loved mine more than anything in the world, even though most of his life he spent more of his time being drunk than sober. I had to brush away a tear from my eyes before Ewan saw it; at last the pair of us settled down, each of us at a seat at the window. It was wonderful just sitting watching the beautiful scenery of the countryside as the train sped on its journey. The night before I had made up some Spam and egg sandwiches and a flask of tea as the journey to Oban was two and half hours and as usual Ewan would be starving. After an hour's travelling we had our lunch then I must have fallen asleep.

Ewan was shaking me saying, 'Mary we are here, Oban. Look at that big ship; is that the one we are going on?' We collected our cases and made our way out to make inquiries about which boat to take for Mull. The man pointed to Quay 4 and we had to hurry as they were getting ready to sail. Ewan raced up the gangway; try as I could I did not have the energy to hurry. A young sailor ran down and took hold of my cases and said, hurry lassie, we are late already then he ran ahead or me. I just reached the ship when the gangway was pulled up and we were off sailing over the grey misty waters. The rain and the mist were back with us again; it had been lovely sunshine all the time we were in the train. It's funny I thought, the lochs and the sea seemed to sense our moods or was it the moods of the water which affected us. Ewan was so excited, he ran from one end of the deck to the other exploring every nook and cranny. I just sat on the deck and took in the wonders of the sea. I supposed it had its angry moods also but then it was calm and misty. It took us one hour to reach Mull; when we docked at Craignure Auntie Kate was waiting for us with a taxi. Ewan ran down the gangway first and straight into her arms. The young sailor who helped with my cases when I arrived carried them down to the quay for me then he said, 'when will you becoming back, miss?'

'Next week,' I said, 'I'll see you then.'

I ran to Auntie Kate and gave her a big hug and kiss. It just seemed a minute till we reached Auntie Kate's cottage. What a lovely garden it had; roses everywhere and the lawn had no weeds on it. Auntie Kate must have had a gardener; no way could she do all the work herself. The rooms inside were a lot bigger than I thought they would be. We were shown to our bedrooms first; I was to sleep in Auntie Kate's room, Ewan in the spare room. Auntie Kate was going to sleep in a made-up bed in the living room. I wasn't going to have that and argued with her until she agreed to let me sleep in the made-up bed.

I went out into the garden. The back garden was full of different vegetables. Of course, with the war still raging, everyone had to grow as much food as possible but the front garden was breathtaking with a lovely smell from the lilac, also the beautiful colour of the lupins and roses. When I got home I would plan my garden like Auntie's. When I went indoors again, the tea was ready. As usual Ewan was first sitting down.

Auntie Kate said, 'will you say grace, Mary, or will I?'

'You, Auntie,' I said, it had been so long since I had said grace before meals; I had forgotten the words. On the table was a bowl of chips and a large dish of peas. On each of our plates was a lovely piece of fried haddock. I felt hungry right away; the meal was delicious, Ewan emptied the bowl of chips; he sure did enjoy himself.

'Young man, when you are finished, do you think you can be trusted to play down at the shore and be able to find your way back here?' Auntie Kate spoke with her schoolmam tone. At first Ewan thought she was angry but before the week was over he would understand why she spoke that way. She was the headmistress of the local school and due to her age and the war she just worked part time. Auntie Kate as it was had a good pension and was very comfortably off. 'Away you go then,' she said, 'I want to talk to your sister.' Ewan was off like a flash, I thought it was a pity he did not have a pal of his own age instead of always being with his older sister.

When we had the house to ourselves Auntie Kate asked me what sentence Donald MacPherson got for killing Nan.

'Five years,' I said; 'that's a wicked family Nan married into.'

'Be careful, Mary, when you go back home.'

'I know,' I said, 'I'll need to get a good dog.'

'Oh there's a dog and cat home in the town, we will visit it the day before you leave for home. We might find something suitable; in the meantime get as much rest and fresh air and enjoy yourself for a change. You sure have had a terrible time of it.'

The rest of our week's stay in Mull was heaven; Ewan and I spent most of our time down on the beach. It was there while I was lazing on the sands that I met my sailor boy again who had carried my cases on and off the boat. I never paid any attention to him but when he stood in front of me and said, 'hello suitcase, girl,' I realised what a handsome young man he was.

Even though I was 19 years old I did not know how to speak to boys of my own age. I was always used to dealing with older people since I was 15. Suddenly, I felt very shy and felt my face blushing. At first thought I wanted to get up and run away, instead I said, 'hello, I never really thanked you for helping me.'

He sat down beside me and we talked. He told me his name was John Lewis and told me my aunt had taught him at school. She was a dragon, but a good teacher. He coaxed me to paddle, saying salt water is good for the feet. The day flew while Ewan, John and I splashed each other and laughed our heads off. Suddenly we realised the tide was coming in so there was nothing else for us to do but make our way home.

'Can I see you tomorrow, Mary?'

'Of course, John,' I said.

'I'll take both of you up to see Torosay Castle; the gardens are magnificent.'

Auntie Kate had our dinner ready for us when we arrived home.

'I see you had a grand time splashing by the looks of you and was that John Lewis you were with?'

'Yes, Auntie, do you know him?'

'Know him, he was always the one to start trouble but it was always the other child who took the blame.'

Our trip to Torosay Castle with John was exhausting; it was quite a climb but well worth it. I had made sandwiches and brought a flask of tea for us. It was just as well as there was no tea room in sight. The gardens were as John had described, magnificent. Every now and then he would slip his arm round my waist when Ewan wasn't looking. I was beginning to wish that it was just the two of us alone up there. I think John was thinking the same. It's funny, when I look back I always seemed to be saddled with someone to look after. I never seemed to be able to do as I pleased. Inside of me I felt angry. 'Why me.'

John said he had to be back on board ship the next day and would most likely see me when going home. I was disappointed that our time together was so short. Ewan and I together would explore the island in the rest of our few days we had left. On our way back home John asked me for my address so as he could keep in touch with me, then he said, 'if that's all right with you, Mary.'

'Of course, John, I would love that,' then he put his arms around me and gave me a big kiss. It was my first kiss from a boy. When he looked at me my face was burning; all of a sudden I felt really shy.

'Come on,' he said, 'I'll treat Ewan and you to tea; how about that,' then the three of us made our way back to town. After tea we made our way along the prom watching the waves splashing on the rocks.

'I am afraid, Mary, its going to rain all day tomorrow.'

'How do you know that?'

'Its in the air, us sailors just know.' When we were near Auntie Kate's cottage he grabbed me and said, 'how about a goodnight kiss.'

'My you are greedy, you already have stolen one.' Never the less he bent down and brushed my lips with a light kiss and waved goodbye.

Ewan and I went into the cottage; Auntie Kate said she was beginning to get worried thinking we had lost our way. 'Were you with that boy Lewis again?'

'Yes,' I said, and Ewan said we were kissing and cuddling up at the castle.

'Hush boy,' Auntie Kate said, 'that's enough. Get your supper both of you and get to bed. Tomorrow we will go shopping.'

'It's to be raining tomorrow,' Ewan said.

'How do you know that?' Auntie asked.

'John said it, so it's going to rain because John said it.'

The next day it wasn't just raining, it was pouring. The waves were lashing against the rocks. It seemed more like winter than late summer but inside the cottage was warm and cosy. The kitchen was like our own big and spacious and plenty of chairs to sit on. The old range wasn't as big as ours. Auntie Kate said the rain would be on for the day so we would have to put on our coats. Ewan said he hadn't a coat so Auntie Kate covered him with her umbrella then the three of us set off in the pouring rain for the shops. I myself didn't care if it rained or snowed, I was feeling so happy and carefree. The first shop we went into was a ladies' dress shop. Not much fun for Ewan but he just followed us inside.

Auntie Kate thought I should have two summer dresses, gloves, shoes and a raincoat. I protested that I'd spent all my coupons before coming on holiday. Auntie took no notice. I felt quite excited looking through all the lovely dresses. At last I picked two, one blue silk with white spots, the other yellow with pink ribbons. My raincoat was in the latest fashion; a dark shade of blue. Auntie Kate attended to the payment; also the coupons. We went to a shoe shop and I got black patent shoes with two straps. While we were there Ewan got fitted with a pair also. At last Ewan was getting attended to. A good strong pair for the young man Auntie had said to the assistant. At last he was suited then we all made our way to a gents shop. It was still raining heavily so it was a matter of how to get shelter in the mens shop as soon as possible. We were in luck, the shop we needed was just two doors down. Ewan and I ran in, Auntie was a bit slower. Ewan was pleased with his new coat. After Auntie paid she said we would all go to Crawfords for tea.

Crawfords was a large tea-room. The little tables were all set; it was the cakes that caught Ewan's eyes and mine. We sat down at the table for three, the waitress came and took our order. Pot of tea, scones, butter and jam and cakes for three. Ewan and I just looked at one another; 'scones first, young man, before you get any cakes.' I just have my little brother a wink.

Since it was such a miserable day we took a taxi home. When we reached the cottage Auntie Kate said she was going straight to her room to rest. I knew what I was going to do, parade about in my new dresses and shoes. Just wait till Sarah and Vera see them; they will be green with envy. Ewan had the same idea as me because he disappeared to his room. After I was tired dancing about in my new clothes I took them off and folded them away till we were ready to go home. I lay on the bed and fell asleep.

I dreamed that John and I were in a big white yacht; John was dressed all in white which showed up the lovely tan on his face. His fair hair was blowing softly in the wind. I, also, was in white lying on the deck at his feet; everything was calm and lovely sunshine. The next minute a gale force wind blew up and both of us were flung overboard by an enormous wave. I felt myself drowning; something seemed to be pulling me under the water. I heard myself scream then I heard a voice say; 'are you all right Mary?' I woke up to find Ewan standing beside my bed. When I was wide awake I said to myself thank God it was just a dream, then maybe, I thought, it was a warning not to get too close to John. Ewan admitted he thought Auntie Kate was nice but he was now feeling homesick.

Both of us were in a better mood the next day; it was calm, warm and sunny. I just read and lazed the day away. Ewan could please himself. My mind wandered back to home and all that had happened in the short space since I arrived then I wondered about Colin. Why was he visiting me all the time when he had a new wife. Also the mystery of my parents death. Auntie Kate hadn't brought the subject up since I arrived; I wondered why. When I got the house to myself I'd make it my point to see into everything. I thought I'd remind Auntie about the visit to the kennels to get me a pup. It was nice to hear the children laughing; they put me in mind of our own family when we were young. Ewan was playing football with three other boys about his own age. I supposed they were down on holiday also. Auntie Kate was lucky living on such a lovely island. My sailor boy John would be busy on the ferry sailing back and forth from Oban to Mull. I wished he was with me just then. Not much fun for a girl on her own. I must have fallen asleep again; Ewan was shaking me telling me to hurry as the tide was coming in fast. I don't know what's wrong with me but I just seem to drift off to sleep every time I relaxed. Ewan had enjoyed himself playing with the boys who were there only for the day.

We hurried home to find Auntie standing at the gate waiting for us. 'Hurry up children, I have a nice meal ready for you; run and wash your hands first boy.'

I was waiting for her to tell me to wash mine but she gave me a big smile. 'You sure are looking a lot better, Mary; I am glad the holiday has given you a rest which you badly needed, now sit down at the table and I'll serve.' I was starving.

'Oh, Auntie, have you forgotten we have to get a pup for me from the kennels?'

'No, Mary, I phoned the owner last night and he said they have the very kind you would like. Tomorrow after breakfast we will all go over there to see it. He will supply the travelling basket for it as well.'

I was sorry I was leaving this lovely kind lady but inside me I was glad I was going home also; with that in mind I went to bed and slept like a log.

After breakfast Ewan and I were so excited; soon we would be on the ferry carrying us back home. Auntie Kate's voice interrupted my thoughts; 'Mary, you are miles away, which dog would you like.'

We had arrived at the kennels, the noise of the barking dogs was terrible. I wanted one like our own Rusty. It was Ewan who spotted one. He led me to a small pen and there lay this little bundle of fur looking up at us with such large, beautiful sad eyes. I went over to Auntie and said Ewan and I had picked one. I was glad to get outside as I was beginning to get a sore head with all the barking that was going on. I felt sorry for all the animals locked up like that. At last the kennel owner came outside carrying my precious bundle in the basket followed by Auntie Kate. I was handed the basket. After a few words with the man we all set out for home. We had just time for a cup of coffee, give the pup some milk and collect our lunch basket.

At last we were on our way; Auntie Kate ordered a taxi to take us to the quay; the ferry was berthed waiting for everyone to board her. I was so excited at seeing John again; Auntie must have read my thoughts for she said, 'I do hope John will help you with the cases.' He must have been looking out for us for he came running down the gangway, took our cases and disappeared up to the boat. Auntie gave Ewan a big hug then me, then she whispered 'remember, Mary, whatever happens the house is yours, take care now, write when you get settled.'

Then we were off on the start of our journey home. Ewan ran up the gangway followed by me; both of us stood at the ship's rail waving to Auntie Kate till we could no longer see her. I was puzzled when after she had given me a hug and kiss she slipped something in my coat pocket. I didn't want to look right away as John was busy working at the other end of the deck all the while watching me. Ewan came up to me and handed me a note; it was from John saying he was sorry he could not spend any time with us as he was on duty. 'I am enclosing my address, Mary, mind and write soon, I love you John.' I felt disappointed at not being able to speak to John, oh well that's life, just when you think everything is rosy in the garden something is sure to go wrong. I just kept standing at the rail of the ship. The sea was in one of her happier moods, the sun glinting on the waves, the warm soft breeze blowing gently, the seagulls screeching quite close to us.

It only took one hour from Craignure to Oban so it wasn't long before we docked. Ewan had disappeared, I had clean forgotten all about him. Oh my God, I hoped nothing had happened to him. The gangway was lowered, everyone hurrying to get ashore. Panic stations were taking over when at last Ewan and John appeared together. I was really angry; I flew at Ewan, 'where have you been and by the way where is the puppy you were supposed to look after it?'

'It's all right, Mary, Ewan was with me, just look at the bottom of the gangway; you will find all your cases and the basket with your little pet safe and sound.'

'Oh I am sorry, John, I was so worried in case anything happened to Ewan.'

'All is forgiven then?' he said.

I just nodded then he put both is hands round my face and gave me a big kiss. I felt my face burning; everything happened so quickly. Ewan looked up at me with a big grin on his face. To overcome my embarrassment I said to him, 'I'll fix you when we get home. Come on we better hurry and catch our train.' As usual we were the last to get on. The porter helped me with my cases and guided us to the seats Auntie had booked for us. I tipped him, he touched his cap and he was off. The next minute the train was moving; another two hours or so to go and we would be home. We settled in and opened the lunch basket Auntie had packed for us. There were Spam sandwiches, a large slice of fruit cake, two oranges and two bananas and a flask of tea. I wondered where Auntie had got the fruit from because the whole week we were on the island there wasn't any fruit to be seen in any of the shop windows. It must be 'black market'; never mind what it was, Ewan and I enjoyed our lunch. As I sat staring out of the train window taking in the ever changing beautiful scenery I felt at peace with the world.

Ewan was asleep, I felt sleepy also but tried to stay awake. I sometimes forgot that Ewan was still a boy; maybe in a way I expected too much from him. I lifted the basket with the puppy in it and laid it beside myself to give Ewan more room to stretch his legs out. I decided to call the little thing Rusty even though its colouring was black and white. The kennel owner said it would become a good guard dog; it better be for my sake. Try as I did to stay awake, it was impossible. Sleep won the battle. It was the voice of Hector's father Ronald that woke me up. He was standing in the carriage; the porter was taking our cases down from the rack. 'It's a good job I came looking for you; I don't know where the pair of you would have stopped. Your Auntie Kate sent a telegram asking me to meet you on this train. We better hurry, we are holding the train up. I'll take this basket; what on earth have you got in it?'

Ronald was not long in running us home; when I opened the front door I was glad to see some letters lying on the floor. Ewan picked them up and Ronald carried our cases into the hall; also the dog basket. He disappeared again then came in with a brown bag and laid it on the kitchen table then he asked; 'did you both have a nice rest?'

Ewan piped up, 'gee,' he said, 'it was great down at the shore.'

'That's fine then,' he said, 'I'll be off now Mary, be seeing you.'

I shut and locked the door and went back into the kitchen glad to be home again. Ewan had taken Rusty out of his basket. The poor little thing could hardly stand. We made a bed for him beside the fire with an old blanket and right away Ewan gave him some milk. I opened the parcel Ronald had left; good, I thought, there was a pint of milk, bread and scones. That must have been Hector's mother who thought of that. They are such a nice family. I got the fire going and while waiting for the kettle boiling I read my letters. The first one was from Vera, who said Mr Smith did need more help and he would give Ewan a trial to see if he was suitable. Billy and she would be home for the weekend at the end of the month so that Ewan could travel back to Angus with them. Ewan was delighted when I told him the news. I opened the other letter; it was from Sarah, Hector was still overseas. She was worried sick in case anything happened to him. 'Every night before I go to bed I'll say a special prayer that he will come home safe. Mind and let me know how the holiday went, love Sarah and Hector.'

When I finished reading Sarah's letter, I remembered Auntie Kate had pushed something in my pocket. I ran into the hall where my coat was, pulled out the letter from my pocket and opened it. There was a short note saying that if ever I needed help to write and let her know right away; she enclosed two ten pound notes. I was beginning to wonder why she gave me so much while the rest of the family, except Ewan of course, never got anything. I put the money away in a safe place then went back to the kitchen. Ewan had placed Rusty on his blanket again and he was fast asleep. I thought that when I had the house to myself I would get some of mum and dad's furniture out of the attic and back in the bedroom. That would give me more room for my clothes; also, I'd have a good rake in all the chests and cases lying about.

There was a loud knock on the front door; Ewan made to answer it but I said I would go. When I opened it Donald's father stood there; he was in a threatening mood. Right away he said, 'what's wrong with the locks?'

'Nothing,' I said, 'I got them all changed before I went on holiday.'

'You had no right doing that, the house belongs to Donald.'

'What do you mean belongs to Donald?'

'Well you see, Nan was the oldest daughter and Donald was her husband.'

'Get off my step at once,' I said, 'or I'll report you to Constable Campbell.'

He let out one big laugh; 'that will be the day, Campbell will do as I tell him.'

Before he could say another word I shut the door in his face and locked it. So he was up right enough at our house while Ewan and I were away. My, I would have loved to have seen the expression on his face when he found he could not get the door open. It would be the same when he tried to get into the back garden; the locked gate would keep him out of there. It's a wonder he never tried to break it to pieces, with the type of temper he had. I'd have to speak to Father Joseph about him when I went to Mass on Sunday. When I got back to the kitchen Ewan asked who it was.

'Oh only that man MacPherson and for heaven's sake keep clear of him anytime you see him.'

'He is a bad man, Mary; him and Donald used to beat us if the work they laid out for Billy and me wasn't finished. What about yourself, Mary, when I go back with Vera and Billy? You will be in this big house by yourself.'

'I'll think of something, Ewan; don't worry.' I looked at the little bundle of fur lying asleep beside the fire. 'Maybe Rusty in a few months time will turn out to be a good guard dog.' What a cheek that MacPherson had coming up to my house like that. I was never going to get any peace from them at all. I had just sat down in mum's rocking chair when the door went again. When I opened it Father Joseph was standing there. 'Come in, Father, I am glad you called; I was meaning to speak to you on Sunday.'

'What's troubling you, Mary?'

I told him what Donald's father had said; also what he had said about Constable Campbell. I sat in the rocking chair, Father sat beside Ewan at the table. At first he never said a word then he said, 'this is serious, Mary. We can't have him threatening you. I'll have a word with Constable Campbell to see what his opinion of the situation is.' I offered tea to the Father but he said his housekeeper would have his tea ready for him. He promised to investigate the MacPherson's claim to my house, said he was glad to see my holiday had done me good and went off.

So much for getting the unpacking done. All of a sudden I felt so tired; I told Ewan to attend to Rusty; take him into the garden, put papers on the floor and leave him a saucer of milk. When all that was arranged the pair of us made our separate ways to bed; before I fell asleep my mind wandered back to the first day I arrived home and was horrified at the terrible state I had found my mum and dad in. Both of them dying of starvation; I was sure the MacPhersons were behind the trouble, and asked God to help me to solve the problem.

It was pouring with rain the next day, the loch was in one of its angry moods; I just sat at the window and watched the waves lashing against the rocks. I could see the MacPherson's farm on the other side through the light mist. I wondered why they were so keen on claiming my house. After all, at mum and dad's funeral Auntie Kate told me the house was mine. Maybe it was them who planted the body of the dead infant in the attic. Ewan came into the parlour, starving. I thought to myself, it is a good job Ewan was in the house with me, otherwise my daydreaming would make me forget all food. I wasn't hungry myself but I supposed I better cook for Ewan, he was still a growing boy. After a lunch of scrambled eggs, toast and tea we set off for the village. I needed bread and I wanted to know if Mrs MacLean had seen anything suspicious while I was away.

Hector's mother was in the garden, 'hello, Mary, had you a nice holiday? You are certainly looking better.'

'I really called to ask you if you noticed anyone hanging about the house.'

'To tell you the truth I was really worried. The MacPhersons, three of them, came over in their boat, they even had Constable Campbell with them trying to open your door. I told Ronald to never let on to anyone that we had seen them. They tried that new garden gate also, but it would not budge; one of the brothers gave it a kick.'

I was more worried than ever, even frightened at the news I had just got; the sooner I got Ewan away the better. I hoped Father Joseph could help me on Sunday. I would have Vera and Billy for the following weekend but for me the state I was in it was a long way away.

Our plans to have tea in the hotel were dashed when Ewan saw Colin Campbell and his wife disappearing into the hotel. Instead, we went to the baker's and bought bread, Scotch pies and a nice cake. Then we went to see Mr Walsh and I bought some of the dog food he recommended. We hurried home scared stiff.

CHAPTER 6

On Sunday after Mass I waited behind to see Father Joseph. 'Mary, I have bad news for you. I spoke to Constable Campbell about the MacPhersons annoying you and he said when your father lay in bed ill that the house was to go to Nan.'

I didn't believe a word of what I had just heard. 'You can tell Constable Campbell that I have the deeds to the house and they are in my name.' God forgive me for telling a bare faced lie in his sacred house but I had to give them something to think about.

'Oh I never knew that, Mary.'

'There's quite a lot you don't know, Father, if you did your hair would turn white with shock.' I was thinking of the little dead baby buried in our garden.

The first thing Ewan and I did when we got home was to take Rusty out to the garden to let him play about the place while we were having our lunch. While I was drinking my tea I thought I'd better write to Auntie Kate telling her about the MacPhersons saying the house was theirs and could she advise me what would be the best course of action to take. While I was at it I'd write to John Lewis, maybe he, also, had got another girl.

I was excited the following weekend when Vera and Billy came home; Vera ordered a taxi to bring them from the station. After hugs and kisses I had a good look at Billy; he seemed to have grown a few inches taller and his shoulders to have broadened out. My, I thought to myself, mum and dad would have been proud of him. He looked so healthy and had a lovely tan or was it just weather beaten. Vera cut in on my thoughts; 'well, has he passed your inspection?'

I just laughed, 'I knew, Vera, you would look after your little brother.'

'That's enough of the little, Mary.'

'Go on, the two of you, up to your rooms with your cases.'

After we had our meal the boys went into the garden and by the sound of their laughter, they and Rusty were having the time of their lives. I was glad

Vera and I had the kitchen to ourselves. While I sat in the rocking chair I told Vera the whole story about the MacPhersons; also Constable Campbell saying that our house was Donald's. I told her, also, how the MacPhersons had a key to our house; 'that's why, Vera, I had to get all the locks changed.'

'Why, Mary, didn't you write to me and let me know all this earlier?'

'There was nothing you could do, Vera; you have your work which comes first. I am glad Ewan will be going back with you and Billy. I'll feel a lot happier when he is out of reach of the MacPhersons. Did you know that Colin got married?' I told Vera about Colin's wife working in the hotel and we decided we would all go there for a meal and get some more information from the waitress.

Vera was missing her boyfriend, Andy Carter, who made her feel somebody special. Tom was all right for dancing with.

The boys came in with a very tired puppy. They gave Rusty some milk and put him in his basket to rest. The two of them then disappeared to their bedroom and in a few minutes were ready to walk to the hotel.

It was warm when the four of us set out down the road to the hotel. It was just like old times laughing and chatting; the boys throwing stones in the loch as they ran ahead of us. 'By the way, Mary, did Constable Campbell ever investigate the broken branches on that tree?'

'No, Vera, I have come to the conclusion that he knows a lot more about father's death than he lets on. I think the best thing for us to do is to try and make friends with his wife; if we see her today we will invite her up for tea.'

'Leave that to me, Mary, if you start asking questions they might be suspicious.'

The four of us made our way to the dining room; it was spotlessly clean and everything in its place. 'You know, Mary, this is the first time I have set foot in this place. My, the furniture is lovely.'

I thought to myself I wonder where Mr Bell the owner got the money to buy it. I remembered as a child when his daughter Mary Kate was in the same class as me, she always seemed to look as if her parents had no money. It's funny really, within a few years there she was lording it over me the last time she visited me. That's another thing I needed to look into.

The four of us found that we were the only guests in the place; the same girl came to take our order. 'What would you like, boys?' Vera asked. Vera ordered salmon, trifle and tea for all of us. I protested about the expense but Vera said if she got the information she wanted it would be worth it. While we were waiting Mr Bell looked into the room; he was quite surprised to see the four of us sitting at the table. He came over to me and said, 'hello, Mary, got company today.'

'Yes,' I said, 'my sister Vera and my brother Billy.'

He looked at Billy as if he was seeing a ghost. 'Quite the grown up young man you have turned out to be. You put me in mind of your father sitting there.'

So that was why he had turned slightly pale. I thought it was a pity the sight of Billy didn't give him a heart attack. The girl came with our order and Mr Bell slipped through the swing doors.

After we were all finished Vera said, 'you lot wait for me down at the loch.'

I was glad to get out into the fresh air again. Billy and Ewan disappeared into Mr Walsh's shop; I just made my way down to the loch. It was the only place except the church that gave me a sense of peace. It was so peaceful just sitting watching all the different shapes and sizes of the boats that sailed up and down the loch. My mind was miles away when I was joined by the boys; 'look, Mary, see what Billy has bought for Rusty.' It was a lovely dog's collar with a lead, a dog's food dish, a big ball and a rubber bone. Now why did I not think of those things before.

'Oh Billy, Rusty will be thinking it's his birthday; he is only a puppy yet and he will enjoy himself with these. He sure will go daft when he gets playing with them.' Vera came running towards us. 'Mary I think we better make our way home, right boys home.' The pair of them ran on in front of us.

When they were a distance away Vera told me all the news she was able to get.

'You would not believe this, Mary, but Alice, Constable Campbell's wife, and Donald are first cousins. MacPherson is her maiden name. Donald's father and Alice's father are brothers. What do you think of that now?'

'Well, I'll be blowed, so that's why Campbell is always with them. One thing for sure from now on, no way will I be confiding in that policeman again. To think that I was silly enough to imagine that he loved me when all he was doing was spying in my house when I was ill. Thank God Billy and Ewan are going away again.'

By the time Donald gets out of jail my brothers would be four and a half years older and able to take care of themselves. I supposed they would always remember the ill treatment that they endured while they worked on the MacPherson's farm. I wondered if I would ever get the real story of how they were forced to go over to the MacPherson's farm while mum and dad were alive. As soon as we went in the door Billy and Ewan made a beeline for the kitchen to give Rusty his toys. The puppy went barking and running around the kitchen. The boys were told to take Rusty into the garden. When peace was restored Vera and I had a cup of tea and one of Hector's special biscuits which I had to hide from Ewan, otherwise he would have made himself sick gorging them. 'Vera, when the boys come back in I am going to ask them straight how it was that mum and dad allowed them to be taken to work on the MacPherson's farm.' I was beginning to doze off when the boys and Rusty came into the kitchen; the two boys looked so happy and healthy, the little pup barking away full of life also. 'Vera and I want to talk to you both,' I said.

Both of them sat at the table then we asked all the questions concerning how both of them were kept on MacPherson's farm.

'I don't like talking about it, Mary, it involves mum and dad.'

'Never mind, Billy, who it involves, Vera and I have got to know.'

'It starts with dad bringing home this fair haired girl from the pub; he was the worse for drink, in fact he could hardly stand. The girl was very stout as if she was pregnant. They were no sooner in the house when in walked Donald, his father and two of Donald's brothers. They accused dad of getting the barmaid pregnant and they pulled him to his feet and dragged him outside. They told the girl to follow them.'

'What was mum doing all this time?'

'Donald's father had threatened her if she moved to help him, then he shouted to Ewan and me, "you two will get attended to next. I warn you if any of you move before we get back I'll see that you pay for it" so, Mary, there was nothing mum and Ewan and I could do but sit still. To me it seemed a long time before they came back carrying dad. The four of them told mum to get a bed made up for him in the parlour and just flung him on it. Donald's father shouted, "see that you attend to him old woman and I warn you don't let anybody know what happened here tonight. As for you two, you are coming with us in the boat to our house, that way our secret will be safe. I will be able to keep an eye on you and don't go carrying lies about us to your big sister Nan." Ewan and I never seen mum and dad alive again.'

Both of the boys started to cry. Vera and I also cried at the thought of what mum and dad, Nan and the boys must have suffered at the hands of that murderous family. After we all settled down I asked Billy, did the fair haired girl come back with them.

'I don't know, Mary, we never seen her again.' So the MacPherson family were the cause indirectly of my parents' death. We all had tea and biscuits, then the boys went up to their room to read comics. When we had the kitchen to ourselves I asked Vera what she thought of Billy's story and come to think of it, if they must have beaten dad at that big tree with all the broken branches where Ewan found dad's wheelbarrow. They must have wheeled dad in it before they beat him to a pulp then carried him home. My, I thought to myself, that was why Constable Campbell was such a regular visitor when I was ill. It was a good thing Nurse Duncan was staying with me; dear knows what would have happened.

'What will you do, Mary, when I and the boys leave tomorrow; you know according to what I have just heard and Donald beating Nan to death I am afraid your life is in danger also.'

'I have been thinking about that for a while; when I was in Mull I bought a small ladies' gun and a box of cartridges. The gun fits in my handbag; I carry it about with me, at night I put it under my pillow. I do wish Rusty was a bit older but that will come in time.'

A taxi took Vera, Billy, Ewan and me to the railway station. The train was on time and as usual packed. My arms were sore waving to them till the train turned the corner. The day was cloudy, misty rain falling but I decided to walk the two miles home; the fresh air itself would do me the world of good. I wished I had one real friend in the village who would help me but the MacPherson clan seemed to be a law unto themselves and now the local policeman Constable Colin Campbell had joined forces with them. What chance did a slip of a girl like me have against them, then something within me said fight them with their own methods. Yes I said to myself, that's just what I'll do. Before I went home I went down to the loch to sit awhile and try to find a way to outwit the MacPherson clan. The loch was covered in mist, I could hear the hoots of the ships sending messages to one another in the fog. The rain was getting heavy and I went home.

After taking off my wet outdoor clothes I made my way to the kitchen; the house felt so eerie and a chill went down my spine. I went back to the front door to make sure it was properly locked and bolted. The back door was all right; this will never do, Mary, give yourself a shake. The little pup woke up, and started running round the table; he was going to miss Billy and Ewan. I supposed I would have to take their place and be a little girl again, running around with the ball to keep Rusty happy. I was like the little pup, missing all my family. First of all I'd better feed him then make myself a cup of tea then both of us could play in the garden. Playing with Rusty would take my mind off other things.

I was exhausted when Rusty and I got back into the kitchen. I locked and bolted the door then lifted the little bundle of fur, sat on the rocking chair and laid it on my lap. The kitchen was quiet, the only sound was the creaking of the chair as I rocked back and forth. Sleep must have overcome both of us. When I woke up it was quite dark. I drew the blackout curtains before switching on the lights. I put Rusty in his basket then made my way up to bed. While I lay in bed I thought, since I am on my own I will clean out the attic; that will keep me busy for a few days as the place had years of dust lying on it. I'd have a good rake in all of mum and dad's belongings then I drifted off to sleep again.

The next morning the sun was shining brightly, not a cloud in the sky. I gazed out over the loch, it was in one of its good moods, so was I. Rusty was already standing at the door waiting for me to let him out. The boys had made a good job of training him. I heard the rattle of the letter box; there on the mat lay two letters. Glancing at them I noticed one from Auntie Kate, the other from John Lewis. Rusty would be starving so I fed him first; he was already in the kitchen when I got back. The little thing with his big unusual coloured eyes looked up at me, tail wagging and barking loudly. The fire in the range was very low so I put on paper, a few sticks then the logs, struck a match to it, filled up the kettle and set it on the hob to boil. I read Auntie Kate's letter first; she said that she was very worried about all the trouble the MacPhersons were causing. 'I have arranged for my solicitor in Oban, to visit you. Enclosed is his card and phone number.' I glanced at the card, his name was Norman Hendry. 'Expect him on Thursday around 2 p.m. The house, Mary, is yours, you have nothing to fear. Mr Hendry will explain everything when he calls to see you. Enclosing ten pounds, look after yourself, love Auntie Kate. P.S. how is the little puppy, has he settled in all right.'

The little thing was sitting looking up at me as much to say, 'yes I am fine.' The kettle was singing away. I made my breakfast then opened John my boyfriend's letter. He was busy sailing back and forth from Oban to Mull; he missed me terribly asking me when I was paying another visit to Mull. He sometimes saw Auntie Kate in the shops but didn't like going up to speak to her. 'I wish you were here beside me, Mary, and I would give you a big hug and kiss. I do miss you so, love John, write soon.'

I missed John also; I was so busy looking after my house and family, I was putting myself last. Once I got the problem of the house settled I'd visit Auntie Kate again. I wouldn't have Ewan tagging along with me. John and I would be free and happy. Now that Mr Hendry was visiting me on Thursday I had to get the whole house cleaned. I took Rusty out for a walk. He had never been out on the road since we brought him home and I put him on the lead. Rusty was not at all pleased at the way he was being pulled along but he had to get used to it. He just sat down at the door step and refused to move. 'All right, Rusty, if that's what you want you can sit there all day.' I moved to walk away and slowly he followed me. I suddenly realised that everything must be strange to him so after a short walk I lifted him up in my arms and carried him to the back garden. There he was in his glory, jumping and running about happy again.

Mr Hendry my solicitor arrived on time in a black Ford car. He was a powerfully built man, beautifully dressed with his bowler hat and walking cane. He introduced himself and said he had come to help me. I took his hat and coat, showed him into the parlour and then we both settled down to discuss the problem of the house. 'Really,' he said, 'there is no problem, the house belongs to you. Mr MacPherson, your sister's husband has no claim whatsoever on your house. I made a cup of tea and while we were drinking it, I told him all the news that Billy and Ewan had told Vera and I about the treatment dad and mum had suffered at the hands of the MacPhersons; also, how they had ill treated the boys and forced them to go with them over to the other side of the loch to their farm. As I was speaking Mr Hendry wrote everything down.

'First of all, Miss Scott, we will pay a visit to the local police station; after they have heard my story and if Constable Campbell is not prepared to do anything about it I will apply for a court order for the MacPhersons never to go near your property again. We will go right away.'

I ran into the kitchen and put some food out for Rusty. Dear knows how long it would be before I got back, washed and put my coat and hat on, grabbed my handbag, locked the door then got into the back seat of the lovely car. It took just ten minutes to drive from my house to the police station. Mr Hendry opened the door for me. Constable Campbell turned pale when he saw the two of us walking in.

'Who is in charge here, Constable?' Mr Hendry asked.

'I am sir,' he said, 'there is no one in charge except me, sir.'

'Very well, I hear that you are related by marriage to Miss Scott's sister Nan's father-in-law. Your police headquarters, I think, are in Oban and I'll call there and make my complaint. In the meantime, Constable Campbell, I want you to tell Mr and Mrs MacPherson and all their family to stay clear of Miss Scott's property. Also stop threatening her and her family.' With that he lifted his hat and stick then guided me out of the door to his waiting car. 'I'll run you home and after I have discussed everything at police headquarters in Oban I'll write you and your Auntie Kate giving you both all the details. Don't worry, I'll put the fear of death into them.'

I felt a lot better, at last something was being done to curb the selfishness of the MacPherson clan. I went straight into the kitchen and let Rusty out into the back garden. I sat on the garden seat and remembered to say a little prayer for the infant who was lying in the cold earth underneath the seat. Rusty was enjoying himself running around in circles trying to catch his ball. I was beginning to wonder why was it that the house was mine and not Sarah's or Vera's. After all both of them were older than me. Sarah was four years older while Vera was one year. No mention of the boys either. I heard knocking on the front door and found Dr McKinnon standing there.

'I really came, Mary, to see if you would like to fill Peggy's place; she is leaving in a fortnight to get married. Do you feel well enough to take the work on? Peggy will show you the ropes for a few days before she leaves.'

'Oh I would love that, Doctor; I would have to get home at lunch time to let Rusty out.'

'Of course, Mary, you get one hour off for lunch; will that suit you?'

'Oh yes that will be fine.'

'Then that's settled, see you a week come Thursday.' I showed doctor to the door; as he was leaving he said he was glad to see me looking a lot better. I let Rusty in before he got up to more mischief. He seemed slightly bigger, his lovely fur coat gleaming with health. He was supposed to be a collie, but he was just a ball of lovable fur. I thought of writing to John Lewis and inviting him to stay, but that would start all the tongues in the village wagging.

The days now were beginning to shorten, autumn was slowly creeping in. I wasn't looking forward to the long dark winter nights again with the black-out all the time and the miserable rations. Before I started cleaning out the attic I checked both doors to make sure they were locked then I went into the big cupboard, slid back the secret panel, put on the light and went into the attic. The skylight windows had blackout cloth tacked on them. I suppose it would stay on till the war was finished. I had carried a pale of warm soapy water, a scrubbing brush, a big sweeping brush; also a feather duster. I noticed standing in the corner a large trunk; I felt quite excited at the thought of all the treasures stored in it. I tried to open the lid but both locks were locked. Just my luck. I fled down the stairs for Dad's keys and just in case none of them opened the trunk I took a hammer and chisel with me in case I had to break it open. I raced upstairs again to the attic, tried all the keys. The very last one which was smaller fitted. I opened the trunk after a hard struggle as the locks were rusty. On the top of the clothes was a beautiful satin wedding dress wrapped in tissue paper. I lifted it gently out of the trunk and held it against me. Holding it in front of me I danced round the room then out loud I said, 'Mary Scott, this will never get the work done,' so I laid the dress on the lid and started eagerly pulling the rest of the other clothes out. My hand touched something cold; a shiver went through my spine. Slowly I pulled the remaining piece of material off. There before my eyes lay the remains of what once had been a beautiful fair haired girl. The next minute I fainted.

I don't know how long I lay there but when I went to get up I was violently sick. I had to get out in the fresh air as quickly as possible. I slid the panel back, pulled all the coats back in place then made my way out to the garden and sat on the garden seat. Dear God, now I have two lost souls to pray for. The young woman dead in the trunk must be the little infant's mother. 'Oh dear God what am I going to do; this house is evil yet Father Joseph blessed it for me.' I felt so ill I thought I was going to faint again; must get to bed. 'Oh dear, the little puppy, I'll leave water and food for him when he wakes up.' Wearily, I made my way upstairs to bed, took two of the sleeping pills Dr McKinnon gave me the last time I was in shock then just slipped off my dress and fell on the bed. The blankets seemed a ton weight as I tried to pull them over my shoulders.

When I awoke I remembered it was Sunday but felt too ill to go out to church. I had to let Rusty out in the garden. The little thing was waiting patiently at the door; I let it out then went and sat on the rocking chair. Tears started rolling down my cheeks; I needed help right away; how to get it was a different matter. My legs felt like lumps of lead and my head felt as if it did not belong to me. I had to push myself to light the fire, fill the kettle and made myself some tea. I drank a cup of tea then fell asleep again. Rusty must have jumped up on my knee while I was sleeping because when I woke up he was sound asleep on my lap. I lifted him gently and laid him in his basket. I tried to get up but my legs would not move. There I was sitting in the rocking chair, the front door locked and bolted; if anything was happening to me nobody would get into the house. The garden gate was also locked; I suddenly realised the danger I was in. No one had a spare key to my house. I would have to give Father Joseph a spare key to keep for me. I should have thought of that long ago. I fell asleep again.

It was dark when I woke up. I let Rusty out again, left food and water for him then I crawled to the front door, pulled the bolt back and unlocked the door, crawled to the parlour, pulled myself on the settee then fell asleep again. It must have been the sounds of the wind and rain lashing against the window pane that woke me up. Rusty was beside the settee whining. 'Oh you poor thing, I am coming.' I put my legs on the floor and stood up. They were still weak but I could walk. Rusty ran ahead of me to the kitchen barking with joy, glad to see me on my feet again. I had to get word to Sarah right away but there was no need to involve Vera or the boys. Whoever murdered that lovely girl and her baby I might never find out. According to Billy and Ewan's story she was alive when the MacPhersons took her and Dad out of the house that night. They brought back Dad nearly dead with the beating they gave him. He was so badly injured that he never moved from his bed again and come to think of it the MacPhersons had a spare key to my house. It must have been them who planted the dead bodies in my attic. How to prove it was a different matter. I wished Nurse Duncan was with me. I would have to bear this heavy burden alone. I was sure Sarah would come as soon as she received the telegram.

I was lucky I didn't need to go to the village; the postman came with a letter for me from Ewan. He said he would send the telegram for me and when he read the message, 'the sun was shining brightly this morning', he looked at me as though I had horns. I paid him the money, he jumped on his bike and was off in the pouring rain. While I was at the front door Rusty ran out; the noise of the waves lashing against the rocks frightened him and he ran back into the house again. I would have to take time and train him for taking him walks out on the main road. I hoped I would be better before starting work on Thursday. It was something to look forward to as the work would help me to take my mind off the last few days of agony I had been through. The day was terrible, heavy rain lashing at the windows all day. It sure gave me an excuse to rest; I opened the kitchen door then sat in the rocking chair wondering if mum knew about the secret in the attic. The MacPhersons were cunning; I am sure they planted the bodies in the trunk. Maybe my sister Nan knew, that's why she was killed. I watched Rusty running out and in at the door, he sure did not like the rain.

Sarah's telegram arrived the next day, 'coming right away, Sarah'. I felt a lot better, two heads are better than one for solving a problem especially one like ours. Late afternoon a taxi drew up at our front door, it was Sarah. After a hug and kiss I asked how on earth she got here so quick.

'Never mind that, Mary, tell me what the trouble is.'

'I think, Sarah, before I give you the news both of us better get a cup of tea. I am sorry I really have not much in the way of eats.' Sarah said that Hector was back in this country and brought a hamper of food, some for his parents and some for us. We had our tea and I told Sarah what had happened. Her first words were, 'oh my God what are we going to do? We will have to get rid of the body somehow.'

'What about letting Hector into our confidence? Maybe he can plant the body miles away from here; he's got his car hasn't he?'

'I don't know, Mary, I'll need time to think, in the meantime do you think you could come with me to the attic so as I can have a look myself.'

The pair of us made our way to the attic, I stood just inside the door while Sarah had a peek; she stood back in horror. I thought she was going to faint but she straightened up to her full height and said 'I'll see what we can do.' As we left the attic Sarah said 'better take that pail of water and brushes with you, Mary,' then the panel was secure and the coats back in place. We were back in the kitchen when there was a loud knock on the front door. It was Hector with a big box of food. He gave me a hug and kiss then he said, 'don't say you have been ill again. The rations people are allowed would not keep a bird alive. Never mind, tuck in to this lot.'

'It's not the rations, Hector, that's made Mary ill, it is something more serious. Oh, Hector, we did not want to involve you.'

'Come on, Sarah, you better tell me, I will be more capable of attending to things.' So Sarah went ahead and told Hector the full story. He was silent for a long while then announced he had a plan.

First, he gave us each of cup of tea, two aspirins and a slice of Dundee cake. Then he wanted me to open the panel into the attic. After that he told us to find three old pairs of dad's socks. It became even more puzzling. 'Find some old dresses and coats to fit you,' Hector said. 'On second thoughts it doesn't matter whether they fit or not for we'll be burning them later.'

Hector broke off to run home and tell his parents he would be late.

When he returned he put the remains of the young woman into a sack and stowed the sack and a spade in the boot of his car.

Sarah and I dressed in the old clothes and pulled the old socks over the soles of our wellingtons so that we would not leave identifiable footprints. We drove off into the stormy night. The three of us sat in the front. Hector had laid newspapers on the floor and he saw me looking at them. 'That's to keep my car clean when we all return with our muddy boots.'

'We are mad, Hector, coming out on a night like this.'

'The blacker the night the better the deed. This is the kind of weather we choose to go out on our raids over Germany. The Jerrys think we British will wait till the storm is over. That's how we catch them out.' The rain was simply pouring down, a gale force wind raging. As we passed through the village not a soul was in sight.

We seemed to have motored for about one hour and a half when Hector stopped. 'This is the spot,' he said, 'come on out. You take the spade, Mary, and I'll carry the bag. Sarah can just follow us.' I followed Hector into the forest where we were a bit sheltered from the heavy rain and wind. We seemed to be climbing uphill all the time. Sarah and I were out of breath. At last we reached the spot where Hector wanted to dig; the ground was quite soft so he wasn't long before he had the grave ready. He laid the bundle gently in the ground and was about to shovel the earth back when I spoke lowly to Hector. 'Wait a minute.' Sarah and I knelt down on the ground and both of us said a prayer for the unknown soul in the ground then I took a small bottle of holy water and sprinkled it on the remains. 'Now, Hector, you can fill it in.'

'While I am doing that you girls gather branches and leaves to camouflage the grave. Now when you have done that take a branch off one of the trees, walk backwards and pull the branch after you. I'll tell you when to stop.'

By the time Sarah and I reached the car we were both exhausted. Hector wasn't in the least bit put about. I supposed he was used to facing death being in the RAF. On the way home the wind and rain never let up. It was just as well as we seemed to be the only ones out. As soon as we got into the house Hector got the fire going. 'I think, girls, when you have changed into proper clothes I'll attend to burning those rags; maybe the two of you could sit in the parlour for a while.' Rusty waggled his way in after us.

'Thank goodness, Sarah, that's off our hands, it was a blessing Hector came home with you. We could never have managed without him. I wonder who planted the bodies there in the first place. The only people who had a spare key to the house were the MacPhersons; they meant the blame to fall on dad. I think, Sarah, that hotel owner Mr Bell was involved in it as well. Dad was always drunk so it was easy enough to plant the blame on him.'

'Well, from now on,' Sarah said, 'we better forget what has happened here tonight. We had nothing to do with the deaths; whoever planted them has been outwitted by two young girls and Hector. Come to think of it, Mary, I am just 23 years although what the pair of us have been through these last four months we should feel like 90. From now on, Mary, think of yourself. Tomorrow you start work at the surgery. On Saturday both of us will clean out the attic. That will give you peace of mind when that is finished then we'll see if Hector will run us somewhere for lunch after Mass. Would you like that, Mary?

Monday, both of us will have to return to base.'

I was thankful for Sarah being home, I could rely on her, Vera on the other hand, you just did not know how to take. Through all the excitement of the past few days I had forgotten Ewan's letter, I had left it in the kitchen drawer. While we were sitting on the settee we got a whiff of a delicious smell coming from the kitchen, the next minute Hector came in with a big apron on, a napkin flung over his arm; 'dinner is served ladies.'

Sarah let out a loud laugh, 'Oh, Hector,' she said, 'I do love you.'

We all trooped into the kitchen followed by Rusty. The table was set for three, a large plate of stew was dished up for us, tinned potatoes, bread and butter and tea. I didn't realise I was so hungry till I sat down and started eating the delicious stew. Rusty was running about daft wondering when he was going to get his share. At last we managed to leave some for him. Shortly after Sarah and Hector left for Hector's parents house. I waved them goodbye, locked and bolted the door and went back to the kitchen to read Ewan's letter in peace. He was happy working on the large farm with Billy and Vera. He thought Billy had a girl; she worked in the house. Vera was still going with Tom Wilson. Mr Smith the owner was very good to him, he always laid out the light work for him. I was glad that at last he was getting shown a little understanding. I put the letter away, got ready for bed; I wondered how I would get on in my new job.

CHAPTER 7

I need not have worried, Peggy wrote down everything I had to do. Always be polite and kind to the patients even though at times they will be cross with you. When they come to the surgery most of them are ill and need to see the doctor. A few, of course, just come for a chat.

Thursday and Friday passed at the surgery without any real mishaps. Peggy was getting married the following week. I gave her a tablecloth as a present and wished her all the happiness with her new husband. I arrived home at 5.30 p.m., let Rusty out in the garden then made myself a meal. I was taken aback at the amount of food Hector had bought me. He certainly wasn't meaning me to starve. I thought Sarah was lucky being married to such a nice gentleman. I wondered if I would ever find one like him. John Lewis was young but he was a bit on the rough side; it takes all sorts to make the world.

Sarah and Hector came to help me clean out the attic; I laughed at the sight of the pair of them with their old togs on and hair covered with dust caps and old shoes. It was a good job they were dressed the way they were, the room was filthy. Sarah and I each had a pail of hot soapy water and scrubbing brush. Hector had the sweeping brush covered with a duster. First of all I said I'd feel happier if the wardrobes and chest of drawers were empty; that way we would be sure there were no more bodies hidden there. Soon the whole attic was thoroughly cleaned out. Sarah and I had just bundled the contents on to the floor in my bedroom. Hector said he would have to attend to a few things for his parents so we were left alone. I noticed Hector had laid three boxes on the floor; one was a large metal one.

'What do you think, Sarah, we should do with all these clothes?'

'I don't know, I think we better just keep them till Vera is home then we can decide what to do with them.'

'We better rake in all the pockets in case something important has been left in them.' I came across some folded papers in Dad's trouser pockets. I was horrified when I read the contents, 'I love you darling, meet me at the usual place. We will wait till the children and your wife are in bed.' I handed them to Sarah, 'I'll throw these in the fire right away. I wonder who the girl was Dad was meeting.'

The front door knocker went. When I opened the door Mary Kate Bell was standing there. 'Hello, Mary,' she said. 'I am home for a few days; thought I would pop in to see you. I tried the garden gate but it was locked.'

We went through to the kitchen. Sarah was busy putting logs on the fire. 'You remember my sister Sarah, Mary Kate.'

'Oh I am sorry I did not know she was home. Dad thought you were just yourself.'

Rusty jumped up from his basket and started growling and barking at Mary Kate. It was the first time I had seen him in that type of mood. I became a bit worried; I wondered what her real purpose for calling was.

'Would you like some tea, Mary Kate? Sarah and I were just going to have some.' Rusty all this time was still barking at her.

'I didn't know you had a dog, Mary.'

'A present from Auntie Kate; he really is lovable once you get to know him,' but inwardly I thought I'll make sure you never will.

Sarah asked her what she worked at and if she had a boyfriend.

'Oh yes I work in my boyfriend's hairdresser shop. I am also a hairdresser.'

'It's a wonder you were never called up, Mary Kate.'

Her face turned slightly red then she said, 'I have bad feet.'

Sarah and I exchanged glances, I think the two of us thought the same 'bad feet my foot'. Both of us glanced down at her expensive high-heeled black shoes.

Mary Kate said she had managed to walk up but her feet were now killing her. She finished her tea. Thanking us, she left and added she would see us at Mass.

'What do *you* think of that, Sarah? I think she came up to see what was going on; maybe her dad sent her to find out the lie of the land. After all, Donald's cousin, Colin's wife works there. I wonder if the MacPhersons have received the threatening letter from Mr Hendry our solicitor banning them from coming near our house again.'

'I never knew about that, Mary.'

'I was going to tell you in my next letter but I was ill. It was Auntie Kate who arranged everything; Constable Campbell I think is involved also. It's just one big hornets' nest.' A loud knock heralded the arrival of Hector with the car.

106

I locked and bolted the door when Hector and Sarah had gone. The fire in the kitchen range was crackling away merrily; I sat in the rocking chair and went through the day's events. I didn't know how I could have managed without Hector and Sarah's help. I must put those three boxes back in a safe place till I have time to look through them. 'Please God don't let me get any more shocks when I open them.' Might as well put them back in the attic; it's as safe a place as any. I just sat relaxing in the rocking chair beside the fire. Rusty had settled down and was fast asleep. I was looking forward to work on Monday; it would take my mind off the terrible recent events.

Hector called for me to run me down to church. When we reached his house he hooted his horn and Sarah came running out to join us. The church was quite packed by the time we arrived. The three of us made our way to our pew; it was already filled with MacPherson children. Father Joseph was coming down the aisle and he noticed the children occupying our seats. He went over to Donald's father and said a few words then Father Joseph showed the children over beside their grandfather then the three of us made our way to our seats. During all the commotion you could have heard a pin drop.

After Mass Hector ran me home so that I could let Rusty out and feed him.

When Rusty was settled down and the doors locked the three of us set off for our lunch. I was looking forward to the drive; I glanced out of the car window and noticed the loch was in a better mood. It was covered with boats, all painted grey. Of course they had to paint them that colour during the war. The leaves on the trees were beginning to turn a golden brown, autumn was slowly creeping up on us. I loved watching the scenery as the car ate up the miles; at last we reached the Black Swan.

Outside it looked like an ordinary pub but inside it was beautiful. The owner knew Hector who had his RAF uniform on. I don't know much about stars or stripes but as we were shown to our table the young RAF men rose from their table and saluted him. Hector raised his hand back then they all sat down again. We were given a private table in a small room, just ourselves there. Hector ordered the food, I could see Sarah was used to lunching out. I thought to myself I could so easily get used to it myself. We had soup, roast beef, Yorkshire pudding, brussel sprouts then ice cream and fruit followed by coffee. Hector had some kind of spirit. I could hardly move when I was finished.

'Feeling better, Mary?'

'Oh, yes, Hector, I have never enjoyed a meal so much.'

'Forbidden fruit always tastes better,' he said. 'I'll leave you two to have a chat together as Sarah and I will be leaving early tomorrow morning and you,

Mary, will be starting work also.'

So Sarah and I had the room to ourselves. 'I have put Dad's boxes back in the attic; I could leave them, Sarah, till the next time you come home. To tell you the truth I am frightened to open them when I am just myself.'

Sarah and Hector left the next morning early. I was sorry to see them go. I was on my own in my new job. I didn't realise there were so many sick women and children. Nurse Duncan was helping Doctor for a while then she had to leave to go to a confinement. Mrs so-and-so was having her sixth baby; the young children were running wild in the surgery. The morning soon flew and I was able to get home for lunch. Rusty met me at the door as soon as he heard the key in the lock and rushed out. While he was running mad about the garden I built the fire up and got my lunch ready. I had beans on toast, something easy, filled Rusty's dishes with water and food then sat in the rocking chair. I always felt relaxed sitting in it, rocking back and forth. Rusty came rushing in full of life, he was lovely to look at; as each week passed he grew slightly bigger and fluffier. He had such an unusual coat.

I got ready to walk back to my work. There was a large queue waiting for the surgery doors to be opened. I didn't realise Dr McKinnon was so busy. I thought to myself, he must be sick himself by the end of the week when all he listened to was other people's aches and pains. I was nearly finished taking all the patients names down when my light was practically blocked by the next patient. 'Name please,' I said, without looking up.

'MacPherson,' he said, 'and you don't need to write it down as I'll not be waiting to see the doctor. Read that,' he said, and he flung a letter across the counter at me. I looked up to see the back of Donald's father going out of the door.

I still wrote his name on Doctor's list. When he asked about him I would tell Dr McKinnon what happened. I glanced over to the other patients but thank goodness they all seemed too busy chatting to one another to notice anything unusual. I thought to myself, dear God don't say I am going to be pestered by that clan even at my work. I put MacPherson's letter in my handbag.

The surgery was busy up to the last minute. I locked the door and gave the key to Dr McKinnon who wanted to know what had happened to Mr MacPherson. I told the doctor about the letter and he asked to see it.

Doctor read the letter then he handed it to me to read. 'Sit down, Mary, after you have read it I think you should take it down to the police station for Constable Campbell to deal with it.'

'Oh no,' I said, 'there is no sense in me going there. Campbell is in with the MacPhersons, related to them by marriage. His wife Alice is Donald's cousin. To tell you the truth, Doctor, I was going to write to Mr Hendry my solicitor when I got home.'

'I think that would be a good idea. Put your coat on and I'll run you home. Don't worry, Mary, I'll see to things at my end.'

I was glad to be home. I took the letter out of my pocket and laid it on the table. All of a sudden I felt dead tired. I lay down on the top of the bed. I thought of the day's events, working at the surgery was interesting. I must have dozed off. It was Rusty barking that woke me up then I heard the loud knock on the front door.

When I opened it Constable Campbell was standing there. 'Can I come in, Mary?' he said. I kept him standing in the hall. He seemed embarrassed then he said was there anywhere we can sit down. We went into the parlour. When we were both seated he asked me if he could see the letter that John MacPherson handed in to me at the surgery. Doctor McKinnon had called in making a complaint about MacPherson harassing me at work.

'There is nothing you can do about it, Campbell, I am going to write to my solicitor tonight.'

'Oh Mary, if you don't make a complaint to me it could cost me my post.'

'You are too related to the MacPhersons for you to judge fairly, or are you frightened of them.'

He just looked down at his shoes then he said, 'please, Mary, can I just see the letter then I will decide what to do.'

'I don't care what you do, I will be writing to Mr Hendry anyway.' I handed him the letter to read.

His face turned white; 'do you think I can keep this, Mary?'

'No, Constable, I haven't read it properly myself.' When he left I read the letter properly and was blazing; how dare he threaten me. He must have got a letter from Mr Hendry when in the note he wrote, 'tell that hound to stay clear of our house, otherwise I'll give some juicy news to the local paper about your dad.' I wrote down a copy of it and enclosed it along with my letter to Mr Hendry. The MacPhersons must have been mad when they received my solicitor's letter barring them from coming near my door. Now Dr McKinnon was telling them to stop troubling me at my work. I just hoped he wouldn't waylay me in the street on my way to or from work.

My first week at my new job passed without any hitches. I was gradually getting to know all their names off by heart. Sometimes I would just have to give some of the noisy children a certain look and they would run to their mum and be quiet for a little while.

I was glad when Saturday came, with it a long lie; not too long because I had Rusty to attend to. I heard the letter box rattle. It was a letter from Vera; I opened it straight away. Tom Wilson was home again on leave; he had asked Vera to marry him straight away. 'I really could not, Mary, I like going out dancing with him and he is such charming company but that's about all. He said he would wait so we still go dancing together. Billy and Ewan are the picture of health; both of them have grown taller and broader. Billy is beginning to look more like his dad every day. How are you liking your new job. We will all be home for a weekend at the end of the month, love Vera, Billy and Ewan.' Well that was something for me to look forward to.

The knocker on the door went again; heavens I thought I was going to get a quiet day today. When I opened it, it was Constable Campbell. I asked him in. He said he needed a copy of John MacPherson's letter to send to Oban. Headquarters had asked for it. He noticed Vera's letter on the table. I just folded it and put it in the drawer then I wrote a copy of MacPherson's letter and handed it to him. He thanked me, bade me good morning and left. I let Rusty back in from the garden, poured myself out a cup of tea and sat in the rocking chair. I thought to myself, any juicy bit of news that went in any paper would be about the MacPhersons by the time I was finished with them. I quite believed whoever planted those poor souls in our attic was bound to be wondering what on earth was happening as no news had leaked out about them. As long as I was alive I would protect my mother and father's good name. I supposed Sarah, Vera and the boys would do likewise.

While I walked briskly down to the shop I thought of Nan's children; I had never seen any of them at the surgery. I often thought of little Helen. I would have so liked to bring her up as my own but under the circumstances it just could not be allowed. It was sad I wasn't even allowed to visit my nieces and nephews; all eight of them. I went to Mr Walsh's first for dog food then posted my letter then to the baker and treated myself to a nice Scotch pie, cream cakes and bread. My coupons had collected with all the food Hector had given me. After I had everything I made my way home. I sat at the lochside for a while; the water was like a sheet of glass. There were only a few boats lying at anchor.

When I arrived home I was glad to get inside as it was becoming chilly outside. Rusty must have heard me come as he was barking and running around the table. I opened the door and he flew out, he was so full of life. As for me I felt half dead. I heated the pie and made myself a nice cup of tea then after Rusty had been fed I took him for a walk. I didn't feel like going out again. I fitted Rusty's collar and lead, wrapped myself up again and the pair of us went for a walk. I took the lead and had to pull Rusty across the road to the forest. Once we were amongst the trees he was in his glory running after the fallen leaves. I wondered who was the new forest keeper since Dad died.

I never seemed to have enough time to do all the things I wanted to do. It was time for us to make our way home; when we came to the main road Rusty followed me quite happily. I locked and bolted the door for the night and went up to the attic and brought dad's smallest box. That would keep me busy the rest of the evening. The locks on the box were easy to open. It contained lots of papers, one envelope was addressed to my dead sister Nan who was the oldest of the family. It also read, 'not to be opened till after my death'. The letter went as follows:

My Dearest Nan,

I do hope when we are both gone that you will forgive your Dad for treating you so cruelly. Many a night I have cried myself to sleep thinking of you my dear lovely girl, but before I say any more I am afraid I must warn you about Donald. Dad and I think your life is in danger; also I have got to tell you the truth about Dad's illness. Your father came home from the hotel a bit the worse of drink. When he came into the house your husband Donald, his two brothers and his father walked in behind him. Also with them was a lovely young girl with long fair curly hair and beautiful blue eyes. She was very stout with child. The next minute the MacPhersons pulled your dad outside; the young girl followed. They beat your dad in the forest across the road; after that they dragged him home dying and flung him on the single bed. He whispered it all to me before he lost consciousness. Also that girl from the bar in the hotel; Donald punched her till she fell to the ground. Her name was Marie Duffy. Dad heard her say Donald was the father of her child. After they flung your dad on the bed they ordered Billy and Ewan to go straight down to the boat and don't dare move from there then they turned to me and said, 'old woman, if you know what is good for you don't dare move from that bed,' then they all disappeared. There was a lot of noise going on upstairs in our bedroom then all of a sudden there was silence. I crept out of the parlour, the house was empty. My Dear Nan, your life is in danger; also I am sorry I can't help you, my hands are tied; your dear dad is dying. The

MacPhersons threatened me if I called Dr McKinnon,
Love Mum xxxx

So that's who the poor girl was we buried in an unmarked grave, God rest her soul and poor Nan never got the warning in time. After the funeral of my parents Nan and I were too busy going through Dad's papers in his desk; we never gave a thought to the attic, in fact I would not have known we had an attic if it had not been for Sarah showing me where it was. Oh my God I thought, my life will be in danger if the MacPhersons find out about this letter. I needed a safe place to hide the letter. In a tin box buried under the stone floor of the outside toilet seemed the best idea. Also, I would have to make a copy to send to Mr Hendry. One letter was quite enough to deal with. I went to bed early with the intention of going to first Mass in the morning. That way I wouldn't see any of the MacPherson clan. They always went to 10.00 a.m. Mass.

I met Flora, Hector's sister coming out of church. We walked together. It was a lovely morning, a bit cold with a nip in the air. When we reached Flora's house she asked me in for a cup of tea, but I had to go home to attend to Rusty and we arranged for afternoon tea instead. I thought to myself, what a nice family the MacLeans were; always willing to help. Rusty was barking at the door as soon as he heard my key in the lock. I set the kettle on the hob and waited for it to boil so I could have my breakfast, just a boiled egg.

When I had finished clearing everything away I went upstairs to the attic again and brought down the box. First of all I made a copy of that terrible letter to send to Mr Hendry. I put the original in the tin box to bury in the outside toilet. In my note to my solicitor I asked him if he would keep the enclosed letter my mother wrote before she died in a safe place and to advise me what was the best action to take to safeguard myself and the family. I sealed the envelope and addressed it, then I took the small tin box to the outside toilet. For the first time in all the 19 years I had been using it I never really looked at it properly. It was in a terrible state; in fact the whole place needed pulling down and a new one built. It certainly wasn't a safe place to bury my little box. I put it back in the big box again. I put that box in the attic. I put Rusty's collar and lead on; he was quite excited, he seemed to know where he was going. The two of us made our way over to the forest; he was in his glory.

After I had laid Rusty's food out for him I made my way down to Flora's house. It was such a lovely cottage, well kept and the garden was a pleasure to walk through. Flora opened the door before I reached it, took my coat and hat then showed me into the parlour. A lovely big fire was burning away in the grate. It was Flora's mother who brought the tea tray in. 'Hello, Mary, glad to see you are looking a lot better and how are you liking your new work? Nurse Duncan says she does not know the secret that you have for keeping the children quiet. Peggy usually let them run wild.'

'Oh,' I said, 'I give them my sweetest smile.' Little did she know.

The tea tray was set with lovely small sandwiches, all different kinds of biscuits and a lovely fruit cake. Flora poured the tea. When I saw all the lovely food I could not resist being a bit greedy. I had a taste of everything, even two cups of tea then I suddenly realised I wasn't in my own house. 'Oh, Mrs MacLean, I'm terribly rude, I really should not have eaten so much but, to tell you the truth, I really enjoyed myself.'

'I am glad, Mary, you are always welcome to call anytime you feel like it.' She asked after Vera and the boys. Ronald, looking the picture of health, came in. He was worried about the shortage of men for the Home Guard. I refused to be the first woman member. 'Oh dear, no Ronald, I'm much too busy.'

'Right then get your coat and hat on and I will run you home.' I thanked Flora and her mother for the lovely tea then I was off home.

Being out all afternoon helped to take my mind off my worries. I did enjoy my tea though, must remember to invite Flora up some Sunday afternoon. I sat in the rocking chair thinking of John Lewis, wondering what he was doing and if he really missed me. Being a sailor he had the chance of seeing lots of pretty girls. When I came to think of it I never seemed to attract boys. I wondered why; maybe I was too bossy.

The surgery on Monday was chock-a-block with babies howling their heads off, mothers looking exhausted. Very few men of course; they would be all away fighting. Nurse Duncan was bossing everyone as usual; Dr McKinnon had the patience of a saint, as for me I just watched and learned. I seemed to be always on my guard against the next catastrophe. In the last six months since I arrived home there seemed to be no end to them. At lunch time Mr Walsh said that he would attend to everything about the toilet and give me an estimate of the cost. I thanked him then made my way home. As usual Rusty was barking his head off when he heard my key in the door.

The following week the men came to build my new toilet; the plumber and joiner. I never let them in the house as Rusty was becoming quite vicious with strangers so I just left the garden gate open for them. Any water they needed they had to carry from the well the same as we did. It took them a fortnight to build it but what a difference. The men told me to pay Mr Walsh. Just before they were leaving Mr Lees the joiner said they had found a rusty tin box in the toilet floor and put it up on the window sill. I thanked him, and tipped the both of them then locked the garden gate and went to inspect our new toilet. I was pleased with it; the men had made a good job of it. It needed painting, of course, inside and out. I collected the rusty old box and let Rusty out into the garden while I went inside to have a better look at the box. According to the look of it, it must have been buried in the ground for a hundred years. The locks were still secure and it was heavy to lift. It would have to be broken open with a hammer and chisel and I couldn't find the hammer. Hector had used it when preparing for the burial of that poor girl. I hoped against hope it hadn't been left by the grave.

Life went on as usual at the surgery. Rusty had grown into a beautiful dog. He was a collie, mongrel of course, with a lovely grey and white silky coat and he had the oddest colour of eyes. Sometimes you thought they were green, other times they changed to blue. He was very protective of me and wicked with strangers. In fact he was a good guard dog, just what I needed.

As we were nearing closing time one day the surgery door opened and a middle-aged lady came in. At first she just stood and looked round the room then she came over to me and said, 'young woman, could you tell me if Dr McKinnon has a young girl on his list. The name is Maria Duffy.'

I had the presence of mind to keep my eyes down on the appointment book till I had time to get over the shock then I looked up into her face. 'Just a minute madam,' I said, 'I'll look through all the names. I am afraid I am new here. I'll ask Nurse Duncan if she can help you.' I brought Nurse through and explained the position to her. She asked who the lady was and received the reply 'Mrs Duffy, Maria's mother.'

'Yes,' said Nurse, 'we used to have a patient of that name. I can't tell you anything about her. They might be able to tell you something at the hotel where she used to work. Mary will show you the way, if you like.'

I accompanied Mrs Duffy to the hotel, showed her the way in then left in a hurry. What a turn up for the books I thought as I made my way quickly back to the surgery.

'My, you weren't long; was the devil after you?' Nurse asked.

'I was only in a hurry to get back in case you were busy.'

'It's funny,' Nurse Duncan said, 'Maria seemed to have disappeared so suddenly. I wondered where she went; she was expecting any day and I was supposed to attend to her confinement but she seems to have vanished off the face of the earth.'

'What like was she, Nurse?'

'My, she was a beautiful girl; natural blonde hair and the most beautiful blue eyes you ever saw. At times I felt sorry for her, she was easy going with the men. Why, with her looks she could have gone far; well that's life, we better hurry and lock the doors. I am going your way, Mary, so I'll give you lift home.' On the way home in the car I asked Nurse Duncan how long it was since Maria left the village and was told about two and a half years, maybe less.

'I don't know her at all. I was only fifteen when Mum and Dad sent me to service. I was terribly upset at the time. It was just after Nan's wedding; I wasn't even invited to Sarah's wedding. Mum said it was a big affair.'

'Yes, Mary, it was, your sister Sarah was a beautiful bride. Doctor and I were at the wedding; Hector is a real gentleman. Here we are Mary, mind and pull your blackout curtains before you put on the light.' I hurried indoors. Seeing Maria's mother at the surgery had upset me.

Rusty was barking to get out. It was pitch black outside but it made no difference to him. I really felt tired and contented myself with feeding Rusty, having my own meal and going to bed early.

I felt better in the morning and called at Mr Walsh's shop to order the paint, also to ask his advice what kind of paint would be best. 'I'll attend to that, Miss Mary, and I will deliver it myself before the weekend.' I made my way to the surgery hoping for some news of that poor girl Maria Duffy. As soon as the doors were opened the place wasn't long filling up. It was nearing lunch time before I got peace to talk to Nurse Duncan and ask for news of Mrs Duffy. I learned she had been to the police station and had talked to Father Joseph. That meant she was a Catholic. Thank goodness, I thought to myself, I blessed the ground where she was buried with holy water and Sarah and I said a few prayers for her departed soul. I believed Constable Campbell would have been taken aback when he heard who the lady in black was. Also he knew a lot more than he pretended to. Will just plead ignorance if I hear the name mentioned again.

On my way home for lunch Constable Campbell caught up to me on his bike. 'Can I come in a minute, Mary? I would like to ask a few questions.'

'Of course, but you will have to hurry as I have only an hour for lunch. Wait here while I let Rusty out in the garden then you can come into the kitchen and ask as many questions as you like while I am getting my lunch ready.'

He was standing looking out of the window watching Rusty running around wild then he turned to me and said, 'I did not know you had a dog, Mary. About that girl Maria Duffy. Her mother was at the station enquiring about her. She seems to think she has gone missing. The last letter she got from her daughter was two and a half years ago. She gave the hotel as her address. I was wondering if your mother or father ever mentioned her name.'

'How dare you ask me such question, my poor parents were on their death beds when I arrived home and in case you don't know it neither of them could eat or drink, never mind speak. As for me I had never heard that girl's name till her mother came into the surgery. Get out of my house at once; to think that I was away for over three years and when I arrive home I find both my parents dying of starvation and not one person in the village offered any help to them.' I got up and went to the front door and opened it.

As Constable Campbell was leaving, he said, 'I am so sorry, Mary, I did not know anything about your parents. You have had a hard time since you came home. I won't bother you again,' and with a wave of his hand he was off back to the village. I was angry, the cheek of him coming here for information. Well he got very little from me. I felt exhausted when I got back to the kitchen. It suddenly dawned on me that it would be old MacPherson who would plant the seed in Campbell's mind. They knew about the bodies in our attic because it was they who planted them there. They must be racking their brains wondering about what had happened to them.

I was just in time for opening; I was beginning to get used to all the aches and pains of the patients. Little did they know about my own heartache. The thought of Christmas buoyed me up for the afternoon. The little presents I would have to buy for everyone. Perhaps Ronald would drive me into Oban to do the shopping. Then, again, I couldn't leave Rusty for a day. At last it was time for going home. I had just arrived home and was taking my coat and hat off when I heard a loud knock at the door. It was Mr Walsh with the paint and a list of what to do, also paint brushes and a bottle of turpentine. He left the tins inside the door and I went to the kitchen for the money to pay him. I got quite a shock at the price. When he got his money he thanked me and said any time I needed help he was always handy at the shop. Since I arrived home he was the only one who showed a little kindness and understanding, except Dr McKinnon, Nurse Duncan and Father Joseph and, of course, Hector's family.

The days never seemed to be long enough for me. I had a million and one things to do but by the time I got home from work I was usually too tired to do them. All I wanted to do was rest. I looked at Mr Walsh's list again to see

116

if he had made a mistake in the prices. I let Rusty out then made my meal. Later I got mum's box down from the attic and laid the box on the kitchen table. Putting aside mum's first letter; the next envelope was a large folded brown one. The paper was very old; I was frightened it would crumble to pieces. Gently I opened it; there were lots of certificates. The first one I picked was mum and dad's marriage lines then Nan's birth certificate then Sarah's then Vera's and Billy's and Ewan's but no sign of mine. That's funny, I thought mine, should have followed Vera's as she was just a year older than me. I pulled the other two folded pieces of paper out but they were mum and dad's birth certificates. I looked through the rest of the papers in the box for my birth certificate, but no sign of it.

I began to cry; the effect of all the terrible things that had happened to me since I came home was taking its toll. I sat in the rocking chair sobbing my heart out, wondering why I had no mention anywhere. Rusty got up from his basket and tried to comfort me. He was too big now to jump up on my knee but he planked his two big paws on my lap. His lovely big eyes looking up to me so pleadingly as much to say, 'I will look after you'. I cuddled him and said, 'Oh, Rusty, what would I do without you.' I dried my eyes, and once and for all I hid those boxes away.

The post delivered three letters the next morning, one from Sarah saying she would be home for Christmas, the next from Vera saying the same; also the boys would be coming with her. The third one was from Auntie Kate inviting me down for Christmas. 'Bring your pet dog with you, P.S. I saw John Lewis the other day, he was asking kindly for you. Try and come dear, at times I feel so lonely, love Auntie Kate.' Well, I thought, that would be quite a good idea to take a trip to Oban then Mull. Vera and the boys could look after the house while I was away. I was feeling a lot happier as I made my way to my work. The loch seemed in one of her good moods, also; the children could howl their heads off to their hearts content and I would just smile back at them. Dr McKinnon and Nurse Duncan were all smiles also; it must be the Christmas feeling. I'd better get some decorations up and buy a bottle of sweets for the children. I hadn't been using my sweetie coupons lately. Just as well using them for a good cause; I'd give them all a sweet each as they leave for home on Christmas Eve.

We closed early on Christmas Eve and as each child left I handed them a sweetie in return for a big smile. One boy about 10 was leaving after I had given him his sweet. He reached the door then came back to the desk again and said, 'please miss, can I have three more for my wee sisters.'

A loud voice boomed out over my shoulder and said, 'Dougal Fraser, out of that door at once or I'll come and give you a skelp on the lug.' It was Nurse Duncan standing at my back, 'three sisters indeed. See that boy, he would take the eyelashes from your eyes and you would never know he had done it.'

'Has he not got sisters?'

'No, but he's got four brothers,' Nurse Duncan said, 'I am telling you, Mary, you keep an eye on Dougal any time he comes in here.'

I could not help but smile to myself thinking how easily I could have been conned by a small boy. It wasn't long before the surgery was empty. I gave Nurse and Dr McKinnon their presents and wished them both a Merry Christmas.

'The same to you, Mary; I'll run you home,' Nurse said. 'Your family are all home, I heard Mrs MacIntosh telling her daughter before you came in from lunch. That's a nice family you have got, Mary, have a nice rest.'

I was left at the door, Billy had opened it before I got my key out of my purse and Rusty came barking with glee nearly knocking me down running round and round. Vera came into the hall, 'what's keeping you, Mary, the meal is ready. Come on, boys, and I suppose you better come too, Rusty, and stop all that noise or I'll put you outside.' We all trooped into the kitchen. Vera had laid the table; it was beautifully set with lovely china which Vera and the boys had bought as my Christmas present. Normally when I arrived home from work I didn't like eating as I was always tired but I was really hungry and looking forward to enjoying my meal. Ronald was going to bring Sarah up later. She was on her own as Hector was away on a secret mission.

I told them that Auntie Kate had invited me to Mull for a few days and, as the train and boat would be uncomfortably packed, I wouldn't take Rusty.

Vera argued that Rusty would pine and that there would be plenty of room in first class. She persuaded me and I gave the boys money to send Auntie Kate a telegram, urging them to hurry before the post office closed.

While the boys were away I brought Vera up to date with all the news about the MacPhersons, Colin Campbell and Maria Duffy's mother.

The boys came back with my tickets. It seemed I needed one for Rusty, and the boys had paid with their own money. Then they were off with Rusty for a walk in the moonlight.

I parcelled up presents, my mind a jumble of unconnected thoughts; has Ina the cook received my card; what to take to Auntie Kate; was Katie the parlourmaid managing to keep Master James out of her bedroom; would I see John Lewis on the ferry.

Billy, Ewan and a boisterous Rusty came in, closely followed by Sarah. The first thing Sarah said was, 'oh, Mary, tell Rusty to lie down so that we all can get moving about in peace.'

It suddenly dawned on me that I would have to get him properly trained, otherwise he would be ruling us instead of me controlling him. I put Rusty outside.

'By the way, who is all going to Midnight Mass?'

Dear God, I thought to myself, I had clean forgot all about it. 'I think, Sarah, we all better go; if I fall asleep during Mass just give me a nudge.'

'Well that's settled, Ronald said he would run the lot of us to church. Hector's mother is not feeling too great so she is having an early night. She is not ill, just over tired.' I liked Hector's mother, I would not like anything to happen to her. I let Rusty in and told him to stay in his basket. Sarah shut the kitchen door then the first thing she said was, 'what's this I hear about Constable Campbell questioning you about some girl called Maria Duffy?'

'So Vera told you the story then. Well I never knew such a girl existed till the girl's mother called at the surgery to see if her name was on Dr McKinnon's list.'

'Its queer,' Sarah said, 'I wonder what happened to the poor girl. Campbell had a good cheek coming to see you, Mary, about her when you have never even met her.'

'Come on, girls,' I said, 'change the subject; it's Christmas Eve. Lets talk about something pleasant like are you still going with Tom Wilson, Vera?'

'No, Mary, I have got a new one, another American, I think I have really fallen in love this time.'

'You have been saying that with them all.'

'I know, Mary, but this boy is different. He is smashing to look at, he is in the American Air Corps.'

'I suppose he brings you plenty of silk stockings.'

Vera went into a fit of the giggles, suddenly we all joined in. To tell the truth we didn't now what we were laughing at. The kitchen door opened, Billy came in followed by Ronald. 'We never heard the door, Billy.'

'Small wonder with the noise you girls were making.'

I dried the tears from my cheeks, it had been such a long time since I had laughed so much. Ronald had arrived to take us down to Midnight Mass. Vera and the boys got in the back of the van while I sat at the front with Sarah and Ronald.

It just seemed like a second when we all arrived at the church; the place was packed. We made our way down to our family pew; thank goodness it was empty; Sarah and I got in first then Vera, Billy, Ewan and Ronald. As usual we were always in at the last minute. All my weariness left me as I knelt down to pray. The crib in front of us was laid out beautifully; when I looked at that babe in the manger my thoughts went back to the little infant I had buried in the garden and I shed a quiet tear for it and prayed to God to give his little soul peace. Mass was half through when Sarah gave me a push and said, 'are you going to Communion?' We all got up and made our way to the altar. Father Joseph's vestments were white, the symbol of purity. The church was beautifully decorated; I wondered where he got all the flowers from. My mind always seems to wander. I said a special prayer for Mum and Dad and my dear sister Nan.

When the service was finished we were about the last to leave the church. Father Joseph was standing in the porch; he wished us all a Merry Christmas. He came to Billy and Ewan and could not believe how tall both of the boys had grown. He told Billy, he was his dad's double, Billy just smiled. Dr and Mrs McKinnon came over and wished us a Merry Christmas. He shook hands with the rest of the family then he and his wife made their way home.

'Mary Scott!' a loud voice bellowed across the path; it was Nurse Duncan followed by a slim small man. 'Meet my husband Bert.' She eyed the rest of the family as she wished us all the best. 'Don't eat too much today,' then we were at last free to go home. We all clambered into the van then Ronald drove us home. 'I am glad we were last to get out of the church.'

'Why?' Sarah asked.

'Because if you lot got out first we would never have got home till morning.'

When we arrived at our house I asked Ronald to wait a minute till I ran in to get their presents. In two seconds I was back; 'off you go the two of you and have a nice time.' I heard the van drive away as I locked and bolted the door. Vera shouted from the kitchen, 'tea ready, Mary.'

I made my way to the kitchen; Billy and Ewan were already sitting at the table taking theirs, Rusty was fast asleep in his basket. How he could sleep with all the noise that was going on beat me. I took my tea sitting in the rocking chair then I noticed a big fruit cake in the middle of the table. 'Oh, Vera, how lovely, where did you get that delicious fruit cake? I must have a bit of it.'

'The farmer's wife made it for us; she thought it would put a smile on your face.'

The boys wanted to open their presents which they knew were lying on their beds. I had bought each of them a shaving kit, underwear, socks and a box of sweets. Vera confessed she had opened hers before going to Mass and gave me a big hug for the nightdress and the money. The boys came running in to the kitchen and the two of them planked a big kiss on my forehead. It was lovely to see their happy faces then they flew upstairs again. Vera just shook her head, 'you sure do spoil them. It's about time you opened yours; they are all beside your rocking chair.'

'Heavens I never noticed them.' The first one I opened was from Sarah, a beautiful hand knitted jumper; then a box of lace edged handkerchiefs from the boys; from Vera a lovely white satin blouse. 'Oh, Vera its beautiful.' It was my turn to give her a hug and kiss.

'This came the day before Christmas Eve; Postie brought it addressed to you, Mary.' Vera pulled the parcel from under the table and handed it to me. I could not get it opened quickly enough so I just ripped the paper off. Inside the box, all covered with tissue, lay a cute fur hat and matching gloves and a note wishing me a Merry Christmas, from Auntie Kate. We took turns trying on the hat. The feel of it was luxury; when I tried it on I felt like a million. 'It sure does something for you, Mary. Better not let Sarah see it or she will be off with it.'

'No fear of that,' I said, 'its mine and I'll wear it when I am visiting Auntie Kate. Oh dear, I forgot all about the Christmas dinner; it's Christmas already and there is nothing prepared. Let's forget about that, it's time we were all in bed.'

We bade each other goodnight and went our separate ways. I peeped into the boys room as I passed their door. Both of them were snoring their heads off. God help their wives if they ever married; the noise they were making was enough to waken the dead.

Christmas Day arrived; it was bitterly cold but it certainly wasn't a white Christmas. I thought I was up first but Vera and the boys had beaten me to it. Rusty was outside running wild as usual. It's great to be young I thought to myself as I watched Rusty chasing his ball. What a laugh, I was only 19 and I felt like 50. My thoughts all day and every day were spent on thinking what I could do for other people.

'Penny for your thoughts, Mary,' Vera's voice brought me back to earth.

'Come on then, sit down and eat your breakfast.'

A plate of bacon, egg and tomato was put down in front of me. 'Oh, Vera, where on earth did you get all that bacon?'

'Never mind where I got it, eat it up, Sarah and Ronald will be up for us all at 1 p.m.'

'Whatever for?'

Billy chipped in, 'that's our secret, Mary, when you are finished you better get all dolled up, and we will clear everything away.'

As I made my way back up to my bedroom I wondered what game they were all up to. It was nice just to have someone to look after me for a little while. Soon they would be all back to their work and I would be alone in this big house except, of course, for my lovely dog Rusty. What on earth was I thinking of, tomorrow I was going to Mull for a few days holiday at Auntie Kate's. At last I was ready. I took my good coat and the fur hat and gloves Auntie Kate gave me. As I made my way down to the kitchen I was thinking of John Lewis, wishing he was here with me.

When I arrived at the kitchen door Vera looked up. 'My, you sure look pretty, Mary. Where did you get that lovely dress; it fairly suits you.'

'She got it in a shop in Mull, Auntie Kate paid for it,' Ewan said. Vera never said anything but I am sure she was thinking, why is it Auntie Kate is always buying for me and never for her or Sarah. I was beginning to wonder myself.

At last we heard the hoot of the van except it wasn't a van but a lovely big black car. We were all so excited when we saw it. 'Hurry up, you lot, we'll never get away if you all stand staring at the car.' Sarah sitting in the front seat was helpless with laughter. Ronald just shook his head. I am sure he was thinking what a mad lot we were. Once we were all settled in our seats Ronald drove off. I had no idea where we were going. Even though it was a bitterly cold day the wintry sun was trying bravely to break through the clouds as we sped past the loch. I noticed it was dead calm; I was sure snow would fall before we got back. Ronald passed through the village; after that I didn't know where we were. We must have been driving about an hour and a half when we stopped in front of this beautiful house.

'Here we are girls and boys; out you get.' I gazed across the water looking at all the different houses. It was then I saw ours standing on its own on the edge of the cliff. We must have driven right round the loch; the MacPherson's house must be quite near. So this was what they were all planning for me. I went over to Sarah and thanked her.

Ronald led the way into the hotel; he seemed to know his way about. Our table was ready set for the six of us. The waiter took our coats and hats then held the chairs for us to sit down. It's funny, all the hotels I had been in were always dimly lit. Of course, there were lighted candles on the table, lovely crackers and all the Christmas decorations which made it feel like home. The waiter filled our glasses; Ronald ordered the first course then we all picked our own second course and pudding. I of course picked turkey followed by plum duff for pudding. We all had fun pulling the crackers then just before we were finished Ronald and the boys stood up and said; 'a toast to all the brave lads serving our country, especially my dear son Hector. May the Lord bring him home safely.' I am sure I saw Sarah wipe a tear from her eyes then we all said, 'to Hector'. Somewhere in the background music was playing 'The White Cliffs of Dover' sung by Vera Lynn. It was so peaceful just to sit and listen to her; she was such a beautiful singer. 'Is that you dreaming again, Mary. That's the third time Ronald has told you coffee would be served in the lounge.'

Soft settees were right round the room and small tables. Ronald had gone to the bar for a refreshment. He asked Billy and Ewan if they would like one. I gave Billy a push and shook my head. 'I am sorry, Ronald, but I am too young and Ewan is only 15 years,' Billy said.

'Oh dear Lord; to look at the pair of you I thought you were twenty at least.' Coffee was served for us; Ronald brought his drink over to our table then he said; 'do you know Mary, I often wondered why you were so protective towards the boys. I didn't realise that they were so young. They look so mature for their age.'

'That's because they have had to stand on their own two feet and fight their own battles. They had to suffer a lot when they worked on the MacPhersons's farm from morning till night and my poor sister Nan had to stand and watch. She, also, was a prisoner.' There was silence for a short while then Ewan started telling us about some of the tricks Billy and him got up to on the farm. By the time he was finished spinning his yarns we were all in a happier frame of mind.

When we all had our hats and coats on ready to leave for home Sarah came over to me and admired my hat. She tried it on and looked beautiful in it; she had the kind of face that would suit a dish cloth as the old saying goes. As we made our way home the light flakes of snow were beginning to fall; the water on the loch looked black, sure sign of a storm. By this time it was fairly dark; a full moon broke through the clouds just for a second. I thought it was bitterly cold outside, inside the car we were lovely and cosy. At last we arrived home, Sarah and Ronald said cheerio at the door to us then they made their way home.

We all made for the kitchen which was the warmest room in the house. Billy put more logs on the range; Ewan let Rusty out. It was the first time he had seen snow; he made to rush out, then all of a sudden he stood still bewildered by the white covering the whole garden. At first he just took a step or two then the next minute he was his usual self running and rolling about in the snow. The boys were as bad as him; they were busy throwing snowballs at one another. Vera was sitting at the kitchen table; I took my coat and hat off then came back and sat in the rocking chair. 'Who was it, Vera, who paid for everything today.'

'It really was Hector; he sent Sarah the money. Ronald of course hired the car.'

'Well I sure did have a lovely time; it was great to get out of the house and forget everything.'

'Mary, when the war is over my new boyfriend, Fred Turner, has asked me to marry him and go back with him to America. I don't like leaving you yourself, Mary. Billy and Ewan will want to work on at the farm. Sarah and Hector will be going their own separate ways, also.'

'You talk, Vera, as if the war was over.'

'Well, according to the way Sarah was talking to Ronald she said Hector told her that the way things were shaping, Hitler could not hold out much longer. Don't say a word to anyone, Mary, about our conversation. Sarah told me in confidence.'

'Well, I sure hope what you say is true; it would be great to get those dirty blackout curtains down and thrown in the dust can. I do hope you will be happy with Fred; give me plenty of time to get off work for your wedding. I would love to be a bridesmaid.'

CHAPTER 8

Ronald and Sarah ran me and Rusty in the van to the railway station. I only took a small suitcase with me. Vera had packed a lunch box for me and Rusty's dish and a bottle of water for him. It was such a long journey for both of us. I was hoping the ferry crossing would not upset Rusty. We arrived on time at the station. The train came puffing round the corner just a few minutes after we arrived. Ronald and Sarah saw me and Rusty safely in our compartment; it was a good idea of the boys to book first class otherwise we would have had to stand all the way to Oban as the train was packed with servicemen and women. As Sarah kissed me goodbye, I whispered, 'I need to speak to you alone, Sarah, when I get back.' She just nodded and hurried off the train as it was beginning to pull out of the station. I took a towel out of my case and spread it on the seat for Rusty to lie on; he jumped up and lay beside me and settle down to sleep. I sat at the window and watched the lovely countryside covered in snow as the train sped swiftly on its journey, then dozed off. The guard asking to see my tickets wakened me. He looked at Rusty sound asleep then he said, 'excuse me, Miss, that's a beautiful dog you have got there. Can I ask what do you feed it on?'

'Oh he has the same food as I have every day; his favourite dish is the left over from the mince and tatties.' He went to pat him but I told him not to touch Rusty as he was vicious with strangers. He just touched his cap and was off shutting the door behind him.

We were nearing Oban when I decided to have my lunch; as soon as I took the lid off the lunch box Rusty woke up. 'So you smelt the food did you?' He jumped down to the floor and put one big paw on my lap. 'Oh, all right, you are just getting two sandwiches and a drink of water. That will do you till we get to Auntie Kate's. Don't look at me like that or you will get nothing.' There were plenty of Spam sandwiches so I gave Rusty another one. I had a flask of tea; I really enjoyed my lunch. I hurriedly packed everything away as the porter was opening and shutting doors shouting next stop Oban.

125

The journey seemed short; I suppose it was because both of us slept most of the time. When we arrived at the quay the ferry was berthed there. People were already boarding her. I hurried up the gangway with Rusty hoping the would not be seasick. No sign of John Lewis; maybe he was off duty. I made my way below deck looking for a comfortable seat for myself and Rusty then I spied John sitting cuddling a lovely fair haired girl. I said to myself, 'there goes my dream.' I just sat down, Rusty lay at my feet; I watched John Lewis with his new girlfriend. I wonder how many girls he has had since I last saw him six months ago. Rusty behaved himself well throughout the whole journey. At last we arrived at Craignure where the ferry docked. After I had picked up my case and stood up to lead Rusty towards the gangway, John Lewis rushed past me pulling his latest love with him; the passengers were all hurrying to get off the boat. When Rusty and I reached the gangway John Lewis was standing at the top taking the tickets; I handed him mine and said 'hello, John,' then I made my way down to the quay with Rusty. Auntie Kate was waiting for me with a taxi. 'Hurry up, child, it's bitterly cold,' then she noticed Rusty. 'Dear God, Mary, is that the little ball of fur you took away with you? My, he is a beauty. If I had known he was going to turn out like that I would have kept him to myself.'

'He will need to go somewhere to do his business; the poor thing hasn't had peace all day.'

At last we were all in the taxi heading for Auntie Kate's cottage. We were all glad to get indoors.

A lovely big fire burned in the grate; the small table was set for tea. I put Rusty's dishes in the kitchen and set out his food first, that way Auntie and I would get peace to get our tea. We had hot muffins and butter and jam, home-made sultana cake and little chocolate biscuits. I enjoyed my tea and was feeling a lot better. It had been a long day but I had so much news to discuss with Auntie Kate that I was beginning to think two days stay as far too short.

'I think the best thing for you to do, Mary, is to have an early night. I'll let Rusty out in the garden before I go to bed and will see you in the morning. I have arranged with my solicitor to call tomorrow to discuss a few problems with us, so off you go and get a good night's rest.'

I was quite pleased to get to my bedroom to rest; Auntie had a big fire burning in the room. I always seemed to be more at home here than at Loch Etive. As soon as I laid my head on the pillow I was fast asleep. It was blowing a gale force wind when I woke up; the sky was black, it certainly looked like more snow. The little window gave a lovely view of the sea where huge waves were lashing against the shore. There wouldn't be any crossing to Oban. I hurriedly washed and dressed then made my way to the kitchen. When I had finished Auntie Kate said I should wrap up and take Rusty down to the shore. It would put colour in my cheeks. I enjoyed my breakfast, scrambled eggs, tea, toast and butter and marmalade.

As soon as Rusty saw me putting on my coat he went jumping mad and we set off for the shore, the only two silly enough to weather the storm. Once we reached the shore I sat in the shelter of a big boulder and watched the huge waves covered with white spray. Rusty was enjoying himself; I thought it funny how he took to Auntie Kate right away; he was always on his guard with strangers. 'A penny for your thoughts, Mary,' a voice said.

I looked up and John Lewis was standing beside me. 'I don't think that's any of your business and before you say another word, I watched you and your latest lady love the whole of the crossing from Oban to Mull so just don't stand there and make any excuses.'

'You might have let me know you were visiting your Auntie and I would have met you at the train.'

'And what may I ask were you going to do with that girl?'

'Oh her, she means nothing to me, Mary, I was just passing the time.'

'In that case you can pass the rest of your life with her because I am finished with you.'

He went to give me a kiss and Rusty flew at him. John got a fright; 'that's a dangerous dog you have there, it needs to be put down.'

'If anyone needs to be put down it's you, now be off with you and don't come near me again.' He was the type of boy who thought he could outwit everyone. Finally, he walked away and Rusty and I made our way back home.

Auntie Kate had lunch ready; 'what kept you, Mary?'

'Oh, that boy John Lewis, he thought he could use his charm on me but thankfully I saw through him in time.'

'I could have told you last night about that other girl he is going with but I didn't like to interfere. Eat your lunch before Mr Hendry arrives. I will attend to Rusty, his basket is ready if he wants to sleep.' The fresh air had given me an appetite and I wasn't long in emptying my plate. Auntie seemed tired and I sent her to rest by the fire while I cleared the table and washed the dishes. She was soon sound asleep. I thought to myself, she must be quite old. Of course, when you are just 19 you think 35 is ancient never mind 60 years. I made myself comfortable beside the fire; it was beginning to get dark early even though it was barely 2 p.m. People were battling against the wind as they walked by our window. Just then Mr Hendry's car drew up at the door. I gave Auntie a gentle shake to wake her up and went to open the door for him. He shook hands with me, said I was looking at lot better since the last time he saw me and hurried into the warm parlour. I took his hat and coat and told him to sit at the fire. By this time Auntie was wide awake; 'could you bring a pot of tea, Mary, then while we are drinking it we will discuss everything.' I wasn't long in setting the tray on the little table with the silver teapot. We all settled down then Mr Hendry asked if I still had the letter my mother wrote about how the MacPhersons beat my father.

'Yes,' I said, 'and I'd better tell you, Mr Hendry, the girl that was with the MacPhersons that night has never been seen since. Her mother called at the surgery the week before Christmas enquiring if her name was on the doctor's list. I told her I didn't know the girl as I had just started work a few months ago. She called at the police station, also to see Father Joseph but I don't know how she got on. I have not seen her since. The girl's name was Maria Duffy. Constable Campbell had the cheek to come and question me about her, as if I knew. You know I was in service for over three years.'

'I think Constable Campbell is over stepping his position. I'll report him to his superior after the New Year and tell them to stop him harassing you once and for all.'

'Also I was wondering, Mr Hendry, what the situation was regarding the house.'

'The house is yours,' Auntie Kate said. 'Mr Hendry will attend to that also. Now, Mary, would you mind leaving the room, Mr Hendry and I have a lot more to discuss.'

I hurriedly made my way to the kitchen without mentioning the box of old coins that was found buried underneath the outside toilet. Rusty was anxious to go out and I opened the door after switching off the light. When he came back he was dripping water all over the place and I had to dry him. At last Mr Hendry left. He just popped his head round the kitchen door to wish me a Happy New Year when it came. He took a long look at Rusty but never said anything. Auntie Kate came into the kitchen; before she could say anything I told her about the coins.

'Oh dear, they are bound to be worth a lot of money and where have you got them now.'

'I have hid the box in the attic.'

'Good, on no account, Mary, tell any of the rest of the family; it would be safer to keep them hidden till after the war then we will discuss the best thing to do with them. Tomorrow Mary I'll treat you to the pictures then tea in the afternoon. Now, after supper you can go to bed early again and rest. I will look after Rusty.' I wasn't long in getting ready for bed and as usual as soon as my head touched the pillow I was fast asleep.

In the morning the weather wasn't much better but at least the rain had stopped. I wrapped up well and took Rusty to the shore enjoying my walk along the sea front; the big waves were still lashing at the rocks. Turning a corner, I bumped into John Lewis. God, he sure is persistent, am I never going to get rid of him, I thought. On the verge of walking past him he said, 'I am sorry, Mary, surely at least we can be friends. There is a good picture at the Regal, Clark Cable is in it. We could go this afternoon.'

'All right, John we'll be friends, as for the pictures Auntie is taking me this afternoon then I go home tomorrow.'

I liked John but he was such a notorious flirt; we walked together along the shore for a while then I decided to turn back and make my way home. I called to Rusty who came running up to me giving John a wary look.

'I don't think that dog of yours likes me, Mary.'

'He really is a big softie but when it comes to me he is very protective. He would not let anyone harm me; I suppose that's the way it should be. See you tomorrow on the ferry.' Rusty and I arrived home out of breath as we raced each other the last few yards. The walk had done the pair of us a lot of good. After I had taken my coat and hat off I made my way to the kitchen. Auntie had our meal ready and said there was a letter for me on the table. It was from Sarah, she asked me to come home straight away as something upsetting had happened at home. 'I won't say anymore Mary but we need you here right away, love Sarah.' I told Auntie who immediately phoned the harbour and learned that a ferry was leaving in half an hour.

While I was getting myself and Rusty ready she phoned Mr Hendry who, as luck would have it, was also crossing and going on to Loch Etive. He called for me, and as we left Auntie pushed an envelope into my hand. We reached the quay in time and Mr Hendry drove his car on to the ferry. After he had locked his car we made our way to the first class. The seats were comfortable and I did not hear the noise of the ship's engines. Mr Hendry pressed a button and when one of the ship's stewards came in ordered a pot of tea for two and a sandwich and cakes for me and a dish of water for Rusty. The waiter returned with everything on a tray and laid it on a small round table beside us. He put the dish of water on the floor for Rusty then quietly disappeared.

'Would you like to pour the tea, Mary?'

I had often watched Lady Ramsay, my mistress at Rutherglen House, so I knew what to do. Mr Hendry wasn't one for conversation, he spent most of his time writing. I think he completely forgot all about me but I was mistaken for he said if I had finished my tea to just press the bell and the steward would clear the table and take Rusty's dish away. He certainly was teaching me how to give orders. When the steward returned I told him what to do then sat back in the comfortable chair until we docked at Oban.

'We'd better get down to the car now, Mary, we are nearly there. My car was last to come on so I'll be first to leave.' When we reached land he said, 'take Rusty for a walk as we have a long journey before you reach home.' He called after me, 'don't be long, Mary, I want to get back to Oban tonight to celebrate the New Year with my family.'

At last we were on our way home, I put a towel on the back seat for Rusty to sleep on; it wasn't only Rusty who slept the whole journey. I, also, fell into a deep sleep. Mr Hendry shook me awake when we arrived home. Sarah must have heard the car because she had the door opened before we arrived. 'I am sorry, Sarah,' Mr Hendry said, 'I can't stay long. If you could let me know what has happened I'll take notes and be off.' Sarah repeated everything that happened that day I left for Mull. When she had finished, Mr Hendry went up to inspect the attic. He assured us he would attend to everything then, wishing us Happy New Year he set off for Oban.

It was when we were all seated round the kitchen table drinking our tea that Vera told me what really had happened. The boys were out tidying the garden when Vera heard a loud knock at the door. When she opened it Constable Campbell and a police inspector were standing there. Vera asked what was wrong. Campbell said, 'we have reason to believe that you have illicit goods hidden in your attic. The inspector here has a search warrant to search your attic right away.'

'To tell you the truth, sir, I don't know how to get to the attic.'

'I saw both your sisters leave on the train, I heard they were going to Mull; may we come in please.'

I shouted to Billy to come right away. Both the boys came in together. 'Run down, Billy, and tell Sarah to come up right away.' Billy flew out of the door, Ewan stayed beside me.

'I thought Sarah went with Mary to Mull.'

'Is that why you came today thinking I would be here myself?' Campbell blushed and just then Sarah and Billy returned.

Sarah was really angry. 'How dare you come to our house without any

130

warning. I will see my solicitor gets word about this right away.'

'Well, Miss—'

'Mrs MacLean to you. Since you have the notice I'll take you up to the attic; as for you Constable Campbell, my husband and I and the rest of the family will take you all the road.' We all followed the two policemen into the attic. The inspector was taken aback; the place was spotless and quite empty. 'Have you got the key to that trunk?'

'That thing is never locked, it's just used to store blankets, sheets, Mum's wedding dress; look for yourself and see.' The inspector nodded to Campbell who opened it and found everything as I said he would then he went over to the crib. Your doll, Mary, was lying in it with a little crochet blanket on top. He took everything out of the crib. 'I want everything put back, Constable, the way you found it then the two of you will go please, leave our house right away. You will be hearing more about this after the holidays.'

The inspector said he was sorry to have troubled us then they left.

Ewan then told Sarah and Vera the story he told me about the night the MacPhersons dragged Dad out to the forest and nearly killed him and about the fair haired girl who worked at the bar in the hotel who went with them but never came back and how both of them were forced to go into the boat while Donald and his father and brothers carried out the brutal hammering they gave father. 'That's right,' Billy said, 'and there wasn't hardly a day went by that Donald or his brothers didn't give us a belting also, we got hardly any food either.' When Sarah and Vera heard the story Sarah asked why nothing had been said about this before. Of course, there hadn't been an opportunity.

'The more you tell me, Mary, the more I am convinced Constable Campbell is involved with Dad's death,' Sarah said. 'Right everybody we must stop being morbid, it's New Year's Eve and we are all going to celebrate down at the hotel. Ronald will be coming up for us in the van after he has driven Flora and her mother there first. I'm going back down to Hector's to change.'

Vera didn't have anything decent to wear. I was wearing the blue dress Auntie Kate bought for me and I gave Vera the pink one to try on. It fitted her perfectly. Then she needed a pair of shoes. God, I thought, will I never have peace to get ready myself. I told her try the bottom drawer of the chest of drawers. When we were all ready to go Vera said we would need some cash; we couldn't let everyone else buy us drinks without returning them.

As last we heard Ronald hooting his car horn. I sat in the front seat beside Sarah, poor Vera she was always landed with the boys in the back of the van. I hoped Ronald did not get too drunk to drive us home. Outside, the hotel was complete darkness but inside the bright lights nearly blinded us. The dining room was beautiful, the little tables with pure white lace table clothes, napkins to match. Our table must have been reserved for us for Ronald led us to a table for eight. Flora and her mother were already seated. Vera and the boys were in there glory, the look on their faces said, 'tonight we are going to enjoy ourselves.' The only thing that spoiled the atmosphere was Constable Campbell and his wife Alice and, lo and behold the MacPhersons all sitting together at one table. I had my back to them, it was Vera who whispered it to me. 'Oh, Vera, let's forget about them and enjoy ourselves tonight.'

The waiter came and Ronald asked us what we would like to drink then ordered white wine for us all. I studied the menu, and decided on the turkey and all the trimmings followed by apple tart and cream. I wondered if I should have brought more money with me. The night was a great success, by the time we all had finished our meal and drinks, everyone was in high spirits. As it was nearing midnight a dead silence settled in the room as we waited for the last chime of twelve to strike then a huge roar went up from everyone in the room. We all kissed and hugged one another and wished each other a Happy New Year for 1945. I think we all had the same thought going through our heads, please God let this war soon be over and everyone's loved ones back home. The band started playing 'Ain't Misbehavin'', Sarah and I were asked up to dance by two strange young men in sailor's uniform. I didn't think it was anyone I knew at school.

'Hello, Mary,' he said, 'I hardly recognised you, it must be years since I last saw you.'

I racked my brain trying to remember who this charming young man could be.

'Don't you remember me; John Campbell, my uncle is Constable Campbell.'

At the moment of that name I froze, John must have felt the difference in my dance because the next minute he said, 'what's wrong, Mary, have I said something to hurt you?'

'Oh no, John, just my mind must have drifted away for a second. To tell you the truth I was thinking of Rusty hoping that he is all right.'

'Is Rusty your boyfriend?'

'Don't be silly, he is my dog,' both of us laughed at the same time, 'and who may I ask are the two good looking young men sitting at your table?'

'Did you not recognise them? They are my brothers, Billy and Ewan.'

'My looking at them is making me feel old all of a sudden.'

'When do you go back to your ship?'

'I have to leave first thing in the morning, how about a walk outside for a breath of fresh air?'

'Sorry, John, I must get back to my guests.' If he thought for a second I was something to play with before he went back to his ship he was greatly mistaken. He led me back to my table. Vera was up dancing. Flora was standing at the bar so I introduced John to Mr and Mrs MacLean then my brothers. He wished us all a Happy New Year then disappeared among the dancers. I tried to remember John when I was at school but I just could not place him at all. Vera was flirting with the young sailor she went up with. Billy and Ewan were still sitting at the table. I managed to persuade Billy to have a dance with a girl despite his protests that he couldn't dance and I danced with Ewan who tried to copy every dancer on the floor. Billy was dancing with Gillian Walsh the grocer's daughter. I hardly recognised her, she looked beautiful, full of laughter. Normally when she was helping her father in the shop her face was as long as a fiddle.

At last the party broke up and everyone made their way home in the black-out. The snow must have been pretty heavy, the whole road was covered with a deep layer of snow, in fact the road was quite dangerous. Ronald had to drive at a slow pace. He and his wife and Sarah sat in the front seat while Flora, Vera and the boys and myself crammed into the back of the van. We were all singing and laughing our hearts out. Ronald shouted, 'less noise at the back there, the Germans will hear you.' Of course, that set us off again. Ronald dropped us off first then he made his way slowly back to his own house. Sarah was staying with them. Rusty was sound asleep so after we all had a cup of tea and a biscuit we made our way to our own separate rooms and to bed. I felt happy and flung myself into bed singing softly to myself.

All the family were leaving to go back to work; Vera, Billy and Ewan off to Angus, Sarah back to Inverness. Ronald was driving them to the station. I thought I would be better saying goodbye to them all as they left the house. After the van disappeared round the corner I shut the door, locked and bolted it.

The big house seemed so silent and empty as I made my way into the kitchen. Lately Rusty had been a bit neglected; he was standing patiently waiting at the door to be let out. You poor thing I thought. When he saw the snow he jumped into it right away, running up and down the garden. I would never really be alone so long as I had Rusty. We loved one another. I sat in the rocking chair and looked back over all the events of the past week.

Monday morning arrived and I was quite glad to get out of the house. The road was still covered with snow and the walking was difficult. The loch was very still and the water looked black, a sure sign of more snow to come. At last I arrived at the surgery, the place was empty. Doctor McKinnon and Nurse Duncan were there before me. 'What's wrong, Nurse?' I asked.

'If you ask me,' she said, 'most likely they will all be in bed suffering from hangovers.'

I got all my notes ready in case anyone was brave enough to venture out in the bitter cold weather. The day wore on, when just an hour before lunch time a mother and her four children came in. That was the lot that morning.

'I think, Mary, you better have lunch with Doctor and me, we don't want you laid up with a broken leg, walking is pretty bad.'

'What about Rusty?'

'I'll tell you what, since the surgery is so quiet I'll ask doctor if you can take the afternoon off. I'll attend to anything that crops up.' She disappeared for a few minutes then when she came back said, 'off you go home, Mary, and mind your feet.'

I was glad to get home, it seemed to have got even colder since I went out in the morning and the road was like an ice rink. Rusty came running to the door to meet me. I piled the logs on the range, made some lunch for myself then settled down in the rocking chair with Auntie Kate's letter and opened the envelope. Inside was twenty pounds, nothing else. I put it away along with the rest of the money I had hidden. That was one thing I would never tell the family. I thought of the box of old coins that was found buried under the floor of the old toilet and wondered what they would be worth. Nobody had mentioned the new toilet and to think I spent the whole day Sunday giving it its second coat of gloss paint.

The rest of the week at the surgery was back to normal, mothers with their fretful babies, boys and girls making faces at one another. Just a few old men, no young ones, they were all away at the front. About a fortnight after the New Year Nurse Duncan told me that Constable Campbell was being moved to Oban. The new police officer, Neil Drummond, coming in his place was a lot older. I thought to myself Mr Hendry wasn't long in getting things attended to. Outwardly I said, 'who told you, Nurse?'

'Oh, I was talking to Campbell yesterday, he seemed pretty upset.'

I am sure he would be, I thought to myself. I wondered how the MacPhersons would react to the bad news. Good news for me and my family, bad for the MacPhersons. I felt a lot happier as I made my way home after surgery was finished. The following Monday when I got home for lunch there was a letter for me lying on the mat from Mr Hendry. I waited till Rusty was attended to and I had finished my lunch before I opened it. There was a letter of apology from the Chief Inspector about the unfair intrusion of the police officers in my house. Mr Hendry wrote that he had discussed everything with Auntie Kate and he was to tell me that I would not be troubled in any way by the police again. Constable Campbell would be leaving at the end of the month. The new one who was coming in his place had been given instructions by the chief himself, on no account were you to be harassed again, 'so I hope, Mary, you will feel a lot happier now. Your Auntie Kate is hoping it won't be too long till you visit her again in Mull.'

I needed to start getting into a routine with the house chores, instead of going out on a shopping spree on a Saturday I seemed to spend the whole day cleaning the house; I never seemed to have time to enjoy myself. Didn't feel like going out anyway, what with the terrible weather and the blackout, it was easier staying indoors. I took Rusty out and stood looking up at the clear sky with a million little stars shining brightly. There was a full moon. I suppose Hector and all the thousands of boys and girls fighting for their country are looking at the same moon, it would be shining brightly down upon them also wherever they may be, God bless them all. I was beginning to feel cold so I shouted Rusty in, shut and locked the door then put the light on.

One morning in May 1945 I was making my way down to my work when I passed Postie on his bike. 'Good morning, Miss, did you hear the great news?'

'No,' I said, 'what news?'

He stopped his bike; 'the war is over.'

I forgot where I was, I flung my arms around his neck and gave him a big kiss. 'Are you sure now that it is true?'

'Of course it is, I heard it on the radio.'

My first thoughts were all the family would be back home again. I hurried down to the surgery to see what news they had heard. I knew it was true before I opened the door. Everyone was dancing and singing and hugging one another. I made my way to the back of my desk; Nurse Duncan was dancing with Doctor, as for me I just sat down and cried. It must have been the pent up feeling I had had all through the war years, never knowing what was going to happen next.

Nurse Duncan saw me crying my heart out, 'my, my, Mary, what's all this for?'

'I am just so happy, Nurse, I felt like crying.'

'It sure is a funny way to have of showing you are happy. Just look at that

135

lot dancing away, they don't look sick to me.' The next minute the waiting room was empty, everyone had left hurrying home with the good news. 'Now did you ever see the likes of that, Mary,' Nurse said then she shouted to Doctor 'I think the end of the war has created a miracle. Everyone has gone home cured.' We all had a good laugh. 'Well, Doctor, we are going home also as the place is empty. Come on, Mary, I'll run you home.' Nurse left me at the door, 'see you tomorrow, Mary, and no more bubbling.' I just laughed.

Rusty was there at the door, 'now what do you think happened today Rusty?' He just looked at me with those lovely big eyes of his; 'the war is over, you silly,' then I danced my way into the kitchen. 'Now when I have had my tea I'll take you a nice long walk, in the meantime out in the garden you go.' I could hardly take it in, peace at last but at what a price; thousands of our lads killed, the cream of the country. I hoped Hector would come home safe and sound.

I gave Rusty his meal then took him his promised walk; when he saw me with his lead he went wild. It was a lovely day and I thought, a walk down to the loch for a change. I sat on a huge boulder and let Rusty splash away in the water. I noticed a small motor boat making its way across from the other side of the loch to where I was sitting. I wondered where it was going and who it belonged to. Where I was sitting no way could they see me. I waited quietly watching to see where they would land. Lo and behold the two men that were in it pulled the boat ashore just below my house. I called quietly to Rusty and the pair of us hurried back to the house.

When I got inside I locked and bolted both doors and ran upstairs to the boys' bedroom which looked out into my back garden. The next thing I saw was a rope ladder being flung over our high wall. I raced downstairs, took Rusty by the collar and stood at the foot of the ladder. It wasn't long before two long legs started coming down the steps then I let Rusty go, 'go get him, boy,' I said. The dog flew at the man and bit his legs. He let out one big howl and disappeared quickly back over the wall. The next minute the ladder was pulled back over the wall. I never got a glance at his face but whoever he was would have to get his leg dressed by the doctor or nurse. It dawned on me that if I had been at work I would never have seen them. I wasn't supposed to be home today. Suddenly, I was worried. I wondered how often that sort of thing was going on and what were they wanting in my garden. They, whoever 'they' were were not expecting me to be home. 'They' certainly got more than they bargained for.

I put the lead on Rusty, locked both doors then set out for Nurse Duncan's house which stood about a quarter of a mile further along the road. Nurse was busy in her garden when I arrived. 'Oh hello, Mary, I am quite pleased you called. Gives me an excuse for downing tools. Come on in and we will both have a nice cup of tea.'

Nurse's kitchen was built on the same lines as mine only not as big. It was just as cosy, a big fire was burning brightly in the range. Rusty sat at my feet eyeing nurse all the time. Nurse Duncan said, 'my, Mary, that's a beauty of a dog you have got there.'

'That's who I am here to talk about, Nurse,' then I told her what had just happened in my garden. 'Whoever it was will have two pretty sore legs after the way Rusty attacked him. I'll have to report the incident to the police.'

'Don't worry about that, Mary, once you have finished your tea I'll run both you down to the police station. In the meantime I'll give Doctor McKinnon a ring and put him on his guard if anyone goes to his house for treatment for dog bites. Between the three of us we will soon find out who the culprit is.'

It didn't take long to reach the police station. 'I'll come in with you Mary, I want to have a good look at our new constable. If he is attractive at all I might fall for him.' She gave me a gentle push as we made our way to the counter and I rang the bell. A heavily built man in his late forties came through to the counter. He was very attractive, his hair black as jet but the hair on the sides of his face was slightly greying. His best feature were his eyes, large and deep blue which seemed to keep staring at you all the time while you were speaking. I made my complaint and he wrote down everything I told him. When I was finished he asked if it was all right to come home with me and have a look at the garden wall. We all piled into Nurse's car and went back to my house. When we arrived I used the garden gate which I opened with the key.

'Is this door kept locked all the time, Miss Scott?'

'Yes,' I said, and took the constable to the actual spot where the ladder had been flung over the wall.

'You don't by any chance have a pair of ladders, Miss? I would like to have a look over the wall to see what sort of drop it is on the other side.' I went to get the steps, Rusty all the time keeping a watchful eye. The constable saw me struggling with the steps and took them from me. Setting the steps by the wall, he climbed up. 'Oh my God,' he said, 'there is somebody lying injured down there on the rocks. I'll have to get back to the station and phone for help.'

Nurse Duncan said she would run the constable down to the station and at the same time, alert Dr McKinnon. Telling me to stay at home, the constable said he would see me next day.

When I arrived at the surgery next morning Nurse Duncan gave me the full story of what happened when she and Constable Drummond left our house. As soon as they arrived at the police station Drummond phoned the lifeguard then Doctor McKinnon and they all went down to the jetty where a boat was waiting to take them to the spot where the man lay injured. When they reached the man it was too late to do anything, the poor young man was already dead. He had been shot in the head.

All of a sudden I felt sick and started crying. 'Sit down, Mary, I'll get you a cup of tea and an aspirin. You have had nothing but shocks since you came home.'

'Tell me, Nurse, did he have the marks of dog bites.'

'No, Mary, he didn't; according to Doctor he had been dead for two or three days.'

'Oh, Nurse, don't say those two men were going to throw that dead body in my garden.'

'I think, Mary, you and Drummond had the same thoughts. The man was a complete stranger to us.'

I called in at the police station on my way home for lunch; the place seemed empty at first so I pressed the bell. Constable Drummond came through from the back. He told me that Oban were taking charge of the investigation into the young man's death and he didn't think he would need to trouble me again. As I left, he reminded me to keep my doors locked.

Having lost fifteen precious minutes of my lunch hour, I hurried home only to be interrupted by Mary Kate Bell from the hotel. Rusty growled at her and bared his teeth. I told Mary Kate to wait outside for a minute or two and I'd walk back to the village with her. Wondering what the little minx wanted, I hurriedly finished my sandwich and settled Rusty then made my way to join Mary Kate.

'Mary, that's a wild dog you have got there.'

'Not really, only to certain people does he behave like that.'

We were silent for a while as we walked down the road together then she said, 'I saw you going into the police station, Mary, anything wrong?'

'Not really, Mary Kate.' I changed the subject and asked how her family were. By this time we had reached the surgery and I asked how long she was home for.

'Just a week,' she said. After that we went our separate ways and I thought to myself, if she thought she was going to get news from me she was barking up the wrong tree. Doctor and Nurse were there by the time I arrived and there was no fresh news about the dead man, except that the MacPherson brothers were supposed to be coming across to make enquiries about him. The waiting room was packed. By the time everyone was attended to I was feeling exhausted and was glad when Nurse said she would run me home. We were nearly at my house when I asked Nurse if she could phone the hospital tomorrow for some news.

'Funny, Mary, I was thinking of doing that myself. I'll attend to that tomorrow.'

I hurried indoors and let Rusty out. Since it was a lovely evening I thought I would take him out a walk after I had had my dinner and a rest. I didn't think that Mary Kate would call again. I sat in the rocking chair with the kitchen door open watching Rusty playing with his ball. Now that the war was over maybe it wouldn't be too long till the family were all back home again. Rusty came running in and wasn't long in cleaning up his dishes then he came over to me and placed his big paws on my lap and looked at me with those lovely big eyes of his, then I whispered, 'how about a nice walk?' he went mad running round the table.

I locked and bolted the back door then the pair of us went out the front way. Once I had crossed the main road and was in the forest, I took his lead off and let him run wild. It was so peaceful walking amongst the beautiful tall trees, it seemed as if it was yesterday that Dad went to look after them every day. I often wondered who the new forester was; nobody seemed to mention him. I sat down on a stump of a tree thinking I would have to write to Sarah and Vera giving them all the news. My mind as usual was miles away when I heard a twig breaking. I looked up and saw Donald's father coming towards me.

The first thing he said was, 'what are you doing here?'

'Out for a walk of course.'

'This is private property and you have no right here. I am forester now.'

'Oh, it wasn't private property the night you and your sons beat my father and brought him home dying.'

His face turned red; 'who told you that, you slut?'

He lifted his hand to strike me when a huge ball of fur flew at him and bit his arm. MacPherson let out one big scream and ran out of the forest. Rusty stood beside me; the bristles of his lovely coat standing on end. I thought at the time he had wandered off but there he was. For the second time that week he had saved me. I sat down on the leaves and cuddled him and whispered, 'good boy, you are always there to protect me.' The tears were running down my face and he started licking me. 'Come on Rusty we'd better get home.' At least I had let Mr MacPherson know that I knew who was responsible for Dad's death. It would give him something to think about.

Nurse Duncan phoned the hospital to see if any patient had been treated for dog bites. The sister at the hospital looked up the records but there was no record of dog bites. Whoever he is would have to show up some time for treatment. I didn't have to write to Sarah, she wrote to me. Hector was safe, his leg scratched by a bullet; his stay in hospital wouldn't be long. I was so pleased to hear he was safe; both of them would be coming home as soon as Hector was well enough to travel. Thank God for that bit of good news. I wrote to Vera giving her all the bad news and asking when she and the boys get leave.

It was a fortnight later that I got word from Vera; she said it would be the end of the month before she and the boys would be back home then she went on to say even though the war was over the country needed to dig for food and it would be a while before they could end the food rationing.

In July 1945 Winston Churchill went to the country; the voters gave Attlee's Labour Party an overwhelming victory over the Tories. Nurse and I worked away at the surgery; I enjoyed my work even though at times the noise of the children crying would make me feel like screaming. The only place I could relax from it all was when I sat down at the edge of the loch and watched the waves gently lapping against the stones. Sometimes it would depend on the mood she was in, I would have to sit further up the bank, otherwise I would get soaked to the skin. When she was angry and the waves came roaring in still I loved her in all her different moods. Rusty also got to understand her moods and like me respected them. September was my birthday month; I would be twenty. I felt old for my years so much had happened to me in the last year. The effects of all the disasters and sadness would always be with me, in some way, till the day I died. When the boys come home I'd get them to tidy the garden. I had meant to buy fruit bushes in February but clean forgot all about them. My mind was kept busy with so many other things; a lot not very pleasant either.

At last the end of the month came and Vera and the boys arrived home. They all looked so well and sunburnt and weather beaten. Rusty went mad when he saw the boys and the boys went mad with Rusty. Vera just laughed, 'Oh, it's lovely to be home again, Mary.'

'Yes,' I said, 'you lot will be dying of hunger, I'll make a cup of tea then we can all go to the village for messages after you have had a rest. Listening to the laughter out there the boys don't seem to be tired at all.'

'As they slept the whole of the train journey they certainly should not be.'

'We will leave them a while, Vera, while we have our tea.' I was so happy to have them home again.

Vera wanted to know if there had been any strange happenings. Just then the boys came bursting in for tea and I said I'd tell her all about them when we had more privacy. While we were having our tea Ewan announced that Billy is walking out with the farmer's daughter, a bonnie looking lass and Mr Smith invited him in to the big house just like one of the family.'

'You will have to invite her here, Billy, the next time you are home. Tell her she will always be welcome to come at any time.' Billy's face just turned red and he never said a word, just gave his brother a warning look. Vera changed the conversation and Billy and his girlfriend were forgotten.

It was a lovely summer day as the four of us made our way to the shops; the boys of course walked faster than Vera and I. I told Vera everything about the boat landing just below our house and the two men getting out. Also, how Rusty and I were at the foot of the rope ladder which they had flung over the wall into my garden. Then when I told her about my setting Rusty on the man as he came down the ladder and Rusty biting into his legs before he disappeared back over the wall she roared with laughter.

'Good for you, Mary, if it was those MacPhersons I hope their legs will rot.'

'That's not all, Vera, when Constable Drummond stood on the steps to look over our garden wall he saw a man lying on the rocks below. When the lifeguard went to bring him back they found he was already dead. Shot in the head; he was a stranger to the village.'

'Oh my God, Mary, somebody is trying to incriminate you. I suppose the men intended to throw the body over your garden wall then maybe hide it in the garden shed then after that thinking that you would be still at work phone the police then you would be charged with murder. Well you certainly foiled their plot.'

Then I told Vera about the encounter with MacPherson in the forest and about Rusty's reaction to Mary Kate Bell which made her worry even more.

We continued on to the shops with Vera telling me not to buy vegetables or meat as she had brought plenty. She thought it would be nice if we could all have an orange and I promised to ask Mr Walsh if he had any. Mr Walsh came to the counter to serve me himself, his daughter Gillian was slyly eyeing Billy. I gave him a list of what I wanted. He disappeared to the back of the shop;

when I looked over at Gillian she was busy chatting Billy up. I thought to myself, you are wasting your time girl, he is already spoken for. Mr Walsh came back with my order; after I had paid him I said, 'you don't by any chance have oranges.'

He stood still for a few minutes then he said, 'I can spare four, Miss Mary, but don't say a word to anyone.' When he came back with the oranges I paid for them and thanked him for being so kind.

We made our way to the bakers; I asked the boys and Vera what they would like. The three of them shouted Scotch pies and cream cakes. I ordered four pies and four cakes, bread and scones. The lovely smell in the bakery made us all feel hungry.

As we set off for home coming towards us was Father Joseph. 'I haven't seen you in church lately, Mary, anything wrong?'

'Plenty, Father, I have been ill. I meant to come and see you when I felt better.'

'Yes, I heard from Constable Drummond about that poor young man; when I have time next week I'll come up for a chat,' then he looked at Billy and Ewan. 'Don't say that's your two young brothers, Mary? They sure have grown.' Billy who would be 18 years in a few weeks time was six feet tall and, like his father, very good looking. The only thing was he never inherited his dad's jolly nature. Ewan was very tall for his age but in looks he took after Mum. Then Father spoke to Vera telling her how well she looked and he asked after Hector and Sarah.

'I do hope, Vera, nobody else crosses our paths till we get home except of course a black cat, it might bring me some luck.'

The boys ran ahead of us carrying the bags. The fresh air was making me feel hungry. We arrived home and got the kettle going. The pies went in the oven. While we were waiting Billy and Ewan took Rusty outside in the garden. 'Oh, Vera I meant to tell you not to mention to the boys about the dead body on the rocks, I don't want them worrying.'

'I would not have mentioned it anyway.'

I set the table for us all and it wasn't long before Vera had the tea ready; the pies were lovely and hot. While I was eating mine I thought I should have bought one for Rusty. He was sitting patiently in his basket, the lovely smell of the pies driving him crazy. I left a wee bit for him. Vera and the boys noticed what I had done so they left some also, Vera saying, 'you sure spoil that dog, Mary, but I can't blame you, he is beautiful. What do you do to keep his coat shining like that?'

'Nothing much, Vera, I just give him a good brushing down every Sunday, the only day I have time.' The boys went up to their room followed by Rusty and Vera and I went out into the garden. We sat on the seat for a little while then Vera said she would like to see over the garden wall. I didn't think it was a good idea but called for the boys to fetch the step-ladders. Billy held the steps while Vera climbed up. When she reached the top she put her hand up to her mouth and let out one big scream. Billy went half way up the steps and helped her down. We sat her on the grass, her face was the colour of death. Ewan went to make his way up the ladder; I shouted to him to come straight down again.

'Billy run in and bring a chair and Ewan you go and get a glass of water for Vera. Hurry up the pair of you.' After Billy brought the chair the pair of us helped Vera on to it; Ewan brought the glass of water. 'Now you, Billy, run and get Dr McKinnon, you, Ewan, tell Constable Drummond to come right away. Mind and lock the front door after you; Rusty come here at once.' Rusty came and lay on the grass beside us. I tried to give Vera a sip of water but it was hopeless, she could not stop sobbing.

At last Doctor arrived along with Nurse Duncan. After Dr McKinnon examined her he said she was suffering from severe shock and he thought it better if she was sent to hospital straight away. 'I'll take her in my car, Mary, Nurse Duncan will come also. We will let you know how things are when we get back.'

I sat down on the chair that Vera had just left and started crying. Constable Drummond just took one look at me then he climbed up to the top of the steps with his pen and notebook. He spent a long time gazing over the wall and making notes. When he came down he would not tell me what had so frightened Vera, but advised me to stay indoors and keep the boys with me.

After he was gone I told Billy and Ewan to run down to the post office and send a telegram to Sarah. Billy read the piece of paper I handed to him then he looked at me as if I was out of my mind. On it I had written our password between us if ever I needed her right away. 'Stop standing there, Billy, hurry up, I'll lock the doors till you come back.' The two boys ran down the road as if the Devil was after them. Rusty had settled down in his basket. I sat in the rocking chair saying a prayer for Vera, hoping by tomorrow she would have her speech back again. I was beginning to think somebody was trying to frighten me and the family out of my house. I felt like trying to find out how I could reach the rocks at the back of our house and find out for myself what Vera saw. Our big house stood at the edge of a steep face of solid rock; I don't know how it looked if I was in a small boat on the loch at the foot of the crags; if Constable Drummond is busy elsewhere this evening maybe Billy and Ewan will come with me and climb the rocks. I went up to the boys' bedroom to have a good look but it was hopeless, the garden wall was at least eleven feet in height which gave our garden a great deal of privacy. Now the way things were happening our garden was no longer private.

I went downstairs to the kitchen again, sat in the rocking chair waiting for Billy and Ewan to return. The way things were going the boys will be glad to get back to Angus. A loud knock on the door brought me to my feet; as I made my way to the door I thought that will be Billy and Ewan back but instead standing on the doorstep was Father Joseph. The first thing he said was, 'Dr McKinnon is just back from the hospital. He told me all that had happened to Vera; I am sorry Mary, as if you have not had enough already. Where are Billy and Ewan?'

I told Father Joseph the boys had gone to send a telegram to Sarah asking her to come. Father agreed that was the right thing to do. Then he gave me the good news that Vera had settled down and was sleeping peacefully. I made some tea for Father then went to the door to see if the boys were coming. In the distance I could see someone. As the figures came nearer I recognised it was Billy and Ewan. I heaved a sigh of relief. The pair of them were out of breath when they reached the door. After they were inside I put my fingers to my lips and nodded towards the kitchen; 'for goodness sake the pair of you, come into the kitchen, take a seat and get your breath back. Tea is made, I'll get you both a cup.' Billy and Ewan just nodded towards Father Joseph, who went on drinking his tea. I cut the boys a big slice of fruit cake. Father's face was expressive when he saw the cake; 'now, Father, you only wanted a chocolate biscuit. If you had asked for a piece of cake you would have got it.'

'Please, Mary, can I have a piece to take home with me?' When we had all finished our tea I asked the boys what kept you so long, was the post office extra busy? The two of them together said it was busy. Rusty by this time had wakened up. When he jumped up out of his basket he was on the verge of making his way to the door when he noticed Father Joseph sitting in my rocking chair. At first he gave a loud bark; as I patted his back and said it's all right boy, go and say hello to Father he just gave two barks then made his way to the door. Billy opened it for him. I was quite surprised Rusty didn't tear Father to pieces when he saw him sitting in my chair.

'Is that the little pup your Auntie Kate gave you the first time you visited her?'

'Yes he is.' Then Father asked what on earth do you feed him on?

'Just whatever I am cooking for myself.'

Father said he would call at the hospital to see Vera in the evening and looked meaningfully at the fruit cake. I took the hint and cut him a slice, hesitated for a moment then cut a slice for his housekeeper. With a big smile he blessed me. I locked the door after he left. The boys were roaring with laughter as they played with Rusty. It was nice and relaxing just watching the three of them. At last the boys and Rusty came in again. I had filled up Rusty's food dishes for him and he could not get to them quickly enough. When the boys had settled down I asked them what had kept them so long, I was beginning to get worried. It was Billy who told the whole story.

'After we came out of the post office a lot of the villagers were standing in a group at the jetty. Ewan and I wondered what was going on so the pair of us ran down to see what all the fuss was about. The coastguard boat was standing at the jetty with Constable Drummond and three other young policemen; also Dr McKinnon. We pushed our way to the front of the crowd to get a better view; when Drummond saw us he came off the boat straight over to us and said quietly, "come with me". Ewan and I could not do anything but follow him. When we were a few yards away from the crowd he shouted at us; "I thought I told you two to stay indoors, you don't mean to say you have left your sister alone in that big house. Get up there the pair of you at once," so there was nothing but to run all the way home. We were glad Father Joseph was with you Mary. So Ewan and I were not any the wiser. Where the boat was going I don't know, it must have been something serious because you could hear a pin drop, the big crowd were so silent.'

I wished I could see Nurse Duncan; no sooner had I said it that a loud knock at the door brought me to my feet. I opened the door slowly and was pleased to see Nurse Duncan. She came into the kitchen, 'hello, boys,' she said, 'and you too Rusty, now give me a paw, just look what I have got for you.' Rusty understood every word, his tail wagging like mad. Nurse opened a paper bag and pulled out a bone, Rusty's friend for life.

'And what have you got for us boys, Nurse?' Ewan said.

'Oh, you will not believe it but I have a bar of toffee for the three of you, you don't think I was going to leave your sister out of all the fun.' We all started laughing at the same time.

'Nurse, I do love you.'

'Be off with you and sit down while I give you the news about Vera. I promised her I would run you and the boys to the hospital tomorrow to visit her.'

'It will have to be in the afternoon, after Father Joseph blesses our garden, he said he would come after last Mass.'

'I would not be free anyway, Mary, till the afternoon and before you go to bed tonight you have to take these two pills to give you a good night's sleep, "doctors orders". Remember, Mary, and take them, you have had a shock also.'

Nurse said she was gasping for a cup of tea. While I was making it, the subject of my getting a telephone in was discussed. Nurse and Dr McKinnon thought it would be useful in emergencies. The boys greeted the idea with such enthusiasm I could visualise the bills being enormous. Still, it seemed a good idea.

Father Joseph, on his way out, had sneakily told Nurse about the fruit cake and chocolate biscuits so, of course, she wanted some too. When she was finished she said, 'that was good Mary, I feel ready to do battle again.'

I knew the two sides of Nurse Duncan's nature, she could be the gentlest of people when attending the very sick people but woe betide anyone who got on the wrong side of her. Dr McKinnon and I knew only too well but both of us thought the world of her, so did Rusty. As she was leaving she said, 'mind, boys, look after your sister the short stay you are home, and mind, Mary, be sure to take those two tablets before you go to bed; see you all tomorrow afternoon.'

I went with Nurse to the door and thanked her for coming up.

'It was worth it, Mary, I still have the taste of that lovely cake in my mouth, bye, Mary.' I shut and locked and bolted the door for the night.

CHAPTER 9

When I woke the next morning it was ten o'clock. I just could not believe that was the time but I felt a lot better. The boys had got the big range going, kettle boiling and Billy had even made porridge. In fact it was better than I ever made. They had had their breakfast and fed Rusty. It was a different side of the boys I was seeing, the two of them able to stand on their own two feet. If Mum and Dad had been alive they would have been as proud of them as I was. I hurried with my breakfast, cleared the table, washed the dishes then hurried upstairs to get ready for church. Billy and Ewan were sitting waiting for me when I arrived down. It was a lovely calm morning as we set out for church, the three of us walking smartly down the road together. I walked between my tall good looking brothers; it's funny I thought to myself how all the family were so tall, even Sarah and Vera yet at 19 years I was only 5 feet 2 inches. Still it didn't seem to bother the rest of the family so why should I worry. At last we reached the church.

I led the way to our own pew; it was empty thank goodness. If it had been the 9 a.m. Mass the place would have been crowded with the MacPhersons, my sister Nan's children, all eight of them. Instead of saying my prayers I was thinking of those poor orphans. I paid attention to what Father Joseph was saying and said a prayer for all the lost souls especially my parents, my sister Nan and the two unknowns Sarah and I had buried; may they all rest in peace. Billy gave me a nudge, 'Communion time,' he said. When I got back to my seat instead of saying all the prayers I meant to say my mind wandered to what was it Vera had seen to upset her so. I hoped by the time we saw her in the afternoon she would be speaking again. God, I needed to say some prayers before leaving the church.

At last the service was over; we were the last to get out of the church. Father Joseph was standing at the door. He promised to be up in about an hour. Ewan remembered that Father Joseph had blessed the house shortly after Mum and Dad had died and wondered why he was coming again. I told him it was to bless the garden.

I prepared a quick lunch of scrambled eggs and toast, then put the leg of lamb in the oven to cook slowly for the evening meal. We had just finished when Father Joseph arrived. 'If you don't mind, Mary, I'll just go straight away and bless the garden.' I went out with him; as he was leaving I asked him to give the garden seat and the ground under it a special blessing. He gave me a funny look, shook his head and carried on blessing the seat and ground. 'I'll have to go, Mary, I have a sick call to make on the other side of the loch.' The next minute we heard the hoot of Nurse's car.

The three of us made our way to the car. I sat at the front with Nurse, the boys at the back, their long legs a bit cramped. 'Did you get a good night's sleep, Mary?'

'I certainly did, in fact I slept in.'

'That's fine, will you be well enough, Mary, to come to work tomorrow?'

'Of course, Nurse, last night's sleep did me the world of good.'

We arrived at the hospital and my mind went back to the last time I was here visiting my dear sister Nan who had been beaten to death by that murdering husband of hers. I was glad to see Vera sitting up; her face still a bit pale. Her eyes lit up when she saw us. I sat at one side of the bed, the boys on the other. 'Oh dear, Vera, I forgot to bring you something.'

'You have brought yourselves, that's enough for me.'

All of a sudden I started crying; Vera had got her speech back, that was the most important thing for me. Billy and Ewan and Vera wondered what on earth I was crying for.

'Doctor said I would be able to go home tomorrow. I think Nurse Duncan will be running me home; she is nice, Mary, even though at times she is a bit of a bully.'

'She has a heart of gold underneath all that shouting.'

Vera just laughed then she asked the boys what they had been up to. We talked of anything at all that might keep Vera amused until Nurse Duncan came breezing into the ward, 'time to go you lot, Vera still needs a lot of rest,' then she went up to Vera and said, 'just you do as you are told, Miss.' I kissed Vera goodbye then Nurse ran us home.

'I am glad Vera is looking a lot better. Doctor thinks she needs another day in bed. I wonder, Nurse, what it was she saw to upset her so.'

Nurse just clamped up; her lips tightened when she shook her head. No more was said until we reached our house when she just said, 'see you tomorrow, Mary,' then she was off.

148

Sarah arrived home while I was still at work; Billy came into the surgery to give me the news. Nurse Duncan saw Billy and she asked if anything was wrong? When she was told why Billy was there she had a look in the waiting room then said, 'just go home with your brother; I'll take over, there are not many patients waiting to see doctor.' I grabbed my coat and hat and made my way home with Billy. The sight of Billy reminded me that he and Ewan should have been back at work. I said they would have to go back next day and would get a certificate for Vera from Dr McKinnon.

Sarah was sitting in the garden when I arrived home. I gave her a hug and kiss. Sarah didn't seem too pleased at being sent for. 'The head staff at the office are none too pleased at the amount of leave I have had lately, Mary, so please don't send any more telegrams for me in the future. I'll need to travel back tomorrow, you forget I have got Hector's illness to worry me, also.'

'If you say so, Sarah, I won't bother you again.' I was pleased the boys were up in their room and never heard what Sarah had just said.

She rose from the chair and said she better get back to Hector's house, her lunch was waiting for her. Without even asking about Vera she was off down the road to the MacLean's house. I could have cried but thought if that's how she is going to behave we were better off without her. She even left to go back to Inverness without as much as a goodbye to Vera, me or the boys. I wondered what the MacLeans had told her for her to behave the way she did.

I saw Billy and Ewan off to Angus early next morning before I started work. I never saw Sarah, in fact it was to be ten years before I saw her again. Nurse Duncan brought Vera home; it was to be the following week before she went back to the farm. The night before she left home I asked her what was it she saw on the craigs that day. With tears in her eyes she said, 'when I reached the top of the steps I saw the body of a man; his head had been split on a sharp piece of rock. He was covered with blood.' I had to hurry to the toilet where I was violently sick.

When I felt a bit better I went back to Vera and put my arms around her shoulders and said, 'pray God you will get the strength to try and forget the horrible experience you have been through. Oh, Vera, when you were in hospital I got the garden blessed. All going well tomorrow I'll see you off at the station, take care dear.'

Next day after work the large house seemed empty except of course for my faithful friend Rusty. I thought to myself so long as I have him I'll never feel lonely. Constable Drummond visited me after I had arrived home from work. Rusty was lying in the garden so he was quite safe. 'I've come about that dead

149

man Vera saw on the rocks. It was Donald's brother, James. The rest of the police and I have come to the conclusion that he was trying to climb your garden wall and break into your house but the craigs being so slippy and dangerous he must have fallen and cracked his head on the sharp rocks.'

'What on earth was he wanting in my house? My parents died penniless and starved to death. There is nothing here of any value.'

'That's what puzzling us, we had to go and bring his father over in the police launch to identify the body. We are still trying to trace the boy's parents, the one that was murdered. I think the best thing to deal with those steep craigs is to seal them off from the public.' He touched his cap and was off.

I called Rusty in, locked and bolted both doors then settled down to make my tea. I was quite surprised at the news Constable Drummond gave me. Later, Nurse Duncan told me it was the MacPherson's boat I had seen drawn ashore beneath my house. The police thought that they were involved in the murder of that young man who was found on the craigs but no way could they prove it. The whole clan of them are so devious. Well, I thought, it was up to the police to catch whoever did it.

On Sunday as I was leaving church after 11.30 a.m. Mass Flora, Hector's sister was waiting for me at the door. 'I'll walk home with you, Mary. Mum got a letter from Hector; he was discharged from hospital last week. He says he walks with a slight limp, nothing serious. Mum also says he is being posted as a diplomat to the Canadian Embassy. Sarah and he are flying out to Canada next week. Dad and Mum are going to London to see them off.' By this time we had reached Flora's house and she shouted 'cheerio' and went indoors.

I could not see the road as my eyes were blinded with tears. Sarah hadn't the decency to write me a note, I had to get the news second-hand from her sister-in-law. Flora must have purposely waited at the church door to give me the news. I was beginning to wonder what the world was coming to. After I had lunch I made my way to the parlour, sat at Dad's desk and started going through all his papers. Most of them were unpaid bills but I was mystified by a large document about the house. According to the layout of the house on paper there should be a cellar but even as children none of us knew about it. I laid the plan on the floor and tried to pinpoint the actual spot it should be. The more I studied it the less I could understand it. I put it away till Billy would be home, maybe he could make some sense out of it. I also came across the plan of the grounds surrounding the house; in fact the main road according to the way I read it cut through our property. I put that paper in a safe place, also.

Rusty came into the parlour, needing to be let out. 'OK, I'll take you for a nice walk.' At the moment of the word 'walk' he went mad. I hurriedly flung on my coat and hat then the pair of us were off out into the bright sunlight. The road was quite deserted and for a while I kept Rusty on the lead. Just as we were passing Nurse Duncan's house she rapped the window pane and beckoned me to come in. When Rusty and I went inside we found Nurse baking. What a mess. Flour all over herself, on her face and hair. To crown it all, nearly all of the kitchen floor was covered with flour, also. When I saw the state she was in I roared with laughter. Nurse wondered what there was to laugh about. I took the mirror from the kitchen window ledge and put it in front of her.

'Oh, Mary, help me tidy up at once, I would die if Doctor McKinnon saw me like this. I was trying to make a few scones.'

That set me off laughing again, I could not stop. The mess of the place all for the sake of a few scones. 'Come on, Nurse, I'll help you clean up.' I took my coat and hat off, rolled up my sleeves and set to work to clean up the mess. 'Well, Nurse,' I said, 'you are the best in your medical profession but you sure are a rotten baker.' That set the pair of us laughing again.

We had tea and bemoaned the rationing which put margarine rather than butter on our toast. Afterwards, we walked a little way and I asked if there was any news of Donald's brother James and his funeral. Nurse said there would have to be an inquest and the police were thinking of putting a DANGER sign at the foot of the craigs. She wanted to know if I had done anything about getting the phone in and was pleased to hear I expected it installed in a month.

Back home again, I wrote to Vera. I supposed now the war was over all the Yanks would be returning home. Maybe Vera would go to America with Fred Turner, that's to say if it was serious between them. Then there was Billy walking out with the farmer's daughter. I wondered if anything would come of that. In September 1945, I would be 21 and I had never really had a boyfriend. I never had the time to go out and enjoy myself. I hadn't met what people call Mr Right. The way I lived I wondered if I ever would.

At the surgery the next day Nurse Duncan spoke to me in whispers about a body of a young girl found in a shallow grave in the forest on MacPherson's land. The government had ordered a certain amount of trees to be felled for timber. It was one of the lumberjacks who had discovered the grave. I just carried on with my work as if nothing had happened but I knew who the person was because it was Hector, Sarah and I who gently laid her to rest there that dreadful night that Hector drove us to that forest. I didn't know then that it was on the MacPherson's land. Maybe Hector knew a lot more then he pretended to know; he sure was a deep one. He was in Canada out of it all, safe and sound with Sarah. At lunch time Nurse said she would run me home. As soon as I sat in the car she told me that Constable Drummond had sent for assistance, also he had sent word to Mrs Duffy as he thought the dead girl might be Maria Duffy. When I reached the house I could not get in quick enough. I let Rusty out in the garden, my mind in a daze; 'dear God don't let them trace anything back to my house.' I made a cup of tea and tried to pull myself together.

It was when I was getting ready to go back to work I noticed the letter lying on the mat; I just glanced at it and put it in my pocket to read later. Back at the surgery a notice was on the door; 'no surgery this afternoon'. I had my own key; Nurse was in the back. 'Oh, Mary, Doctor was called over to the MacPherson's farm this afternoon; the old lady had a heart attack, that's why surgery was cancelled so off you go home and relax.' Little did she know what was racing through my mind.

'Thanks, Nurse, I'll do a bit of shopping first before I go home,' then I was out in the fresh air again wondering what was going to happen next. I made my way to the shops. I needed bread, a Scotch pie and a nice cream cake. One thing where Hector and Sarah were, there would be no shortage of food. No food rations or clothes coupons to trouble them. Sarah had the style, she would fit nicely into her new world with Hector; good luck to both of them.

After I had finished my shopping I was making my way down to the loch when I ran into Mary Kate Bell. 'Mary,' she said, 'did you hear about the dead body they found this morning on the MacPherson's land. Dad was just telling me about how that poor girl disappeared without trace; Maria Duffy was her name. We were all wondering if it could be her; of course Dad says she worked as a barmaid before he took over the hotel. Anyway he would not know anything about her.'

'How long is it, Mary Kate, since your dad took the hotel?'

'I think it would be about three years, I am really not sure. I'll ask him when I get home.'

I said, 'I was away from the village for three and a half years so I really would not know her or what she was like. Now I am going down to the loch to rest awhile and get peace. Bye, Mary Kate, see you later.'

I made my way down to the water edge. The loch was in the same mood as myself, turbulent. I sat down and read my letter. It was from Vera saying she was marrying Fred Turner in three weeks time, also enclosed was the wedding

152

invitation. They were getting married in St Mary's R.C. Church. Mr Smith was arranging the wedding breakfast. 'Don't let me down, Mary, I need you as my bridesmaid, bring Rusty also. Billy and Ewan are quite excited. After the wedding we will be sailing on the *Queen Mary* to America. To tell you the truth, Mary, I am beginning to take cold feet wondering if I am doing the right thing. I do wish Mum was here to help me; write soon and let me know.' I thought to myself, of course I would go, dear knows how long it will be before I would see her again. Vera would be the third sister married. Once she was in America with her new husband there would be just Billy and Ewan. I sat beside the loch for a while watching the waves swirling around just like the thoughts in my brain. Thank goodness Vera's wedding would keep me busy during the coming three weeks. I popped into the post office and sent a telegram 'delighted to come to your wedding, Mary'.

Rusty was waiting patiently at the door when I opened it. 'Come on then, boy, I'll let you out.' I did the usual things, logs on the range, filled the big black kettle and placed it on the hob, put my pie in the oven thinking I should have got one for Rusty. I opened a small tin of Spam for myself, stupid fool that I am. When the tea was ready and my sandwiches made up I took the pie out of the oven and gave it to Rusty. It wasn't long in disappearing. I enjoyed my tea and as soon as everything was cleared away I wrote to Auntie Kate. Since I came home two and a half years ago there seemed to be nothing but deaths surrounding me.

When I arrived at work next day, I told Nurse about Vera's wedding; also I would need time off.

'That's all right, Mary, you are due a week's holiday anyway, when is the wedding?'

'In three weeks time, in fact I was thinking of going to Oban for my outfit.'

'No need. There's a lovely ladies' shop just opened on the other side of the loch. Get Mr Ross to run you over in his boat. He doesn't charge very much. I'll tell you what, on Saturday both of us will go over, I'll speak to Mr Ross myself.'

Saturday turned out a glorious day; the loch was beautiful and calm as Mr Ross's boat sped across the water to the other side. We told Mr Ross to come back for us in two hours then climbed the hill to the hotel for tea before going shopping. It was the hotel we had gone to for Christmas dinner. Funny how it just seemed like yesterday. Nurse ordered tea and cakes as soon as we sat down. Our table looked out over the loch. 'That's your house, Mary, up on the hill.' It took me a while to finally recognise it in the distance. Funny looking at it from that side of the loch, it looked a lot bigger than I thought. My mind just then went back to the cellar of my house wondering what secrets it held. The cakes were delicious, I wondered where they got them from. 'I'll pay, Nurse.'

'You will do nothing of the kind.'

'But you paid Mr Ross coming over.'

'So what, come on, we better start shopping.'

The clothes in the new shop were out of this world. The sort of suits that Sarah wore. Nurse told the young assistant I was looking for a bridesmaid's outfit for a church wedding. She picked a beautiful sky blue dress and jacket. 'The changing room is here, try it on. I'll get your friend for you.' The material itself was simple luxury; I tried it on and it fitted me like a glove. I didn't realise I had such a tiny waist. The lovely shade of blue suited me. I stepped outside the changing room to let Nurse see me.

'Oh Mary you're beautiful. Yes,' she said to the assistant, 'she will take that.'

'I'll see about a hat, bag and gloves, Miss, to tone with them. The shoes, Miss, you will get in the next room.' The assistant decided on a white hat with a ribbon matching the dress, white shoes, bag and gloves. At last we were finished. The whole lot came to two pounds, ten shillings. Thank goodness I had enough money to pay. We made our way to Mr Ross's boat. It took me all my time to keep back the giggles I felt when I saw the expression of amazement on his face when he saw Nurse and I were laden with boxes and parcels. He helped us into the boat then he said, 'I'll drop you both near your house, Mary, if that's all right with you Nurse?'

'That will do just fine, Mr Ross, it's a bit much for Mary to carry all those parcels. I suppose you know Mary's sister Vera is getting married in three weeks time.'

'I never heard it called in the church on Sunday.'

'No, Mr Ross, she is getting married in Angus.'

No more was said till we reached the other side of the loch. Mr Ross handed us our parcels. We thanked him then made our way up to my house. Nurse, who said she was feeling her age, came in for a rest and a cup of tea. She and Rusty greeted each other joyously. 'When I see Rusty, Mary, I often wish I had got a dog years ago. Then again it would have been neglected as I would have been too busy delivering babies. The poor beast would have starved to death.'

Nurse prattled away happily until she had to leave. She told me I was going to make a lovely bridesmaid and perhaps it wouldn't be too long before I was a bride.

154

I had plenty to think about after she left. Had Billy and Ewan enough money to buy new suits for the wedding? I wrote to them, enclosing two pounds each. Then I wrote to Vera asking for the name of a hotel where I could stay the night. Finally, there was a letter to write to Auntie Kate. Then, to cap it all, Constable Drummond arrived with the news that Vera would have to attend the inquest on James MacPherson next Friday.

The day of the inquest arrived and I went with Vera. The coroner was very sympathetic. Vera just had a few questions to answer; the verdict was death by misadventure. Vera and I were allowed to leave by the side door. Constable Drummond drove us home. I practically had to carry Vera upstairs to bed, made the tea and slipped two aspirins into it. She would never taste them, I had put plenty of sugar in her cup. After a good sleep she would be back to her normal self and ready to return to Angus. I thought to myself, why is it it's always me who has to take the blunt end of the stick?

In the morning Vera was still asleep, I went to early 9 a.m. Mass glad to get out in the fresh air. When I made my way to our family pew it was already filled with the MacPherson's children, my sister Nan's children. I told two of them to move over to their grandfather's pew then I knelt down to say my prayers my thoughts on Vera's wedding. What sort of young man was Fred Turner? I had heard people say that you never know a man until you have lived with him. I hoped he would take care of her.

At last Mass was over; I waited behind to speak to Father about the banns for Vera's wedding. When I discussed it with Father he thought it better that he should announce Vera's and Fred's coming wedding. 'After all, this church is really her parish. By rights,' he said, 'the couple should see me first.'

'Well, it's not easy for Fred as he is still with the American Air Force. Vera, by the way, is at home just now; she had to attend the inquest on James MacPherson's death. I left her in bed, Father, she was very upset when we arrived home yesterday; also, she has to travel back to Angus this afternoon.'

'In that case, Mary, I'll pop in this afternoon and see her, bye now Mary.'

I made my way home hoping that Vera would be well enough to travel back to Angus. I was glad when I reached the door. Vera opened it for me; she was looking her old self again. 'Breakfast is ready for you, Mary, I have had mine. Rusty has been fed and is running around mad outside.' I was quite hungry; it was scrambled eggs, dried eggs of course. I enjoyed them just the same.

'Father Joseph is coming up to see you, Vera, before you go back. Its about the banns.'

'You did not by any chance come across our birth certificates, Mary, while you were going through Dad's papers?'

'Yes, Vera, I did, I'll get yours for you.' I wasn't going to tell her I found everyone's but my own. I left the front door unlocked for Father. Vera went upstairs to pack and I made up a lunch box for her; it was a long train journey back to Angus.

Father arrived; I left him and Vera alone in the parlour to talk about her private business. After a while I went into the parlour and asked Father if he would like a cup of tea. 'Thanks, Mary, but I'll need to hurry back, Vera and I have arranged everything. She will tell you all the details herself.' I locked the door after he had left and Vera and I went into the kitchen. She thanked me for finding her birth certificate and said that Father Joseph would be calling the banns at Mass. I asked her if there was anything special she wanted as a wedding present.

'Do you know what, Mary, do you remember the lovely lace table-cloth mum had, well I would love one like that.'

'Come up to the attic, there's a big box inside the wardrobe there, I am sure it is full of linen.' The pair of us raced up the stairs giggling; sure enough the box was full of all kinds of linen sheets and beautiful hand embroidered table-cloths. 'Take your pick, Vera.' She picked a beautiful table-cloth and a pair of linen sheets.

We made a parcel of the table-cloth and sheets and tied it to Vera's case. Vera was curious to know what sort of dress I was going to wear at the wedding. Over a last cup of tea I told her the colour was sky blue but wouldn't say any more. I never mentioned about Sarah going off to Canada without a word nor that the MacLeans were keeping themselves to themselves. I saw Vera safely on the train. As soon as it turned the corner I went to the booking office and booked our first class tickets for Angus then made my way home. Once again some of the small boats on the loch had been repainted; it was nice to see some bright colours again after the drab colour that covered them during the war years. It's funny, when I had the house to myself I always felt contented; I liked to see the family then I was glad when they went back to work.

I opened the house door, grabbed Rusty's lead and as soon as I said 'walk' he was out of the door like a shot. We made our way down to the loch and Rusty ran out and in the water. He really was the picture of health. I wondered if I could start fishing, but since I came home there was no sign of Dad's fishing tackle anywhere; he used to keep it in the cupboard in the hall. I wondered what happened to it; maybe the MacPhersons helped themselves to it also. Rusty and I made our way home. I dried him when I got him in the kitchen.

After I had my tea I studied the map of the house trying to find out where the cellar lead from. The map itself was a bit complicated for me; maybe there was a sliding door in one of the ground rooms like the one that leads to the attic. I thought the parlour would be the best room; that large room with the bay windows overlooking the loch and I tried all the walls to see if there were any knobs sticking slightly out of the wall. The wallpaper in the parlour was a delicate shade of pink with tiny pink and white roses on it; it must have been lovely when it was new, but it was faded and drab like everything else in the room. I didn't realise it was so dirty looking till that afternoon. The curtains also needed to be changed. I supposed there weren't any to change with. When I got back from Vera's wedding I would arrange to get painters in and get it made respectable. The more I studied the room the more disgusted I became.

When I arrived at the surgery the next morning Doctor said that Nurse was out on call. There weren't many people in the waiting room. As the morning wore on the waiting room was getting a bit overcrowded. It's funny how everyone seemed to take ill on a Monday morning. On a Friday, pay day, the women are so busy shopping they have no time to be ill and the few men left in the village would rather head for the hotel for their usual pint than visit the doctor. At last it was lunch time. Nurse hadn't arrived back. I locked the door and said cheerio to the doctor, glad to get out, the noise of the children was beginning to give me a headache. I did some shopping – bread, pies, cakes, sausages and stewing beef then hurried home. Rusty was at the back of the door as usual, also a letter from Auntie Kate. I filled Rusty's water dish up and put his pie in the oven along with mine. While I was waiting for the pies heating I read Auntie Kate's letter. When I opened it a few postal orders fell on the floor. She said she was delighted to hear Vera was getting married and enclosed a ten pound postal order for her as a wedding gift. She also wished her and her future husband all the happiness. She was surprised to hear about the remains of that poor girl being found on the MacPherson's land; would I let her know the outcome of it. 'I do hope you are looking after yourself, enclosing twenty pounds for you. Mind and don't go short of food. How are the boys and that lovely dog of yours? Love Auntie Kate.'

That lovely dog of mine had smelt the pies and was jumping around daft. I put Rusty's pie in his dish first, that way I got peace to eat mine. I sat in the rocking chair looking out into the garden; it was getting out of control. What I really needed was someone to help me. If Ewan could come home for good and do all the odd jobs I needed done it would be a great help to me, then again it would not be fair to Ewan; he was young and was entitled to live his own life not tied to my apron strings.

I was late for work and got quite a few sullen looks from the older women even though I was only a few minutes late. I just smiled and opened the door for them. Nurse wasn't there and it was nearly closing time when Nurse arrived back; she went straight into doctor's office, the both of them speaking in low voices.

At last she came over to me and said that's Donald's mother had died. 'Of course, she has never really recovered from the stroke she took that day the grave was discovered. I left Father Joseph there speaking to the children; they are lovely children, Mary, that little Helen is so like your sister Nan. Nan will never be dead as long as that little girl is alive. She is the spitting image of her mother.'

For no reason at all I started crying.

'Oh I am sorry, Mary, I didn't mean to upset you.'

'It's all right Nurse, for a minute my mind went back to the day we lost Nan. She was so young; just 25 years. She never really lived.'

'Are there many patients left?'

'Just three.'

'Good, I'll run you home as soon as you are finished.' I was glad of the lift home as I was feeling very tired.

CHAPTER 10

I was glad when the day finally arrived for Rusty and I to set out on the long journey to Angus even though it was pelting with rain and the loch was covered with heavy mist. As usual the train was packed with service men and women. I was glad when Rusty and I arrived in our first class compartment. I laid a towel on the seat for Rusty, put my small case on the rack and settled down for the long journey ahead. I had sent Vera's ten pound postal order on to her with Auntie Kate's best wishes. It was great just to sit and watch the beautiful scenery as the train sped swiftly on its way. The guard came and checked my tickets, all the time keeping an eye on Rusty. I asked the guard to let me know when we were at my destination. Rusty jumped up on to his towel and soon we were both sound asleep. When I woke Rusty had his big paws on my lap and was looking up at me with those lovely big pleading eyes of his. The train had stopped at a small station and the guard popped his head round the door. 'Here we are, lassie. I'll take your case, you attend to your dog.' I followed him off the train and tipped him.

Only three other passengers got off the train besides me. They had quickly disappeared and Rusty and I were left standing alone. Just then an old banger of a car came round the corner. A stout middle-aged man came out of it and made his way towards me. As he drew closer he put me in mind of my dad; the same brisk walk, rosy cheeks and a big wide smile on his face. Before he reached me he held out his big hand and said 'you will be Mary, Vera and the boys' sister. I am Mr Smith, sorry I am a bit late and please excuse the state of the car, that daughter of mine ran off with my good car.'

'Don't worry, Mr Smith, Rusty and I will be fine.'

He looked down at Rusty, 'that's a lovely dog you have there, I think I'll hide mine till you go home.' I could not help but laugh my head off. 'My, Mary, you sure look bonnie when you laugh. You have such a lovely smile; did anyone ever tell you that before?'

'I am afraid not, Mr Smith.'

'The name is John, cut out the mister.'

I felt at ease with the boss of the farm right away, so did Rusty. Both of us settled in the old banger, me in the front beside John and Rusty in the back seat. It took us about an hour before we eventually reached the farm. I was amazed at the size of the house, in fact it looked more like a castle.

'Come on, Mary, into the kitchen, that's the room everybody uses, and I better hide that lovely dog of yours from Catherine or she will want to keep it. I'll get Patsy to show you to your room. Rusty will be quite safe outside in the back yard.'

Patsy was a bonnie healthy girl of sixteen; she looked older than her years. Lovely rosy cheeks, very dark blue eyes and short black curly hair. She gave me a shy smile as she showed me up a long flight of beautifully carpeted stairs then, at the end of a long corridor, she opened the door for me and said 'this is your room, Mary, I hope you will be comfortable. I'll bring you up a cup of tea then you can rest; don't worry about that lovely dog of yours, the master is looking after him,' then she shut the door.

I could not believe my eyes as I looked round the room; the big four poster bed with the beautiful lace linen sheets and pillow cases to match, a pink satin bedspread and quilt to match. The dressing table at the window had hand crocheted mats with mirror brush and comb silver edged. The wash stand had a large bowl and a jug filled with warm water, the soap dish beside; hanging on the rail were two pink towels. Vera and the boys had told me they lived in huts and here I was in this beautiful bedroom. A knock on the door brought me back to earth; it was Patsy with a tray with a small pot of tea, milk and sugar and two small hot scones thick with jam. 'Dinner will be at seven. You will have the chance to see your sister and brothers after dinner. Master says you are to have dinner with him and Catherine.'

I enjoyed my tea; the hot scones just melted in my mouth; I thought to myself, no shortage of food here. When I was finished I filled the basin with the warm water, undressed and washed then brushed my hair, lay on the bed, pulled the satin quilt on top of me then fell asleep. It was comfortable in that lovely bed.

Patsy standing at the foot of the bed shaking my legs woke me up; 'you will have to hurry, Mary, dinner is about ready.' I jumped out of the bed, splashed water on my face to wake me up then pulled on one of Auntie Kate's lovely dresses, brushed my hair then made my way down the long staircase. Patsy was waiting for me at the foot of the stairs and she led the way to the dining room. John and his daughter Catherine were already seated at the large polished table.

'Come, Mary, sit beside me,' John said. He got up and held the chair out for me; 'what's this I hear, slept all afternoon; you must be tired.'

'Well, John, I am a working girl, the days are not long enough for all the odd jobs I have to do after I come home from surgery. I was thinking of getting a help in at the weekend to do the housework. I seem to be tired all the time.'

'Why don't you stay on longer than tomorrow. You are welcome to stay on as long as you like.' Catherine gave her dad a quick look then started playing with her fork.

'Thanks, John, but I have to head back home tomorrow after the wedding, I have my own house to attend to; also my work.'

No more was said; another young girl came and served the soup course. I had a proper chance to size up the table; it was beautifully set. The silver and the crystal glasses sparkled in the late evening sunshine; the salt and pepper cruets were like the ones the Ramsays used. Vera and the boys never once mentioned anything about Mr Smith's wealth; of course, maybe they were never in this part of the house. Whoever the cook was, she certainly was good; the lamb chops were cooked to perfection along with all the trimmings. Vera and the boys were right when they said they were well fed. I was glad when dinner was over as I wanted to see Vera and the boys and poor Rusty. Inwardly, I was gasping to leave the room right away but then again it would have been the height of bad manners to do so, so I just sat at the table. Catherine now and again would give me a side glance without speaking to me. I was beginning to wonder what was going on between father and daughter. In a way I felt like the fly trapped in the spider's web. At last I could stand it no longer so I stood up and said, 'excuse me, I would like to see Vera, Billy and Ewan to discuss things for tomorrow's wedding. Also I would like to see Rusty.'

'Oh that can wait till tomorrow, Mary, the workers will all be retired for the night. You know they are all up at 5 a.m.'

'But it's Vera's wedding day, you don't expect her to work tomorrow?'

'Of course I do, I expect every ounce of work out of people who are employed by me. I am afraid you won't see them till morning.' The tone of his voice had changed; Catherine just sat at the table saying nothing.

Well, I thought to myself, if that big farmer with all his wealth thought he was going to dominate me like his workers he was in for a shock. I had dealt with better men than he was with his big fat belly and false smile, I'd play him at his own game. 'In that case I'll take Rusty for a walk.'

'I am afraid, Mary, Rusty is locked up for the night.'

I just could not believe I had heard right then I shouted, 'how dare you shut my dog up; he has never been locked up before.'

'Well, there is always a first time, Mary, you are a guest in my house and while you are here it would be better if you abided by our rules.'

Here I was in this strange big house which was like a castle, practically a prisoner. I put my best smile on and pretended I didn't suspect anything wrong. 'Oh well, I suppose I'd better wait till tomorrow to see everybody; you don't mind if I go for a walk or is that out of bounds also.'

'Of course, you can go. Catherine will go with you in case you get lost.'

'By the way have you got a phone? I promised Doctor McKinnon and Nurse Duncan and Auntie Kate I would phone them from here; I gave them all your address, also Constable Drummond.'

The two of them stood still and looked at one another then John said, 'there's a phone in the village; you can phone tomorrow. Off you go now the pair of you.'

I gave Catherine a big smile and we set off briskly. Catherine made no attempt at conversation and I felt she was a guard over a prisoner. I took a good look at my surroundings as I walked ahead. All I could see was miles and miles of farming land, not a house to be seen. All at once I became afraid, even if I was to run off I knew I would not get very far. I'd have to play a waiting game to see what the pair of them were up to. 'I suppose, Catherine, we better go back, it's getting late.' She never answered me but followed me back to the house. I went straight to my room. There was no lock on the door. I didn't like the look of that, still there was a handy chair. I could jam the door with it before I went to bed. The best plan, I thought, was to sit at the window until dark, make up the bed with pillows as though I were in it and sleep underneath the bed with a cushion as a pillow. I emptied the big water jug then placed it at the edge of the bed underneath the quilt, settled down under the bed and went to sleep. If the fat farmer tried to crawl under the bed his big fat belly would prevent him.

I don't know how long I had been sleeping but a loud crash woke me up; it was the big jug breaking into a million pieces. A loud curse then a scream rent the room. He must have stood on one of the jagged broken pieces of the jug. From where I lay all I could see was two big fat feet and the rim of his striped night shirt. He was limping out of the room but he was going in the opposite way to the door. So, he had a secret way in; it was a good job it was dark otherwise he would have seen the chair jammed against the door. I got up right away, made the bed up properly, pretended it was slept in, lifted the

162

chair from the door, washed with the same water I had used yesterday, dressed for the wedding, packed my other things then sat at the window and dozed till daybreak.

At last the farm was stirring, with the tramping of heaving boots in the farmyard, the cows mooing, and the hurrying of footsteps in the house. I just sat still at the window waiting patiently for Patsy to come to my room. The knock came, it was the strange girl who served at dinner. 'I have brought you a cup of tea, Miss; Master says to be ready at 7.30 to go to the wedding, it's a bit of a journey.' I was glad of the tea, it warmed me up.

At 7.15 a.m. I made my way downstairs; the place seemed empty. I went into the kitchen. It was empty so I ran upstairs, grabbed my case, made my way to the back yard and found Rusty tied up. The rope was so short he could hardly move. I flew into the kitchen, grabbed a kitchen knife from the drawer, ran outside again and cut the rope and set Rusty free. I put his lead on to be on the safe side then the pair of us made our way to the main road. I could not understand how such a big farm could be deserted after all the hustle and bustle earlier on. There was something fishy about the whole affair. I stood at the side of the lonely road wishing some kind of transport would come into view. At last a horse and cart moved slowly towards us. There was just one man sitting with the reins in his hand. When the cart was quite near me I stepped out into the middle of the road, put my hand up to stop it. The man looked quite amazed to see me and Rusty out on the road. 'What can I do for you miss, anything wrong?'

I explained that I was supposed to be bridesmaid at my sister's wedding and had become hopelessly lost. The man was sympathetic. He knew where a wedding was to be held at a Mr Smith's farm and would take us there. After what seemed an age we arrived at the farmhouse. It was only when I failed to see any sign of Vera, Billy and Ewan I realised I was at the wrong wedding and remembered that Vera was to be married in church.

By this time I was so thoroughly bewildered and frightened I just wanted to go home. A fat man showed me to a telephone and I phoned for train times then phoned Nurse Duncan, asking her to meet me. The fat man said he would arrange for someone from the wedding party to give me a lift to the station and he would organise some food for me. I waited outside.

A young girl came out with a tray of food and a dish of water and food for Rusty; he was starving. The tea tray was set with different kinds of sandwiches, hot scones and biscuits. I had two cups of tea; I was simply parched. I left one and threepence on the tray when I was finished; it would help to pay for

Rusty's food also. At last the wedding party were leaving; the young couple ran to the car. Everybody was laughing and shouting; the stout man came over to me and said he would take me to the guests who had kindly offered to run me to the station. The car was pretty full but Rusty and I managed to squeeze in. I was nearly suffocated by Rusty who had plonked himself on top of me. When we arrived I could not get out of the car quickly enough. I turned to thank someone but they were all running to catch the train which was ready to leave. Rusty and I started running also and managed to board it as it started.

At last we were alone in our compartment; I shut the door, put the towel on the seat for Rusty, seated myself at the window and heaved a big sigh of relief. Rusty jumped up on the seat beside me and we both settled down, comfortable and at ease for the first time since I had left home. It wasn't long before the pair of us fell fast asleep. Rusty wakened me with his loud barking. When I opened my eyes the porter was frightened to come in. I grabbed hold of Rusty and told him to sit down quiet then asked the porter if anything was wrong. 'I was just going to waken you Miss to tell you this is Loch Etive when your dog flew at me.' I could not get out fast enough. As we passed the porter I slipped him a shilling and hurried off the train. Nurse Duncan was waiting for us.

'Hop in, both of you, I have a surprise for you both.'

'What I have been through the last two days I badly need one, only if it's a good one.'

'Oh it's good all right, wait till you get home.' Before we reached the house I could make out two young men standing at my door with their backs to me. Nurse stopped the car, 'that's your surprise at the door.'

As we reached the door the two young men turned to face me; it was Billy and Ewan. You could have heard my laughter at the other end of the village. Rusty went wild dancing about. 'What are you waiting at the door for?'

'Oh, Mary, it's locked and you're the only one with a key; we arrived yesterday. Nurse Duncan put us up for the night at her house.' The boys went in first and Billy picked up a letter that was lying on the mat and handed it to me. 'It's for you, Mary.' The lot of us made our way to the kitchen and we all settled down at the kitchen table.

'Well, Billy, what's the trouble that both of you are home?'

'It's a long story. I suppose you have already guessed by now that both of us have been sacked through no fault of our own. Vera and Fred had to get married a day earlier as the Queen Mary was sailing that night. All the service men and their brides had to board otherwise the American Air Force would not take any responsibility for them after that date. After Vera and Fred left for their honeymoon Mr Smith called the two of us into his office, said he no longer needed our help and we were to leave immediately; "here are your wages for a month, I want you both off my land right away." Well, Mary, what could we do but hitch a lift to the station and come home. '

'What is this man Smith like, your boss?'

'Oh he is on the fat side, he always has a big cheery smile for strangers but it hides a cruel streak in him. I have seen him ill using the young girls when they first start work. I used to feel sorry for them but there was nothing I could do as I did not want to lose my job. Vera, of course, was able for him; I think that's why before he never troubled us.'

'What sort of house does he own?'

'Oh it's enormous, in fact it's more like a castle.'

'Yes, Billy, he met me at the station yesterday; also he took me to his castle as a guest but he never told me Vera and Fred were married the day before. He said I would see you all after dinner. Poor fool me believed him; it was only after dinner I began to sense something was seriously wrong. Call it sixth sense if you like because when I asked to see you he made the excuse that you would all be in bed sleeping. He sure has plenty of money, boys, going by the beautiful furnishings in the whole house. The food also was out of this world. No, he didn't take advantage of me; it was the other way round. I sent him limping out of my bedroom.'

Both of them roared with laughter. 'How did you and Rusty manage to get to the station?'

'That, too, is a long story so it will have to do for now. How are you both for cash?'

'Oh we are fine, Mary, don't worry about us.'

I suddenly remembered the letter I put in the kitchen drawer. When I opened it I was surprised to see it was from Vera telling me not to come to the wedding. The letter must have been delivered after I had left for Angus. A knock at the door heralded the arrival of Nurse Duncan with the boys' luggage. She stayed for a cup of tea. We discussed the prospects of the boys getting work. I didn't want them staying around Loch Etive while the MacPhersons were still a danger. Then, after telling me to enjoy the rest of my holiday, Nurse went home to feast on the chicken the boys had given her.

I went into the larder to see what the boys had brought and couldn't believe my eyes. It was packed with potatoes, turnips, cabbages, leeks, a leg of lamb, two chickens, a cooked ham and goodness knows what else. Goodness only knows, too, how they had managed to carry it all. Back in the kitchen, Billy was scrambling eggs and Ewan was setting the table. I was told to sit down. It was nice to be bossed and looked after by them.

On Sunday morning the three of us made our way to 11.30 Mass. Our own pew was empty when we arrived. I looked across to the opposite seat to see if any of the MacPhersons had come but there was only the grandfather with a heavy scowl on his face. How God could suffer that look; all of a sudden I remembered where I was and asked God for his forgiveness at thinking such thoughts in his house. I suddenly looked up and noticed it was a strange priest saying Mass. Dear God, I hoped nothing has happened to Father Joseph. The first person I met was Gillian, Mr Walsh's daughter. I asked what was wrong with our own priest.

'Nothing, Mary, he is just on holiday.'

I was thankful that's all it was. Billy and Ewan came over beside me. 'I think Gillian you have already met my brothers?'

'Yes,' she said and a slight colouring of red spread over her cheeks. 'I have to go, Mary, Dad will be waiting for me, bye all', then she hurried away.

The three of us made our way home. 'I think, Billy and Ewan, if the pair of you could tidy up the garden for me while I am at work it would make me happy.'

'We were going to do that anyway; also your windows badly need cleaning and lots of other jobs we will get attended to but, for today, after lunch Ewan and I and Rusty will disappear and give you an afternoon's rest and peace.' Those two young men had more wisdom in their little finger than the whole lot in the village. I wondered who they got it from, it certainly wasn't from Dad. I thought it would be Mum; she was always the one to solve all our problems when we were young. After lunch the boys and Rusty disappeared and I went down to the loch, taking a book with me to read but most of the time I just sat at the water edge and watched all the different kinds of small and big boats sailing by with their lovely brightly coloured sails. Where my house was situated high up on the craigs gave us a lot of privacy. While I could sit and see everything that was going on, nobody could see me. That's why I loved my loch; I often looked upon her as my protector. She gave me a sense of well being. At peace with the world again I set off for home to get tea ready for the boys. When they returned they were laughing and breathless and Rusty was soaking. They had all been playing at the loch side near Nurse Duncan's house.

'I hope the pair of you have not been making a nuisance of yourselves?'

166

'No, Mary, she was with us, we had great fun.'

'Dear God Almighty what next. Was Nurse Duncan soaking also?'

'Yes, she was, so are we, we were all trying to bath Rusty in the loch.'

I turned away from the boys to try to hide a big smile on my face. I could just picture the three of them trying to keep Rusty still for a minute in the water. 'I'll see Nurse about this tomorrow. You two, in the meantime, get right upstairs and get into dry clothes; I'll attend to Rusty.' I grabbed a towel and started drying him. 'You poor soul,' I said, 'what were they doing to you?' He looked up into my face and I could have sworn that he was laughing. 'So you had a good time also,' then he just gave me a loud bark and lay in his basket.

Next morning I rushed downstairs to grab a cup of tea before heading down the road for my work. The boys must have been up early, there was a roaring fire in the range, a pot of porridge made and the tea made but no sign of the boys. I was just going to take a cup of tea but the sight of the porridge made me hungry so I helped myself to a plateful which I thoroughly enjoyed, gulped my tea then hurried down the road to work. I began to wonder what Billy and Ewan were up to. The surgery was packed when I arrived, the usual Monday morning blues. No sign of Nurse Duncan. I called first patient please.

It was about 11.30 a.m. before I could straighten my head up; there was a tap on my shoulder. It was Nurse with a cup of tea for me. I looked at her and said, 'I thought you would be in bed with a cold with the soaking you got yesterday.'

She burst out laughing. 'I had great fun with Rusty and the boys. We will need to do it again.'

'Not with my Rusty you won't.' She just went away laughing.

At lunch time I was in a hurry to get home to find out what the boys were up to. As soon as I arrived home I hurried into the kitchen. My lunch was ready for me. Spam and tomato sandwiches and two cream biscuits. I wondered where they had got the tomatoes from as I hadn't seen any in the larder. I hurried and finished my lunch then made my way out to the garden. What a transformation had taken place. It was beautiful. The boys must have been up early to turn my garden from a wilderness to this. There were brightly coloured plants and bushes covering the surrounding of the lawn, the patio tubs had new plants in them also. I hoped they hadn't used up all their money. I sat down on the garden seat then remembered to say a prayer for the little unknown infant who lay buried at my feet. I wondered what happened to Maria Duffy's body after they found it on the MacPherson's land. It was soon time for me to get to work. I locked the door then walked briskly down the road to the surgery. There were only two patients in the waiting room when I arrived. Nurse Duncan was already in the doctor's office; when she came out I asked her if she had heard any news about Maria Duffy's body.

'I am busy, Mary, I'll give you the news later' and I had to be content with that. As the afternoon wore on the waiting room became more noisy, the poor mothers all looked half starved and dejected. What a life it must be for them.

I had to make my own way home; Nurse and Doctor were called away on a case. When I opened the door I expected Rusty to meet me and Billy and Ewan at home but all was silent, even the fire was out. By now I was beginning to get really worried. I lit the fire and got the kettle boiling, I then went up to the boys' bedroom to see what clothes they would have on. It was their good suits that were missing. After I had finished my tea I sat in the rocking chair wishing the boys and Rusty would come home. As usual I dozed off; I was wakened by loud knocking on the door. Before I opened it I could hear Rusty barking; thank goodness they were home. The three of them burst into the house full of laughter.

I flew at the boys; 'where on earth have you two been all day. Do you see the time, it's 9.30 p.m.'

'Oh, Mary, we are no longer children, I'll soon be 19 and Ewan 17. You are just acting the very same way as Mum and Dad used to when they were living.'

'I was worried, Billy.'

'We are both sorry; sit down and we will make you a cup of tea and tell you where we went today. You will not believe this Mary but we all went to Mull to visit Auntie Kate; oh she was delighted to see us and especially Rusty. You know, Mary, I felt quite jealous of Rusty; did you not Ewan? Well, to cut the story short, we landed lucky; both of us are employed on the Torosay Castle gardens. It was all arranged by Auntie Kate, we have to start work in ten days time.'

'But I thought you were going to take a month's holiday.'

'Ten days is long enough for us, isn't that right Ewan? We will be glad to get back to work.'

'Before I go to bed, thanks, boys, for the lovely surprise; the garden is beautiful.'

I was making my way upstairs when Billy handed me an envelope, 'Auntie Kate told me to give you that.'

When I reached my room the first thing I did was to read Auntie Kate's letter. She was delighted to see Billy and Ewan. 'Such nice boys, Mary, you should be proud of them as I am. I phoned a friend of mine at the castle and told him they were looking for work. By the end of our discussion he decided to take them on. The boys gave me a big hug when I gave them the news; hope you are keeping well yourself, enclosing a little something for you.' It was two ten pound notes. I put them away beside the rest of Auntie's money. 'P.S.' she wrote, 'don't worry about the boys, they will be fine, love Auntie Kate.' The worry of the whole day melted away as I fell asleep.

At work the next day I asked Nurse about the Maria Duffy affair. 'Oh, Mary, I don't suppose you will rest till I tell you. Well, when you go home at lunch time tell the boys you are coming to my place for dinner then I'll give you all the news. Can I get a bit of peace now?'

The day seemed to pass quickly then Nurse and I were racing along in her car to her house. The dinner was practically ready so it wasn't long before we were discussing the Maria Duffy affair. 'It seems they had to leave the body lying as it was found till a pathologist arrived from Edinburgh to examine the body then it was removed carefully to Edinburgh for forensic experts to study the body to find out how long the poor girl had been dead. We were told, Mary, just between ourselves, that she had been dead about four years or more. Also they were able to tell that she had just given birth to a child; now the search was on for the child. The police are still busy on the case. None of the MacPhersons have been arrested as the experts say that the body had just been buried in the forest for a short while. How they are able to tell these things I don't know but the police are busy night and day on the case.'

Dear God, I thought, don't ever lead them to my garden. I was glad only Sarah and I knew the secret of the little grave and that of the dead mother. I wondered what made Hector pick that forest to bury the mother. Did he have a spite against the MacPhersons.

In the ten days that Billy and Ewan had left before they were to go to work, they sawed logs and packed the shed up to the roof, cleaned all windows, had garden perfect and Rusty run off his feet.

CHAPTER 11

It was in 1948 Aneurin Bevan, Minister of Health in the Labour government managed to get the bill for the National Health Service on the Statute Book. It was a great victory for all the poor families in Britain. It meant every person from the oldest to the new born babe had the right to free health care and medical attention when ever needed. All the workers in the country had to contribute a few pence per week from their pay packets to help towards the cost. I was delighted when I heard the news; not for myself but for all the poor ill patients who came wearily into our surgery. Often as not, Dr McKinnon never received a penny as they had no money. Doctor and Nurse would get a steady wage now as the government would be paying them; as for me it gave me a lot of extra work as every man, woman and child was issued with an identity card with their special number on it. Doctor was allowed 2,000 patients on his list but in the village and across the loch they amounted to only 800.

At that time my work involved marking each patient's number opposite their name and address on their medical charts for Doctor and Nurse, often after my day's work was finished. I would take a bundle of the medical cards and doctor's charts and make them all up; the next time the patient came back I would hand them back their medical cards which they kept themselves. It was a lot of extra work but I didn't mind when I saw the smiles coming back to the tired mothers' faces. Of course, our waiting room became a bit overcrowded; I supposed Doctor would have to look for bigger premises. That would take time and money.

Also that same year my dead sister Nan's eldest son Michael went out in his grandfather's boat one lovely afternoon on the loch; one minute the weather was beautiful, the next the loch was covered in heavy mist. The loch that night was in one of her secretive moods; the boy who was only 15 years old never returned. The boat was found four miles further down the loch. It was upside down but no sign of young Michael. Special divers were brought from the Holy Loch near Glasgow; also a dredger to drag the loch. For a whole month the search went on but no sign of Michael; I was heartbroken. They say the sea always gives back its dead but I don't think that saying goes for my loch. Michael's father Donald MacPherson was due out of prison the following week; owing to the sad circumstances of his eldest son he would be sent home, his prison sentence would be finished anyway. Five years was a long time; I for one was not looking forward to seeing him again; in fact I was a bit frightened, also sorry for him. During the five years he had been in prison for killing his wife, he had lost his mother, his brother and now his eldest son Michael. Such a waste of a young life.

The following Sunday when I attended church I noticed the other MacPherson children sitting in their grandfather's pew but no sign of their father Donald. I didn't want to see him anyway. During Mass Father Joseph asked us all to remember young Michael in our prayers. When I got out of the church Flora, Hector's sister was waiting for me. She told me that Hector had said in his last letter to his mother that Sarah was expecting her first child. I pretended I knew all about it.

During the past four months, Katie Fraser had been coming in every Saturday morning for three hours to clean my house. She was 15 years of age, well built for her age and a cheery personality. She was a good worker; her mother had a large family and what little money there was the father made sure he drank it all. It was Nurse Duncan who recommended her. She said, 'Mary, the poor girl needs money and you need help with that big house.' I was glad I took her on; I didn't need to tell her what to do. As soon as she arrived every Saturday morning at 9 a.m. I would have a big plate of porridge ready for her, she made her own tea. After that she disappeared and cleaned the whole house. Then, when she was finished, I paid her and gave her a few extra things for her mother. The arrangement worked out fine for both of us; in fact I was getting quite fond of Katie. Most Saturday afternoons I would take Rusty a long walk; that way the pair of us got a bit of exercise and good clean fresh air. Often Rusty loved to run out and in the loch; sometimes if the wind was raging Rusty loved dodging the big waves in the loch.

My life seemed to be all work and no play. I needed to discuss with Nurse about getting time off and Rusty and I could spend a week in Mull at Auntie Kate's; also I would be able to see Bill and Ewan again. I took a good look in the mirror at myself, I had very pale skin, beautiful dark blue eyes and my jet black curly hair needed cutting and shaping. I thought it was about time I gave myself a little pampering. A bathroom installed in the house and soaking in a nice hot bath would do me the world of good. No more running out to the outside toilet in the hail, wind and snow. I'd make it my point to see if Mr Walsh could arrange everything for me. I had the money so in that sense I could get the workmen to start straight away. Also I could get a sink in the kitchen with running water from the tap instead of having to carry it everyday from the well. In fact the whole house needed papering and painting. New curtains and chintz covers for the chairs and settee in the parlour. With these thoughts in my mind I fell asleep.

When I arrived home from work at lunch time there was a letter lying on the mat. After I had my lunch I sat in the rocking chair and read my letter. It was from Vera; she was so madly in love with Fred; also they were expecting their first child. Fred, she said, was doing so well with his garage business that he had to take on an assistant. 'You will need to come over for a holiday, Mary; it's a vast but beautiful country but there is no place to beat home or our lovely loch.' If Mum had been spared and she had heard of Sarah and Vera's new arrivals she would have rushed for the baby patterns and knitting needles.

When I saw Nurse Duncan in the afternoon I asked her when my holidays were due.

'To tell you the truth, Mary, you should have had them long ago but since this new Health Scheme has come out both of us have been run off our feet; in fact, Doctor was just saying yesterday that you needed help so he thought if we got a young girl in next week you could show her the ropes for a fortnight then you can go on holiday for a month. You sure need a well earned rest.'

'Oh that will be lovely, Nurse, I am very tired and the house is needing such a lot done to it. Have you anybody in mind for the job?'

'Yes I have; she is Katie's cousin Sadie Fraser, just left school. She seems a bright little thing, clever at the school so it should not take long to show her the ropes. Now we better get on with our work; the patients will be thinking we are on strike.'

As soon as surgery was over I flew down to Mr Walsh's shop to see if he could order the bathroom suite and kitchen sink. As soon as I entered the shop he came straight over to me. I explained to him what I wanted.

'It will take a month before I could get the suite and sink for you; also you will need a plumber and joiner. I'll attend to everything for you, Miss Mary.'

'I'll need an estimate of the cost for the whole of the work before the men start.'

'I'll see to that also; when the order arrives I'll let you know.'

Gillian went to the door and opened it for me. When I was leaving she

172

said, 'hello, Mary, how is all the family?'

'I have just had good news; Sarah and Vera are both expecting. The boys of course are still working at the castle in the Isle Of Mull. Next time I write to Billy I'll tell him you were asking for him,' then I hurried up the road glad to get home for a rest.

At last my month's holiday arrived; I had already written to Auntie Kate giving her the time and date Rusty and I would be arriving in Craignure. The night before we left for holiday I gave Rusty's coat a good brushing till his fur shone. I also had a bit of pampering done to myself; got my jet black curly hair shampooed and set, treated myself to a whole new rig out, everything to match, in case I met a dark handsome stranger while on holiday. The morning of our departure arrived; I made sure all the windows and doors were securely locked then Rusty and I set out on the walk to the station. It was a glorious day with a slight nip in the air. The loch was dead calm; I never tired of watching her just to see what mood she was in. I had already booked our first class tickets so I knew that Rusty and I would be comfortable during the long journey to Oban.

When we arrived at the station the train as usual was already in so it was just a matter of asking the porter to show me to our seats. At last we were settled down; the porter put my small case on the rack for me. I tipped him, he touched his cap and Rusty and I were alone at last. I covered the seat with his towel then he jumped up and settled down beside me for the long journey ahead. Before long, however, I fell asleep, it's funny but I always seemed to be tired all the time; let's hope the rest and sea air at Auntie Kate's will do me the world of good. Rusty had fallen asleep as soon as the train had started. I must have slept the whole journey; when I woke up the porter was opening and slamming doors all along the train shouting 'Oban'. I jumped up, grabbed my case, put the lead on Rusty and hurried off the train then it was a brisk walk to the ferry.

I travelled first class, that way I wouldn't see John Lewis cuddling another girl. One of the crew showed Rusty and me the way to a comfortable lounge then he asked if I would like anything. I ordered tea and cakes for myself and water for Rusty. The steward admired Rusty and, like so many others, wanted to know what he was fed on. When we reached Craignure I expected Auntie Kate to be there waiting for me with a taxi ready to take us home but there was no sign of her. I was sure I told her the date and time I would be arriving. I had to get a taxi myself. There were a few of them standing in a line on the quay so Rusty and I got into the first one and told him the address to go to.

While I was sitting in the taxi I had time to wonder what had happened to John Lewis, I hadn't seen him when I came down the gang plank. We arrived at Auntie Kate's house and I had just reached the door when it was opened by Mr Hendry, Auntie's solicitor.

'Come in, Mary, sorry no one was at the boat to meet you; your auntie has been ill for a while now. She didn't want you troubled, that's why I was told not to worry you. Doctor is with her just now. I am afraid it's bad news; they don't think she will last through the night.' All this time I was still standing at the door in shock, my feet seemed to be glued to the floor, I just could not move them.

Then a nurse came up to me and said, 'you poor child, come and sit by the fire, I'll make you a nice strong sweet cup of tea.' I sank wearily into the big cosy armchair beside a big blazing fire.'

Rusty sat at my feet whining all the time, he seemed to sense something awful was about to happen to both of us. When nurse brought the tea I asked her if she could get some food for Rusty. I don't know how long Mr Hendry and I sat there in silence then I heard Nurse's voice say, 'I think, Mary, you better get to bed, you have had a long day. There isn't anything you can do for your aunt so come on I'll take you to your room. It's all right I'll see to Rusty.'

In the morning I dressed hurriedly and went into the kitchen. The place was empty except for Rusty who welcomed me with his usual jumping around. The place seemed to have a deadly calm about it; all at once a shiver went right through me. Suddenly, I felt afraid, too frightened to move then Nurse came breezing into the room.

'Did you have a good night's sleep Mary? I'll make you some breakfast. By the way, Mr Hendry will see you as soon as you have finished your tea. He is in the parlour, he has been up all night. Drink your tea child, Mr Hendry will give you all the news.'

I thought to myself I was no longer a child, I was 24 years old and I wished she would stop calling me that. I gulped down my tea then Rusty and I made our way to the parlour. Mr Hendry was dozing in front of a big roaring fire. I slipped quietly into the big chair opposite him. Rusty lay at my feet and I gazed into the ever changing flames thinking of far distant places. It's funny when you sit watching the flames you visualise all sorts of faces and figures. I was day dreaming as usual when Mr Hendry's voice brought me back to earth. 'Had a good night's rest, Mary? If you'll excuse me for a few moments I'll go and tidy myself up, just relax there, I'll be back shortly.'

I felt like going into Auntie Kate's bedroom but some sixth sense held me back so I just sat and stared in the fire again. Nurse brought a breakfast tray in for Mr Hendry, with a cup for me. Mr Hendry came into the parlour. I noticed that he had washed, shaved and had changed into a clean white shirt with a black tie. His salt and pepper coloured hair was brushed neatly back off his face. 'Good,' he said, 'Nurse has brought me some breakfast, would you like to pour? Better pour one for yourself also, you will need it.'

I filled both our cups then put sugar and cream in Mr Hendry's. Both of us were silent as he ate his breakfast. I just sipped my tea wondering how Auntie Kate was and wishing I was sitting beside her bed comforting her through her illness.

Mr Hendry pushed the tray aside and said, 'I am sorry, Mary, that I am the one to break this dreadful news to you but your dear aunt passed peacefully away in her sleep at 2.15 a.m. I was sitting beside her till the end.'

At first I wondered what he was talking about, I just could not believe I had heard right. 'No, she can't be dead, it was only two months ago Billy and Ewan paid her a visit and Billy said in his letter she was fine and she was so pleased to see them.'

'Your aunt has been ill for a long time now; the boys would be too young to notice.' It was then I started crying, the sobs racking my shoulders. Nurse came in, put her arms around me and said, 'come on, dear, you better lie down for a while. I'll get you another cup of tea, be undressed and in bed by the time I come back.' When she appeared again with the tea she stood over me till I drank it all. 'Now just you rest, child, Mr Hendry and I will attend to everything.' On her way to the door she turned back and pulled the bedroom curtains shutting out the bright sunlight.

In my mind I was saying Auntie Kate can't be dead but I knew in my heart she was gone. She was the only person I could really trust. Nurse must have put something in my tea because it was dark when I wakened. I washed and dressed then made my way to the parlour. I was taken aback at the number of people old and young sitting round the room. Mr Hendry rose at once and told me to sit beside the fire. Everyone in the room was dressed in black, the men, of course, with their black ties then the parish priest arrived. He went straight into the bedroom, everyone in the parlour rose from their seats and followed him then Mr Hendry beckoned me in. Within myself I felt frightened.

I didn't know what to expect. Auntie Kate's coffin was laid on a table beside her bed and everyone was taking their turn at standing beside it and saying a little prayer then it came my turn. Mr Hendry came beside me and said, 'it's all right, Mary, see how peaceful she looks.' At first I was afraid then slowly I opened my eyes. Yes she was peaceful, also beautiful; to me she still seemed alive. I gently touched her cheek. I was surprised, it felt so soft against my fingers. I said a prayer then moved on as the priest said a prayer and blessed the coffin. I heard him saying he would arrange for the coffin to be taken to the church that afternoon. After we left the bedroom everyone went home each one shaking my hand and mentioning their names to me as they went. As soon as the last person had left I had forgotten all their names. I wished I had been paying more attention to them. The way my mind was I felt as if I was dead also. Nurse came hurrying into the parlour, 'come, child, into the kitchen, I have made something nice for you. Sit down now and I want to see that plate clean before you leave the table. I noticed you haven't eaten since yesterday.' I thought to myself don't say I slept the whole day and night. The bully said 'stop dreaming and start eating.'

Oh dear God, where do those kind of people come from, then I thought of Nurse Duncan. At first she was the same but then I grew to love her, even though at times she did bully me but within my heart I knew she would not let anyone harm me. All of a sudden I said to Nurse, 'where is Rusty?' I heaved a sigh of relief to see Rusty was sound asleep in a large box padded with a coloured blanket. As I rose from the table the nurse said Mr Hendry wanted to see me in the parlour. Before he could say a word I asked him about Billy and Ewan.

'It's all right, Mary, I have notified them of your aunt's death. They will be arriving any moment now. Sit down, Mary, I want to speak to you. The Requiem Mass for your aunt will be at 10.30 a.m. tomorrow, there will be a large crowd there. You already know your aunt was a well loved and respected schoolmistress in the town. The teachers and the children from the school will be in church to sing the hymns during the service. I have arranged everything so what I really want to say is when your brothers arrive, the three of you better buy some clothes suitable for the funeral. Here is a card; go to the Nairns main shops and just show this card then pick something to suit the occasion. Here are your brothers now, so as soon as possible make your way to the shops and get everything you need.'

Billy and Ewan came into the room, I gave them each a big hug then Mr Hendry shook hands with them and disappeared. Nurse came hurrying in with three cups, tea and sandwiches. She stood for a few seconds then I suddenly remembered I had not introduced the boys to her. She shook hands with the boys, and gave them both a big smile. 'Now drink your tea then off the three of you go and get your shopping done. I'll look after Rusty.'

Poor Rusty I thought to myself he will be wondering what is going on. I had hardly said two words to him since I arrived in Mull.

After we finished our tea the three of us set out to the shops. I bought a black dress, cardigan, woollen coat, small hat, stockings, shoes, bag and gloves then I handed the card to the boys. 'Get dark navy blue suits, white shirts, black tie, black shoes.' Off the two went while I waited for mine to be parcelled up. A middle-aged lady in a black dress came over to me and said there was no need for me to wait. All the items would be delivered in the afternoon, including the purchases my brothers were making in the gentlemen's department.

Before going back to the house we walked along the shore. The Oban ferry was moored at the quay. I was glad to get a breath of fresh air. I think the boys were also. 'Did Mr Hendry send for you, Mary?'

'No, Billy, I just came down on the spur of the moment to visit Auntie Kate. Mr Hendry was already here; Auntie Kate had been ill for a long while but she didn't want to worry any of us. I don't know what I am going to do without her kind and wise advice which she often gave me in her letters.' The three of us walked on in silence just staring out to the angry sea. 'I think boys we better turn back, Mr Hendry will be wondering what has happened to us.'

On our way back we met the nurse with Rusty. When he spotted us he flew like mad toward me. I gave him a big hug and whispered, 'I sure do love you,' then he went to Ewan and Billy. The boys took to their heels with Rusty racing after them. 'Oh dear,' I said to Nurse, 'I think the boys have forgotten themselves running and laughing with Rusty while dear Auntie Kate is lying in the house.'

'It's all right, Mary, your aunt's coffin was taken to the church half an hour ago, that's why I thought I would show off your lovely dog. By the way my name is Joan Munro, just call me Joan. Mr Hendry employed me to nurse your aunt; she loved you a lot, Mary, she never seemed to tire of talking about you. Oh, I forgot she gave me an envelope to give to you. I'll give it to you as soon as we get back to the house.' We all arrived back just as the shop van drew up to the house with our order. Joan told the men to put the parcels in my room and tipped them. After giving me the envelope from my aunt she made tea for all of us. We were all busy drinking our tea when Mr Hendry walked into the parlour; he nodded to us all then sat in the big chair beside the roaring fire which Billy had risen to give him. Joan came in with another two cups, one for herself and one for Mr Hendry. I laid my cup down and attended to his then I offered him a sandwich but he just shook his head. It was a good job he didn't want any because when I looked the boys had scoffed the lot. I glanced over to Joan but she just smiled as if she understood. I wondered if she had any brothers of her own.

After tea Billy and Ewan made to get ready to go back to the castle but Mr Hendry stood up and said, 'I have booked a room at the Crown Hotel for both of you tonight; Requiem Mass is at 10.30 a.m. tomorrow; everything is all arranged. Dinner is booked for you also; try to get a good night's sleep.' The boys said goodbye to us and left for the hotel.

'Sit down, Mary, I wish to speak to you,' Mr Hendry said. Joan disappeared into the kitchen with the tea tray shutting the door quietly behind her. When Mr Hendry felt sure we were alone he told me after Auntie Kate's funeral there would be the reading of the will. 'Part of the will, Mary, I'll leave till the nurse and your brothers have left to go back to work; when you have heard everything you will understand. Have an early night tonight, tomorrow will be a long sad day and, Mary, don't offer to help with any of the work, Nurse is well paid to do it. After all, this is your house now.' With that he got up, put his coat and hat on; as he was leaving he said, 'the car will come and collect you and your brothers and Nurse and take you all to the church. Be sure and be ready for 9.30 a.m.'

I was up quite early; all night I had been wondering what Mr Hendry meant when he said now the house was mine. I dressed in my mourning clothes and hurried down to the kitchen for breakfast. Joan was busy at the table. 'Your breakfast is ready for you, Miss Mary, in the parlour; Mr Hendry is already there.' I noticed the 'miss' in front of my name, I think Mr Hendry had spoken to Nurse. According to him I was the owner now.

'Good morning, Mary, did you sleep well? No I don't suppose you did. It will take you a long while to get over your great loss. Please pour my tea and try to eat something, it will be a long service.' Just then Billy and Ewan arrived; they looked handsome in their dark suits. I realised how good looking the pair of them were, what with their faces glowing with the picture of health I was proud to be their sister. Mr Hendry just wished them good morning and explained to them that they had to come back to the house for the reading of the will. 'Everything is arranged at the hotel for the meal after the funeral. I'll have to go to the church first to see that everything is in order; the car will call for you, Mary, and the rest; see you in church.' With a nod he was off.

He was no sooner out of the door when the boys burst out laughing. 'What an old fuddy duddy, he is so old-fashioned.'

'Don't talk like that, boys, and remember we are on our way to Auntie

178

Kate's funeral.' Just then a large limousine drew up at the door.

I hurried to my bedroom, put on my coat and hat and gloves, grabbed my bag. When I reached the door Nurse and the boys were waiting for me to get into the car first. When we arrived at the church the place was packed. Mr Hendry was at the door waiting for us then he led us right down to the front pew. Auntie Kate's coffin stood in front of the altar with four candles lit, two at the top and two at the bottom. All the school children were in the choir with their teachers. By the looks of the crowd the whole school must be at the Requiem Mass. At last the service started; it was only when the children started singing the hymn 'How Great Thou Art' that I started crying; the sobs were racking my body. I was thinking how poor Mum and Dad, my dear young sister Nan had gone forever and now dear Auntie Kate. It took me a while before I felt a bit calmer then I followed the coffin out of the church. Billy and Ewan were behind me then Mr Hendry and Nurse.

We made our way to the cemetery where Father John said the final prayers as my aunt's coffin was laid to rest. Everyone seemed to disappear; all of a sudden I found I was the only one left standing at the grave. I felt Nurse's arm round my shoulders and she whispered, 'we have to go to the hotel, Mary, Mr Hendry's waiting, so will the rest of the mourners.' I just let myself be led away in a daze. When we reached the hotel there were so many people there; they were all helping themselves at the buffet.

'Come on, Miss Mary, you will need to eat something.'

'A cup of tea then. Oh, Joan, where are the boys?'

'Don't worry about them, before you can say boo they will have that sideboard empty. I'd better snatch some sandwiches before they disappear.'

I gave a little smile to myself, glad that Billy and Ewan weren't too upset by their aunt's death. Of course they had attended quite a few funerals in their young lives.

Nurse came back with my tea and sandwiches; 'come on, now, you will have to eat something, Mr Hendry is watching you like a hawk. Eat something, Miss Mary, otherwise I'll be in the black books.'

Mr Hendry called me over beside him; as everyone left they shook hands with me, of course I didn't know anyone but they were all Auntie Kate's friends.

The car was waiting to take Mr Hendry, Nurse and the boys and me back to the house. After I took my outdoor clothes off I made my way to the parlour. Mr Hendry, Nurse, Billy and Ewan were already there; also a stout lady and a younger person sitting beside her.

'Make yourself comfortable, Mary, I will start reading your aunt's will.' Mr

Hendry's voice sounded far away, in fact I felt quite faint. Then I heard, 'to my two nephews Billy and Ewan Scott I leave the sum of one hundred pounds each; to my faithful nurse and friend one hundred pounds; to Craignure School where I was proud to be headmistress for most of my life I leave the sum of two hundred pounds to be used for the children's benefits. Miss Hardie the headmistress now will attend to that. I am afraid ladies and gentlemen that's all I have time to read just now, excuse me. I will see you later, Mary.'

He shook hands with the stout lady and the young one then he was gone. For a few seconds we all sat in silence then Billy and Ewan said they would have to get back to work.

The lady rose, came over and shook hands with me. 'It's been a sad day, Mary, we will all miss her so much. She will not be dead so long as you are alive; you are the spitting image of her when she was young. Goodbye, Mary, we will let ourselves out.'

Billy went to the door and opened it for them then Ewan rose also and both of them left.

Joan said, 'I think, Miss Mary, you better lie down for a while and rest, I'll take Rusty a walk along the shore.' I went to bed glad to get time to myself; poor Rusty, he would be thinking I no longer cared for him. So much had happened in the last few days, I never had time to think about him or myself. I lay on top of the bed, my mind going back to the reading of the will. I didn't remember my name being mentioned; maybe she never left anything to me. Sarah and Vera were not mentioned either. With those thoughts in my mind I fell asleep.

It was Joan who brought me back to earth; 'hurry and get washed and dressed, dinner is ready. Mr Hendry is in the parlour.' When I got to my feet I felt a lot better. In the parlour a big roaring fire made the room so cheerful looking; a small table was set for two. I hadn't eaten much all day; now with the lovely smell drifting in from the kitchen I was looking forward to dinner. Mr Hendry was a man of few words so all he said was, 'feeling better, Mary?' Nurse brought in the soup, chicken I think it was and I enjoyed it; then roast beef and all the trimmings. When Nurse came in with the tea Mr Hendry said 'when you have cleared everything away, Nurse, Miss Mary and I have things to discuss, therefore, we don't want to be disturbed by anything or anybody. If anyone calls just say we are not at home.'

As soon as I had finished my tea Mr Hendry opened his briefcase and took out a pile of papers. Before he started reading them he got up from the big chair and locked the parlour door. 'That will make sure we are not interrupted.

Now, Mary, I want you to listen carefully,' then he started reading the rest of my aunt's will. 'To my daughter Mary Ann Clark I leave the whole of my estate, the Craigshill House in Loch Etive, also my Sea View cottage in the Isle of Mull to do with as she pleases and all my monies. Mr Hendry will advise and help her in every way. The deeds of the cottages will be handed over as soon as possible after my death to my daughter.'

I never heard any more; I collapsed in a dead faint at his feet. I don't know what had happened but when I opened my eyes again I was in bed, Nurse bending over me. 'Now drink this. Mr Hendry is worried sick, so I'll run and tell him you are all right now.' My mind went racing round and round thinking I was no longer sister to Sarah, Vera, Billy and Ewan. The whole family I was brought up with were my cousins. Mum and Dad were really my auntie and uncle and Auntie Kate was my real mother. I was her illegitimate child. Now I was beginning to understand why it was me who was sent away to service at the young age of 15 years.

Later on why it was me who was sent parcels at Christmas and none of the rest of the family got any. Also the letters always with money in them. It was a blessing I never told any of the rest of the family about the money.

The next morning when I went into the parlour Mr Hendry was sitting in his usual big chair. After the breakfast table was set for us I said that I would need to be getting back to Loch Etive as I was expecting the workmen to install my new bathroom suite and also the sink in the kitchen.

'I'll attend to that, Mary'.

'But I have arranged everything with Mr Walsh.'

'That's all right I'll see him. I think you'd better stay another week here, it will do you good. Nurse will attend to everything. I also have a few more documents for you to sign and a few legalities to attend to. We also have to order a headstone for your mother's grave; all that takes time. You will be provided with your own bank book and cheque book. Just in case you don't realise it, Mary, you are now a very rich young lady. I'll advise you as much as possible before you go back home as you call it. From now on there is no need for you to take any responsibility for Billy and Ewan, they are quite capable of looking after themselves. As for Sarah and Vera, instead of them being your sisters they are your first cousins.'

'Did Mum tell you about the dead bodies we found in the attic after I came back from service?'

'Yes she did; I am following that case closely, don't worry your pretty head about it, things will sort themselves out in their own good time. Now off you go and take Rusty a walk along the shore, the air should bring a bit of colour into your cheeks, you are far too pale anyway.'

It was a relief to get out of the house with Rusty. He was so happy to be with me again, just the two of us. When we reached the shore I took his lead off and let him run wild. How he enjoyed ducking out of the way of the big waves. I sat down on a large stone and pondered over the last few days. The outcome of the events was to change my whole style of living. I had enough money to live comfortably so I didn't need to work at the surgery any more. I would miss Nurse Duncan and Dr McKinnon. After I had trained Sadie properly I would leave; in a way it was too much for me; I was always tired. I would just keep Katie on, maybe two days a week, that way I could get the house back in order. As for Sea View Cottage I could rent it out and get a bit of a steady income. I'd discuss it with Mr Hendry.

A shadow fell across my legs; a voice said 'a penny for your thoughts, Mary.' It was John Lewis the sailor as brazen as ever. He sat on the stone beside me then he said the whole town had been in mourning since my aunt's death and offered his condolences. It took me all my time not to burst out crying.

'You will not be coming back now that she is gone.'

'I don't know, I haven't given it too much thought.'

'No, I don't suppose you have. It was your lovely dog I noticed first then I looked around for you. I am glad to see you again.'

'Don't say that, John, I am sure you have a girlfriend in every port as the saying goes. Don't say you haven't been with a girl for two years. That's how long it's been since I last saw you.'

His face turned slightly scarlet. 'Well, Mary, what do you expect me to do, live a hermit's life till you came back?'

'No but you could have come to Loch Etive to visit me. You get holidays don't you?'

'Often I thought of doing that but, then again, some party or other seemed to come up, and how was I to know I would be welcome. After you left me standing at the picture hall and you never turned up.'

'Oh John, I had forgotten about that, I am so sorry. When I arrived back at Auntie Kate's that day there was a telegram waiting for me saying I had to return home immediately and I had no way of contacting you.'

'Can we at least be friends? In case you don't know it, Mary, I love you. Of course, I am a notorious flirt as you already know, but lying in bed at night alone it's you my thoughts turn to. Come on, I'll walk you back home. When you are feeling better and are over the shock of your aunt's death mind and write to me. Here's my address'; he slipped a piece of paper into my hand then gently kissed me on the cheek. I got to my feet and called on Rusty; he came bouncing up to me. When he saw John he sniffed at his heels for a few seconds then ran ahead. 'Still the protector I see. I would not mind having one like him myself. It's funny when I was at school and your aunt was the headmistress us boys used to call her the old dragon. At that time she could not have been very old. It's funny when you are young you think everyone over twenty had one foot in the grave. Here we are, Mary; I'll say good-bye then; mind and write, Mary.'

As I reached the door Mr Hendry stepped aside to let Rusty and me in and he asked who the young man was. When I told him he just nodded and left. Joan hung up my coat and hat then went to make a pot of tea.

I sat in the big comfortable chair beside the blazing fire; everything in the cottage was spotless yet I never saw Joan doing any housework. Joan came in with the tea tray and biscuits. I asked her who does the housework?

'Oh we have a day woman coming in at 7 a.m. Your aunt employed her so in the meantime Mr Hendry said she was to carry on as usual till all the details are settled. She comes in and cooks the dinner also.'

I gave a laugh, 'and I thought what a marvellous cook you were.'

It was Joan's turn to burst out laughing. 'Me cook; I even burn the toast. I have seen Mr Hendry sniffing in disgust but he never says anything. He knows I am good at my job and that's nursing. Now tell me who was the young man who brought you home.'

'Oh, Joan, I met John Lewis years ago; Auntie Kate taught him at school. She said as a boy he was such a rogue, I suppose he still is. I think he must have kissed the Blarney Stone, he's got such a gift of the gab, but to tell the truth as soon as I arrive home I forget all about him so in a way I can't very well be in love with him.'

I wondered what he would say if he knew I was Auntie Kate's illegitimate daughter. I wondered what any future would-be husband would do. I hadn't realised until then the stigma that was attached to that dreadful word. Before I came to Mull for a holiday I was part of a family, two brothers and three sisters. Now I was only their cousin; in a way I was nobody. I didn't even know the name of my father. Auntie Kate covered up her deceit well. There she was the prim and proper headmistress of the local school, the teachers and children showing her the greatest respect while I the unwanted one was hidden away among her sister Helen's family. At that moment I hated my long lost mother. What right had she to abandon me as if I was an old dish cloth. I'd speak to Mr Hendry and ask his advice whether from now on I should use my real name Mary Ann Clark or keep to the name I was brought up with, Mary Scott.

All of a sudden I felt very tired and went to my room and flung myself on the bed. For a while I just lay listening to the birds singing in the tree outside the bedroom window then sleep took over and all my tormenting thoughts disappeared. It was Joan who woke me. 'Mary, dinner is ready, Mr Hendry is waiting; you know what he is like.' I thought to myself, who the blazes does he think he is anyway. It's my house, he is living on my money that's paying for all his meals and his services and comforts. Let him wait till I am ready so I just took my time, washed and changed then went into the parlour. Mr Hendry had finished his dinner and mine was cold. He opened his mouth to say something and closed it again when he saw my expression, for I was about to explode. I ate my meal, which Joan had re-heated, in silence. When I had finished Mr Hendry said 'your aunt's headstone is being placed at the graveside tomorrow. Father John will be blessing it. I'll drive you to the cemetery at 3.30 p.m. after that we will discuss what to do with the cottage and I need you to sign all the deeds and documents. Also, I'll have ready your bank book and cheque book then if you feel up to it you can go home. I'll let you rest now.'

After he had gone Joan came into the parlour; 'why, Mary, who stood on your tail. Your face was like thunder when you came in for dinner. I think Mr Hendry was taken aback.'

'To tell you the truth, Joan, I am sick to the teeth with him; he treats me as if I am a child.'

'Look, Mary, in case you don't realise it Mr Hendry knows you have suffered a great loss. Anything he does is for your benefit. I suppose you will be shutting up the house before you go home.'

'That's what I'll be discussing with Mr Hendry tomorrow after we come back from the cemetery.'

At 3.30 p.m. sharp the car with Mr Hendry in it arrived at the door to take Joan and me to the cemetery. Outside of the warm parlour it felt cold and dreary; maybe it was the way I felt myself. The anger was stirring in my breast again thinking, why oh why did I have to bear so much trouble in my young life. Why was it me who was sent for to come home to find my real aunt and uncle dying instead of Nan, Sarah or Vera. The boys of course were too young. Why was it me they all turned to for help when I was just their cousin. A nudge on my arm by Nurse brought me back to cold reality. We all got out of the car together and made our way to my mother's graveside. Father John arrived shortly after us with two altar boys. A few prayers were said and the headstone blessed then we all made our way back to the car and home.

Nurse and the morning cleaner, Mrs Morrison, were witnesses to signatures on the various documents then were asked to leave the parlour while Mr Hendry talked to me in private.

Mr Hendry handed me my bank and cheque books. I looked at the name on both of them and was pleased to note Mary Ann Scott. Impulsively, I threw my arms around his neck and gave him a big hug. Mr Hendry was taken aback.

'Why, Mary what was that for?'

'Well, when I saw Scott on my books I knew my secret would be safe with you.'

'Thank you, Mary, I think you have been through enough without going all through the red tape to change your name. As you say, your secret is safe with me. When you arrive back home things will go on as normal. You are still the sister all the family depend on. Before I finish I would like to ask you if you still want me to act as your attorney?'

'Of course I do, Mr Hendry, no way could I manage without you.'

'In that case while you are at Craigshill House I think you should let Sea View Cottage to a respectable couple. That would give you a steady income. I'll attend to that side of the affairs; also, Mary, I have sent most of your mother's belongings on to Loch Etive. They belong to you and here is your mother's jewel box and the key. Also, I think you should have a few more days' rest. Nurse will be here as long as you stay to look after you. She has got her instructions what to do when you leave; bye for now, Mary, I am always ready to come if at anytime you need help,' then he was off. I sat down in the big comfortable chair beside the blazing fire, my mind racing round in circles going back to the last ten days since I arrived at the cottage. I looked round the cosy room; to think this was all mine, also Craigshill House in Loch Etive. It suddenly dawned on me that I was a very rich lady yet inwardly I didn't feel any different. I suppose gradually I would get used to my new wealth. My mind went back to the three and a half years I spent scrubbing from morning till night, stuck down in the dark damp kitchen of Lord and Lady Ramsay's mansion.

Nurse broke my train of thought by saying that a young man was at the door asking for me. It was John Lewis with a big smile on his face. 'I was wondering, Mary, if you would care to go for a walk with me. We could take Rusty along with us.' I quickly put on my coat and hat, gathered up Rusty's collar and lead then the three of us raced for the shore. The cold fresh wind helped me to forget everything for a while and Rusty was a joy to watch running ahead then back again. I don't know who was acting mad, John or Rusty. At last I reached my favourite rock where John and I settled down, Rusty still running wild out and in the stormy waters. John put his arms around me and gave me a big hug and kiss. At that moment I would have loved to have loved John then. I thought, would he love me if he knew the full story about me. Inwardly, I just could not bear it; I was illegitimate. If we were to get married my secret would be out and I just could not allow it. So I sat with John and pretended we were so in love with one another. I don't know how long we stayed together in the shelter of the rock; it was the tide that brought us to our senses. We rose and called for Rusty who came running up to us soaking wet. We made our way home arm in arm with Rusty following us. I was sad that soon I would have to say goodbye to John for good. I'd stay another day then leave for home.

When we arrived at the cottage I asked John in for tea. In front of the blazing fire the tea table was laid for two; John sat in Mr Hendry's big chair while I made myself comfortable in mine. John must have been as hungry as I was for it wasn't long before all the plates were empty. It was the first time in days that I had really enjoyed my food. Joan came in and cleared the tea tray away. 'I am going out for a walk, Miss Mary, Rusty has been fed and is in his basket so I'll leave the two of you in peace.' She left the room and closed the door quietly behind her.

John then stretched out his arms and pulled me gently on to his lap. After awhile we started petting and kissing; I knew what I was doing was wrong. I was leading him on. I had no intention of seeing him again after I was back home, but I still had another full day to love John. I heard Joan's key in the door; 'you'd better go John, I'll see you tomorrow.'

'Do I need to leave Mary, it's so nice and comfortable here and this is your house now, you must be well off now.'

All of a sudden a cold fear went through me. I knew John was a rogue; was he scheming now about the cottage. 'I don't know, John, to tell you the truth I haven't given a thought to anything except Auntie Kate's death.'

After I had kissed him at the door he said 'I'll see you tomorrow, Mary.'

'Yes, John,' I said and closed the door on him; tomorrow I would leave for home. If John was planning any wool pulling over my eyes he was in for a shock. Joan was surprised when I asked her to pack my things ready for me to leave next day.I went back into the parlour and cried my eyes out thinking of what might have been. I was in no position to love anyone. Wearily, I made my way to my bedroom; there was no room in my heart for love. I was the odd one out; with that thought I went to bed and fell asleep.

I slept a lot later than I had intended to; quickly I washed, dressed then hurried through to the parlour. The breakfast table was set for me; Joan popped her head round the door. 'Bacon and egg, Mary? You have time to catch the early ferry with twenty minutes to spare. I have ordered the taxi to take you and Rusty to the quay. I'll be coming to the ferry to see you off, so take your time and eat a proper breakfast, you have a long journey ahead of you. I have packed a lunch box for you and something for Rusty. Here is your first class ticket for you. Mr Hendry has attended to everything so settle down and eat your breakfast.'

I wrote a note to John apologising for leaving so suddenly as some expected business had turned up and I had to return home. 'Do hope you will forgive me love, Mary.' I gave it to Joan to give to John when he arrived. It was with a weary heart that I left the cottage and John behind. If he really loved me it was up to him to come to Loch Etive and tell me; time will tell. Joan saw Rusty and me settled comfortably on the ferry. As the boat moved away from the quay I waved to Joan and in my heart whispered goodbye my love, dear John. A tear rolled down my cheek; quickly I brushed it away then Rusty and I settled down on the short sail to Oban. The sea was its usual angry self but it was so relaxing watching the changing face of the powerful sea.

At Oban, Mr Hendry was waiting at the foot of the gang plank to meet me. 'I'll attend to your luggage, Mary, your compartment is booked for you on the train; take Rusty a short walk before you board, it's a long journey.' When Rusty and I arrived in our compartment all my luggage was on the rack but no sign of Mr Hendry. I glanced out of the window as the train started to pull out of the station and there was Mr Hendry, hat in hand. With a slight nod of his head he disappeared. I thought to myself that's the kind of gentleman I should marry, someone to take care of me; then again I did not love him. For a while I watched the beautiful countryside hurrying past as the train sped on its way then Rusty and I both fell asleep. It was Rusty barking who woke me up then he placed his two big paws on my lap. 'Oh hungry are you?' I opened the lunch box and gave Rusty his then I settled down and had my tea and sandwiches. At Loch Etive the porter stood outside my door making signs.

When I opened the door he said he would take my luggage off the train for me but he was frightened of the dog. I took Rusty out of his way, hailed a taxi and told the porter to bring my luggage over. I gave him a generous tip which brought a beautiful big smile to his face then I turned to the cab driver and said 'Craigshill House.'

'Where is that, Miss? Never heard of it.'

I thought to myself neither had I till I went to Mull. To the driver I said, 'I'll show you.'

The driver brought my luggage in. I paid the fare then tipped him. He went away happy. Rusty and I were back home, the pair of us at ease at long last. The first place I made for was the rocking chair in the kitchen. I always felt at home here. I wondered if there were any letters for me on the mat. Most likely the cases would be covering them. I hadn't shut the door. Quickly I rose, shut and bolted the door. Yes there was one letter, it was from Mr Walsh saying the workmen would be installing the bathroom suite and the kitchen sink on Monday.

CHAPTER 12

It was about closing time when I finally arrived at Mr Walsh's shop. As soon as he saw me he hurried towards me. 'I am so sorry, Miss Mary, to hear of the loss of your dear aunt. I suppose you are down about the men starting work on Monday, if that's all right with you?'

'Of course, Mr Walsh. I do hope they will be completely finished in a fortnight's time as I will have to be back at work; also I would like an estimate of the whole of the work.' He gave me the estimate then ran and opened the door for me. I made my way to the surgery; Nurse Duncan met me with open arms and invited me to supper that evening at seven.

I felt a lot happier as I made my way home after buying a couple of Scotch pies and cakes at the bakers first for myself and Rusty. It was good at last to relax in my rocking chair and watch Rusty running wild in the garden.

Nurse Duncan gave me all the local gossip. Donald MacPherson was courting Mr Walsh's daughter Gillian. Half his age, more fool her; she must be hard up for a man. Especially a murderer just finished five years' sentence for killing my eldest sister Nan. Also he was the father of eight children. What on earth was she thinking of. Sarah, my sister married to a diplomat in Canada had a baby girl. She hadn't the decency to write to me herself; it was Flora, Sarah's sister-in-law who told Nurse Duncan. The new baby was called Helen after her grandmother Scott. The old man MacPherson hasn't been seen outside the house since the sudden death of his wife and eldest son who was found dead on the craigs at the foot of my garden. Dr McKinnon's surgery was chock-a-block; in fact they needed to get more help. I was going to tell her that I would be leaving for good but just hadn't the heart to tell her then.

'Oh, Mary, I am sorry, here I am gossiping away and forgot to give you my sincere sympathy at the loss of your dear Aunt Kate. Are you keeping a lot better? It must have been a terrible shock for you.'

'Mr Hendry was a great help; he attended to everything. I'll be pretty busy during the next fortnight; the workmen are starting work on Monday installing my new bathroom suite and kitchen sink. Could you contact Katie and tell her I'll need her help on Monday?'

'I'll do that for you, Mary. My that will cost you a pretty penny getting all that work done to the house.'

'Yes, I suppose it will, but when it is all finished it will save me a lot of work. Also give me a lot of pleasure soaking in a nice warm bath.'

It was getting late when Rusty and I made our way home. The nights were getting a bit chilly but the brisk walk did me the world of good. After seeing all the doors locked and bolted and Rusty settled I made my way up to bed thinking how it would not be long before I'll have the luxury of my new bath.

On Sunday morning at Mass when I went to go to my pew all the MacPherson children had filled it up. Father Joseph noticed my predicament; he came right down from the altar and after he had said a few words to the children four of them moved over to their own father's seat and I was allowed in my own pew. I glanced over to the MacPherson's pew and there was Donald scowling at me. If he thought he had a right to my pew he was greatly mistaken. After the service I spoke to Father Joseph about saying a Mass for my Auntie Kate. The Father told me that Mr Hendry had phoned to make all arrangements for it.

Flora MacLean, Hector's sister was waiting for me. 'I'll walk with you, Mary; sorry about your aunt's death.'

I wondered what news Flora was fishing for; I wasn't long in finding out. 'Is it true, Mary, your aunt has left you her house in her will?'

At first I was struck dumb; the cheek of her asking such personal questions so soon after the funeral. 'Who told you that fairy story, Flora?'

Her face turned slightly red. 'I heard someone talking about you in the post office.'

'Well, Flora, whoever it was, you can go back and tell them to get their facts right.' I changed the subject by telling her I had heard that Sarah had a baby girl called Helen.

'Yes, Mary, Mum is going over to Canada for the baby's christening.'

I didn't think Nurse Duncan knew that or she would have told me. Well to me it didn't really matter. Sarah left in the huff and she could just stay in it for all I cared. By this time we had reached Flora's house so I just wished her good morning and walked on home to a breakfast of bacon and egg.

The house was in a complete turmoil for the next fortnight. Katie Fraser, the girl I had employed, was kept busy carrying pails of water from the well for the workmen. At times I felt like screaming. I think so did Rusty. I had to tie him up outside in the garden otherwise he would have had all the workmen's legs torn to pieces the first day they started work. At last the work was all finished. I had a lovely bathroom and a lovely new kitchen sink at my side window. For the first time in my life I had the luxury of having hot and cold water at my fingertips. The terrible mess the workmen left had to be cleaned up in four days as I would be starting work on Monday. A loud knock on the front door sent me hurrying to it. When I opened it Katie and her mother stood there.

'I have come down with Katie,' Mrs Fraser said, 'to help you clean up the terrible mess Katie was telling me about if it is all right with you, Miss Mary.'

'Of course, Mrs Fraser, I was just wondering how I was going to manage; just call me Mary. Both of you better have something to eat before you start. Katie get a move on and make the tea.'

'Could you show me, Mary, how the water runs and which is the hot and cold.'

As I showed her she went around like a child with a new toy. 'Now don't you worry your pretty head Katie and I will have the house like a new pin. Just you and that pretty dog of yours stay out of our way. Better take a walk the both of you.'

I left my helpers to clean the house then Rusty and I made our way down to the loch. I sat looking across the dark grey waters; looks like a storm's brewing I thought. I wondered how Nan's children were being looked after. Did their father beat them as he had beaten their mother. Donald should have got ten years instead of just five. I wondered if he still thought my house was his and certainly wasn't looking forward to meeting him face to face again. The look he gave me at Mass was full of hate. We had been away long enough and I raced Rusty back home to find Mrs Fraser finishing the front steps.

'That's the filth all scrubbed out, Mary; if you could just give it a few minutes to dry.' She stood with her hands on her heavy hips and said, 'my, you have a lovely view of the loch. Those MacPhersons on the other side; that Donald one is a bad bloke, mark my word. Right, Mary, we can go in now. Katie and I will make our way home.'

'Just a minute, Mrs Fraser, I have something for you.'

'Now, Mary, I just came down to help. To tell you the truth I wanted to see that new fangled bathroom of yours and how the water runs. Wait till I tell the neighbours.'

I just laughed and handed her a small envelope; 'be off home the pair of you and thanks for helping me out.' As they left I said to Katie, 'see you tomorrow?' As Rusty and I stepped in the spotless place had a different appearance to it. It was home again; the clean smell took me back to my happy childhood days never to return. When I went to the bathroom I was delighted with the perfect work the men had done. On Monday I'd pay the bill, which was quite a sizeable amount. In a month or two I'd get the painters in to decorate the whole house which was badly needing done. I hoped Auntie Kate's trunks arrived before work on Monday.

The trunks arrived on Saturday morning; I got the men to carry them up to the big cupboard in my bedroom so it was with an easy heart that I set out for my first day's work after a month's holiday. Some holiday, it seemed an eternity since the day Rusty and I set off for our holiday in the Isle of Mull. I reached the surgery; the place was packed. The children gave big smiles, so I wasn't forgotten after all. Sadie Fraser, Katie's cousin was coping quite well.

Nurse Duncan caught my eye and beckoned me in to the back room. 'Doctor is away across the loch to the MacPherson's house; since that Donald has come home there has been nothing but trouble. To tell you the truth, Mary, Doctor seems to think he is ill treating the children. When Doctor calls he makes out that the child has fallen so the little girl is sent to hospital for further investigation. The police have been notified. Constable Drummond is already over at the house. Between you and me Mary, he should never have been let out of prison. Oh, here is Doctor, run and help Sadie, we seem to be getting more patients by the day since the N.H.S. came into force.'

By the looks on the mothers' faces they were all pleased to see me back again. At the end of the week I would have to tell Dr McKinnon and Nurse that I would be leaving. I'd stay long enough to train another girl. I just could not possibly stay on as the house needed too many repairs. Also I had the cottage in Mull to keep an eye on. At lunch time Nurse said she would run me home.

'Give me a few moments to go to the baker.'

'While you're there, Mary, get me a Scotch pie also.'

In a way I was happy to be back at work; it was a pleasure working for Doctor and Nurse. At times Nurse could be a right bully. It was funny, the side of her nature she showed to me was always the kind side. I wondered why. After I was served at the bakers I ran out to Nurse's car. In five minutes I was home. I gave Nurse her pie then ran up to the door. Rusty as usual waiting for me and a letter was lying on the doormat. I hurriedly lifted it up and made my way to the kitchen and let Rusty out. The letter was from Vera, full of praise about the beautiful baby girl she had. Her name was Nan. 'I

192

thought of dear Nan the minute I clapped eyes on my new baby girl. Every day I seem to see Nan's lovely face in her.' She asked about Auntie Kate; how she was keeping.

The tail end of the queue was disappearing into the surgery as I made my way through the door. 'Late as usual, Mary, that will never do,' Nurse's voice boomed in the air. Doctor just shook his head. I was always late anyway. The afternoon passed quickly; Sadie was good at the book-keeping. I wondered who would get my place. I was in the middle of getting ready to go home when Nurse said Doctor wanted to speak to me. I hurried through to his office; knocked on the door and went in.

'Sit down a minute, Mary, I want to talk to you. Mr Hendry has been on the phone to me; he thinks you haven't had enough rest since your aunt's death.'

I cut in; 'Oh, Doctor, I know what you are going to say. Mr Hendry is quite right; I was thinking of handing in my notice on Friday. In a way I didn't want to leave you in the lurch.'

'I think, Mary, for a long while you will have to take it very easy. I see you have a good girl in Katie helping you in the house. As from tomorrow you can stay at home. You trained Sadie well so she can train the new girl we are starting on Monday.' For no reason at all I burst out crying.

Nurse came in to the room with a cup of tea. 'My, what's this; the tears are not because you're leaving us? Here, dry your eyes at once. We'll keep in touch. I have still to see that posh bathroom of yours. Mrs Fraser hasn't stopped talking about the water running out of the taps. It was the talk of the surgery for days. I'll run you home, Mary, now drink up your tea and Doctor wants you to take this tonic three times a day. You are far too pale.' I shook hands with Dr McKinnon and joined Nurse in the car. 'Now dry your eyes, Mary, you are not going to the other side of the world. I'll tell you what, every other Sunday in the afternoon we will take turn about and visit one another. That way we won't lose touch. My turn first on Sunday, I must see that bathroom.'

'Oh, Nurse, you are always one step ahead of me.'

She gave me a side look and said, 'don't you believe that Mary Scott, that brain of yours whirls round faster than the speed of sound. Here you are, see you Sunday.' After I and Rusty had our meal I wrote to Vera and the boys.

Katie came three mornings a week, the money she earned helped to feed the children. Their father certainly didn't bother to look sideways at them. I wondered if it would be safe to get Katie's cousin Dougal Fraser down to clean up the garden. He should be 17 or 18 years old according to my calculation. I'd see what Katie said. When he was a boy a bigger rogue you could not get. I always had a little laugh to myself when I thought of how he tried to get three extra sweeties for his sisters at Christmas when he didn't have even one. All brothers he had. I remember jumping when Nurse shouted at him and going to give him a skelp on the lug. After a lazy week I laid out the plans for decorating the whole house. It would cost me a lot of money but in the end if I wanted to sell it would increase its value. I supposed I'd better ask Mr Hendry's advice first, just in case the tradesmen tried to double deal me. When I did phone him he said he would arrange everything. If I could manage a day in Oban he would take me to the best shops to pick the papers, paints and furnishings. That way I could see what I was getting.

It was about two weeks after the painters had started work when the awful incident happened. It was a Saturday morning. The painters had all left early; Katie had cleaned up the mess after them and was finishing off washing the front steps. I was standing with my back to the open kitchen door writing out my list for shopping in the afternoon when I felt enormous hairy arms grab me round the neck, then a voice which made the hairs on the nape of my neck stand up in fear. It was Donald MacPherson. 'Well, my pretty high and mighty one; at last I have got you where I want you. I'll tame you as I tamed your haughty sister Nan.'

The next minute he lifted me by the neck with his big hairy hand and laid me flat on the table. One big hand he put over my mouth, with the other he struggled to pull my pants down. I was desperate; time was short. I knew he intended to rape me, then my old technique came to my aid. I opened my mouth wide and dug my teeth into his little finger. With one roar he let go of me and I let out one big scream. Next instant a huge ball of fur jumped on the table and Rusty sank his big teeth into Donald's neck. Another big howl rent the air. I managed to get down off the table before Katie came into the kitchen. Donald had pushed past her running out of the house, knocking the bucket of water over in his hurry while Rusty was gripping at his legs. I managed to tell Katie to shout Rusty back then I collapsed to the floor.

The next thing I remember was lying on top of the bed and Nurse Duncan bending over me. 'So, you decided to come back to us again. Doctor will be here in a few moments. Katie told me the whole story, Constable Drummond has also been notified.'

I started howling again.

'Now, now, Mary, try to stay calm. Katie has brought some tea, now drink it down. Oh, here is Doctor.'

He came into the bedroom, took one look, said a few words to Nurse and

194

disappeared. Katie came back into the room. 'Right, Katie, help me get Mary undressed and into bed, Doctor is going to give her an injection. To tell you the truth I really don't know how much more the girl can take; she must be made of iron.'

At last sleep made me forget everything.

The following Monday when Constable Drummond came to see me I was able to give him an account of what happened. He told me my story matched Katie's. As he left, Father Joseph came in to give me Holy Communion and he promised to get in touch with Billy and Ewan. Katie came into the room carrying a bowl of soup then her mother Mrs Fraser followed her. 'You don't mind me interfering, Mary, but I thought a nice bowl of home made soup would do you the world of good. The men working downstairs were all asking for you. The boss said to tell you the work will be done to perfection.'

Nurse Duncan breezed into the room as Katie's mother left. 'I would keep her out at the other side of your door, Mary, if I were you. I know you are not well enough to deal with her just now but when you are better watch Katie too. There's too much fast talk in that family. Did you know also that they are second cousins to the MacPhersons? I'll look around for another girl for you. Just tell Katie you are short of money; that you had spent too much on the house and that you will have to call a halt. That will make her look elsewhere in a hurry, also that mother of hers.'

Mary Scott v. Donald MacPherson case never came to trial. Donald instead of going to a doctor to be treated for his wounds went straight home to bed where he bled to death. It seems when Rusty attacked Donald his sharp teeth had sunk deep into his jugular vein. The verdict of the coroner was death by misadventure. My beautiful dog Rusty was ordered to be put down. I cried for weeks every night in bed thinking how cruel life was. My dear loving friend had to die because he protected the one he loved most in the whole world. Billy and Ewan came home for a week but it was a quiet house without Rusty. The boys also seemed to have changed; of course they were no longer boys. Billy was 23, Ewan 21. Both of them had girlfriends also. One evening after supper we all went out to the garden. There was a slight nip in the air. While we were walking Billy said, 'Ewan and I were wondering where you got the money from to decorate the whole house; also that lovely new bathroom suite.'

'Why, Auntie Kate left me money in her will the same as she left you two. You might tell me what you did with yours.'

Both of their faces turned a deep red then Billy said, 'sorry Mary, we should not have asked. I see you have spent your money well, we didn't. Since then both of us have learnt our lesson. We have grown up a lot since. When you are feeling better I think you should come to Mull and get another puppy for company.'

The boys' stay passed all too quickly; one thing they had done for me was to leave my garden in lovely condition. There was crazy paving in different parts of the ground, four lovely evergreen bushes, plants, the lawn cut and the edges all trimmed, two apple trees, four gooseberry bushes, black-currants, raspberry canes also, two rows of strawberry plants. 'That's all the rough work done, Mary, all you will need to do is keep it tidy. Now that winter is drawing near there should not be much work for you to do till the turn of the year. Maybe if you are kind to us we might come for a week in the spring and tidy it up again. By rights Mary you should be getting a boyfriend of your own.'

'Do you ever run across John Lewis in your tracks, boys?'

The two of them remained silent then Billy said, 'it was him who swindled us out of our money Auntie Kate gave us. We were stupid enough to be lured into a gambling den. Of course Ewan and I lost every penny.'

If I had any notion of getting in touch with John Lewis it was completely wiped out of my mind after hearing Billy and Ewan's story. I always knew he was a con man. After I saw Billy and Ewan off at the station I made them promise to write to me and send a photo of the lovely girlfriends. I wondered what Gillian Walsh would do now that Donald was dead. I'd call in at the shop on my way home and see what way the wind was blowing. The walk from the station would do me the world of good; I had been confined to the house far too long. When I arrived at Walsh's shop it was Gillian who came to serve me.

'Hello, Mary', she said, 'feeling better?'

'Yes, Gillian, I am, in fact I think the long walk from the station has done me the world of good.'

'I heard you have got the whole house refurnished.'

'Yes, in fact the cost has left me quite broke but why worry, I am still young and able to earn my living.' She was purposely steering clear of Donald MacPherson; for someone who had just lost their future husband she was in her element as if a burden had been lifted from her mind. Maybe Donald was blackmailing her father and marrying Gillian was his asking price. After all when Mr Walsh died Gillian, his only daughter, would inherit the shop and everything else that went with it. Donald MacPherson was always a schemer.

196

While in the village I called at the bakers also. Mrs Fraser and Katie were already there. When I went in the chatting stopped; as Katie and her mother left the old woman just gave me a nod. I bought the few things I needed then made my way down to the loch. I thought what a great difference having money makes. When the Frasers thought I had plenty of money they were all over me; now a nod of the head was all I could get. I supposed they would have spread the news all through the village, more fools them. Still it was better that way; I would not be pestered by any of them. Nurse Duncan was quite right; if you want to get rid of anybody plead poverty. Inwardly, I was smiling away to myself, I felt as if a heavy load had been lifted from my shoulders After I had got over the shock of the attempted rape by Donald MacPherson the fear that I always felt at the mention of his name had finally left me. From now on I'd stand on my own two feet. I had to do it when I was 15 so why not again at 25.

When I opened the door I always thought my lovely Rusty would be there. The house was so empty without him. I was able to manage the house myself now, carpets, curtains, furniture all new and so easy to keep clean and the whole place had the lovely smell of fresh paint. The telephone, which had been installed a week earlier, rang. It was Nurse Duncan inviting me over for tea the next afternoon. She had some news for me which she didn't like to give over the phone. 'You never know who is listening in, Mary. Do you think you could manage to bring me two Scotch pies.

'Oh, Nurse.'

'Call me Meg, Mary, you are not working in the surgery now.'

'Of course, I'll get the pies, terrible to think I have to bring my own tea with me.' Both of us laughed. I went to bed wondering what the special news Nurse, Meg, had for me.

The next morning I went to the village and arranged with Frank Lees, the joiner, to put a peep-hole in my front door then I spent the rest of the day going through mother's trunk; it was full of the most beautiful dresses and twin sets. I found a photo of my mother when she was a young girl. I must be like my father as I didn't see any resemblance at all to the girl in the photo. My real mother must have been wealthy according to all the beautiful clothes that filled the trunk, including two luxurious fur coats wrapped in layers of soft tissue paper. I put everything back carefully folded in their own special paper then locked the trunk again, opened the panel to the attic. I hauled the heavy trunk up the few stairs into the safety of my secret room. After I had a good look around I went down the stairs again into the big store cupboard then slid back the panel again. I had a nice little hoard there. Given time I'd spend an afternoon looking through my real mother's jewel box. I never was one for wearing rings and things.

While I was making tea there was a loud knock on the door. At first I was frightened to open it but at last I forced myself to see who it was. Standing on the doorstep was the joiner, Mr Frank Lees, the handsome young man with the mass of black curls. He made the peep-hole and camouflaged it with a lion's head door-knocker. I looked out of the peep hole and could see Mr Lees as clear as a bell. I asked how much it was and paid him, shut the door and watched him walk down the road.

It was time to go to Meg Duncan's. Meg opened the door as soon as I reached it. 'Hello, stranger' she greeted me.

'The same yourself,' I said. 'Here are your pies.'

'Oh thanks, Mary, I just took a notion for one.'

'My that sounds bad, Meg, especially the position you are in. It's only pregnant women who take notions.' Both of us burst out laughing.

At last I got the news I had been waiting for. It seemed the foresters were looking over the forest across the road from my house when they came across a piece of a girl's dress among the branches of one of the big trees. Constable Drummond said they thought it was a bit torn from Maria Duffy's clothes. They now knew for sure, according to the experts, that it was the actual spot where she was murdered. The investigations were brought nearer home to my very door. I thought that when Donald MacPherson died all my troubles would be over; no such luck. Little did they know who had actually buried the body on the MacPherson land. Meg for one would take heart failure if she knew. My only crime was giving her a decent burial.

After a short pause I said, 'do you know, Meg, after my parents' funeral Father Joseph went with me to bring back Billy and Ewan from the MacPherson's farm and Ewan said that Dad's barrow was across the road. When we went for it the branches of the big tree were all broken. Vera and I reported it to Constable Campbell. At the time he said he would look into it but I don't think he bothered. That was seven years ago; now this has turned up.'

'You'd better report that to Constable Drummond, Mary.'

'Do you really think I should? Campbell might get into trouble for doing nothing.'

'Well that's his funeral, if he noted it down at the time he has nothing to worry about so I still think you should report it for your own sake. By the way, that Mary Kate Bell is expecting. I am beginning to wonder if she is married. To tell you the truth I didn't like to ask too many questions. She is on our panel. Of course, she is home for good, staying at the hotel. I don't think her father is any too pleased.' I wondered what happened to her posh boyfriend, the hairdresser. It would be just like the thing for her to be jilted. Always too big for her boots. Meg's voice cut through my thoughts. 'Better watch out, Mary, she doesn't sook into you for lodgings. It seems the new barmaid at the hotel has put it about that Mary Kate and her father are always at loggerheads.'

The evening just flew by then it was time for me to go home. 'How about a week today, Meg, for dinner after surgery and we can exchange all the news.'

'That will be fine, Mary, I am really looking forward to seeing that posh house of yours.' As I walked home I didn't realise how quickly it got dark. It was at such times I missed my Rusty. I felt a bit frightened as I hurried along the road as if someone was watching me. At last I was home and got the door opened, shut it quickly behind me, locked and bolted it then slid to the floor. I sat there for a good ten minutes then rose and peeped through the spy hole.

There was a heavy dark shape disappearing down the road. All my old fears of the MacPhersons came back again. I wondered if that shape was Donald's only surviving brother out for revenge. I had been beginning to feel on the top of the world, all my worries forgotten, now this. Maybe I would be better with a boyfriend, that way I would not be such a lone target. The next day was the end of the month, I'd get the month's rent from the cottage in Mull. While that income came in there was no need for me to work. Vera had never answered my letter telling her of Auntie Katie's death. I supposed Flora had told Sarah. No word from her for five years. I didn't even know why she left in the huff; maybe in some way she found out I wasn't her sister, just her cousin. There was no sense in worrying about her, and I went to bed to forget.

Next morning the ground was covered with heavy frost. The loch was in one of her secretive moods, covered in heavy mist and dead calm. I hurried and piled the logs on the big range, filled the black kettle from the tap. No more running outside in the freezing weather to the outside toilet or to the well for water. It was a pleasure to move around in my warm comfortable kitchen.

After breakfast I wrapped up well and walked briskly down to the bank. I wasn't struck on any of the male clerks at the bank, they all seemed as if they carried the weight of the whole world on their shoulders. They were all stuffed shirts, never even took the time to smile. The good morning they gave was through tight lips that never moved. My turn to be attended came; I was served by a young man, immaculately dressed, beautiful navy blue suit, pure white shirt, blue tie with tiny white spots, jet black, shining straight hair brushed straight back off his face. When I handed him my book he just nodded without looking up. After he was finished filling it in he held it in his hand for a few seconds then looked up into my face. If he thought I was going to give him a smile he was in for a shock. I just took my book and wished him good morning as I made my way to the door. I could feel his eyes boring into my back; I thought to myself if there was just a few pounds in my book instead of four figures he would never have looked up at me. I'd make sure he was out of the race.

From the bank I went to the hotel in search of tea and cakes. Mr Bell himself took my order then sat down beside me and had the cheek to ask how much my bathroom suite had cost. He looked put out when I told him I had no idea as Mr Hendry had attended to everything.

Constable Drummond came in and we both exclaimed, 'ah, the very person'. I told him the story Vera and I had told Constable Campbell and he was grateful for my help.

The constable warned me to always lock up properly as there were some very funny goings on. I assured him I always did and, in addition, carried a small gun. He asked me if I had a licence for it and, when I said I hadn't, promised to help me with the application for one.

Although it was cold I sat beside the loch for a while. I liked to watch my lovely loch whatever her mood. On the way home there at the side of MacLean's house stood Flora; she must have been waiting for me. 'Hello Mary,' she shouted then she made her way to the front gate. 'My', she said, 'you are looking well. Did you know Hector and Sarah and the two children are due home tomorrow? Eachan is a year and a half now.'

'You and your parents will be quite excited. Sorry I won't be at home, I am leaving for a week's holiday to the cottage in Mull tomorrow, bye for now, Flora.' If she thought she had pulled a fast one on me I pulled a bigger one on her. That morning when I got up I didn't realise that before the afternoon was over I would be planning to go to Mull for a week's holiday. If Sarah thought I was just going to sit waiting for her she had another thought coming. I didn't know why I had always to get news about Sarah through the MacLeans, she could quite easily have written me a short note or maybe she is too high and mighty. Little did she know how well off little Mary was and little Mary had no intentions of telling her. I'd play the innocent poor girl then I remembered

I could not go to the cottage for a holiday as it was let. I'd stay at a hotel and while in Mull pay Billy and Ewan a visit.

The rest of the day I spent cleaning and polishing the furniture in all the rooms, mopped out the kitchen and bathroom floors then the front steps. Then I cleaned the outside toilet, also. It is always handy if you are working in the garden.

On my way to Mull I enjoyed the first hour of the journey watching the beautiful scenery as the train sped quickly on its way. The rest of the train journey I slept. When I arrived at Oban station I had to hurry to catch the ferry. The crossing to Craignure was calm; as soon as I set foot on the quay I hailed a taxi to take me to the Crown hotel. It was a small place but very homely and comfortable. After I had changed and washed I made my way to the dining room for lunch. For the time of the year the place seemed quite busy. I was put at a small table with a lovely view of the sea. In a way I was happy to get away from Craigshill House in Loch Etive and out of the way of Sarah and Hector and the children. I finished my lunch, wrapped up well against the chilly wind then made my way to see Billy and Ewan.

I thought I had nothing to do but walk into the Castle grounds but I had an entrance fee to pay first. The beautiful gardens were vast; to keep the size of these grounds in the perfect condition that they were in took a lot of men. There was no one about so I went into the Castle. There were plenty of uniformed men walking about; also a young woman leading a group of tourists through the large cold rooms. I asked one of the men how to find out where the boys worked. I was then told I would find the gardeners' cottages at the foot of the long winding road leading from the Castle. So I had paid my fee for nothing. It was a good thing I had the whole afternoon to make my way down again. I was shown Billy and Ewan's cottage but nobody was in, so I just pushed a note in the door telling them where I was staying then slowly made my way back to my hotel. I enjoyed the walk and liked nothing better than watching the sea with its changing colours.

I went into the dining room for tea before going to my room to rest till dinner time. I got the shock of my life to see Sarah and Hector sitting at another table at the window. I wondered if they had noticed me coming into the hotel as from where they were sitting they had a clear view of the entrance. Quickly I drew back and made my way to my room then I ordered tea and cakes to be brought up to my room. A young girl brought my tea to my room; the cakes were delicious. I felt a lot better after I finished my tea and ready now to do battle. I phoned the cottage; Mrs Forrester answered. I asked her if she had any callers. 'Yes, Miss Mary; a young couple called; they wanted to stay the night. The wife said she was your sister Sarah and it was important that she see you. I told her that I could not let her stay without permission.'

So I was right. Sarah knew about Auntie Kate's cottage and wondered why should she should get permission from her little sister Mary. She was too intelligent a person not to smell a rat and she was the type of person to go to any lengths to get her own way. If she thought because she was the eldest of the family she was entitled to a share of the cottage she could think again. I stayed the rest of the evening in my room having dinner sent up. For safety's sake I'd leave for home in the morning, asking for my bill to be sent up along with my breakfast. That settled I got ready for bed and sleep. As I was dozing off I suddenly remembered that I had to call at the cottage. I could do that on my way to the ferry.

In Oban I made my way to Mr Hendry's office; when I said who I was I was shown in right away. As I entered the room he rose from behind his large desk covered in papers, held out his hand and said, what a nice surprise it was to see me. He rang a bell and ordered tea. After the tea was brought and we were alone I explained what had happened during the last few days. 'I think Sarah seems to think that she being the eldest of the family, that the cottage should be hers.'

'Don't worry, Mary, I'll write to her and tell her by law the cottage is yours. She doesn't need to find out that you are just her cousin. By the way how long is it since she arrived back?'

'Two days ago.'

'I see; she hasn't been long in showing her hand.'

'I would not mind so much but I have never had as much as a scrape of the pen from her or Hector. I get what little news there is from Flora MacLean whenever it suits her.'

'Don't worry any more about this matter, I'll deal with it; go now and spend a few hours in the shops before you return home to Loch Etive.'

I didn't need to buy anything so I went straight to the railway station where I boarded the train for home. Back home I hoped I could get into the house without anyone seeing me so when the taxi drew up at the door I hurriedly paid and slipped quietly into the house. A small white envelope lay on the mat. I picked it up and made my way to the kitchen. It was a note from Sarah saying she had called and got no answer. Now why should she call when Flora would tell her I was in Mull and she had the cheek to follow me there. Hector's mother and Flora must be looking after the children. I hoped the two of them were not thinking of blackmailing me over Maria Duffy's body. If they did they were in for a shock. It was Hector who carried the remains to the forest where she was buried so they were all involved in it. If they thought they were going to squeeze money out of me they could think again.

I made myself some scrambled eggs. I had half a dozen nice fresh ones in the larder. My mind went back to the harsh rationing days and thought of how kind Hector was to us then. He used to stock up our food cupboards and never say a word. Maybe I was being a wee bit too harsh on them. The shrill noise of the phone ringing made me jump to my feet. It was Billy phoning during his lunch break. He could not understand why I did not stay any longer. When I asked him if he had seen Sarah and Hector he said no. Oh, how I missed Rusty, even just sitting looking at his lovely big eyes made me feel better. The phone rang again, it was Meg Duncan asking me over for a chat.

I hurried along the road to Meg's, glad to get into her cosy parlour. Meg said, 'what do you think of your sister Sarah? She had the nerve to go up to the Fraser house and ask Katie and her mother where you got the money from to do up the whole house and that stupid woman told her all about your new bathroom.'

'Where is she now, Meg?'

'I heard she went to Mull straight away to find out for herself.' I had a secret smile to myself; I had outwitted them this time. By the time they get back from Mull Mr Hendry's letter would be waiting for them then Sarah would realise that little Mary is not so stupid as she thought.

I had a long lie in bed the next morning; I don't know why but I was feeling very tired. I was just finishing my breakfast when there was a loud knock on the door. I looked through the spy hole and there were Sarah and Hector standing there. When I opened the door I was taken by surprise; both of them threw their arms round me and were all smiles. 'Do you want to come in to the kitchen, I'm just finishing my breakfast.' I don't think either of them heard because they stayed in the hall eyeing everything up.

Sarah said, 'you don't mind if we look around.'

'Of course not' I said, 'I'll come with you.' It was my house and no way were they going to rake through my rooms.

'The Frasers told me all about your bathroom; it must have cost a bit of money?'

'Well, yes, it was a necessity; it was misery running out to the outside toilet in all kinds of weather. By the way, why the sudden interest in the house now; when you and Hector left you never as much as let me know you were gone;

also you never wrote. It was Flora who gave me the news about the children.'

'Well it seems according to Flora that Auntie Kate had left you a lot of money and Hector was just saying that by law I was entitled to my share. This house must be worth a pretty penny.'

'Well if you want the full information you better contact my solicitor.'

'I have already done that, Mary; also I received a letter from him this morning and if Mr Hendry thinks that's the end of the matter he can think again. Hector will write to our solicitor. You know, Mary, Hector knows a lot of people in high places.'

'Is that why you cut me out of your life; because I was a nobody just back home to nurse your dying mother and father? I had spent three and a half years scudging as a miserable low paid servant while you with your well paid position, you never even took the time off to visit your dying parents.'

'Oh, that's all in the past now, I mean to get my share of anything that's going and my husband Hector here will go into all the details.'

'If that's the way you want it, Sarah, I am afraid you and Hector are in for a hard battle; possession is nine tenths of the law.' They looked at each other in silence then I said, 'for old times sake how about a cup of tea?'

It was Hector who said, 'thanks, Mary, but we have no time, Sarah and I have a lot to attend to.'

I thought to myself I bet you two schemers have. Out loud I said, 'how long are you staying?'

Abruptly Sarah said, 'I don't know', then they made for the door. Sarah as usual, with her pretty head held high as if she owned the world. She was a law unto herself. I thought, no way were they going to take my house and cottage, which were legally mine, from me. I piled the logs on the range, filled the big black kettle with water and set it on the hob; put on my warmest coat then made my way down to the surgery to ask Doctor for a tonic.

When I arrived there the place was packed; I went to the desk. Sadie gave a big smile; 'oh you're back. We heard you had gone to Mull. Your sister Sarah and that stuck up husband of hers were here asking where you were. I told them I didn't know; even if I did I would not tell them. Is it Dr McKinnon you want or that smashing young assistant of his? He sure is a good looker. Just sit down, Mary, I'll try to squeeze you in earlier.'

'Is Nurse in?'

'Oh, yes, you will soon hear her howling.'

My mind went back to the time I had just started working in Sadie's place. I nearly jumped out of my skin when she howled at Dougal Fraser. I thought to myself that coarse voice hides a loving, kind heart. The sick she nursed saw the gentle side of her. That's why I loved her so much, I knew the true Meg; not the side she showed at the surgery. I sat down and waited my turn. The children were running wild as usual; the tired looking mothers scolded the children who managed to escape the occasional slap that was meant for them. At last it was my turn. Sadie showed me to Dr McKinnon's room. He was standing looking out of the small window. He turned round, 'Oh, it's you, Mary, you're certainly looking well. What can I do for you?'

'I really came for a tonic; I am still feeling very tired all the time.'

'Yes, Mary, even though you are looking better it will take some time for you to feel top form. I'll give you the same tonic you had before. Come and see me if it doesn't help. I hear your sister Sarah is home running around mad.'

I left the room then bumped into Nurse. 'Oh, Mary, Sadie told me you were here; sit in the waiting room, I'll run you home after we are finished.' I was glad to get in the car as the rain was pelting down. Meg came in for a lunch of tea, Scotch pies and cream cakes. 'My,' she said, 'you sure are cosy, and that bathroom of yours. I see now why it's the envy of the village. You know Mary I miss that lovely dog of yours. Will you be getting another one?'

'Not just yet, I need time.'

After we were both sitting at the fire I told her the whole story about Sarah and Hector wanting the share of the house and how she was going to do everything in her power to get her share. 'I always knew she was a greedy one. It's funny, it's only since I got the house refurnished that Sarah sees nothing but pounds, shillings and pence in front of her eyes. She says she just wants her share but it's not hers it's mine by law.' I told Meg what happened in Mull.

She burst out laughing; 'good for you, Mary. I for one would never have thought of doing that; so you gave them both a bit of running around.'

'Have you seen the children, Meg?'

'No, but I suppose it won't be long before I do; with young children you never really know what mischief they get up to. I don't know how long they are home for but I'll try and find out and phone you. Have to run now; oh did you meet our new doctor? Since he arrived all the young girls have suddenly taken ill. Between you and me there's nothing wrong with them. Sadie always puts them down for Dr McKinnon. When they come out their faces are like fiddles. To tell you the truth I think Sadie wants to keep him for herself. His name is Peter MacInnes. I think you and him would get along together. I'll give you a ring, Mary, if I hear any news,' then she ran to her car quickly to get out of the heavy rain. My mind went back to Sarah wondering what dirty trick she had up her sleeve.

I spent a few minutes going through all of Auntie Kate's papers. I might find some clue. When I looked back I wondered where Mum and Dad got the money to pay for Sarah's lavish big wedding. Funny how they could find money to spend on her with not a scrape of the pen from Mum or Dad during my three and half years at service. I thought I'd just tell Sarah that I am not her sister but Auntie Kate's daughter. That would wipe the smile off her smug face. I went to the attic, where I kept all my private papers, to make a hole in the floor to hide my little boxes. While I was in the cupboard downstairs getting the tools the door knocker went. I just sat on the floor, waited a few seconds then went to the spy-hole and saw the back of Constable Drummond disappearing down the road. I went back up to the attic with the hammer and chisel and some nails. It was hard work prising up the planks of wood, even though they were old they were solid. At last I managed to get one plank up. First, I put in the tin of old coins that was found underneath the old toilet. Then there was my box of all the money Auntie Kate had sent me throughout the years. I sealed it properly then I laid it beside the coins and my mother's jewel box. I kept the lovely sapphire ring, the ruby brooch and the pearl necklace then I placed the box of jewels in a tin box, sealed it and put it under the floor board, replaced the plank then nailed it down. There were bits of white wood showing so I ran down stairs, went to the garden, took a handful of wet mud, locked and bolted the back door then flew up the stairs and spread the muck all over the plank. Tomorrow when it had dried I would rub most of it into the wood then sweep the rest away, push the wardrobe back in its place. Another knock came to the door. It was Constable Drummond. I quickly opened the door and let him in. His face was very solemn. 'Sit down, Mary, I am afraid I have bad news for you. Your sister Sarah and her husband were in a bad accident.'

'Were they travelling fast in the car?'

'No, Mary, they went out on the loch in Mr Ross's boat. They said they were going fishing. The coast guard was called out by Mr Ross as he was worried. They said they would be just two hours but it went on to six hours and no sign of them. What with the poor visibility and the severe storm raging he sent for help. The coastguard found Sarah lying on the rocks with her leg broken, half in the water. Hector, God rest his soul, lying dead on the sharp craigs just at your garden wall.'

'Oh my God,' I said then fainted.

I don't know how long I was out but when I came to Nurse Duncan was bending over me. With her was the new doctor, Peter as they all called him. 'Well, Mary, you do give us all some frights,' a male voice said. 'We better get her to bed.' I felt myself getting carried upstairs and put on the bed then the male voice said, 'when you have settled her, Nurse I'll give her a jag.'

'I'll stay the night with her, Doctor, then I'll get a girl to stay with her tomorrow. She has been through a lot.' Nurse Duncan sat with me till I fell asleep. It was late the next day when I woke; a young girl came into the bedroom carrying a tray. 'Nurse Duncan told me to stay with you all day. I am Rose Walsh, Gillian's cousin.' God, I thought, everyone in the village is related one way or another. 'I have brought you some breakfast; Nurse said I was to look after you. She also said "make sure she eats her breakfast" so, Miss Mary, if you could just sit up I'll fix the pillows and settle your tray. Eat something I don't want Nurse roaring at me.' I didn't feel hungry but for peace sake I did eat. My mind went back to the events of the previous night. So Hector was found dead on the other side of my garden wall and Sarah must have been trying to climb the rocks as well and fell. The loch had protected me again. I wondered if there was a secret entrance from the garden into my house. If anyone knew Sarah would.

Rose came into the bedroom followed by Father Joseph. 'I just heard the news, Mary; I called at the MacLean's house first. It's a dreadful thing that has happened. I just stayed a short while. Sarah, by the way, is in a critical condition; the surgeon in charge doesn't know yet whether she will lose her leg or not. She lay in the water so long. She must be a strong lady to have survived the terrible conditions of last night.'

'I am sorry to hear that, Father, but what on earth were they doing on those dangerous craigs, especially when the weather was so bad and too dark to see anything. Did Mr Ross get his boat back?'

'Yes I understand the coastguard brought it back for him. Just you rest, Mary. That young Dr Peter was telling me that you gave them all a fright. I'll need to attend to the arrangements for Hector's funeral. Those poor children; it will be weeks before they will really feel the great loss of their father; as for Sarah, only time will tell. It's a blessing the children have such nice grandparents and their Auntie Flora to look after them.' Rosie saw Father out and she locked the door after him. I gave her strict instructions to always keep it locked. I still felt very weak. I heard the word 'shock' mentioned when I was coming round.

There it was again, the loud knock on the door. The next minute Nurse Duncan came breezing into the room. 'And how is the patient this morning,' she shouted.

'Oh, Meg', I said, 'you have got a voice like a fog horn. Any word about Sarah, Meg?'

Her lips went tightly together then she said, 'whatever the pair of them were doing they were up to no good.'

'It's funny, Meg, I was thinking the same; so was Father Joseph. I don't think the MacLeans will want to nurse her when she comes out of hospital. With all the money Hector had she should be quite comfortably off.'

'Well, Mary, I heard a different story; it seems Hector was discharged from the Diplomatic Service. He had some gambling trouble. That's why they came home. According to the haughty way Sarah spoke to me he was still a secretary to the British Embassy in Canada. She would of course bluff it out.'

'So that's why she was trying to get her hands on my house, to pay her husband's debts.'

'I am afraid so, Mary; here's Rosie with our lunch.' When Rosie left the room Meg said, 'by the way that young doctor was quite concerned about you. He said he will call to see you if he has time.' Meg shook her head; 'that's a nice pot of tea Rosie has made, I am not moving from here till you finish that lovely bit of fish on your plate.'

'You know I quite believe you take delight in bullying everyone.' Another roar of laughter rent the air at the same time as this charming smashing looking young man stood in the doorway. Nurse wondered what was wrong as I was staring at the door.

When she looked round she jumped up and, 'it's you, Dr Peter, I never heard you coming in, I'll go downstairs till you have seen Mary.'

He came over to the bed with his hand outstretched and said, 'I am Dr Peter. I just called to see if you were all right.' I don't know what came over me but I could not speak. He took my pulse which must have been racing then told me to rest. 'I'll see Nurse on my way out, bye now.'

It was the first time in my life that I felt my heart beating so fast. After I shook hands with him I said to myself don't be stupid Mary, he has all those young girls to pick and choose from.

Meg came rushing into the room. 'Time I was off, Mary, Doctor was quite pleased with you. He said to get up this afternoon for a while. Now what do you think of him? Small wonder all the girls are running after him, especially Sadie. She goes about all day with those sheep's eyes of hers, watching him all day. If she doesn't stop it she will lose her job. I have already told her.'

'Poor Sadie,' I said. Poor me is more like it. I wished Dr Peter would get married and we would all get some peace.

I must have dozed off; it seemed just like a minute since lunch and there was Rosie shaking me and holding the tea tray. Nurse Duncan was on the phone saying she will be calling in on her way from work. After you have had your tea and I have washed the tea dishes, is it all right with you if I go home as mother needs me.'

'That's quite all right, Rosie, to tell you the truth I'll be glad to get up.'

Rosie took the tray away. I made my way slowly downstairs to the kitchen where Rosie was busy putting on her coat and hat. I handed her the pay and thanked her for looking after me. Through my spy hole I watched her with all her abundance of energy skipping down the road. It was lovely just to watch her, so young and full of life with not a care in the world.

While in the hall I phoned the hospital and enquired about Sarah. The news was not good. The hospital was worried about the effects of lying in the cold water for so long and could not make an accurate assessment of her prospects for recovery. I put the phone down then made my way to my cosy kitchen. Rosie had piled the logs on the range and the wood was merrily crackling away. Sitting in my rocking chair I started dreaming about Dr Peter. I wondered how old he was; he looked so young. I hoped he was about 30, that way I would be 2 years younger than him. I could still picture him in my mind. Small wonder all the young girls were madly in love with him. Another knock came to the door; it was Flora, Hector's sister. We went into the kitchen and I asked if she had the latest news about Sarah. Without waiting for a response I went on 'what on earth were the two of them doing on the craigs anyway on such a night?'

All I saw was the tightening of her lips then she said, 'Mum was wondering if you could keep the children, Helen and Eachan, till Sarah comes out of hospital.'

'Why, Flora, should I look after the children? They are your parents' grandchildren, your mother's responsibility not mine; I have been ill myself and still don't feel too great. After all, Flora, it was your brother and sister who never wrote to me for years.'

She burst into tears; 'the house has been in a turbulent state since they arrived and since Hector's death Mum has taken to her bed. Dad is busy running after her and I am left with the children.'

'Well, Flora, the only solution to your problem is to get help in till Sarah

209

comes home.'

She was taken aback then she said, 'Mum says anyway half of the house belongs to Sarah.'

I stood up and drew myself up to my full height and said, 'how dare you come into my house and talk to me like that. Just go back to your mother and Sarah and tell them I said no. If it's too much for you all to look after the children put them into an orphanage.' She burst out crying again. 'Your tears, Flora, won't cut any ice with me so just dry your eyes. In case you don't know it, Flora, I was sent to service at the young age of 15 where I slaved for three and a half years while Dad's precious Sarah was sent to college. I have suffered a lot and I had to stand on my own two feet. Nobody helped me, so tell your parents that I am really sorry but taking care of either the children or Sarah is out of the question and while you are on the subject, the house here is mine. I have all the title deeds to it.'

'I am sorry, Mary, I never knew that part of your life.'

'I am sorry also, Flora, if you think me hard but I have already been through too much.' With that out in the open we parted friends.

Meg Duncan came in after surgery was over. She wanted to know what had been happening and I told her the story about Flora and the children.

'You did the right thing, Mary, refusing to take the children. You yourself are not strong. Oh, by the way, Dr Peter wants to see you in the surgery some day next week. Sadie has already been told. I am going to the hospital on Sunday. Would you like a run in and you can visit Sarah. I think you should go, Mary; after all, she is your sister and she is pretty ill.'

'All right, anything for a quiet life.' After Meg left I locked and bolted the door, attended to the back door as well. I sat in my rocking chair and went over the day's events thinking I certainly didn't have a dull moment. At last it was bedtime so I could sleep and forget all the day's happenings. Sleep didn't come easily, I tossed and turned thinking of Hector and Sarah and the children. It was the small hours in the morning when I eventually fell asleep, and late in the morning when I woke.

I hurried downstairs; there on the mat lay a letter. I lifted it, pushed it in the kitchen drawer, to read when I had had my breakfast. I finally settled in my rocking chair and opened my letter. It was from Vera with a photo of herself and her husband and the children. They were all looking the picture of health. Fred, of course, had put on weight. I didn't know who the children were like; they were beautiful anyway. In her letter she said she was sorry to hear of the loss of Auntie Kate. She wanted me to go to America for a holiday. She had already asked Billy and Ewan to go out there for good as there was plenty of work. There was time to reply to Vera's letter before going down to the village. I told her all the news about Hector and Sarah trying to take my house away from me, Hector's death and the danger of Sarah losing a leg.

When I called at the surgery to see Dr Peter Sadie was her usual self. As I sat down to wait my turn I felt everyone had suddenly fallen silent. I supposed they had heard of Hector's death and Sarah's accident; also the news that I had refused to look after Sarah's children. Flora would make sure of that. I went in to see Dr Peter, the surgery by that time nearly empty. I hoped he wouldn't take too long as I had the shops to go to before they shut. The first thing he did was to take my pulse. As soon as he touched me my stupid heart started racing again. Oh dear, I thought to myself, what on earth is wrong with you Mary, then he sat down and said he would like me to get a chest X-ray. Knowing that I had no means of transport to the hospital, Doctor said he would arrange for the ambulance to take me. He rose and opened the door for me. I felt my face flushing as I left. Thank God I left by the back door, I could not bear anyone seeing my face so flushed. The wind was bitterly cold so if my cheeks were flushed when I went into the shops I would blame it. Luckily nobody noticed. I was quite annoyed at myself for feeling the way I did.

By the time I had been to all the different shops it was getting quite dark. I had just started walking when Meg drew up in her car. It was a relief to get the lift home. I thought maybe I'd better get a car myself. Of course I would have to take driving lessons. It was pitch black by the time I let myself in.

I forgot to call on Father Joseph to find out the time of the Mass for Hector. By rights the MacLeans should have let me know. It was Meg who gave me all the information about Hector's funeral while she drove me to the hospital on Sunday to see Sarah. The post mortem on the body had delayed the funeral.

When we went into the ward to see Sarah I hardly recognised her. Her left leg was bandaged from her toes to the top of her hip. The left side of her face was completely covered also. Meg said we would have to be very quiet as she was still on the danger list. Just sit beside her bed for a while. Meg went off to see the ward sister. I sat beside Sarah; the thought of her and Hector climbing those craigs in that terrible weather puzzled me. I supposed it would be a long time before I got the truth from her. Meg came hurrying back into the ward. Sister had said Sarah was heavily sedated so there wasn't any sense in waiting any longer. I rose from the chair, bent over the bed and kissed Sarah lightly on the forehead. For the children's sake I prayed for her to get better.

211

I followed Meg into the car and she said, that sister said there was not much hope; we all would just have to pray. 'I don't understand, Mary, since you came home to stay everyone who has dared to go near those craigs has died.' It had puzzled me, also; my loch protects me. She said how sick she was of those young girls crowding into the surgery to see Dr Peter when there was nothing wrong with them. I told Meg she had been young once herself. She agreed, but denied ever being that brazen.

I think the whole of the village attended the Requiem Mass of Hector MacLean's funeral. I sat in my own pew; the MacLean's pew was on the other side of the church. I didn't like to look round. The Mass seemed extra long; maybe it was me, I was always feeling tired. The graveyard was at the side of the church. It was a bitterly cold day with a blustery wind and I thought everyone would be happy when the service was over. I never went to the breakfast which was held in the hotel; just made my way slowly home. I never got an invitation to the funeral so I thought it best to make myself scarce. At home in my cosy kitchen I made myself a nice cup of tea and sat in my rocking chair. I seem to feel happier when I am sitting in it. A loud knock on the door gave me a fright. I thought to myself am I never going to get a minute's peace and went to the spy hole. There was Dr Peter standing at the door. Before I even opened the door my knees felt like jelly at the sight of him. Oh, Mary, I said to myself pull yourself together and stop making a fool of yourself. I forced myself to open the door.

'Mary, I saw you leave the graveyard early so I thought I would find you at home.'

'I was just having a cup of tea, Doctor, would you like one?'

'That's just what I need, I was frozen standing there waiting on the service finishing. What I came to see you about was your X-rays. Remember to go to the hospital on Friday. It will most likely be a week before I get the results. Come and see me in a week's time; remember to make an appointment with Sadie.'

'I sure will, Doctor, and what's your opinion of Sarah's chances of walking normally again?'

'Dr McKinnon is in charge of the hospital. I'll make inquiries for you and let you know. Don't worry she is in safe hands. How long is it since you lost your parents?'

'Oh it's more than ten years.'

'I am afraid I'll have to move otherwise I'll fall asleep, it was my turn to be on call last night.' When I asked Dr Peter how he got on with Meg Duncan he roared with laughter and said he was frightened to death of her. I said that I was, too, but still thought the world of her and that set us both off giggling. He was still giggling as he left, saying he was glad he had called. That makes two of us, I thought, and prayed it wouldn't be long before he called again.

At the hospital for my X-ray I took the chance to nip into the ward and visit Sarah. She was propped up in bed; her leg still strung up and still covered in bandages. I thought she was asleep so I sat quietly on the chair beside her bed then I heard a weak voice say, 'Oh, it's you Mary; it's nice of you to come and see me.'

'How do you feel now, Sarah? Is the pain still unbearable?'

'Yes, Mary, it is but I am thankful they didn't have to take my leg off. Dr McKinnon told me it will be a long time before I'll be able to walk so in a way I should be thankful. Were you at Hector's funeral, Mary?'

I thought to myself what a silly question to ask me, as her mother-in-law would have told her everything. To Sarah I said, 'yes I went even though I didn't get an invitation. I would not have known the time or day of Hector's funeral if it had not been for Nurse Duncan telling me.'

'Thanks for saying that, Mary, Hector's mother and Flora told me a completely different story. I am beginning to realise that they have been feeding me and Hector a pack of lies all those years. Now that I have nothing to do but lie in bed all day I have plenty of time to think things over and when I look back all those years I see now how they pulled the wool over my eyes. I am ashamed I believed the horrible lies they told me about you; that was why I never said goodbye to you when Hector and I went to Canada. Also do forgive me for ignoring you all those years. It's funny, it had to be this big accident which would bring me to my senses.'

'I was very hurt, Sarah, but meantime don't say any more, just rest and get better. I'll have to leave you as my ambulance is waiting.' I don't think Sarah heard me; all the talking she had done had tired her out; now she was fast asleep. I made my way to the ambulance thinking at least I had got part of the reason why Sarah had turned against me all those years, yet the MacLeans to my face were as sweet as butter and behind my back sticking the sharpest of blades in my back. I wondered why and Flora had the nerve to come to my house and ask me to look after their grandchildren.

The ambulance dropped me at my door; as soon as I arrived home I put some more logs on the range. The kettle was singing away to itself so I just made myself a cup of tea and thought of poor Sarah. As she said it had to be that accident which would bring us closer together again. I was beginning to get a bit suspicious of Hector's father Ronald MacLean; maybe he was involved with Maria Duffy's death. There must have been some battle the night my dad was beaten up and killed according to all the broken branches of that big tree. I could tell the police a lot of news but I dare not. I was one of the three who buried her; finding out who placed her dead body in Mum's trunk and her new-born child in our crib was a different story, so for the families' sake I better keep quiet.

There was an insistent knock at the door. Before I reached the door a loud voice shouted, 'it's only me'. There was only one person in the whole wide world who owned a voice like that, Meg. I opened the door; 'hurry and shut your door, it's freezing out there.' She hurried into the kitchen; with her back to the blazing fire she said, 'my, that's better. I am just back from the Fraser's house. The children must be frozen. They were all running about with their coats and hats on in the house; they have no coal or wood for their fire.'

'When you are going home, Meg, could you run up to them again; I'll give you plenty of wood for their fire, also flour, sugar and some tea. How about some blankets.'

'Yes, Mary, if they are old, not any new ones otherwise they will be in the pawn shop tomorrow.'

'I think, Meg, you have been standing long enough at that fire, sit down and I'll make you a cup of tea. I have a nice fruit cake I got at the bakers. I don't know if you will like it.' During tea I told Meg about my conversation with Sarah when I was at the hospital for my X-ray.

'Right enough, I have never been inside the MacLean's door, they are "private". I don't know who their doctor is. By rights Sarah should not be in a N.H.S. hospital. It's up to Dr McKinnon what happens next. All the same I am glad both of you are speaking again. Well, Mary, I better be on my way; I'll help myself to the logs for the Frasers. If you get the other things ready; mind now, just old blankets and, by the way, Sadie has already made your appointment for Dr Peter, next Friday.' She rushed out to the woodshed while I got things ready in the house. The poor children I thought, and that drunken father doesn't give two hoots for them.

Friday came for me to visit Dr Peter; when I went to the desk Sadie said Dr Peter had said I was to go in as soon as I arrived. She gave me a chair outside Dr Peter's door; 'just go in, when the other patient comes out. I'll deal with the rest of them.' My knees were shaking at the thought of seeing him again. When my turn came I walked into the office looking at everything but him in case I gave myself away.

214

'Good morning, Miss Scott, just a minute till I phone through to Nurse to bring your X-ray plates.' Nurse came breezing in; she just nodded to me and handed the X-rays to Doctor. The two of them spoke in quiet tones then doctor sat down at his desk, Nurse standing beside him then he looked up and said, 'I am afraid I have bad news for you, Miss Scott; the X-rays show you have a shadow on your left lung. It will mean either the hospital for you for six weeks or, if you prefer, you could rest at home. The trouble is, at home there is always the risk of you getting out of bed when nobody is about. The only cure is complete rest in bed.'

I burst into tears; Nurse said, 'now, now, Mary, it's not the end of the world. Come into my room, Sadie will bring you a cup of tea. That will give you time to think things over. That's why you were always complaining of feeling tired. Dr Peter will see you again to discuss things then I'll run you home. If you would like my advice I suggest you go to hospital for six weeks; that way you have a proper chance of getting better. You are still young so what is six weeks in a lifetime.' What Meg said was true. I was just finishing my tea when Doctor came to talk to me.

'Yes,' I said, 'I'll go to hospital.'

'I am glad, Miss Scott; you have made a wise decision. I'll attend to all the arrangements so be ready to go into hospital a week come Monday. I'll visit you when I have time. Nurse said she would run you home. In the meantime rest as much as possible.'

Oh dear, I thought to myself, no way now would Dr Peter give a second thought to a sickly girl like me but I was wrong. Every Sunday in the following six weeks he visited me in all kinds of weather. That year it seemed was one of the worst winters in twenty years. Each time he came he brought me a new book that had just been published which kept me occupied all week. At last my six weeks were up.

During my last week in hospital Sarah had visited me in the small room I had to myself. She was on crutches; her face was still badly scarred on the left side but if she pulled her face forward it was hidden. She said when she got stronger that she would get plastic surgery done. 'I am so thankful, Mary, that I never lost my leg. I suppose I'll always suffer some pain with it. Dr McKinnon was very pleased with me today. I wasn't allowed to visit earlier as the sister said you had to have complete rest. We will make up for that when both of us get out of hospital.' Sarah gave me a big hug. 'I better get back to my room before that dragon of a sister sees me.' Both of us laughed.

When the ambulance arrived to take me home I felt like a schoolgirl again, starting out on our summer holidays. I had the same feeling. I felt a lot better and happier within myself. The day before I arrived home Meg had lit the fire in the big kitchen range to heat the house for me coming home; also put two hot water bottles in my bed to air it. When the ambulance driver saw me inside Meg met me at the door. 'Come into the fire, quick; I've got a bowl of hot soup ready; that busybody Mrs Fraser brought it down. To tell you the truth I am sure she knows everything I am going to do before I know myself. I had just lit the fire yesterday and before I could wash my hands there she was on the doorstep with that sly smile of hers, holding the bowl of soup out to me saying, "for Miss Mary, can I see her?" "Sorry, Mrs Fraser, Mary is not home yet. I'll put the soup in the larder till she comes home." "Oh I thought she was home, Nurse". "Sorry", then I shut the door. I think, Mary, I'll tell Rosie Walsh to call in for a week or two till you are on your feet proper and keep that witch Mrs Fraser outside your door.' After I had finished the bowl of soup I sat in my rocking chair so happy to be home. The six weeks in hospital had taught me a lot.

CHAPTER 13

I didn't need to go down to the surgery for the results of my X-rays; Dr Peter brought the news up to me as the weather was so severe. I could tell by his face everything was OK. Over a cup of tea I told Doctor that the spell in hospital had set me thinking. I wanted to join the Red Cross. Also, I thought I'd take driving lessons and buy a small car to avoid imposing on Nurse Duncan so much.

'Nurse told me what you did for the Fraser family.'

I blushed and said, 'oh, it was just a little help. I don't understand those fathers who drink every penny they have and never think of their wives and family.' All of a sudden I thought of my own father, now my uncle, how he died starved to death and his wife with him; all because he, also, put drink first.

Dr Peter rose from the table and I followed him to the front door; just as he was on the verge of opening it he turned to me and gave me a big hug and kiss. 'Oh, Mary, I do love you; all the times I visited you in hospital I wanted to shout it out to everyone I met but I could not. You were my patient, still are. I'll talk it over with Dr McKinnon and he can take you on as his; until then, I'll have to be discreet. If that's all right with you, Mary.'

I just nodded my head, 'right love; a big goodnight kiss.' The two of us clung to one another. I was wishing he did not need to go but at last he broke free and disappeared quickly out of the door. Slowly I shut and locked the door; please God some day as my husband I'll shut and lock the door to keep him in. I had two good reasons for being extra happy; one was my X-rays were clear; just a slight scar left as Doctor said, also I was in love, really in love for the first time in my life.

The next fortnight Rosie came in every morning, lit the fire then brought my breakfast up to me; also tidied round the house. I always went for a walk down to the loch after Rosie had gone home. Funny, all the six weeks I was in hospital there were no letters from Vera, Billy or Ewan. I was sure I wrote

217

them about Sarah's accident. Maybe Sarah got word but she never mentioned their names the last time I saw her. I wondered if the MacLeans got the letters and kept them back from Sarah. With Meg coming for dinner, I peeled vegetables my mind going back to the drudgery in the Ramsay's kitchen.

A knock at the door heralded Meg's arrival. When I opened the door she could not get inside quick enough. 'My, that's a lovely smell, what's cooking?' Her eyes opened wide and she gasped when I served her a big plate of lamb chops, roast potatoes, brussels sprouts and different sauces, followed by Eve's pudding. 'You must be feeling better, Mary, if you tackled this lot yourself.'

'Yes, Meg, I am. When I was ill I didn't care if I lived or died; now that I am better it's great to be alive; also I feel so happy.'

'Don't tell me Dr Peter has got you under his spell also?'

I turned away from Meg in case she saw my face blushing. When I calmed down I said, 'what do you mean, Meg?'

'Well, I saw your sister Sarah yesterday when I was at the hospital and all she could talk about was that charming Dr Peter. God, I am sick of hearing Dr Peter this, Dr Peter that; now I know what it feels like to want to murder someone.'

'Oh, Meg, don't say he gets on your nerves that much?'

'Yes, he does, I just hope he gets a girl of his own soon or I'll go nuts.'

I was going to tell her about Peter and me but I changed my mind and asked her if there was any news about Sarah.

'The plaster has come off her leg and foot but she will need a long spell of therapy. Through time she will get plastic surgery for that scar on her face.'

'Did she give you any news for me?'

'No, Mary, all she could talk about was that Dr Peter.' I thought to myself I do hope talking about him is the only thing she does, otherwise I'll soon put a stop to it. All her life Sarah always had her own way, this time as far as Dr Peter went he is mine; I'd make sure of that.

After Meg left I went straight to the phone and got the operator to put me through to Vera's number in America. After a while I eventually got through and asked Vera if she had written to Sarah since her accident. Vera said that she and the boys had written twice but there had been no response. I suggested she should write again, telling Sarah what had happened, and send the letter care of me for it seemed as if the MacLeans were trying to cause trouble. As we rang off it suddenly dawned on me I hadn't even asked how all the family were keeping. I sat in the rocking chair and dreamt of Peter. The way things were going I needed to dig my claws into him. There were too many people racing after him; of course I'd have to let him do all the running. It's amazing how time flies when you are happy. Rosie's fortnight would be up on Saturday; I felt quite capable of looking after myself again.

On Monday I called in at the bank and got my book made up. The rent from the cottage had to go in. Why is it every time I go into the bank I feel as if I am in a funeral parlour. All the cashiers go about with long faces; you would think the way they looked at you it was their money they were handling instead of ours. My turn came; I said 'please make my book up' and pushed it through the opening. The young man with his stiff white collar and black suit just looked at it without looking up. I could just picture what was racing through his head when he added up the figures. God I got a shock; he looked up and gave me the loveliest smile I had ever seen. 'Terrible weather, miss', then he handed me my book back. I gave him my sweetest smile, wished him good morning and left.

I was glad to get out of that dreary place. While in the village I got a few messages. A call at the post office first for writing paper and stamps then Mr Walsh's shop then the baker. When I was coming out of the post office I ran into Mary Kate Bell; a very slim Mary Kate. 'Oh, Mary, I heard you were ill; keeping better?'

'Yes, Mary Kate and what did you get, a boy or girl?'

She hesitated then said, 'didn't you hear, I lost the baby?'

'I am sorry.'

'Don't be,' she said, 'in a way it was all for the best. I sure did get my eyes opened. I have grown up since and I have no intention of letting any man take advantage of me again. In fact it will be the other way around. I'll run rings round them. I suffered, Mary, and before I am dead I'll make sure I don't suffer that same torture again.'

What she said made me think I'd have to tread carefully too. I am single and men could so easily think I am an easy target. With that thought in my mind I made my way home. I glanced at the loch as I reached the door. The water was black, sign of a storm; also cold enough for snow. I hurried into the house, took my outdoor clothes off and made my way to the warm kitchen. It's amazing how I love the kitchen best in my lovely big house. It's times like this that I miss my beautiful dog Rusty. I would like to get another one but if anything happened to it I just could not bear it.

It was a week later when a letter arrived for Sarah; also one for me. They were from Vera. She was sorry to hear I had been in hospital so long. She wanted to know what happened to Auntie Kate's cottage. I wonder what made her ask that question; I suppose Sarah must have written earlier to Vera about it. That time she and Hector were trying to take the house off me. I wondered if Sarah will carry on the fight once she gets back to full health. I'd be ready for her. Later I phoned Meg asking her if she was going to the hospital.

'I'll be going next Saturday, want a lift in Mary to pay Sarah a visit?'

'Oh, I would love that Meg, I have got a letter for Sarah; it was addressed to me so I'll take it in with me. Let's hope the roads won't be blocked, it's started to snow quite heavily.'

Saturday arrived and what Meg feared most happened; the main road was blocked. It had snowed non stop for two days. Nothing for it now but to stay indoors and keep warm. The phone rang. When I answered it the voice of Dr Peter sent my heart thumping again. He asked what I was doing and when I told him just sitting by the fire he said he wished he was with me. We talked generalities about the weather for a little then he asked me to the cinema with him in Oban to see *Random Harvest* once the snow had cleared away.

The snow lasted for three weeks; the loch was dead calm. I kept indoors as much as possible. Meg brought me the essentials that I needed from the shops. Dr Peter phoned me regularly to say he loved me. It was exactly three weeks to the day that Meg managed to run me to the hospital to visit Sarah. During that time everyone seemed to have been hibernating. Sarah was pleased to see me and thanked me for the letter from Vera. She sat down on the big soft chair and lifted her bad leg up on to a stool then she read Vera's letter. If she read it once she read it three times then she laid it on her lap and said; 'what do you make of those two red faced liars, those mealy mouthed-in-laws. Vera here in her letter is asking how I never mentioned the last two letters she wrote to me. All the time I have been in hospital they have been keeping back my mail and I suppose Hector's private papers.'

'I think, Sarah, you better get in touch with your solicitor at once and get him to attend to your affairs right away. Mention Vera's letter to him but if I were you I would not mention to the MacLeans what you intend to do. If you like write a letter right away; I have stamps in my handbag and Nurse Duncan can post it for you on our way home.' I stood over her, urging her to hurry, until the letter was finished and the envelope addressed and stamped. I made my way to the door and who was standing talking to the hospital doctor but Ronald MacLean, Sarah's father-in-law. I went back to Sarah and told her to hide Vera's letter quickly. She pushed it behind the chair cushion and as I was giving Sarah a farewell hug Ronald came into the room. 'Oh, Mary, Doctor was telling me you were in visiting Sarah'.

'Yes, Ronald, we saw a lot of each other during my six weeks in hospital.' He didn't look at all pleased but gave Sarah a big smile. 'I'll see you again soon, Sarah,' I shouted as I waved goodbye.

Meg and I returned home, posting Sarah's letter on the way.

The church was full to the door on Sunday. I hurried out first to make sure I could grab Flora. She came out of church with her niece and nephew trailing behind her looking none too pleased with herself and I asked her what was the trouble.

'I am sick to death looking after Sarah's children morning, noon and night. It's time Sarah was out of hospital and looking after them herself. Mum says it would be a good idea if Sarah and the children moved in to her old home again with you.'

'Oh, she did Flora, well you can go back and tell her my house, Craigshill House, is mine and no way is her family moving in. Does your mother forget that Hector's and Sarah's children are also her grandchildren and it's hers and your dad's, also Sarah's responsibility to take care of them, not mine. As for the size of the house, I think your house has four bedrooms, mine has just three. For goodness sake, Flora, why don't you just take a day away from the house and leave your mother to look after the children. Come on I'll come into the house with you.'

As soon as we got in the door an angry voice shouted, 'hurry up, Flora, where have you been, I am starving.' Flora was going to run up the stairs to attend to her mother.

'Flora, stay where you are, let her shout her head off; those poor children need to be fed first.' I took the children's outdoor clothes off and hung them up then I made their lunch. I made Flora sit at the table with the children then I went into Mrs MacLean's bedroom. The old woman was sitting up with a black shawl wrapped round her shoulders. She let out one roar when she saw me. 'What are you doing here, you nobody.'

'If there is anyone in this room a nobody it's you; you useless old woman, lying rotting away in that bed, never giving a thought to your sick daughter or your neglected grandchildren.' She was flabbergasted at the way I spoke to her. 'Also, if you don't want your daughter landing in hospital for six weeks like me you better give yourself a shake. If you want anything to eat move out of that bed and get it yourself.' I went back into the kitchen; little Helen and Eachan greeted me with a big smile. 'I have some children's books and toys Flora, I'll look them out for the children. By the way, play sick,' I whispered into Flora's ear, 'when your mother comes down; that's the only way to get her moving, bye for now.'

The following Sunday after Mass there was no sign of Flora or any of the children. Meg called me over to her car. 'Hop in, Mary; did you know Sarah was home from hospital for good and what do you think of miss Flora, she left home the same day as Sarah got home. Nobody seems to know where she has gone.' I told Meg about the previous Sunday and what I had said to the old woman. Meg stood still for a minute; 'my, Mary, I didn't know you had it in you. From what I hear the MacLeans are blaming you for upsetting Flora. Well, Sarah's home now; she will just have to take charge of the children and keep the old woman in her place. I think she will have to keep that Ronald one in his place. It seems he spends most of his time at the hotel drinking and gambling every night and leaves in the small hours of the morning.'

I had just finished lunch when the phone rang. It was Dr Peter inviting me to a drive in his car. Not wanting him to be seen calling for me we arranged to meet on a lonely part of the road. As I neared the MacLean's house I hoped none of them would see me and when I turned the corner I got the shock of my life. Peter's car was there but standing close up to it with the front door open was Sarah dressed in her Sunday best, laughing and chatting to Dr Peter. When I drew level with the car Sarah said, 'I was in the village; Doctor was kind enough to offer me a lift.'

I made to walk on but Dr Peter put his head out of the window and said, 'I'll give you a lift to the village, Miss Scott.' I turned back and got into his car; I could feel Sarah's eyes boring into my back. I thought to myself I'd have to watch that one. At last we were alone, just the two of us. All of a sudden I felt quite shy. I think Peter sensed how I felt. 'Don't be afraid, Mary, I love you. I would not harm you for the world. I know a little tea room about an hour's drive from here; we will drop in for a cup of tea.' The car raced along the road and we came to a stop at a lovely cottage. The first thing that hit me as I went through the door was the delicious smell of home baking. Peter took my arm and led me to a small table set for two placed near the big open fireplace. Huge logs were burning away; the flames shooting now and again up the wide chimney. 'Happy?' Peter whispered, 'I have ordered tea; it will be here in a moment.'

An elderly lady dressed in black set the table for us. There were home baked scones just off the girdle, fresh cream, strawberry jam, butter and angel cakes then she said, 'is that all, Master Peter?'

I was wondering if I had heard right. 'Day dreaming again, Mary? Come on the tea will be getting cold. I suppose you heard the lady calling me Master?

222

Well, it's our own place, now tuck in and eat up everything. This place is our secret just between the two of us. Someday, Mary, when I get on my feet I intend to make you my wife; of course if you want to?'

'You know I do, Peter, I love you with all my heart.'

After we left the cottage we drove on for another half hour then Peter brought the car to a stop on a side road. The car lights went out then Peter pulled me into his arms. The next minute our lips met; the two of us were lost in each others embrace. Oh how happy I felt, hoping the night would last forever. At last we broke apart; 'oh dear look at the time, I am on duty in three hours. I better get you home before the village stirs.' Peter gave me one long kiss before he dropped me off at my door; 'see you soon, Mary,' then he was off down the road. I went straight to bed where I dreamt of Peter.

It was late the next morning when I woke; in fact it must have been the knocking on the door that woke me. When I eventually got to it Sarah was just walking away. She turned and came back in, 'my you sure are hard to waken. Been on the tiles all night have we? I was just wondering if you and Dr Peter made a night of it last night. In case you don't know it, Mary, I have got my eyes set on Peter and what I want I get. You should know that by now.'

'Why, Sarah, you must be at least ten years older than him; also do you never think he can have his pick of all the silly young girls in the village. You must be mad thinking he will fall for a cripple like you with nothing but your dead husband's debts and you with two young children; grow up, Sarah, be your age.'

Sarah made to grab my hair but I stepped back in time; her face was distorted with anger. 'How dare you talk to me like that; you are nothing but a nobody.' She sat down on the chair and burst out crying.

'If you are in trouble of any kind I advise you to see Father Joseph. He is the best person to help you. When Mum and Dad lay starving to death it was him I went to for help. There was no one else in the world I could turn to. Neither neighbours, you, Hector nor Vera cared. The boys of course were too young. So you see, Sarah, trouble knocks at everyone's door and you will just have to face up to it.' All of a sudden the tears stopped. I could feel her eyes watching every move I made. I wondered what scheme she had up her sleeve. You could hear a pin drop in the kitchen, it went so quiet. I thought to myself, a calm before a storm.

'I was thinking, Mary, you could sell this house and I would get my half share. Ronald sent me up to discuss it with you.'

'Oh he did, did he. Well you can go back to him and tell him from me that my house is not for sale. He can sell his own if he wants money to pay for his and his son's gambling debts.'

She rose in such a hurry that she knocked the full cup of tea all over the table. As she made for the door she said, 'I'll tell the police about the child buried under the garden seat.'

'Just do that Sarah and while you are at it tell them it was Hector's father who killed your own father; also Maria Duffy.' As she left I said, 'don't ever come near my door again, some sister you are.' I watched her through the spy hole walking down the road with a slight limp.

It was late afternoon before I got home from the shops. Meg stopped me. 'I need to talk to you, Mary, hop in. We will have lunch at my place; put your bags in the back of the car.' I could sense there was something wrong as Meg sat tight-lipped at the wheel of the car. Meg said, 'what do you think Ronald MacLean battering Sarah. She came limping into the surgery with her head covered in blood. It seems after she had left your house whatever was said, Ronald went raving mad. He grabbed a heavy stick and struck Sarah on the head; he went for her again but she lifted a chair to protect herself. By this time the children were screaming on the verge of hysteria. Sarah managed to get out of the house leaving the two screaming children. Doctor Peter called the police and Ronald is in police custody. I think Dr Peter would like Sarah to stay with you; also the children.'

I thought to myself what soft yarn has Sarah spun to young Dr Peter. Out loud I told Meg all that had happened that morning. 'No way, Meg, am I having her in my house again.' I also told her how she intended to have Dr Peter for herself.

'I am glad, Mary, I heard your side of the story, Sarah told us a completely different version. I'll discuss it with Dr Peter when I get back after lunch. I'll suggest she be sent to hospital; the children of course will have to go into care. Ronald of course will be charged with assault.'

Meg dropped me off on her way back to work. I told her I would be going to Oban next day and she offered to run me to the station for the nine o'clock train. Next, I telephoned Mr Hendry saying that I was coming in to see him and he volunteered to meet my train.

At 8.30 a.m. sharp Meg arrived the next morning. I was waiting for her so in a matter of minutes we were on our way to the station. 'I've just got time to drop you off, Mary; what train are you coming back on?'

'The 4.30 p.m.'

'Right I'll come back for you. After our tea, I hope at your place, we will discuss the day's events.'

When I arrived in Oban Mr Hendry was waiting on the platform for me. He first took me to a hotel where I enjoyed tea and toast and marmalade while watching him eat, with astounding speed, a heaped plateful of bacon, sausage, egg, tomato and fried bread.

As soon as we reached his office Mr Hendry placed beside the blazing fire a small chair. He asked me what the trouble was. I told him everything about Hector, Sarah and the rest of the MacLeans. When I had finished he said the best thing would be to take legal action against Sarah and Ronald MacLean. He re-emphasised that they had no legal right to my house. I left the office feeling a lot happier and I treated myself to a few new dresses, skirts, jumpers and shoes.

I felt on top of the world again; I was thinking of Peter when I was trying on all my new clothes wondering if he would like them. Meg met me at the station on my return journey. The porter helped me with my boxes. When we reached her car I could not help but roar with laughter at the expression on her face. 'Why, Mary, are you going to start a business; hurry up and get in the car, some folks have all the luck. You will have to wait in the surgery till it closes in another ten minutes otherwise you will have to carry all those boxes home yourself.'

Meg drove me home. Over tea she gave me the news that Sarah had been detained in hospital with a wound more serious than first thought. The children were being looked after in a good home across the loch and Ronald was still in custody. Later, we opened my parcels. The last parcel was for Meg – a full length wool dressing gown. There were tears in her eyes when she tried it on and said, 'this must have cost you a fortune.' Still thanking me, Meg left for home. All of a sudden I felt dead beat; I put all the new clothes in the parlour and went to bed. I just took my dress and shoes off and fell into bed and sound asleep.

It was early morning when I woke and I felt a lot better. The phone rang; it was Peter wanting to know if Sunday after church was all right to meet again. 'Yes, of course, love, usual place with the car, bye for now.' I set to and cleaned the house from top to bottom, all the time thinking of Peter and Sunday.

Sunday came again, I could hardly keep my mind on my prayers thinking of Peter. When I came out of church Flora MacLean was waiting for me. 'Can I walk home with you, Mary?'

'Of course, Flora.' I wondered what was coming next. I didn't have long to wait.

'I suppose you heard Sarah is in hospital again. She asked me to give you

225

this letter.'

I took the letter and put it in my handbag. 'Tell your mum I was asking for her, bye Flora.'

Once I had settled down in my rocking chair I opened Sarah's letter. It was more of a scribble than writing. It took me all my time to make out the words. She said she was sorry for everything she had said and would I forgive her and come and visit her in hospital as she was so lonely. 'Flora had her hands full looking after Mum; she has never got over the shock of Hector's sudden death, now Ronald being in jail doesn't help matters. I hope they keep him there for life. Scum like him should not be allowed to live.' I agreed with her. I supposed in times of trouble you had to put aside the hurt the other person had caused you.

I hurried with my lunch then got changed to meet Peter. It was still cold so I wrapped up well and set off. When I arrived at the spot we had arranged to meet there was no sign of Peter. I hoped nothing had happened to him and kept on walking. I really felt stupid walking down the road and didn't know what to do. Still no sign of Peter. Eventually, I made my way home disgusted at being stood up. I'd make sure he never does that with me again. Inwardly, I was blazing as I let myself in the house. I locked and bolted the door, finished with men. Peter, I supposed, thought I was easy fish to catch after the carry on in the car. I changed into my house clothes and put my Sunday best back in the wardrobe.

The phone started ringing. I wasn't in the mood for answering it. At last it stopped. The phone rang again and I answered in case it was Meg, which it was. Sarah had taken a turn for the worse, Dr Peter was called in at the last minute to help the surgeon as Dr McKinnon had been called out to a patient on the other side of the loch. So Sarah had to go and spoil my Sunday with Peter after all. I felt so angry with Sarah; why was it she got at me even when she was on the danger list. I was beginning to get real sick of being second best to her. A loud knocking on the door made me jump. It was Peter; quickly I opened the door. Before I could shut it properly he pulled me towards him and gave me a big hug and kiss. 'Oh, Mary, I missed you; forgive me, love, for not turning up this afternoon. I was called to the hospital. Your sister Sarah passed away this afternoon. It was too late for the surgeon to operate. I am sorry to be the one to be the bearer of this sad news for you. I can't stay, Dr McKinnon needs my help.' He gave me another bear hug and a long sweet kiss then he was gone.

I phoned Vera to tell her of Sarah's death. Apparently, they were all too busy to come over for the funeral – so she said anyway. I was beginning to lose my temper at always being lumbered with everything.

Father Joseph made the funeral arrangements and Sarah was buried three days later. Ronald was allowed out of jail to attend his daughter-in-law's funeral. It was a very private service. It was a Requiem Mass, of course. There was no sign of Mrs MacLean senior at the burial. Flora was there looking pale and ill. Ronald was escorted by two police officers and led away immediately after the service. Poor Flora was left standing crying her eyes out. I went over and put my arms around her and asked her to come home with me for a while. I wasn't long in getting the tea and bacon and egg made for the two of us. When she sat at the table I slipped her two aspirins. 'Here, Flora, take these, they will make you feel better. Come on now, dry your eyes and eat something, you must be starving. I don't suppose you ate anything this morning? Don't let your mother get you down, Flora, sometimes help comes from the most unexpected quarters. When you are at your lowest, just drop everything, get out of the house, even if it is just a walk to the shops. When you get back home you will feel a lot better. The trouble won't disappear but you will get the strength to carry on. Also, say a wee prayer now and again, it helps.'

'Thanks, Mary, I feel a lot better, I enjoyed the bacon and egg.'

'Anytime you want a chat just come, that's to say if I am at home.' She waved goodbye as I shut and locked the door. Poor lonely girl, she would just have to grow up the hard way as I had to.

The following Sunday there was no hold up for Peter and me, we set off in the car to a different part of the country where we had our tea in a hotel. I liked the cottage best but we could not go there every Sunday. After our tea we drove around till we found a quiet spot where we spent the rest of the evening cuddling and kissing in the car. Our courtship lasted for years. During that time I don't know how often Peter and I fell out over some silly patient who I thought was getting more of his time than I should. Then we would make it up and both of us were in seventh heaven again. Three months before we were to get married our engagement was announced in the local newspaper. Everyone in the village was taken by surprise, even Dr McKinnon and dear Meg.

When I met Meg in the surgery she congratulated me and said, 'my, you sure are a deep one. All those years, how the pair of you managed to hide your secret love meetings for so long I don't know. Thank God he is getting married at last. You will let me help you to pick your trousseau, Mary?'

During the three months up to the wedding I took driving lessons. I think the instructor was a bundle of nerves each time he gave me my lesson. After I had finished the twelve lessons I sat my test and passed. I think the instructor was delighted to see the back of me.

Arrangements for the wedding kept me occupied. I wrote to Vera, Fred and the boys, inviting them over. Meg was delighted when I asked her to be matron of honour and Mr Hendry graciously agreed to give me away. Father Joseph said he would arrange a rehearsal.

My phone rang, it was Peter. When I lifted the receiver he said 'hello sweetheart, happy? Will next Thursday be all right for you to go to Oban to pick your ring. Dr McKinnon gave me the day off. If Nurse Duncan had her way she would be coming also. I'll call for you at 9 a.m. sharp. It's lovely, Mary, no longer need we be secretive. I will be able to leave my car at your door without the whole village gossiping about us.'

I laughed, 'they will be doing that just now anyway. Do you think when we are in Oban you could help me pick my new car for me? I passed my driving test yesterday.'

'Good for you. I'll have to go, bye love.'

Thursday morning arrived, the sun was shining but it was a bitter cold wind. March of course, you never knew what kind of weather the next day was going to bring. Peter hooted his horn. I ran out and slid into the front seat beside him then off the pair of us raced down the road through the village with all the heads, young and old gazing after us. The first thing we did when we arrived at Oban was to go to a hotel for lunch. After our lunch we made our way to the jeweller's to pick my ring. The manager seemed to know Peter. He came towards us and shook hands with Peter then Peter introduced me. Peter and I were taken into a small room at the back of the shop. A young man brought in four trays of rings followed by the manager. The rings were beautiful. The manager asked in what month I was born and, when I said September, he produced a lovely sapphire surrounded by small diamonds. I was worried about the expense, but Peter said nothing was too good for me.

We then went to see about my car with Peter advising me to pay for it in instalments. I knew what I wanted and went straight to it – a blue Mini. Peter settled all the details, including delivery, with the salesman then we set off for home.

The following week my new car was delivered, I was so proud of it. Mr Lees the joiner called; he thought there was enough room to place the garage at the side of the house. Erection would be no problem as the garage would come in sections. I thought such lovely black curls were wasted on a grown man. Hair like that should belong to a girl. I wondered if he's married.

A letter came from Vera saying they would all be arriving ten days before the wedding. She wanted to know what colour I'd like Ann's dress to be. That was when it dawned on me how many preparations still had to be made. Peter interrupted my thoughts. He telephoned to ask if I would go with him to meet his parents on Sunday. It meant staying the night as they lived in Moffat, too long a double journey for one day. I blessed him when he said his sister Elizabeth could help with the wedding preparations.

I was feeling very nervous when Peter called for me on Sunday. He noticed it right away as soon as I got into the car. 'It's all right, Mary, there is nothing for you to worry about; in fact they were all excited at the thought of meeting you. Mum thought I was never going to settle down. We will stop at the cottage that you fell in love with, on our way down, and give the old lady our exciting news about our wedding.'

'What connection is she to you, Peter?'

'She was our cook before she got married. She lost her husband five years ago, that's how she opened the small tea-room to try to make a living.'

Peter introduced me as his future wife. The old lady was delighted. She disappeared for a moment or two then came back with a decanter of sherry and glasses. In front of the log fire she raised her glass to us and toasted our good health.

We continued on our way. I fell asleep and when I woke the car was surrounded by people. We had arrived. Introductions were made but I was so tired I couldn't take it all in. Peter's mother told me to lie down and rest until dinner and Elizabeth, Peter's sister showed me to my room.

The MacInnes always dressed for dinner and I hadn't brought any evening wear. Elizabeth came up trumps and lent me a gown. The dinner passed without a hitch; the food was delicious.

The gentlemen went to the smoking room for their coffee while the ladies went into the drawing room. Peter's mother called me over to sit beside her on the settee; the maid passed the coffee around. Everyone seemed to be talking all the time. There was one young girl beautifully dressed in a plain black dress; it must have cost a fortune the way it was designed. Every time I looked at her she would just stare right through me. I asked Peter's mother who she was. 'Oh, she is our next door neighbour, Peter and she used to play together when they were children. We always thought someday they would get married; she was a bit upset when she heard Peter was marrying you. Are you always so tired, child, or was it the long journey?'

'I have had such a lot of arrangements to attend to lately; also the long journey didn't help. I feel very refreshed now.'

The rest of the evening was spent in pleasant, general conversation.

The weekend just flew; I was glad to get Peter to myself again just the two of us in the car. I loved to snuggle up to Peter while he was driving, he made me feel so secure. Inwardly, I wished tomorrow was our wedding day. We stopped again at the cottage on the way home for tea. As we were leaving the old lady handed me a small parcel and handed Peter something then she wished us all the happiness on our wedding day. When we arrived I asked Peter in for a cup of coffee. After our coffee we made straight for the bedroom where we spent the next three hours making love. At last Peter said he would need to move himself as he was on duty in a few hours time. One long last kiss and he was gone. I just lay on the bed as he had left me, exhausted after our love making.

The phone rang. It was Meg trying to locate Peter. Dr McKinnon had been taken ill and Peter was needed immediately. I told her Peter was already on his way to the surgery. While she was on the line I took the opportunity to ask her to come to Oban with me to help choose my wedding dress.

It was a lovely day when Meg and I set out for our trip to Oban, the loch was in one of her happy moods with the bright sunlight glinting on her waters. When we reached Oban the first place I made for was the Crown Hotel. I saw Meg giving me a side look but she never opened her mouth. As we went through the swing doors the doorman touched his cap and wished me good morning. Meg followed me into the dining room. 'Breakfast first, Meg', I said, 'and no arguments.'

Meg knew the little shop which specialised in bridal dresses. The gowns in the window were beautiful but I wanted my dress made to my own design. I explained what type of satin and lace and pearls I wanted for my wedding gown; also I wanted a long lace veil. The manageress took my measurements, and I was told that as I would need two fittings I hadn't allowed much time.

I still needed shoes, stockings and a 'going away' suit and I wanted a little 'thank you' gift for Meg who had been such a help. All she wanted was a little teapot. We soon had everything and made our way towards the station and home.

When we arrived home it was beginning to rain so the pair of us hurried back and forth between Meg's car and my house till we had everything in the house except of course Meg's little teapot. Also, I had left a cosy pair of slippers for her as a surprise when she arrived home. 'Do you never keep any sherry or brandy in the house?'

'No, Meg, we saw enough of drink when poor Dad was alive. In a way I think the hard drink played a big part in killing him.'

'Well, Mary, I could have done with a drop of brandy in my tea. It's always handy to have in the house.'

The next three weeks flew by. The first call of the bans of our marriage was called on Sunday between Dr Peter MacInnes and Mary Scott. Elizabeth had sent all the invitations out. It was to be a Nuptial Mass. Elizabeth was also attending to all the floral arrangements in the church and the purvey which was to be held in the village hotel. I don't know what I would have done without her help. I had one last fitting for my wedding dress; it was beautiful. Also I had designed the floral headband to keep my veil in place. After I had paid for everything the manageress said it would arrive by special delivery next week. True to form it did arrive in a large box covered in layers of white tissue paper.

The following week Vera and Fred and little Ann and young Fred arrived; also Billy and Ewan. The sleeping arrangements were sorted out: Vera and Fred in one room, the boys and little Fred in another, and Ann and me in the third. It was good to have the house filled with happy voices again and to see Billy and Ewan busy tidying up the garden.

The following weekend we made our way, Peter and I, to his parents' home. Elizabeth rushed out to the car to meet us, 'and how is the future Mrs P MacInnes?'

'Nervous', I said.

'I have a good idea, Mary, how it must feel. Never mind, mum and I have practically everything in hand.'

We discussed what we were all going to wear at the wedding then I went up to my room to rest before dinner. At 6.30 p.m. I jumped out of bed, washed and dressed then made my way down to the dining room. There was nobody about then I heard voices in the garden. Peter and his mother and brother James were enjoying a joke.

'Can I join in?'

Peter's mother looked up. 'Oh, Mary, come here child and sit beside me.' I wished she would stop calling me child. I was 32 years soon to be 33. Maybe it was because I looked younger than my years. I had the figure of a young girl, only 5 feet 2 inches, very pale but lovely blue eyes and a sweet smile, specially for Peter. Dinner was announced and we all went in. Peter's father never had much to say but, to me, he seemed the kindest of men.

When the ladies were all seated in the drawing room drinking coffee Elizabeth said she would have to steal me away for an hour from Peter to discuss the wedding arrangements. She wanted to check the invitation cards to see if she had missed out anybody. At last everything was settled and we went back to the drawing room. Peter and I took a turn in the garden then sat on a seat by the lilacs. The air was heavy with the scent of flowers. Our bliss was interrupted when Peter was summoned to the phone. Dr McKinnon was ill again and we would have to return first thing in the morning.

We arrived back home in time for lunch; Peter dropped me at the house then made straight for the surgery. It was after surgery hours that Meg called. 'I was sorry, Mary, to break up your special weekend but I was at my wits end wondering how I was going to manage alone, what with Dr McKinnon so ill and no doctor at hand to help with the new babies. Mrs Weir had to be sent to hospital, she had such a difficult birth. Your poor Dr Peter never had time to take his coat off when he was called away.'

'It's all right I quite understand; you forget I worked in the surgery and I know what it's like, chaos all the time. Come on, Meg, let yourself rest and I'll make some tea for us; also I have a little something to put in it to steady your nerves.'

Meg told me of the urgent need to bring another doctor into the practice as Dr McKinnon was utterly exhausted. Inevitably, the conversation turned to the wedding and Meg declared it would be just her luck to be called away to some young mother in labour.

Vera and Fred and their family returned as Meg took her leave. They had been talking to Father Joseph who wanted Peter and I to confirm that the time of the wedding rehearsal was convenient. Then they chased me out to the garden while they prepared the dinner. I sat on the garden seat and said my usual prayer for the soul of the little infant in the cold earth underneath my seat. As I sat looking at the garden I noticed all the different flowers and bushes that Billy and Ewan had planted for me. The lawn had been cut and trimmed; the whole garden was beautiful, the boys must have worked non stop to get everything done so quickly.

Three days before the wedding we had our rehearsal of our duties that we all had to carry out on the big day. Dr McKinnon wasn't any better so Peter was left with the heavy load of the whole practice. Elizabeth had everything arranged, the flowers would be put in the church on the eve of our wedding. My bouquet and the bridesmaids' flowers were also attended to. Peter managed to get a young locum in to help him out. His name was Dr John Murphy; also Meg got a young nurse to help her. During the Nuptial Mass I was sure I'd find Peter and Meg fast asleep, both of them worn out. However my wedding eve arrived;

you could feel the excitement in the air. Elizabeth had seen to it that everything was in order. Vera took my beautiful satin dress out of its box and hung it up to get all the creases out of it. I had just one string of pearls to go with my dress. My satin underwear was laid out on the big chair at the foot of my bed, my white satin shoes beside my dress. The veil and the rose band for my hair were spread out on the settee so everything as ready. As I sat in the rocking chair I fell asleep dreaming of my loved one, soon to be mine.

CHAPTER 14

The sun was streaming in the window as I awoke on my wedding day. Vera true to her word brought my breakfast tray up to me. 'Now, Mary, I want to see clean plates all round when I come up for the tray again.' Vera disappeared, I wondered why the house had suddenly gone deadly quiet. I went downstairs to see.

Standing in the big hallway was Constable Drummond and the new young doctor. Vera was crying her heart out, her head lay on her husband's shoulder. Meg came out of the kitchen straight over to me, put her arms round my shoulders and said. 'Now, Mary, you must be brave, I am afraid we have bad news about Peter. You better tell her, Doctor, because I can't.'

'Dr Peter was sent out on a call to the other side of the loch. It was a lovely night when he left but a heavy mist covered the loch so quickly, in a matter of minutes visibility was nil. We don't know what happened, but this morning when I arrived at the surgery there was no sign of Peter. Of course, we called the coast guard as there was no boat on the jetty. Peter's boat was found five miles on the other end of the loch turned upside down with no sign of Peter. I am afraid, Mary, Constable Drummond said that Peter has drowned.'

'Oh, no,' I shouted and went running through the house screaming. Meg tried to catch me but I knocked her down out of my way. I must have gone mad. As in a dream, I felt people carrying me away, where to I didn't know.

It was six months after careful nursing night and day by my dear friend and nurse, Meg, before I passed through the hell I was living in to the everyday world of life. At first I didn't want to live but with Meg's nursing and bullying me I made it back to the normal world. Later I heard the whole story of what really happened that dreadful morning. The whole village was in shock, people could hardly believe what had happened. The church dressed in flowers for our wedding ended as a funeral parlour. Peter's family left for home right away heartbroken by the loss of their lovely son. In a way not knowing what really happened to him. The dredgers had come up from Clydebank to dredge the loch but no Peter was found. The loch was in one of her secretive moods.

Vera and Fred and the children with Billy and Ewan went home after three weeks, they could not afford to stay longer. Doctor McKinnon passed away, also, during the long spell I was ill. I missed him terribly. It was he who nursed me through my first illness. I used to think that my loch protected me from my enemies, but now she had become too possessive; she did not want me to be loved by anyone else. That's why she took my beloved Peter and left my heart filled with hatred.

As I sit in my rocking chair thinking of that dreadful morning thirty years ago, it just seems like yesterday. I was never the same; the light of my life was lost even though I am still living in my big house, Craigshill House, and very comfortably off. I go about my everyday life wearing a thread-worn coat, down at the heel shoes. The children of the village address me as Miss Mary, maybe it's my imagination but as they pass me by I catch a gleam of sadness in their young eyes. My best friend and nurse is still alive. She tries now and then to coax a smile from me, but to no avail. Vera and her husband Fred come over from America to visit me, usually at Christmas time. Ann and young Fred are both married and have children of their own. It's funny to think of Vera as a grandmother. I am of course their great aunt or rather their second cousin. Let's hope they never find out the truth. One thing I was glad of, Peter never found out I was illegitimate. I have had to live with that secret most of my life. Mr Hendry my solicitor has passed away. In his place is a young upstart who thinks he knows everything but has a long way to go before he becomes as high in my opinion as my Mr Hendry.

My beautiful wedding dress, veil, headband, satin shoes and my white silk stockings still lie in the boxes where Vera packed them away that fateful morning. They are all in my attic; I never visit the place now. In my will I have left my house to Meg to be used as a rest home for all the weary half starved mothers in the village who have large families. Meg will know who to pick. A week's rest at Craigshill House with plenty of food and rest and a little bit of pocket money for them during their stay. Meg, of course, will rest along with them as she is old, also. She will hold the purse strings and see that the carers look after the sick tired mothers. I will sell Sea View cottage in Mull; the funds going to the upkeep of the Rest Home. Also, after I die, I'll leave a letter to Meg telling her where the box full of gold coins is hidden so that the home never runs short of money for its upkeep.

The murderer of the beautiful young girl Maria Duffy and her new-born child were never found. Police still keep an open file on the case.

As I stand at my parlour window and gaze over the loch I whisper: 'Goodbye my darling Peter, sleep softly my love: Rest in Peace. Goodbye loch, you spiteful, jealous old woman.'